"Your ankle, m

Mercy igno[...] her face. She'd ne[...] ced such a close encounter with a man like Lord Ashby, not even with Andrew Vale, whose wife she'd had every intention of becoming.

He sat down on the chair from which Mercy had fallen and leaned over to rub the injured joint. "Ah, I believe it may be somewhat the worse for wear."

"Shall I go and find someone to assist you?" Mercy asked.

"No. I managed to walk up here on my own, and I will proceed as before." Nash stood abruptly and made his way to the door, limping significantly.

"My lord, you are obviously in pain," she said, quickly going to his side. "Please allow me to assist you."

She'd done it before, on the road, when he was a complete stranger, touching him in a way no proper lady would ever consider doing. She moved close to him and, even though he was a great deal taller than she, took his arm and draped it over her shoulders.

He expelled a long breath when he leaned upon her, his hand over her shoulder, dangling precariously close to some highly sensitive territory.

"Where are we going?" she asked.

"To my bedchamber."

Romances by **Margo Maguire**

Margo Maguire

Seducing the Governess

AVON
An Imprint of HarperCollinsPublishers

This is a work of fiction. Names, characters, places, and incidents are products of the author's imagination or are used fictitiously and are not to be construed as real. Any resemblance to actual events, locales, organizations, or persons, living or dead, is entirely coincidental.

AVON BOOKS
An Imprint of HarperCollins*Publishers*
10 East 53rd Street
New York, New York 10022-5299

First Avon Books paperback printing: March 2011

Avon Trademark Reg. U.S. Pat. Off. and in Other Countries, Marca Registrada, Hecho en U.S.A.
HarperCollins® is a registered trademark of HarperCollins Publishers.

Printed in the U.S.A.

10 9 8 7 6 5 4 3 2 1

This book is dedicated to my husband, the greatest brainstorming partner ever, and to my three kids. I couldn't be a prouder mom.

Acknowledgments

Many thanks to my agent, Paige Wheeler, who helps me to keep my eye on the next level; and to my editor, Amanda Bergeron, whose clear critique and sharp insights were invaluable.

Seducing
the Governess

Chapter 1

Windermere Park, the Lake District
Early Spring, 1816

"Captain Gavin Briggs to see you, Your Grace," said Timmons, Windermere's valet. He used that supplicating sickroom voice that never failed to irritate the Duke of Windermere.

His Grace grunted and tried to raise his head, but a wave of dizziness forced him to put it back down. "Well, bring him in here, damn it!" He couldn't fling out his curses with enough vehemence anymore—yet another irritation. "Don't waste my time," he muttered. What little he had left.

"Do not rile yourself, Your Grace," said Rhodes, his personal physician. "You will do no good—"

"Get out, Rhodes."

"Your Grace, I think—"

"I already know what you think," Windermere grumbled, his voice a shadow of what it had once been. It was not so very long ago that he'd been a potent young man, a man in his prime with the world at his feet and all that. He'd had a beautiful bride . . . Isabella.

A grimace of pain distorted his face. "Go."

His powerlessness grated. He was the great Duke of Windermere.

And he was all alone.

Bella had borne him two children, and had betrayed him by dying in childbed with the second. The younger, his son and heir, had contracted cholera or some such horror in London and succumbed a year ago, unmarried and without issue. For the first time in three hundred years, there was no direct Windermere descendant.

"I know, Bella," he whispered, as he felt a bit more of his life seep out of him. "Soon."

"Beg pardon, Your Grace?" Rhodes asked.

Soon he would join his beautiful Bella. But only if he made amends. Bella had come to him in his sleep, and she'd been quite clear. Windermere could only join her if he put things to rights.

The duke didn't like to reflect upon his errors. He could not bear to consider what he'd done to his daughter, Sarah. Only in the past fortnight had he considered the possibility that he'd been wrong to disown her when she'd wed her cocky barrister. 'Twas only since Isabella had begun haunting his dreams . . .

Perhaps if he'd allowed Sarah and her husband to come to Windermere Park with their daughters, they wouldn't have moved down to London and had occasion to cross the filthy Thames in a damned storm.

But Windermere had been so very angry. Sarah had defied him for the sake of . . .

Bah. What did he know of love? Of tenderness. Once Isabella had been lost to him, there'd been naught but a burnt-out shell of an organ in his chest.

His sigh was more of a choked sob. Despair was what it was. Something with which the mighty Duke of Windermere had had little congress. For all his life, he'd had nearly complete control of the people and events around him. But even now, the mincing son of a distant cousin paced in a gallery somewhere below his sumptuous but vacuous bedchamber, awaiting his death.

It sickened him.

The doctor stepped away from his bedside, and a young, vigorous fellow with dark hair and sharp blue eyes came to him and bowed formally. "Your Grace, you sent for me?"

"You're Briggs?" he rasped.

"Aye."

"Rhodes tells me I haven't much time."

"I can see that, Your Grace," said the captain without dissembling. Windermere approved of his direct manner, though he could not embrace the subject matter.

"I have two granddaughters. I want you to find them."

"Find them? I don't understand. How were they lost?"

The duke felt a constriction in his chest. "I sent them away when they were infants."

"Away where?"

"I . . . I do not know. I did not wish to know at the time."

Briggs narrowed his eyes as he looked at him. The insolent jackanapes. "I cannot produce them from naught, Your Grace. I'll need something to go on.

When did this happen? Where were their parents? From where were they taken?"

Windermere wondered if the lad would have the ballocks to speak to him so directly were he not so ill. He suspected the man would. He'd been a bold and daring agent for the crown during the wars with the pompous little French arse, and it was said he always found his man. "Of course you will need information, you impudent rogue. You will have access to all of Rolf Newcomb's papers."

"Newcomb?"

"My steward. The one who took the girls away after their parents died."

"I take it Mr. Newcomb is no longer—"

"Been dead for years. Took the girls from their parents' servants in London and gave them away to families hither and yon."

Briggs made a low, quiet sound of derision. "You're serious?"

"Dash it all, do I look like a man with the luxury of being frivolous?"

"No, you do not, Your Grace," he said, keeping a measuring gaze upon him. "But what of your heir? I saw Baron Chetwood and his wife in the drawing room. Surely they will not be pleased to know you are searching for other heirs to diminish their new-found wealth."

Windermere felt his lip curl in disgust. He could not have wished for a more contemptible heir than his distant cousin's worm of a son. In their few meetings since John's death, Chetwood had demonstrated a callous disregard for anything but the vast treasures he would inherit on Windermere's death. Neither he nor his wife cared anything for the revered title or the heavy burden of responsibility it entailed.

And Windermere silently admitted to his late wife that he had not lived up to his responsibilities, either. He'd lost everyone.

He closed his eyes briefly, then looked up at the man who stared down at him with cold disapproval in his eyes. "No doubt you can handle Chetwood."

"Will he cause trouble?"

"Perhaps. Can you do it? Find them?"

"I can find anyone, Your Grace. But it will take some time."

"Time," Windermere said, regaining some semblance of authority, "as you can see, is something I do not have. Find them. Bring them to me. They will each receive a generous dowry out of my estate, and you will earn a boon far above your fee."

"How much?"

The duke would have chortled at the man's brass if he had the energy. "Ten thousand pounds. A fortune to a man like you."

That vast sum got the captain's attention.

"I'll want it in writing, Your Grace. And I'll have it whether or not you're alive when I bring them to you."

"You push too far, Briggs," Windermere said. "You'll get but half if I'm dead first."

Briggs shook his head. "You said yourself—you are a man without much time. I'll have it all, Your Grace, or you'll find yourself another bloodhound."

Chapter 2

The Lake District
Spring, 1816

The sensation of floating adrift did not abate even when Mercy Franklin stepped off the rocking mail coach into the sodden road that felt anything but solid. She no longer had any anchor, any substance. "Normal" no longer defined her life, not since she'd learned that her father and mother were not truly her parents. Reverend Robert Franklin and his wife, Susanna, had taken her in under circumstances unknown to Mercy, and raised her as their own.

And now they were both dead. Her questions would go unanswered, at least until she got up the nerve to open Susanna's journal.

Mercy feared what she might read on those pages—whether the words would touch her heart or sadden her, she did not know, for her dealings with her parents had been strained from her earliest memories. She was hard-pressed to recall any demonstrations of affection, and yet she remembered every admonition and castigation she'd received over the years. She knew how her parents felt about her—she just hadn't known why they'd been so cold and remote—until the day Susanna died.

Collecting her luggage into both hands, Mercy glanced around at the setting in which she found herself. Naught looked familiar here, so far from St. Martin's Church and the town of Underdale that had been her home for the last twenty years. She had been squeezed and jostled over at least one hundred rugged, mountainous miles, and her head ached. Her legs felt like jelly, and she knew it would take more than just a moment to settle her stomach.

Yet there was no time. Mercy needed to move on. She had a living to earn, and had been able to find only one acceptable way to do so.

Sidestepping a deep puddle, she set down her traveling cases in the damp grass, hoping the gray skies would not open up and drench her before she reached Ashby Hall. She suppressed a wave of unease and reached into her portfolio for the letter she'd received from a Mr. Lowell, a man with some position of authority at the Hall.

The mail coach will leave you at the top of the fell above Ashby Hall. Go round the curve and through the turnstile. From there, the path will bring you directly to the Hall.

So it wasn't much farther now. Her new home, so far from Underdale. So far from everything she thought she'd known to be true.

Mercy might have blamed Susanna Franklin's strange and unexpected revelation on some horrible deathbed dementia, but her mother had been entirely lucid up until the end. And her words made a peculiar kind of sense, even though it was difficult to credit Susanna's account of a man bringing her to Reverend Franklin's rectory as a little child, and bidding the Franklins to raise her as their own. It didn't seem possible. The Franklins couldn't be anything other than her true family.

Yet Mercy knew the story must be true. Susanna Franklin's breath had been short and painful at the end, but she had spoken in earnest.

The gray skies opened up and Mercy scrambled to put away Mr. Lowell's letter before it was ruined. With all due haste, she gathered her heavy traveling cases and followed his direction, and as she rounded the curve in the road, noted that the ruts were already overflowing with muddy water from a previous rain. She stepped over and around each one as best she could, but the mud sucked at her shoes, and she feared they would be ruined before she arrived.

As she struggled to manage her luggage, the sudden sound of horses startled her, and she scuttled off the road just as a group of men on horseback rounded the curve at high speed and came upon her. Some of them wore the ragtag remnants of army uniforms, but none of them even noticed her cowering in the trees alongside the road. They splattered mud onto her simple brown woolen coat, and as the last man rode by, he turned and caught a glance of her shocked face.

Without so much as a twitch of his thick, dark mustache, he turned back to follow the others, as only a despicable barbarian would do.

With her already sour mood worsening, Mercy wiped the spray of mud from her cheek and resumed her walk, hoping she'd soon reach the turnstile. Perhaps she'd find a well where she could draw water to wash some of the mud from her clothes and face before meeting Mr. Lowell. It was unusual, to say the least, for a gentleman to be the person in charge of hiring a governess for the earl's niece, but it had been Mercy's only offer of employment. Unconventional or not, she desperately needed the position.

Her father had died suddenly last summer, leaving barely enough for her and Susanna to live on. Mercy had questioned her mother regarding their finances, but her only answer was that Reverend Franklin had made many investments that had gone bad.

They'd lived in a borrowed cottage and relied upon the kindness of her father's parishioners. But after Susanna's short illness and death, it had become clear that Mercy needed to make her own way.

She'd had to find employment.

She held tightly to her traveling cases and stepped back into the road, just as another horseman galloped into sight. He saw her a moment too late and his horse reared, throwing him to the muddy ground.

Somehow, Mercy managed to stay on her feet, but she gave a startled cry. As soon as the massive horse had ambled away, she collected herself and called out to him. "Are you injured, sir?"

He sat up gingerly, and when he shoved his hat off his face where it had slumped, Mercy noticed his scars. One side of his face had been injured—probably burned. A thick webbing of damaged skin marred the peak of his cheek and his brow, and clouded the eye in between. Likely he had not seen her in the road.

Mercy could not imagine what cruel fate had marred such a striking face. His nose was nicely shaped, his jaw square and strong and slightly cleft, indicating a more potent masculinity than she'd encountered in any other man. His lips were neither too thin nor too full, but were stretched into a solemn line that indicated a fair degree of irritation.

Mercy immediately realized he was not the kind of man she ought to be alone with, not when she could feel his powerful physicality even from where she stood.

Fortunately, he did not look at her, but scowled and reached for his ankle through his highly polished Hessians. And as he did so, Mercy wondered if her conscience would allow her to slip away without further congress. Without offering her assistance.

"Aye," he muttered. "Injured." His tone was wry, as though such a simple mishap could hardly be called an injury. He gave an incredulous shake of his head, then tried to rotate his foot, but grimaced with discomfort.

She took a step toward him. "Sir . . ."

He glanced up and caught her eye. Mercy stopped in her tracks and held her tongue, doubtful that he was a man who would willingly accept assistance.

"A mild sprain, I think."

"Oh dear."

A muscle in his jaw tensed. "You'll have to help me take off my boot."

"I beg your pardon?"

His voice was stern and his words carried the tone

of command. "The boot must come off now, else the swelling will prevent it coming off later. Come here."

He glared at her with his good eye, its clear gray color going as dark with annoyance as the murky storm clouds above. "Do you plan to stand gaping at me all afternoon? I am quite certain I cannot be the only one who hopes to get out of the weather sooner rather than later."

Mercy gave herself a mental shake. She had no business ruminating upon his beautiful, scarred face or allowing the rumble of his deep, masculine voice to resonate through her, clear to her bones. He was an overbearing boor, in spite of his pleasing features, and the sooner she was done with him, the sooner she could be on her way.

Mercy had experience in dealing with an autocratic man, for her father had been one, and more severe than most. He had never approved of her speaking her own mind. And yet her usual demure manner did not suit the current situation in the least.

"You would not be in this position had you taken more care around that curve." Mercy nearly clapped her hand over her mouth at her rude retort. But this man was not her father.

She raised her chin a notch and mentally dared him to reprimand her.

"You're an expert at riding, then?" He did not bother to hide his sarcasm.

Mercy let out her breath when he did not respond as her father would have done. "Hardly."

She glanced about for an optimum spot for her bags and set them down. Swallowing her misgivings, she approached the man once again. "But I know the difference between good common sense and foolhardiness."

He made a rude noise. "Like stepping into the road in front of a galloping horse?"

"I did not hear you coming after that last bunch of ruffians . . ."

He waved off her words. "I haven't got all day." He raised his foot in her direction.

"I'm afraid you'll have to manage on your own, sir. It is hardly proper—"

"What are you, a priggy society miss?" he said roughly, giving her the once-over with a critical gaze. "Give the boot a good heave and be quick about it."

"I am no prig, sir." But even as she denied it, she wondered if it was true. Was she a prig?

No. She was a well-bred lady who knew better than to dally with a handsome rogue on an isolated stretch of road.

"Then kindly give me a moment's assistance," he said impatiently, "and I will depart your precious piece of road."

Mercy had never felt so awkward in her life, though she found it oddly invigorating to speak her mind for a change. After years of responding so carefully to her father and every other member of the parish, Mercy's tongue felt surprisingly loose with this stranger.

She placed her gloved hands on the boot and pulled, ignoring the ignominious position in which she found herself. She couldn't even imagine bending like this over Mr. Andrew Vale's foot. *He* had been the perfect gentleman who'd asked her to marry him, not a wretched horseman who thought nothing of running down people in the road.

"You'll never get it that way. Turn around," he said.

"How am I to—"

"You'll have to take my foot under your arm and—"

She dropped said foot and he grimaced in pain. "I'll do no such thing."

"You'll barely have to touch me, I promise you." Mercy detected a hint of amusement in his tone. He was actually enjoying this. "I've done this many times before. Go ahead. Turn around."

She huffed out a harsh breath and did as she was told, gingerly taking his foot in hand once again.

She jerked the boot away while he leaned back and pulled in the opposite direction.

"You have a very fetching backside," he said, just as the boot came off. Mercy lost her balance and took a few quick steps forward, landing in a deep puddle in her path, destroying her shoe.

Chapter 3

Every shred of Mercy's dignity disappeared. In place of it came an odd little coil of sensation wound tight in her stomach. It was a fierce pang of attraction that she knew she should not feel—not for such a brazen rascal. Still, it was not altogether unpleasant, and as her skin heated, her breasts tightened almost painfully. Somehow, she refrained from pressing her hands against them to make them stop.

No one had ever said such a thing to her, and she knew she should be outraged. She *was* outraged. So much so that she yanked her foot out of the mud and went for her luggage.

And tried to ignore the altogether unacceptable notion that he was watching her backside even now.

"Now if you'll just collect my horse for me . . ."

Mercy could not believe the man's audacity. She turned just as he put his foot down carefully and examined his ankle.

"Collect your . . . ?" She shuddered involuntarily. Whether it was from the cold and wet or the prospect of approaching the enormous animal, she was not quite sure. "I know naught of horses, sir. Surely you can manage." Although she did not see how.

" 'Tis a gelding, lass. He will not hurt you. Just approach him where he can see you. And move with some purpose. He needs to know you're in charge."

Mercy had never felt less in charge, unshoeing men and speaking aloud of gelded animals, but she saw no choice but to try to collect the massive creature.

The drizzle might have stopped for the moment, but she was a chilled, sodden mess. It was beyond annoying that this stranger made her feel self-conscious about her appearance, with her bonnet sagging around her ears and the dampness making inroads through the wool of her coat. It hugged her figure far too personally, and Mercy could not help but think the man was enjoying the sight she presented.

"Aye. That's it," he said, keeping a measuring gaze upon her, his lips quirked into a vaguely mocking smile.

"Take hold of his reins and start walking this way."

Mercy did so, as far from its mouth as possible. She spoke quietly to it. "Come now, be a cooperative horse."

Luckily, it turned to follow her.

"Now," said the man, shaking his head in disbelief. "I'll need your assistance to stand . . ."

Mercy closed her eyes to gather her patience, then reached out one hand. He took it, and she braced herself as he rose from the ground, balancing upon one foot.

He clucked his tongue and the horse went right to him.

"Why didn't you do that before?" she asked, so annoyed with this brash stranger.

"Do what?"

"Make that sound. The horse clearly understood what it meant."

"He was too far away."

She released his hand and started to walk away, disbelieving him. He'd enjoyed her discomfiture a bit too much.

"One more thing."

She halted. "I really must be on my way, sir."

He gestured toward the horse. "I'll need your assistance in mounting."

"I cannot imagine how," she said disagreeably. "I'm reasonably certain I won't be able to lift you up."

His mouth quirked at her sarcasm, and Mercy felt her stomach drop to her toes. She'd had previous occasions to appreciate a handsome face—Andrew Vale's, in fact—but this man's rugged beauty struck some deep chord within her.

No doubt he was quite the roué, and it was entirely improper for Mercy to linger here with him.

He handed her his boot. "All I need is your shoulder for support until I can— Ah, that's it."

With surprising agility, he managed to swing his leg over the horse's rump and seat himself in the saddle. Then he reached over to take his boot from her, and Mercy hastened away from the big man and the perplexing warmth that had unfurled inside her as he braced his hand upon her shoulder.

She retrieved her luggage and started back on the path toward the turnstile.

"You have been extremely helpful."

"If that was your thanks, then you are welcome, sir," she said without looking back. "Now, if you'll excuse me, I must make haste before the rain starts again."

"Of course."

He said something else, but Mercy could not hear him. In any event, she wanted no further unsuitable conversation with him. The sooner she put some distance between herself and the handsome stranger, the better.

She trudged on to the turnstile, where Ashby Hall came into view. Mercy's heart sank as she gazed at the massive, bleak stone and timber structure ahead. It was nestled in a wide dale, with tall, craggy fells all around it, and though the rain had stopped, the Hall and all its outbuildings were now enshrouded in a thick mist.

Ashby Hall was a cold and unwelcoming structure—certainly not a home, especially for a young child.

Shuddering nervously, Mercy went through the turnstile. The place seemed to have started out as a crenellated medieval castle, and been transformed over the years into a stately mansion with peaks and turrets and all manner of rooftops. But as grand as it might once have been, now it seemed to be sagging under the weight of disdain and neglect.

Huge trees towered over the edifice, their skeletal limbs rising over the Hall like gigantic monsters with gnarled, black limbs. She looked toward the gardens and saw that they, too, needed attention.

Mercy never thought she would miss the vicarage where she'd spent her childhood, or even the small cottage she'd shared with her mother during those few months after Reverend Franklin's passing. But now that she saw Ashby Hall, she wondered if there hadn't been some other course to take.

She straightened her shoulders and slogged on. Ashby Hall—as dilapidated as it might be—was Mercy's immediate future, along with the little girl who lived within, in need of a governess.

It was not the future Mercy had anticipated, for she'd hoped to marry Andrew Vale and start a family of her own, in a home where she could be mistress of her own life, without the kind of strict governance practiced by her father. She'd felt stirrings of affection for Reverend Vale and knew she would have made him a good wife. But her father had refused his offer, and Mercy feared she knew why.

Though Reverend Vale was a clergyman like her father, he had not been rigid enough. Reverend Franklin had viewed him as lax, and Mercy could not deny that it was his tolerant attitude that had made him so very attractive to her.

Unfortunately, she had not concealed her enthusiasm for the match, and her father had deemed her eagerness unseemly. Besides, anything Mercy might desire of her own volition was likely wrong for her.

No doubt her father would approve of her present path.

It took another quarter hour to reach the gates of the Ashby estate, passing low-lying, flooded fields and an overgrown orchard on her way. One of the huge, wrought-iron gates in the stone wall that surrounded the house had come loose from its upper hinge, and its base rested upon the cobbled drive. Mercy swallowed hard, wondering if she could actually live there. She did not need a palace, but Ashby Hall was a disaster.

She would go inside and warm herself, then decide what to do.

But what *could* she do? The small bequest from her father had been pitiful, and she'd used it to pay for food, medicines, and doctors during Susanna's illness. Mercy had considered writing to Mr. Vale to inform him of her parents' demise and to inquire whether he had any interest in resuming his courtship.

It was a humiliating proposition, since Mr. Vale had not contested her father's refusal of his proposal the previous summer. Clearly, Andrew had borne a great deal of respect for the older clergyman, and had not wished to challenge him.

But it would have done Mercy's heart good to know someone cared enough to fight for her.

Hesitant to write, Mercy had exhausted every possibility for employment at home, but there were few opportunities for a young lady in her position. There was no need for another school in Underdale, and no one wanted to hire the late vicar's daughter as a servant. When she'd failed to find employment, there'd been no option but to advertise for a position in a great household, doing something about which she knew very little—being a governess in such a household.

Mercy had never anticipated such a wreck of a house when Mr. Lowell had written her of Ashby Hall and the child who was in need of a governess.

She braced herself for as cold and bleak a welcome

as the house seemed to offer, and went around to the back where she assumed there would be a servants' entrance. Finding no convenient well for water with which to wash her face, Mercy took out her damp handkerchief, and used it to wipe the mud from her exposed skin. Then she glanced at her reflection in one of the windows.

She looked like some pathetic drowned creature.

Sighing with resignation, she rapped upon the door.

The heavy door swung open and a tall, lanky, young red-haired man peered out at Mercy. His hands were the size of platters and his feet like small boats. But his face was friendly. "Aye, miss?"

"I'm Miss Franklin, here to see Mr. Lowell."

He looked at her blankly for a moment, and then stepped aside and said, "Come in, miss."

Whatever the young man's reticence, Mercy only hoped to get warm and dry. She entered a back corridor near a kitchen and set down her traveling case.

"You're drenched through, aren't you, miss?" the lad said, leading her into a large kitchen where two other men were occupied preparing food at a long worktable. Mercy's stomach growled at the wonderful aromas that bubbled up from the stove. "Come this way. You can get warm in here."

The heat from the kitchen felt wonderful, but Mercy felt ill at ease. She believed she recognized the cooks as two of the riders who'd splashed mud on her. The one with the heavy mustache, definitely.

She gritted her teeth with frustration, aware that she had to make a good impression here, in spite of the kind of men Lord Ashby employed. Mr. Lowell's letter was the only response to her advertisement, which had come just in time, before the last of her money was spent.

Her stomach fell when it occurred to her that it might have been Mr. Lowell whose horse had startled and thrown him in the road. Who else would have been dressed as a gentleman and riding behind the ruffians in the kitchen? Mercy did not know how she would face him now, after his outrageous remarks and their biting interchange.

And yet there was naught she could do now besides pray that she would not have to meet him again. Thankfully, it was far more likely that the Ashby housekeeper, or even the child's nurse, would outline her duties. Even so, she looked down at her stained coat and nearly despaired. She could not face the woman like this. "I'd like to . . . er, is there a place where I might change into dry clothes before I meet with . . . Mrs. . . . er . . . ?"

Her question seemed to perplex the young man, who scratched the side of his head while the other two turned around to look at her. The one without the mustache tipped his head toward a closed door.

"The pantry, Corporal Childers?" the young man asked. "Oh, aye. The pantry will do, eh, miss?"

He picked up a lamp and ushered Mercy into a small room lined with shelves stacked with food staples. He handed her the lamp and then stepped away to the door. "Well, I'll just leave you then, miss. Oh, and I'm Henry Blue. Just sing out if you need anything."

Chapter 4

Nash Farris, Lord Ashby, rubbed his left eye in a vain attempt to clear his vision, even though he knew it was useless. The tissues had been damaged in and around his eye, a small forfeit, considering he should have lost his life.

And what a life it was. He almost laughed. But for the haughty little piece he'd met on the road a bit earlier, his life was naught but a cruel jest.

His best friend, Lieutenant John Trent, had died in Nash's place on a battlefield in Belgium on the eighteenth of June last year. And Nash's elder brother, Arthur, had met his own end here in the Lake District alongside his wife, on the very same day, in a weird and horrific coincidence, making Nash the Earl of Ashby. It was made all the worse since their eldest brother, Hoyt, had been killed in a shooting accident less than a year before that.

No wonder the people around Keswick were saying the Ashby earls were cursed. They were waiting to see what tragedy would befall the third Ashby son. He supposed he should thank the fates he hadn't broken his neck in his fall from his horse that afternoon.

Nash stood abruptly, and then sat right back down. There was significant pain in his ankle, and he knew he should have his valet, Sergeant Parker, bind it and put it up to keep it from swelling any more. He could not pace, as he'd been wont to do since returning to Ashby Hall with a few of the men who'd served with him at various times over the past thirteen years.

Nash was not meant for the life of a country gentleman, especially on an estate that was in such dire need of competent stewardship. What did he know of sheep and wool and grazing lands?

More, what did he care?

He was the dashing Captain Farris, favorite of the ladies and menace on the battlefield, a man whose life had seemed charmed.

But it had all been abruptly and forever altered at Waterloo during the first French onslaught through the gates at Hougoumont Farm. John Trent had shoved Nash away from a French saber, taking the fatal jab himself. Nash had recovered to fight fiercely, bringing Trent's killer down while the Guards managed to close the gates against the enemy, trapping a number of them inside.

They'd made the farmhouse a fortress, but the French were undeterred. As was Nash. He became a man possessed to ensure that Trent had not died in vain. French troops would not take the Hougoumont.

The French continued their assaults throughout that fateful afternoon, attempting to breach the walls via the woods and orchards, but failing. Their howitzers fired incendiary shells inside, setting the house and barn afire. Smoke and artillery fire filled the house and the walled yard, and a sudden explosion threw Nash into a stone wall, cracking his ribs. His vision was impaired by a trail of blood dripping from his scalp, and when a burning beam fell upon him, he was trapped.

By all accounts, everything happened quickly after that, but Nash could not remember the rest of that day or the next several. His men had saved his life, pulling him from the burning rubble, but he did not feel quite thankful. He had his life, such as it was. But everything that had ever mattered was gone.

Nash had not been groomed to be earl the way Hoyt had been, and had not spent more than a few weeks every year at Ashby since leaving for school. Even his stubborn but well-educated brother Arthur had failed at running the estate. And if Arthur could not make a go of Ashby, then Nash doubted he'd have much more success.

He'd been lacking in successes lately, including the reaction of the comely young woman he'd encountered in the lane. Not that he'd been attempting to garner her favor. On the contrary, as his reputation bore out, he had no use for innocent young things, and his mishap had been highly inconvenient. He was lucky he hadn't reinjured his mended ribs.

A knock at the library door interrupted his restless mood and pointless ruminations. Ashby's steward, Philip Lowell, entered the room. Lowell was several years older than Nash's thirty-one years, a powerfully built man with light hair and eyes. His unfailing favor with the ladies reminded Nash of his own prowess before his injury, but that was a lifetime ago. Of late, Nash had encountered very few women who were unaffected by his scars.

Lowell entered the library but stopped short when he saw Nash sitting with his foot elevated on an ottoman. "What happened to you, my lord?"

Nash put his foot on the floor. He was no invalid, to be coddled or indulged. Especially by his handsome steward, an unscarred dandy with ambitions that seemed to exceed Ashby's immediate potential.

"Naught of interest." Besides becoming earl and the sole guardian of Hoyt's daughter, the only remarkable thing that had happened to Nash lately was the silly accident in the road today. The attractive young woman had captured his interest as nothing else had done in recent months. He'd almost laughed at her brusque dealings with him.

And then he'd felt the undeniable stirrings of arousal at her spirit. No timid miss was she.

There hadn't seemed to be any point in asking her name. It seemed quite clear that she wasn't staying in the area. She'd had traveling cases, and it seemed logical that she'd been waiting to catch the mail coach when his men had driven her off the road.

He put thoughts of her aside, for he was quite aware of the effect his scarred countenance had upon women these days. Nary a one could look upon him without revulsion. Or worse, pity.

And yet it seemed the woman in the road had not even noticed his marred face. He wondered now if she—or any other woman—could ever . . .

He gave a slight shake of his head to banish the long-dead stirrings of lust she'd managed to arouse. There were far more serious matters that faced him. Besides the fact that he was now a peer of the realm, the kind of injuries he'd sustained at Waterloo had made him unsuitable for active duty. He couldn't shoot worth a damn anymore, and his impaired vision and frequent headaches would make him a liability to his company. So would his waking night-mares—the flashes of memory that came to him so sudden and startling he could barely stay on his feet when they hit him.

Nash could not hide from the knowledge that his face was irreparably damaged. The doctors in the field might have been optimistic about his vision re-turning and the ugly red scars diminishing, but Nash was far more pragmatic about it. Besides, after all he'd lost, this was trivial.

"I had a minor accident on the road," he said in answer to the steward's question. "What do you want, Lowell? Have you some more bad news about the sheep? Or is it about the flooding in the west fields again?"

"Neither, my lord."

Nash didn't think he would ever become used to hearing himself called by his father's title. As the youngest son, he'd never meant to accede to the title, which was why he'd joined the army. Bought his commission and gone to war, like a good many other second and third sons. Who would have believed his two elder brothers would die in their prime?

A shard of pain shot through him at the thought of the two of them, gone.

"It's about Lady Emmaline, sir. Her new governess."

Figuring out what to do with his little niece was problematic. Lowell had left her in the care of the nurse hired by Arthur's wife, but Nash had sacked the woman on sight and put Henry Blue—the youngest of his men—in charge of seeing that the child came to no harm. But Blue was inadequate at best.

Little Emmaline barely remembered Nash, and to make matters worse, he knew his scars frightened her. So he did the only thing possible. He avoided her.

"Brilliant. Where did you find a governess who will work for no pay?" His sarcasm was not lost on Lowell, who chuckled.

"I fear this is an expense we must pay, my lord."

Nash knew he was right. And fortunately, he would not have to give the woman any money right away. That would not be required until the end of the quarter at the earliest, which would give him time to raise some cash. He hoped.

"How does she compare to that shrew of a nurse who was here when I arrived?"

"I have not met her yet, my lord. But I think she will be somewhat different. Her letter sounded rather more civilized than Nurse Butterfield."

"Is she a Keswick woman?"

"Ah, no. If you remember, Reverend Swan's wife spoke to me of Lady Emmaline's situation one Sunday last month. She suggested I read the advertisements for a governess."

If only a governess was all that Emmaline needed. Nash remembered agreeing with Lowell's suggestion to find a governess, but he had just arrived at Ashby and there had been so many other issues to attend to. "Now that you remind me, I do recall."

"I found only a few advertisements, and hired the most promising one."

"Who?"

"A woman called Mercy Franklin."

"Mercy? What kind of name is that?" Nash wondered aloud.

"She was a vicar's daughter—she wrote that he is now deceased and so she must earn her fortune."

"Her fortune as a governess," Nash said dryly.

Lowell did not reply. "I understand she has arrived. Would you care to speak to her now?"

Nash smiled for only the second time since he'd come back to the Lake District. The first occasion had been less than an hour before as he sat on his arse in the road.

"Aye. Now would be perfect."

Something was a bit off, but besides encountering two of the men who'd raced past her in a haze of mist and mud, Mercy could not put her finger on it. She'd never been in an earl's home before, so she didn't know exactly what to expect. Surely, something grander. Not that Ashby Hall wasn't large, for it was absolutely huge. It was just that everything inside seemed as shabby as the outside.

There was an abundance of activity in the large kitchen, and the cooking aromas had set her stomach to growling. Mercy put aside her hunger as well as her trepidations, and went into the pantry to change.

She felt vastly uncomfortable removing her clothes in the small closet so near the kitchen with those ruffians who'd run her off the road, but there was no help for it. She could not meet the housekeeper in her soaking wet gown. She put on her best dress, a gown of dark blue with white collar and cuffs. Without the benefit of a mirror, she took her hair out of its pins and smoothed it down before twisting it into a knot and refastening it at the back of her neck. She'd had years of practice at this, using only the tiny mirror her father allowed her—to guard against the sin of vanity. Still, he had never abided anything less than a perfectly tidy appearance.

There had been many rules at St. Martin's rectory. Reverend Franklin had required that Mercy be silent until spoken to, and spend one hour every evening on her knees while she read a passage of Scripture that he had chosen for her. She was not allowed to read any material or participate in any activity without her father's approval.

The reverend had believed that the only pleasure to be taken from this life was in strict and pious behavior, and atonement for one's sins. Not that Mercy had ever had a chance to commit any. She had been a conscientious and obedient daughter who'd served her father's parish in every way he'd seen fit.

She just hoped her work on Sundays with the youngsters would help her know what to do with the earl's niece.

Kitchen sounds and smells met Mercy as she stepped out of the pantry, and she carried her wet things toward the voices. "Here, let me take all that," said Henry Blue when he saw her carrying her wet coat and the one mourning gown she owned. "I'll lay it all out by the fire, miss."

"Does the housekeeper know that I am here?"

She made her voice sound as confident as possible, although her stomach was churning as it had been ever since receiving Mr. Lowell's offer of employment. Not even the difficulties she'd faced after her mother's death had unnerved her as much as having to move so far from the home she'd always known, to a position for which she had little knowledge and no real experience.

At least she'd had a few informative letters from her friend Claire Rogers, who'd moved away from Underdale more than a year ago to London to become governess for a wealthy family there. It was Claire's letters that had given Mercy the idea of advertising for this position, and a few hints on how to comport herself once she landed a post.

"Housekeeper, miss?" the young man asked, sounding puzzled. As though he'd never heard of such a person.

Mercy's heart sank. "Yes. Isn't there a . . ." She moistened her lips. "Who is to give me my instructions?"

"Mr. Lowell knows you're here. I went to tell him while you were changing clothes. I'm to take you to the library straight away and . . . well, I'm sure he'll tell you what you're supposed to do."

She eyed her wet clothes, neatly laid out on the hearth, and her traveling cases standing nearby, and wondered if she could possibly make this dark, bleak place her home. Bolstering her resolve, she followed Henry Blue and faced the fact that she had no choice but to stay at Ashby Hall. The Franklins had no other relations on whom Mercy could rely, and she didn't know who her own people were, either.

On her deathbed, Susanna had not been able to recall the name of the man who'd brought Mercy to them all those years ago, but she'd certainly remembered him hinting at her origins. Mercy felt a weight in the pit of her stomach at the memory of her mother's disapproving words.

Only a fallen woman would abandon her offspring, Susanna had said as she lay pale and trembling beneath her bed linens with fever and chills. Mercy's adoptive mother had kept her wits throughout her illness, but the lung fever had robbed her of most of her breath. She had said little during her last hours of life, but in her last moments, had revealed the most significant piece of information Mercy had ever learned.

With that extraordinary revelation, bits and pieces of Mercy's childhood had come to make some kind of sense. It brought a new dimension to Mercy's understanding of her parents' strictness. Considering what the Franklins believed of her mother, it seemed obvious they had feared Mercy would succumb to the same temptations that had caused her own mother's downfall.

And yet she would have thought marriage to a bona fide clergyman was exactly what they'd want. What better way to keep their adopted daughter on the straight and narrow path? But her father had refused Reverend Vale.

Mercy suddenly thought of the man who'd been thrown from his horse and understood how a woman might be persuaded to surrender to such a man's dark good looks and brooding manner. The horseman was temptation personified.

But Mercy was nothing like the mother who'd

abandoned her. She had the wherewithal to resist any man, in spite of what her adoptive parents might have thought of her *or* her true mother.

Following Henry through a maze of stone corridors, Mercy slowed, her worries and trepidations getting the best of her. She did not doubt that the fallen horseman had been part of the barbarous group that had nearly knocked her off the road near the turnstile. And two of those men were in the kitchen now.

"Miss?" Henry asked when he realized she was no longer following him.

Mercy gave him a wavering smile and caught up as she prayed the injured horseman was not the man who had hired her. She had been anything but respectful to him, and he had made at least one undignified remark. The heat of embarrassment burned her cheeks as she thought of his words, so inappropriate for a man to make to a maiden, and a stranger at that.

As they walked through the dim, medieval corridor, their footsteps echoed hollowly. "The library is just through there," said Henry, pointing to a set of pocket doors that had darkened with time.

"Thank you," Mercy replied as Henry took his leave. She stood outside for a moment and checked to make sure her collar was straight and her hair well contained. She gave a brief knock at the door, and a blond man with a nicely trimmed mustache answered. He was only a few inches taller than Mercy, but solidly built, and possessed of an engaging smile.

"Miss Franklin," he said as he stepped aside for

her to enter. He bowed with an impressive flourish. "I am Philip Lowell. Welcome."

Mercy felt almost giddy with relief. In spite of the fact that there was no housekeeper to conduct her interview, at least Mr. Lowell was not the blackguard on the road. "How do you do, Mr. Lowell."

The man was handsome in a conventional way, with a healthy, ruddy complexion. His light hair was thick and fashionably cut, and his smile hinted at charm to spare. Though Mercy sensed that he would find favor with every young lady in the parish, she found nothing intriguing about him, felt no pull of attraction.

It was clear proof that her father had been entirely wrong about her propensities.

The room behind Mr. Lowell was large and dimly lit. The beveled windows were in need of a good washing, but the number of books on the shelves made Mercy's eyes grow wide. She wondered if Lord Ashby would object to her borrowing some of these volumes for her own personal reading. She did not care that they gave off an odor of dust and disuse, or that the deep red draperies were in need of a good beating. Having met Mr. Lowell, her misgivings eased, and the possibility occurred to her for the first time since her arrival at the turnstile, that Ashby Hall might suit her very well.

The smell of the peat fire permeated the room, and when Mr. Lowell led her farther into the library, Mercy was startled to see a man sitting in an overstuffed chair near the fireplace, with his leg conspicuously elevated on an ottoman.

A great rock, the size of a Castlerigg standing

stone, lodged in her throat, and Mercy wished she could go away and hide. Instead, she pressed one hand to her breast, closed her eyes briefly, and forced a composure she did not feel, chastising herself for neglecting to consider this possibility.

And yet she never would have thought an earl would be quite so . . . She gulped when the word *earthy* came to mind. He did not appear at all the way she had expected a nobleman to look, with his plain, gentleman's clothes and lack of ornamentation.

And yet it was this stark, strapping physicality that made him so very intriguing. It was what made her knees go soft like pudding when her eyes drifted to the sensual mouth that was quirked in the vaguest hint of a smile.

Chapter 5

Mercy reined in her unseemly reaction to Lord Ashby, aware that he would likely dismiss her on the spot. He could not possibly want to hire an insolent, cheeky—

"Lord Ashby has a few questions for you, Miss Franklin."

Lord above! Why could she not have kept a civil tongue in her head? She could very well have assisted the man quickly and gone on her way. But no . . .

The earl tipped his head, which happened to be turned slightly so that his scars were not visible. His profile was even more striking than she remembered it. "At your service," he said.

Mercy knew that was patently untrue, but she kept her peace for a change.

"You've come a long way, Miss Franklin?"

She was grateful he did not refer to her dreadful conduct on the road. "Yes, my lord. From Underdale."

"Ah. At the seashore."

Mercy nodded, her mouth suddenly too dry to speak. If only she could have assisted him without having to tuck his leg so indelicately under her arm . . . If only he had not mentioned her . . . derriere.

She felt a prickle of some unfamiliar and unto-ward sensation creep up her spine.

"Mr. Lowell tells me that this is your first govern-ess post."

Mercy swallowed the Castlerigg stone, but it lodged heavily in the pit of her stomach. Clearly, he intended to torture her before dismissing her. "That is correct, my lord."

"Tell me: How have you occupied yourself for the past twenty . . . whatever . . . years? And what quali-fies you to be my niece's teacher?" He allowed his glance to rove over her form for a moment, and the prickle in her spine settled into her lower back.

Mercy could not allow him to rattle her.

"I lived with my parents in Underdale. My father was vicar at St. Martin's Church." No need to tell the arrogant man that she wasn't really Reverend Franklin's daughter, that the Franklins suspected Mercy had been her true mother's immoral misfor-tune. "He died last summer. My mother passed away only recently."

"My sympathies, Miss Franklin." He spoke softly, and a rogue shadow crossed his brow. But then he took a deep breath and addressed her again. "You appear sufficiently stiff-backed to fill the role of gov-erness. Stringent discipline, and all that. Tell me, Miss Franklin, I assume this post was not your first choice of avocations. Were there no opportunities for you to marry in Underdale?"

"My lord . . ." said Mr. Lowell in a cautionary tone, but Mercy turned to him and spoke before he could continue.

" 'Tis quite all right, Mr. Lowell. I do not mind

setting Lord Ashby's mind at ease." She returned her full attention to the earl. "I received two proposals of marriage in Underdale, but both were rejected by my father."

Ashby scowled, the expression reminding Mercy of the harsh looks he'd given her while lying injured on the road. "On what grounds? I cannot imagine that there were two scoundrels in all of Cumberland who would vie for the hand of a vicar's daughter."

Mercy clasped her hands together, feeling altogether out of her element. Her life had been thoroughly fixed and predictable in Underdale—at least, until the deaths of her parents. The people of the parish knew the Franklins well, and afforded her the respect and deference she was due. But here at Ashby Hall, her life would be subject to the whims of her employer.

And he was a rascal at best.

"The first young man was a local fisherman who my father believed would be unable to provide for me as he saw fit." She was not ashamed of her past or of James Morland's proposal. He was an honest, hardworking man with a small fishing boat of his own. And he'd courted her quite properly. Mercy had done naught to earn disdain from anyone, not even a roguish earl.

"And the second?"

Mercy shook her head slightly and hedged. "My father was vague in his rejection of Reverend Vale."

"Vale? Another reverend? I wonder . . ." He looked at her speculatively, and Mercy resisted the urge to squirm. "But here you are, Miss Franklin, ready to teach my niece."

"Yes, my lord," she said, and suddenly realized what had seemed so "off" about the house. She had not seen any women here; no housekeeper, and not a maid in sight. Henry Blue had addressed Mr. Childers as corporal, and the men on the road had worn old army clothes. They seemed to have turned the place into an army installation. Not quite what she would consider an appropriate environment for a young girl.

"You have not yet met my niece, Miss Franklin. How do you know you'll be able to manage her? Or that your severe manner won't terrify her?"

"*Severe* mann—" She stopped and took a deep breath, moistening her lips at the same time. She needed this post, at least temporarily. "I'm sure I'll fare much better with your niece than a battalion of soldiers can do."

"Correction. *Former* soldiers," he said, confirming her suspicions.

"And ruffians, at that." A muffled sound came from Mr. Lowell's direction, but Mercy did not turn to look at him.

For some reason, Lord Ashby brought out the worst in her. She wished she possessed better control of her tongue before those brazen words had a chance to slip out.

Perhaps she *wanted* him to dismiss her before she could even begin.

In any event, there'd been absolutely nothing wrong with her manner prior to meeting Lord Ashby. And since her parents had dictated her mode of grooming and dress, she knew they were perfectly proper, in spite of the fact that she was not wearing her mourning gown at the moment. It had been soaked in the rain and was drying by the fire in the kitchen.

She sighed inwardly and decided she must try to redeem herself.

"I would not call my manner severe, my lord. 'Tis merely sensible. Beyond that, I spent much of my time with the parish children and we got on well enough. Famously, in fact. I am sure your niece and I will carry on just fine together."

She thought she sounded convincing. At least, convincing enough for him to allow her to stay and try with the child.

He rubbed the side of his head, and Mercy wondered if his facial damage was the result of battle. She supposed the injury could be what made him so irritable.

Sympathy for the trouble the earl must have endured was out of place here and now. He had not yet indicated his approval of her as his niece's governess and could send her away just as easily as keep her.

Mercy slid her lower lip through her teeth and forced her nerves to settle as she took a surreptitious glance around the purely masculine room. A large desk occupied one corner, and the heavy, crimson draperies framed the filmy windows behind them. She had already noted that they were dusty with age and neglect—obviously, none of Lord Ashby's men had taken note of their disreputable state. She hoped the nursery was kept in a more acceptable condition.

"You'll do, Miss Franklin."

"Thank you, my lord."

Mercy's heart pattered with relief.

She had a home, at least for the time being, and a means to earn a living. She wondered if she ought to speak of her salary now, for Mr. Lowell had not mentioned it in his letter. Never having sought employment before, she was unsure of the proper protocol.

Nor did she know how to broach the subject. She should not be embarrassed to ask about the wages she intended to earn, but being in need stung deeply. "D-does your niece have a nurse, my lord?"

Lord Ashby made a low sound, and Mr. Lowell quickly answered the question. "No, Miss Franklin. Emmaline is an independent child."

She'd forgotten Mr. Lowell was in the room. "I beg your pardon?" she asked, turning to him.

"Private Blue looks after Lady Emmaline for the most part," Lowell explained. "And Corporal Roarke spells him when necessary."

Mercy frowned. "Mr. Lowell, you said in your letter that Lord Ashby's niece is eight years old."

"Correct."

"It does not seem altogether proper that two . . . young men are responsible for such a young child. She should have a nurse to care for her."

"I sacked the damned harpy on sight," Ashby snapped. "Which is why Lowell has summoned you, Miss Franklin." He turned to Mr. Lowell. "Have one of the men bring Emmaline to us here."

Nash was likely making a gross mistake in allowing Miss Franklin to stay at Ashby Hall. He'd ordered his men to stay clear of the young women in Keswick, and they were starved for female attention.

He did not know how they would react to having Miss Franklin in their midst day in and day out.

His own reaction was less than stellar, and for that reason alone, he should have sent her back to Underdale. But then they would be back to having only Blue and Roarke to keep track of Emmaline, dash it all. He knew it was an unsuitable situation.

But his options were limited.

He hoped Miss Franklin's audaciousness would appeal to Emmaline, perhaps even draw the child out of herself. As much as the new governess attempted to appear the proper, straitlaced vicar's daughter, Nash thought the young lady might actually be too softhearted to be effective with his niece. In spite of what he'd said about her stiff manner, Mercy Franklin was the very opposite of the peevish nurse he'd dismissed on the day he'd arrived at Ashby Hall.

Which had led to his present predicament. He was in desperate need of a female to deal with Emmaline. Nash feared something was wrong with Hoyt's daughter, for she was far too quiet for a child her age—not that he knew a great deal about children, but he'd seen plenty of them during his campaigns abroad. Not to mention that he'd once been one.

But that was a long time ago. Before his brothers had died. Before John Trent had put himself in the way of a bloody Frenchman's saber on the field at Waterloo.

"My niece is quite shy," he said to Miss Franklin. "She barely speaks."

"Even to you, my lord?"

"*Especially* to me." She was as fragile as his mother's bone china, and Nash hardly knew what to say to her, or how to deal with her. Not that he particularly wanted to. That was why he now had Mercy Franklin.

Now that her bonnet was gone, he saw that the young woman's hair was as black as her brows, as glossy as a raven's wing. Nash could not help but wonder how it would look if she allowed its waves to fall loosely about her face. She would be stunning, and a man would have all he could do to keep from sliding his fingers through it and pressing his face to its lustrous bounty.

He curbed his reaction to her and gestured to the chair across from him. Surely she would confine Emmaline and herself to the nursery and classroom for the most part. He couldn't imagine any reason why she might spend time in the drawing room or kitchens. Or in his presence.

Nor did he want her to. She was young, her skin perfect, the blush upon her cheeks a reminder of all that Nash would never have . . . never allow himself to have.

He could not bear yet another loss.

"Why especially to you, Lord Ashby?" she asked.

"Are you blind, Miss Franklin?" he said angrily.

"No, my lord. My vision is quite good."

"Then you can see what my niece observes every time she looks at me."

Her throat moved as she swallowed thickly at his harsh tone. Obviously, she'd seen his scars, even if she had not visibly recoiled from the sight of them. Perhaps a vicar's daughter was accustomed to dealing with the sick or injured, and was inured to such ghastly sights.

He changed the subject. "Tell me what you know of governessing while we wait for my niece."

She lowered herself onto a straight-backed chair near the fire and he caught a subtle whiff of flowers. Lilies, if he was not mistaken. "I know that a child of eight should be able to read and write. She should know something of England and the world, and have the ability to pursue her talents."

"Her talents?"

Miss Franklin nodded. "We all have talents, do we not?"

"She is but a child, Miss Franklin."

"Even children have certain aptitudes, my lord."

Nash remembered having had a noteworthy talent for climbing. Trees, cottage roofs, the gabled roof and high turrets of Ashby Hall. He'd loved looking at the world from a perch far above where he could see for miles. He was lucky these days if he could see his own boots.

"What is your particular aptitude, Miss Franklin?"

She hesitated for a moment. "Plants, my lord."

"Plants?"

"Yes, plants. And insects, of course. I have an interest in botany, therefore, I've made a point to learn all I can on the subject."

"And insects?"

"They often have an intimate relationship with plants. And honey bees are quite essential."

Nash felt heat rise on the back of his neck as he watched Miss Franklin's lips form the words. Intimate relationship, indeed.

The door opened and Emmaline came into the library, followed by Mr. Lowell.

Nash had seen the child at least once daily since his return to Ashby Hall the previous month, out of guilt more than anything. He did not care to form a bond with the girl—or with anyone. The losses of the past few years had taught him the folly of trusting his heart to the whims of fate.

Fortunately, Emmaline was not particularly charmed by her unsightly uncle who knew more about swordplay and artillery fire than dolls and tea parties. Still, he had a responsibility to his orphaned niece. In the absence of a nurse, Miss Franklin would do.

Emmaline came into the room, looking slightly disheveled and more than a little uncertain, and Nash realized how dreadful the situation had gotten. It wasn't that Roarke and Blue were bad fellows, but they were not nursemaids.

Emmaline's light blond hair was loose and uncombed, but at least her face was clean today. Nash did not go to her, for she would just cringe away from his touch. And besides, she appeared so fragile, he was a bit afraid to lay his big hands upon her, for fear she might break.

"Emmaline, this is Miss Franklin, who is to be your governess." He was certain Emmaline had not cared much for Butterfield, the nurse he'd dismissed. Lowell and the ancient butler, Grainger, had told him the woman had been engaged by Arthur's wife. And Georgia had been far more interested in becoming a grande dame of society than a child's guardian.

Georgia had kept a haughty housekeeper as well, and the woman had resigned the day after Nash sacked the nurse. She'd called his men "barbarians and plunderers," and Nash had not been sorry to see the back of her, either.

To be sure, it was unconventional to staff a noble household with former military men, but the group of men Nash had brought to Ashby had nowhere else to go and were willing to work for their keep. They only needed some direction, not that Nash knew how to run a household, much less an estate.

Or a child. Emmaline stood still, her pale eyes turned to the direction of the fire. And Nash was reminded again of his unsightly injury. He couldn't very well blame Emmaline for not wanting to look at him.

"How do you do, Lady Emmaline?" Miss Franklin said, coming to stand before the child. She suddenly dropped down to one knee and took the girl's hand. "I am very pleased to meet you, finally."

Emmaline's eyes flickered away from the fire and came to rest upon the hand Miss Franklin held. "Hello," she said in such a quiet tone Nash could barely hear her.

"Would you like to show me the nursery?"

Emmaline appeared uncertain, but her throat moved as she swallowed and gave a slow, tentative nod.

"Good," said Miss Franklin, rising to her feet. She kept Emmaline's hand in her own and flashed a quick look at Nash. "If that is all, my lord?"

He gave a brief nod and she started out of the library.

"Allow me to escort you, Miss Franklin," Lowell said, leaving with her. "The nursery and governess's quarters are in the north wing."

Chapter 6

Mercy was finally able to breathe normally once she left Lord Ashby's presence. It was clear that Emmaline was going to be a challenge, but at least Mercy would not need to have many more dealings with the girl's uncle. She'd gleaned as much as she could about the occupation she was about to embark upon from Claire's letters. What she knew was hardly enough, but Claire had mentioned that children and their nurses and governesses generally kept out of the way of the adults of the household. Holding Emmaline's hand, they returned through the great hall, past a dreary drawing room, to a wide stone staircase that led to a gallery above.

"Shall we go up?" Mercy asked.

"This way," said Mr. Lowell from behind. Mercy had nearly forgotten he had come along, for she had trained her complete attention on her young charge. The child was as thin as a waif, and abnormally subdued. Mercy could not help but wonder if this had always been her way or perhaps she still grieved the loss of her parents.

Mercy knew how that felt. Even though her feelings for the Franklins were mixed with confusion now, the sense of being entirely alone was daunting.

The upstairs gallery was wide, but encased in shadows, so Mercy could barely see the heavily framed paintings that hung at intervals on the cold, gray walls. There were groupings of tables and stiff-backed chairs, but Mercy had the distinct sense that they had been unused for quite some time. She hoped the nursery was not quite so cheerless.

"I apologize for the darkness up here. We should have lit the sconces."

"I'm sure that would help," Mercy said, but she doubted it. As she walked down the long, wide gallery, she could almost feel the weight of the dreary old house settling onto her shoulders. She did not know how she would be able to tolerate living within these medieval walls with a handful of rowdy soldiers to keep it running, and the smoldering perusal of Lord Ashby every time he looked at her. Of course, she'd seen his scars, but it was horribly rude of him to mention them to her the way he'd done. It wasn't as if they detracted from the man's appeal. If anything, they made him even more interesting than . . .

The thought of contacting Andrew Vale returned with a vengeance.

But Mercy wondered how awkward it would be if Mr. Vale had wed someone in the months since he'd visited St. Martin's and proposed to her. If that were the case, she did not think a letter suggesting a renewal of their courtship would be quite welcome. Perhaps she could write without directly suggesting that he renew his suit. She did not know if he was aware of her parents' deaths, so she could inform him of the drastic change in her life. And if he was still unwed, he could act upon that knowledge.

Or not.

Mercy did not want to think of that possibility, not when she could see no other option than remaining here in this run-down, isolated, uncivilized Hall.

"The original Hall was built in the fourteenth century by the first Earl of Ashby," said Mr. Lowell. "But additions have been built over the centuries. And a few modernizations."

"It's a very old earldom, then," Mercy replied. She wondered if Mr. Lowell was trying to impress her with the longevity of Ashby since it clearly had no other claim to distinguish itself.

They went around a corner and down another long corridor, finally reaching an open door halfway down. Inside was a wide bank of mullioned windows that provided light for the room, dreary as the day might be. At least the furniture was not as antique as what Mercy had seen in the rest of the mansion, but had been furnished fairly recently, perhaps by Emmaline's mother.

Mercy wondered what had happened to her, but did not want to ask Mr. Lowell while Emmaline was present. She had very little knowledge of Emmaline's parents—only that the girl had been orphaned and left in the care of her beguiling but oblivious uncle and his men. She needed more information.

Glancing about the classroom, Mercy found it clean, with everything neat and orderly. Far more neat and orderly than Emmaline herself. The child wore a pair of hose that might have been white at one time, but were gray and dingy, and stained. Her pale blue gown was soiled at the bodice and cuffs, as though no one in this house had ever heard of a laundry tub. Mercy was going to have to see about acquiring a nurse for Emmaline, for there was far more to do for the young girl than just academic instruction.

She turned to Mr. Lowell. "Thank you for escorting us here, sir. I believe we'll manage just fine on our own now."

"Are you sure, Miss Franklin?" he asked, seeming inclined to linger. "It seems so very . . . abrupt."

"Yes, we'll be fine. Thank you, Mr. Lowell." She turned the tables and escorted him back to the door, shutting it after him. Then she returned her attention to her young charge.

"Well," she said, silently vowing to do something about Emmaline's appearance in spite of the absence of a nurse. The Franklins had not been wealthy people. Mercy had done plenty of sewing, and had helped with the daily housework. She'd assisted with the laundry hundreds of times, and knew what needed to be done to improve Emmaline's wardrobe. "This is an excellent room for our lessons. Where do you sleep?"

Emmaline pointed to an adjoining door, and Mercy went to it. She pushed it open and saw that the room beyond was completely tidy, appearing almost as though no one occupied it, certainly not a little girl. There was an abandoned little dressing table, and Emmaline's narrow bed had been made up tightly and had a plain brown blanket folded neatly across its foot. Opposite the bed was a low bookcase that stood against the wall. It contained a perfectly even row of books, meticulously arranged from tallest to shortest, including a number of volumes Mercy had not been allowed to read as a youngster. Several dolls were lined up on top of the shelf, evenly spaced and sitting at attention.

But for the beautiful framed watercolors hanging on the walls, the room seemed a far too sterile, too barren environment for a little girl. Even Mercy's bedchamber in her parents' austere home had displayed more embellishments than this room. Mercy could not imagine what Lord Ashby had been thinking in assigning his men to the care of his niece.

Nor did she know quite where to begin with the little girl who stood so still and quiet. Surely such reserve was not natural.

"Does your uncle call you Emmaline?" Mercy asked.

The little girl looked up at Mercy as if she'd grown wings and was about to fly away.

"What about your parents? Did they always call you Emmaline?"

"My papa called me Emmy."

"Would you mind very much if I called you Emmy?"

Her rigid stance seemed to melt a little and she nodded.

"You have a great number of books, Emmy," Mercy said in an attempt to further engage her.

Emmaline nodded.

"Do you have a favorite?"

Emmaline knelt down and picked out a large book with sturdy covers that appeared to have been made by hand. She handed it carefully to Mercy, who knelt beside her to look at the book.

"This is beautiful," she said as she turned the pages, admiring the delightfully detailed watercolors and the stories written in a clear but fanciful script on the pages opposite the pictures. She turned to the first leaf and saw an inscription that warmed her heart.

"For my darling Emmy ~ May there always be magic in your life. From your most devoted Mother."

Mercy guessed Emmaline's mother had painted the pictures in the book as well as those on the walls. "'Tis lovely, Emmy. I can see why it's your favorite."

Emmaline nodded and took the book from Mercy's hands. Very carefully, she closed it and put it back on the shelf. Mercy wondered how long Emmaline's mother had been dead, and what had happened to her father. But it was clearly not appropriate to ask the child, who seemed so delicate she might break with the first untoward word.

The child was not exactly skittish, but withdrawn. There was no light of curiosity or delight in her beautiful blue eyes. She kept them downcast as much as possible.

"Have you ever had a governess?" Mercy asked.

"No," Emmaline replied softly.

"And I have never been a governess before," Mercy said with a smile, hoping to get past some of Emmaline's shyness. "You will have to help me do a good job."

Emmaline looked at her sharply, and Mercy suppressed a smile at the girl's sudden flare of interest.

Now that she had some idea of how to engage Emmaline, she glanced around. "Where do you suppose my room is? Can you show me?"

They stood, and Emmaline took Mercy's hand. Leaving the nursery, Emmaline took her across the corridor into a stale chamber with a narrow bed and a dusty wardrobe. It had obviously been unused for quite some time, but there were large windows similar to the ones in the nursery that looked out over a grove of tall beech trees that were just beginning to bud. Beyond it were the tall fells and the path she'd traversed to reach her destination here.

With a thorough cleaning, the room would do. And yet Emmaline would not. As a vicar's daughter, Mercy had come into contact with the parish children, and yet none was as quiet and reserved as Emmaline.

Presumptuous or not, she needed to ask Lord Ashby a few questions about little Lady Emmaline.

As soon as his niece and her governess quit the room, Nash turned his attention to his injured ankle. As inconvenient as that was, it was far better than thinking about Emmaline's sad eyes or Miss Franklin's enticing ones. He neither needed nor wanted any new entanglements.

Yet it had been amusing to tease the girl when she'd stopped to help him in the road. He'd been surprisingly engaged by Miss Franklin, half drowned as she was with her soaked bonnet plastered over her hair. The situation had been absurd, but the delicate outline of Mercy Franklin's face had compelled him, with her high cheekbones and daintily pointed chin. Nash considered that her eyes had to be the clearest green of any he'd ever seen, and they'd watched him warily, even critically.

But it was her plush mouth that had captured his attention. That, and the lushly feminine form that had been patently obvious in spite of her prim coat.

Who would have thought such sharp words could have emanated from those enticing lips? Who would have thought Nash would feel such acute arousal for a young woman who had accused him—to his face!—of being foolhardy.

He almost laughed aloud. She had been so busy scolding him, it seemed she had not even noticed the damaged side of his face or his filmy eye, despite the fact that he had done naught to hide them.

Nash turned to look at the fire. Miss Franklin was a puzzle he had no intention of solving. He needed answers to several far more important other questions, which had been the purpose of his visit to Keswick's magistrate earlier in the afternoon.

He wanted to know who had been present when his eldest brother, Hoyt, had been shot and killed. He wanted to know what Hoyt's relationship was with each of the men who'd gone deer stalking with him that day, and if there had been any reason one of them would have wanted him dead.

Lowell had not been present for the day's deer stalking, but there had been an inquest, of course. And Arthur had written Nash to say that the investigation had been conducted with all due consideration. With so many hunters spread out in the wooded land north of the Hall, it had been impossible to know who had fired the fatal shot. And since no one but Arthur stood to gain from Hoyt's death, the death had been ruled accidental.

After more than a decade in the army, Nash knew

it was possible for a stray shot to kill someone. But it was also possible for a man with a grudge to misfire, or to shoot wild, "accidentally" injuring the man he despised. Nash had seen it happen.

Yet he'd never known Hoyt to have an enemy in the world, unlike Arthur, who'd been a toplofty prig all through his youth and beyond. Hoyt had been a gentle, good-natured sort who'd lost his wife three years earlier. His few letters after Joanna's death indicated he had not yet recovered from her loss. He seemed to think he never would, which surprised Nash, since theirs had not been a love match. Clearly, Hoyt had developed a strong attachment to Joanna.

Unfortunately, Nash's trip into Keswick that afternoon had yielded naught but a nastily bruised ankle and the beginnings of a wicked headache. Keswick's magistrate, Mr. Peter Wardlow, had offered nothing new about Hoyt's death, even though he'd been present at the hunting party that day.

Nor could he say much about the accident that had killed Arthur and Georgia. The magistrate had investigated their deaths, of course, and found only that the ground he'd traveled on the high road to Braithwaite had given way under their carriage wheels.

Nash remembered the stretch well. It was a dangerous piece of narrow road, but a careful—a *sane*—driver would never have driven too close to the edge of the cliff. Nor would he have taken it too fast.

Mr. Wardlow's report had mentioned heavy rains in the days before the accident. And Philip Lowell had spoken of Arthur's stubborn insistence on traveling to a local baron's house party at Braithwaite in spite of the poor road conditions. Nash could easily believe it of his brother. Arthur had never changed from the headstrong youth who refused all sorts of advice—even their father's.

The three brothers had been close, each of them with his own particular strengths, and perhaps his own weaknesses. Hoyt had been far too mild-mannered, but he was as kindhearted as a man could be. Arthur was by far the most intelligent of the three brothers, but he was laughably stubborn. Nash had more physical prowess than either of his brothers, and his father had dressed him down more than once for frightening his mother with his dangerous feats of daring. But the three Farris brothers had stood for one another in their boyhood scrapes and backed each other up at school.

Life at Ashby Hall was painfully hollow without his brothers.

Philip Lowell returned to the library and stood across from Nash. He bore a familiar expression—of a man whose interest had been piqued by a woman.

No doubt Miss Franklin found favor with the man's unblemished visage. "I take it your little foray up to the nursery went satisfactorily?" Nash asked, unable to check his caustic tone.

Lowell gave a nod. "Aye. Miss Franklin seems to have matters well in hand."

"Which matters would that be?" He felt unaccountably irritated that Lowell had taken the opportunity to dally with Emmaline's governess. The woman was to manage his niece, and nothing more. Certainly not to flirt with Lowell, the youngest son of a Gloucestershire baron.

Nash did not know why Lowell had stayed at Ashby after Hoyt's death. Surely Arthur had been a difficult, off-putting master, and the estate had declined under his inept management. Nash could easily imagine his middle brother taking control of all his accounts and giving the steward little more than a few schoolboy assignments. But Lowell's assistance in deciphering Ashby's account books had been invaluable to Nash during the past month.

Lowell was not much of a sheep man, however. Hoyt had had a head shepherd who'd resigned on Arthur's accession, and of course Arthur had deemed such a man unnecessary. According to Lowell, Arthur felt that since he'd grown up in sheep country, he knew how to manage the herd.

He could not have been more wrong, as was blatantly evidenced by his ledgers and account books.

Nash hoped that with an infusion of capital and the right advice on rebuilding and managing the sheep herd, the Ashby estate could very well become a thriving estate again in a few years.

"What did you think of the report Mr. Wardlow showed you, my lord?" Lowell asked.

Nash had looked over the official accounts of his brothers' deaths, the interviews with possible witnesses and servants who had knowledge of the events. Nash rubbed the mounting ache at his temple. "Which?"

"The, er . . . shooting incident."

"Hardly sufficient. There was not even a list of the guests who went out hunting with Hoyt that day," Nash said, frowning. "You were not here even for part of the day, Lowell?"

"No, my lord. I was down in Grasmere that day. But I believe your brother's usual guests would have been present for the hunt."

No doubt. But Nash had been away for years, in active military service. He knew only a few of the most prestigious men of the district these days, and next to nothing about running an estate.

Nash thought of the hundreds of entries he'd read in his brothers' journals and wondered if he would ever be able to make sense of them. He'd seen ample evidence of Arthur's pigheadedness in his receipts and ledgers, and it seemed he'd become even more arrogant after his marriage to Georgia.

"Wardlow mentioned some of the men who'd been at the hunt—and they, no doubt, can identify the others."

"Will you send them queries?" Lowell asked.

"Perhaps," Nash said, although another idea had come to him just before his fall on the road. Before he'd encountered the ever-so-distracting Miss Franklin with her lush curves and impertinent mouth. "I've not entertained since my return to the Hall. Perhaps I should host a house party."

He really couldn't afford it, but he was going to need to establish connections in the district. As Earl of Ashby, Nash was the highest-ranking nobleman in the vicinity—though perhaps the poorest.

But social gatherings were generally rife with gossip and information. A casual party with all the notables of the district could very well afford Nash the opportunity to find answers to the questions he had about Hoyt's death. If he used his existing funds carefully, he could manage it.

First on his list of guests would be Sir William Metcalf and his wife, old friends of the Farris family. Their son, Jacob, had been a constant companion of Nash and his brothers, but he'd been killed a few years back, during the Peninsular Campaign.

Nash realized he'd put off his visit to Metcalf Farm far too long. Sir Will might even know something useful about Hoyt's death. Something that would put Nash's mind at ease.

"You'll need servants in order to entertain, my lord," Lowell said. "Proper servants, and not just old Grainger and your men."

Nash nodded, and the ache in his left temple responded with a sharp burst. He shut his eyes for a moment and it subsided, freeing him to consider the matter at hand.

He'd inherited a modest sum from his father, which had grown somewhat over the years. It was certainly not enough to correct all of Ashby's failings, but he'd heard an old adage that one needed to spend money to make money.

Nash believed it would be well spent on an Ashby party, not only because it would provide a setting for idle talk and reminiscences about past events here, but because it would afford an opportunity for him to meet his neighbors and see if any of them would be interested in investing in Ashby.

Nash had spent the past few weeks with Lowell, assessing what improvements the Ashby estate needed and estimating what it would all cost. Like Sir Will and most of the other landowners in the district, Ashby had always depended upon sheep's wool and good mutton for its wealth. But it was clear even to Nash that the herd needed to be restored and they needed a competent head shepherd to manage it. In less than two years since Hoyt's death, it seemed to have dwindled to naught.

In addition, Arthur had allowed the arable fields to lie fallow for his entire tenure. The orchards were overgrown and there was flooding in the south fields. The roof of the Hall leaked in spots, and most of the rooms were musty and neglected. Worst of all were the risky investments Arthur had made that had plunged Ashby deeply into debt.

He looked over at Lowell and caught him scowling. "Aye, it'll cost me, but a house party will give me an opportunity to become acquainted with as many local landowners as I can," Nash said. "And I'll need those connections for the long term."

Lowell's expression lightened somewhat. "Church, too, my lord."

"Church?"

"You might consider attending—it's a good place to meet people. To talk to other farm owners in the district."

It had been a very long time since Nash had gone to church. He'd deemed it a pointless endeavor ever since Waterloo. He'd seen action in many a battle, but the carnage at Hougoumont Farm . . .

He turned his face toward the fire but the movement hurt his head. He rubbed his aching temple again. "You did well enough in finding a governess for Emmaline, Lowell. Perhaps you can ask if they've heard of an available sheep manager when you attend church Sunday morning."

"I'll ask Reverend Swan. He and his wife know

everyone in the parish . . . maybe in all of Cumbria."

Nash had some connections, too—wealthy officers he'd known in the army. He had already written to a few of his closest friends, asking for modest loans, but it would take time to receive answers from them.

"You approve of Miss Franklin, my lord?"

He glanced up at Lowell's sudden change of subject. Nash had had absolutely no idea what to do with Emmaline. After thirteen years in the army, and most of those years at war with France, he was accustomed to dealing with men—especially of the rough and ready sort—like those he'd brought to Ashby Hall with him. What a mess. He was lucky the walls were not crumbling around him.

But wait—they were.

"She'll do."

A light tap at the door interrupted his train of thought, and Lowell opened it to admit Miss Franklin, alone. Her posture was just as stiff as it had been during their initial interview, but this time, Nash noted a gleam of pique in her eyes.

"May I have a word with you, my lord?"

"Leave us, Lowell," he said, enjoying the disconcerted expression Miss Franklin quickly tried to hide.

"But my lord—"

"That's an order, Lowell." Not that the man wouldn't seek out Mercy Franklin at a more convenient time. The steward exited the room, but left the door open.

"Close it, Lowell."

The man did as he was told.

"Abandoned your charge already, Miss Franklin?" Nash asked. For some perverse reason, he enjoyed goading her.

"On the contrary, Lord Ashby," she said, her feathers most amusingly ruffled. "She is with Mr. Blue at the moment. I wanted to speak to you outside her presence."

He gestured to the comfortable chair opposite him. She sat on its edge, her back fiercely unbent in her proper, dark blue gown, though her features were anything but prim. He could not recall any other woman with eyes so sharp a green, or skin that looked so enticingly soft. Miss Franklin might try to remain completely aloof, but her demeanor was sabotaged by the most sensual mouth Nash had ever seen.

Dark buttons marched from the high waist of her gown to the collar at her throat, and he found himself shifting in his seat as he imagined her unfastening each one when she made herself ready for bed. No doubt her underthings appeared plain and white and just as stiff as her demeanor, but they would slide ever so softly from her shoulders before catching on the tips of her breasts.

Nash allowed his eyes to return to her face, where he noted the most delectable flush of color on her cheeks. He had a feeling he was going to enjoy this encounter far more than he ought.

Chapter 7

Gavin Briggs made the obligatory visit to his father's estate near Durham, but relations between them were not improved. Lord Hargrove still resented the fact that Gavin could not tell him about his work during the war.

And Gavin despised his father for turning out his sister when she'd become pregnant.

Gavin had been away at the time, of course, for he'd been employed by the foreign office, engaging in clandestine activities, of which many were still ongoing in France and Russia. He would not risk the identities and lives of his peers, just to placate his arrogant viscount father who had no real need to know what information the Foreign Office was obtaining about England's newest potential enemies. The information his father wanted about Gavin's work would be reduced to gossip, puerile and trivial.

And Gavin would have none of it.

Of course Viscount Hargrove had shown his anger by pulling in the purse strings, which made it imperative that Gavin find the granddaughters of the Duke of Windermere and win the substantial reward promised by the duke, and quickly. There was a fine property Gavin wanted to purchase down in Hampshire, where he could bring his sister and her child, and give them a home. But the gentleman who owned it would not wait forever. Gavin needed to come up with some funds to show old Mr. Wickford he was in earnest. He intended to retire to the country as a gentleman farmer, a good many miles away from his spoiled family.

His disgust was not limited to his father. He despised old Windermere for disowning his daughter. The aging duke should be horsewhipped for what he'd done to his granddaughters twenty years back. But that would only hasten the old gaffer's death. Gavin wanted to see Lily and Christina Hayes spit in His Grace's rheumy old eye.

Just as Gavin wished he could see his sister spit in their own sire's. Not that it would change anything. His family lived an insular life west of Durham, without any real knowledge of the war and the circumstances that made lesser people desperate.

At least Gavin had the opportunity to win a significant treasure if he found the children—young women now. He had the skill and the wherewithal to track them down. This particular puzzle was going to be a challenge, however, since the steward who'd handled matters was long dead, and Sarah and her barrister husband had drowned in the Thames nearly twenty years before. Gavin had to go back to their roots, to the place where they'd spent their married years, and see if there was anyone in London who remembered them.

More important, he needed to find someone who recalled what had happened to their children.

It was a difficult task, but not impossible.

Nash closed his eyes and took a deep breath, chiding himself for lusting after the tidy little governess. He'd bedded some of the most sophisticated women of Paris and London, and yet he found himself bewitched by this sassy, black-haired wench who didn't know when to keep silent.

"Lord Ashby, are you unwell? Should I call some—"

"Not at all," he said, annoyed that she would think of him as infirm. He was in possession of as much strength and stamina—if not the good looks—as he'd always had. If he could just see an end of these headaches . . . He lowered his hand from his aching temple. "You had something to tell me about my niece?"

"Not exactly, my lord. I'd hoped to ask you about Lady Emmaline's past."

Nash's brows came together. "Her past? She is a child. How much past could she possibly have?"

A charming little crease appeared between her brows, and she bit her lip the way she'd done earlier, eliciting the very same reaction he'd experienced before. Instant arousal. " 'Tis likely that many things have happened to her, my lord. The loss of her parents, for example."

Nash repositioned himself in his chair. "Is that what's made her so quiet?"

"Possibly."

He had not really considered whether Emmaline

still grieved for Joanna and Hoyt. She'd been little more than an infant when her mother died, and Hoyt had been killed more than two years later. But Miss Franklin's words caused him to understand there could be more to his niece's reticence than he'd assumed. And giving Miss Franklin a brief history of past events might assist her in Emmaline's education and care. An added benefit was that talking would give him something else to think of, other than that row of buttons nestled so sweetly between her breasts.

"Emmaline's father was my eldest brother, Hoyt, who became earl after my father died. His wife, Emmaline's mother, died bearing a son, five or six years ago." Nash had been involved in some very heavy fighting in Portugal during that time, and the dates were unclear in his memory.

He noted a pained expression crossing Mercy Franklin's fine features. "Emmaline would have been about two years old, then?"

He shrugged, unwilling to revisit the grief he felt at the loss of his brothers, even the pretentious Arthur. They'd been close in age, and Nash's mother used to call them her three little lambs, running together all over the grounds as though their childhood would never end.

Nash looked toward the fire and found himself rubbing the side of his head against the unremitting ache there. "I have it on good authority that my niece is eight years old."

"How long has it been since her father passed away?" Miss Franklin asked quietly.

"Two years ago this fall."

"Which would have made Emmaline six years old at the time."

"You have a way with numbers, Miss Franklin. A very laudable talent for a governess."

"Has she had any schooling at all?" she asked, ignoring his sarcasm.

"I haven't any idea."

"But you—"

"Arrived here just over a month ago," he replied.

If only he had met this woman on the dance floor at Lady Richmond's ball a year ago, before Waterloo . . . Paying court to a beautiful young woman was the best possible diversion for an army officer anticipating battle.

Or for a damaged man, seeking to forget.

"I have little knowledge of Emmaline's history," he said abruptly. "And since I cannot help you any further . . ."

"I don't understand."

"Of course you don't. It's all very complicated."

And so was his attraction to the wench. His life would never be the same. With a good bit of his face burned off and his brothers and closest friends dead, he did not care to forge any more alliances than necessary.

Mercy saw a restlessness in Lord Ashby that went beyond his bruised ankle. She sensed that he would be up and prowling the room if he could, if not for the injury to his limb. She ignored his implied dismissal.

"My lord, if I am to be an effective teacher, I will need to know somewhat more about my pupil."

"If you think to scold me, Miss Franklin, then you must think again." He stood, in spite of the obvious discomfort in his ankle, and took the few steps necessary to reach the fireplace, limping slightly. He rested one hand against the mantel and eased his weight off his hurt ankle, then rotated his foot as if to test it. "I am a soldier, not a nursemaid. You will have to ask Emmaline what education she has experienced before my arrival here."

"My lord, she is so very reticent—"

"She is shy, Miss Franklin."

"Abnormally so. And she has no nurse, no one to take care of her." Mercy stood and approached Lord Ashby, refusing to be intimidated by this tall, arrogant man whose features were so hard and sharp they seemed to have been carved from stone.

"Which is why Lowell summoned you."

"My lord, your niece is surrounded by soldiers—or former soldiers, I suppose. Are there no . . . In a house this size, is there no housekeeper? Are there no maids?"

"My men are managing adequately."

Mercy wondered how the man could be so dense. "My lord . . . who was responsible for Emmaline after her father's death?"

"That would have been my next brother, Arthur, and his wife."

It took less than a moment for Mercy to realize that this brother must also have died, else the present Lord Ashby would not be earl. "You mean to say . . ."

He clenched his jaw tightly before he responded. "Yes, Miss Franklin. My two elder brothers both met with untimely deaths, leaving Emmaline in my admittedly inadequate care."

Mercy could not imagine the grief and uncertainty the child must have felt upon losing her parents and then her uncle. Emmy must feel far more adrift than Mercy did.

"And her aunt . . . ?"

"Georgia died in the same carriage accident last year that killed my brother."

Mercy swallowed. So much tragedy in Emmaline's short life. She kept her eyes trained upon Lord Ashby's and spoke quietly. "Have you spoken with her, my lord?"

"Spoken? About what?"

"About . . . well, anything, I suppose."

He rubbed the side of his head the way her father used to do when it pained him, which was often. "She does not speak much, does she?"

"No," Mercy replied quietly. Lord Ashby was obviously out of his element with Emmaline, and likely grieving for his brothers as well.

It was becoming clear that he intended for Mercy to function as governess, nurse, and companion to Emmaline. And since she had nowhere else to go at the moment, she supposed the situation would have to do. For the moment, at least, until she decided whether to write Andrew Vale. "My lord, I've examined the nursery and schoolroom, and there are a few supplies that will be needed."

"I'm sure you'll find everything you need somewhere about the house, Miss Franklin."

"Do I have your permission to take what I need for Emmaline's lessons?"

"Of course. Feel free to scour the place for all the slates and chalk we possess."

Nash's ankle improved significantly by keeping off it for the rest of the evening, but he had Sergeant Parker bind it for him, just to give it some additional needed support. Unfortunately, Parker could do naught about the lascivious thoughts of Miss Franklin that continued to plague him in spite of all the reading he still needed to do.

It had been some time since he'd shared intimacies with a woman, and nearly a year since any female had looked at him without disdain—or worse, pity. Yet Miss Franklin hardly seemed to notice the dull gray of his injured eye or the scars that surrounded it. She must be so intent upon her new profession that his disfigurement escaped her.

His eyes felt strained as he read through the last of the ledgers kept by Hoyt's estate manager. Ashby had been solvent at the time of Hoyt's death, but not as profitable as it had been in prior years. Improvements to the arable land had drained some profits from the estate, but Hoyt and his tenants had stood to reap a better return in future years.

Unfortunately, Arthur's training had not prepared him to manage an estate, and Lowell indicated he'd refused the steward's help. Arthur was a university-educated clergyman, and had been insufferably pompous after receiving his divinity degree. The mulish nature he'd exhibited in boyhood had only been made worse by the achievement.

For all that they were brothers, Nash didn't know how Arthur's parishioners had tolerated him. 'Twas likely they'd been delighted with his accession to the earldom, for it meant he and his lofty wife would move on, away from his church in Thursby.

And now Nash was stuck with the estate Arthur had ruined.

He needed cash, and though some of his former fellow officers had promised to lend him money if need be, the greatest and easiest infusion of wealth would be through a rich wife.

Nash had never planned to marry, but he was the last of the Farrises. Now that he was earl, with an estate to bequeath to an heir, he understood he had a duty to improve Ashby and produce said heir so the title would not revert to the crown. For he had no other relations in his line.

Nash tried to think of a likely marital candidate. He'd spent nearly a year in London during and after his recovery, and met several belles of society. None had been of any interest to him, and he'd been naught but a curiosity to them, a scarred survivor of Waterloo with a bankrupt title.

He sighed and closed Hoyt's ledger. It was still early in the year, the social season having just begun. Nash supposed he could return to London and see what young heiresses were available on the marriage mart—one whose father would not care that Ashby Hall was at least three hundred miles from London, and a dark and dismal wreck of a place.

But he dreaded the thought of it.

Mercy's priority that evening was to make her bedchamber habitable. She could start on Emmaline's lessons tomorrow, but she had to sleep in this room tonight. By the way her eyes watered and nose twitched when she'd opened the drapes to look outside, she knew sleep would be impossible until she eliminated a significant amount of dust from the room.

She'd learned precious little from Lord Ashby, but it was enough, perhaps, to understand how shaken Emmaline might have been with the loss of both her father and her uncle in such short order. Mercy didn't know how close she'd been to either man, but Emmaline's favorite book was the one her mother had made for her. Surely that said something, especially since Emmaline had been little more than an infant when her mother died.

In spite of her young age, Emmaline must have felt bereft at her mother's loss. Just as Mercy must have done, though she could not remember anything about her life before being taken in by the Franklins. She did not want the same to happen to Emmaline.

Keeping Emmy with her and giving the girl little tasks to keep her occupied, Mercy swept and dusted her bedchamber. It was as medieval as the great hall, with stone walls and dark wood paneling around the fireplace that matched the heavy door. It was not a warm and welcoming room, but she determined to make it so, at least for the duration of her employment at Ashby Hall.

Mercy ventured down to the empty kitchen for a bucket of water, and returned to wash every surface of the room. With Emmaline's help, she located the housekeeping cabinets and found some clean linens for the bed. By the time she'd made the room habitable, she was tired enough to crawl into the bed—but just as hungry. "Soon we'll go and find some supper. How does that sound, Emmaline?"

The little girl nodded, observing Mercy carefully, as though she didn't quite know what to make of her new teacher.

She did not say much, but Mercy talked enough to make up for Emmaline's reserve, telling the child about the life she'd left at Underdale. She avoided speaking of her own recent losses, only mentioning her friends and the gardens she'd kept both at home and at her father's church.

Mercy still did not know what to think of the couple she'd known as her parents, or of the mother who'd abandoned her. A number of the ill-fitting pieces of her life at Underdale began to make some kind of sense with Susanna's revelation, though Mercy did not think she would ever fully understand why the harsh Reverend Franklin had ever agreed to take her in. He'd never enjoyed the affections of his adopted daughter. Why hadn't he just handed her over to the parish?

Mercy mused that maybe it was because Reverend Franklin believed Susanna should have the companionship of a daughter. Not that Susanna had ever been a warm, maternal type of woman. She'd always been stingy with her affections, perhaps because Mercy was not her own.

Mercy wondered about the woman who had given her life. Who was she? What had made her abandon her little daughter? Had it been easy or heartwrenching for her?

Mercy supposed the answers to those questions

might very well reside within the pages of Susanna's journal. Now that she was temporarily settled at Ashby Hall, she was determined to summon the courage to read through her mother's memoir. Likely she would find nothing more than what Susanna had already told her, though her mother's memory might have been at least partially impaired by illness at the time she'd revealed her twenty-year-old secret. She had not been able to answer any of Mercy's questions, but whispered apologies to her dead husband for divulging their secret.

Apparently, no one was to know Mercy was not their natural child.

Though Mercy might learn more from her mother's journal, the thought of reading Susanna's innermost thoughts caused an uncomfortable constriction in her chest. She'd had two mothers, one who'd held little—or perhaps no—affection for her, and the other who had abandoned her.

She put aside her disquieting thoughts and chatted as she made the bed. "Perhaps when the weather changes, your uncle will allow us to plant a small garden." Plants and the peace of a garden were what she knew, what comforted her, and the tightness in her chest eased, just thinking about fresh shoots taking root in the grounds outside her window.

She hoped Lord Ashby would allow them to plant. The Hall might begin to feel more like home to Mercy if she could grow her own flowers and plants. And she thought it possible that an interest in botany might help to bring Emmaline out of her introversion.

"My papa liked to grow things," Emmaline said quietly.

"Did he have a garden?"

Emmy nodded. "A big one. With pots and trees."

"Perhaps you'll show me."

The little girl lowered her eyes. "It's all dead."

Mercy sat down beside her. "We'll get some seedlings and make it grow again. In honor of your father. How does that sound?"

Emmaline brightened, and looked directly at Mercy, something she had not yet done. "Very good."

Mercy touched Emmaline then, running one hand lightly across her shoulder and down her arm. It was not much comfort, but when Emmaline let out a tremulous breath, Mercy wondered if it was not the beginning of a bond between them.

There was one last task before the bedchamber would be usable. In spite of the overwhelming fatigue Mercy felt after her long day, she pulled a chair over to the window. Lifting her skirts out of the way, she stepped onto the chair and reached for the top of the draperies. "These musty old things must be beaten before I will allow them to remain in here," she said to Emmy, stretching precariously to reach the rod. She did not mind sleeping with these windows bare since they overlooked the vast, empty fells that surrounded the Hall.

"In my home, we used to take out all the draperies and carpets every spring and autumn, and beat them in the yard with sticks," she said, remembering the unusually relaxed atmosphere of the household during those times. Reverend Franklin always hired additional help for the big cleaning days, and with everyone working so hard to make the house ready for winter or to clear away the winter stuffiness, Mercy's parents were more relaxed and lenient than at other times of the year. "My father was a very meticulous man who liked—"

She leaned a little bit too far, and lost her balance. Sure that she was going to fall, she grasped the air for purchase on something—anything that would break her fall. She heard Emmaline's squeal and a man's harsh oath.

Lord Ashby.

She did not know how he happened to be there at just the right moment, but he caught her against his chest—his powerful arms around her derriere, the very backside he'd so inappropriately admired while she was assisting him in the road. His face was level with her bosom.

Right then, Mercy was certain it would have been better to fall. Her nipples tightened against her chemise, and she was very glad the dark muslin of her gown prevented him from being able to note the change. It would not do at all for him to realize she was reacting to his touch in such an indecent manner.

She could not help but notice that he smelled of shaving soap and leather. And when his hot breath warmed her chest, her heart seemed to stop. A prickling sensation skated up her back, along with a heated awareness of his strong arms around her. He held her tightly, saying naught for a moment as he looked into her eyes.

It felt as though time stopped and all the air suddenly drained from the room.

A glossy, black tuft of his hair fell across his forehead, and Mercy resisted the urge to blow a light puff of air across it. She sucked her lower lip through her teeth and released it slowly, unable to take her eyes from his remarkable face.

A muscle in his jaw flexed once, the sight of which jolted Mercy to the present. Embarrassed by her unseemly, foolishly potent reaction to this man, she looked away while he loosened his grasp and allowed her to skim slowly down the length of his body. She felt every inch of his hard, male form as she slid down his length, and when she touched the floor, her legs wobbled unsteadily.

He did not immediately take his hands away, and Mercy forced herself to take a step back, ignoring the heat that suffused her face. She'd never experienced such a close encounter with a man, not even with Andrew Vale, whose wife she'd had every intention of becoming.

She wondered if she'd have reacted to Mr. Vale in such a wanton manner. She pressed one hand to her breast as though she could contain the highly inappropriate awakening of those wayward sensations.

"You must ask one of my men for assistance with such chores, Miss Franklin. Henry Blue is nearly always about."

"I will, my lord." Her voice came out as a strange croak.

Lord Ashby tipped his head slightly at the sound and sat down on the chair from which Mercy had fallen, and leaned over to rub his ankle. In the past few moments, she had completely forgotten his injury.

"Oh! Your ankle, my lord. Are you—is it—all right?"

"Ah, I believe it may be somewhat the worse for wear." Grimacing, he looked up at the curtains. "Lowell should have realized your room would need attention and taken care of it."

Mercy looked at Emmaline and saw that her eyes had grown as wide as the blue ocean at Underdale, probably mirroring her own. She guessed that in Emmaline's case, it was because she'd never seen her uncle in such a strange situation. For herself, it had more to do with the burning sensations that still prickled the tips of her breasts and some madly sensitive place deep inside that had never been touched before.

Perhaps Lord Ashby was slightly more shaken than he wanted to let on, for Mercy had not expected to hear any form of contrition from Lord Ashby's lips. Mr. Lowell, indeed.

"Sh-shall I go and find someone to assist you?" Mercy asked. "Mr. Blue, perhaps?"

"No. I managed to walk up here on my own, and I will proceed as before."

He stood abruptly and made his way to the door, limping significantly. Mercy realized he must have reinjured his ankle in his rush to prevent her from falling. "My lord, you are obviously in pain," she said, quickly going to his side. "Please allow me to assist you."

She'd done it before, on the road, when he was a complete stranger, touching him in a way no proper lady would ever consider doing. She moved close to him and, even though he was a great deal taller than she, took his arm and draped it over her shoulders.

He expelled a long breath when he leaned upon her, his hand over her shoulder, dangling precariously close to some highly sensitive territory.

"Where are we going?"

"To my bedchamber."

Chapter 8

Miss Franklin's steps faltered nearly as much as Nash's, although he knew her misstep was not from pain. She was truly the innocent vicar's daughter—the very mention of a man's bedroom disconcerted her.

The contact of her body against his had been her first shock. She'd stiffened at first, but then Nash had felt her soften in his arms. And his body had reacted in a manner he'd sorely missed since his injuries.

The urge to take her into his bedroom and have one small taste of her was absurdly intense. He'd always had better control of his cravings than this. But he found Miss Franklin surprisingly engaging. None of the ladies he'd met on the continent or in London had managed to interest him as she did, with her blunt reprimands and her apparent indifference to his unsightly scars.

"Where is your b-bedchamber, my lord?"

"Only a few doors down." Hoyt's wife had relocated the nursery rooms after Emmaline's birth, wanting her child to be closer to her.

He knew that Hoyt and Joanna had shared a bedroom, too, something not even their parents had done. Hoyt and his wife been close—far closer than any husband and wife Nash had ever heard of, and in the years after Joanna's death, Hoyt had never considered taking another wife. Nash doubted he'd taken another woman to his bed, either.

There was a time when Nash thought he'd understood Hoyt's devotion. Now, it seemed pure foolishness. Why would a man make himself so vulnerable? Life was far too fragile to form such an attachment.

Nash's ankle was really much better after Parker had bound it, so he did not need to lean too heavily upon Emmaline's governess as he hobbled down the corridor. He'd managed to get all the way up the stairs and into the master wing without assistance, but he did not want to relinquish his contact with Mercy Franklin. Not yet. She smelled like dust and cleaning materials, but she also bore an underlying floral scent that was wholly female and utterly delicious.

"You are aware that I do not hold you responsible for my sprain," he said.

She made a delicate snuffling noise. "That's very generous of you, my lord, since your fall was not my fault."

"No? You lunged into the road just as my horse rounded the curve. Startled him."

"I hardly lunged. Not with a heavy traveling case in each hand."

"Came out of nowhere, then."

"Not quite," she replied. "Your men nearly trampled me when they rode past. I was trying to gather my possessions and get back onto the road when you appeared."

"My men?"

"I had barely half a second to get off the road when they barreled through."

His men had been pent up for weeks doing chores in the moldy old house, and Nash had allowed them to ride into Keswick with him that afternoon. He knew they could be unruly at times, especially when confined to barracks for extended periods of time. Even with their frequent foot races and fencing bouts, they had been edgy and impatient with one another.

Miss Franklin was correct—they'd been going far too fast on that stretch of road.

"My men are not reckless," he lied, but their banter was far too enjoyable to surrender the point.

Her shoulders stiffened beneath his arm. "I beg to differ, my lord. Any one of them might have run me over. Or any other unsuspecting traveler."

"We don't have very many travelers this far out of Keswick. But I daresay the mail coach races past at far greater speed than any of my men." They reached the door of his bedchamber, but he was loath to release her.

"I was on that coach, my lord, and I can assure you that we never galloped at the same speed your soldiers did."

"Former soldiers, Miss Franklin."

"Whatever they are."

"You will find they're a harmless bunch."

"But they are not proper servants, are they?"

"Of course not. Each man—with the exception of Lowell—fought under my command during various campaigns over the past decade."

"Their loyalty is commendable," she said, and Nash caught more than a hint of mockery in her tone. He did not explain that they'd come to Ashby only because they had nowhere else to go, no form of employment to keep them. With Napoleon defeated and so many soldiers returning to England during the past year, they were extraneous, their skills on the battlefield now useless. A young vicar's daughter from Underdale could not possibly understand the difficulties these men faced.

Or could she? She'd come all the way to Ashby Hall to find work. He didn't understand why her father would have refused two suitors—both of whom sounded perfectly acceptable for a woman of her station. And now her father was dead and she had no means of support besides that which she could achieve for herself.

"Is this it, my lord?" she asked when they reached his room with its door standing ajar. It was obviously the only other inhabited room in this wing, and he fought a tremendous desire to draw her inside, to test the softness of her skin and the warmth of her lips.

"Aye." He took his arm from her shoulder and limped into the room, turning to give her a slight bow. "Thank you for your assistance, Miss Franklin."

"No, I must thank you for your timely appearance, Lord Ashby. I might have done myself some serious damage . . ." she said, her eyes quickly darting to the wide bed behind him. ". . . if not for your quick . . ." A deep blush colored her cheeks. "*Lord above*," she whispered, and then spun away, marching quickly back to the nursery where Emmaline awaited.

And it was only then that Nash realized that his headache—his sole reason for coming up to his bedroom—was gone.

Mercy could not imagine what had gotten into her, arguing with Lord Ashby as though he were nothing more than an obstinate shopkeeper. Her face burned at the thought of their close contact, of the way he'd held her, his face level with the stays of her corset.

Worse was the way he'd practically embraced her as they walked to his bedchamber. No man had ever draped himself over her in such a way. If he'd dipped his hand just an inch, he'd have grazed her breast with his fingers.

A phantom sensation sizzled through her, and her knees went weak. *What if he had touched her there? How would it feel? Would she . . .*

Mercy shook her head in disgust, stopping to compose herself for a moment before continuing on her path back to her bedchamber where Emmaline waited for her.

Clearly, she needed to distance herself from the man who seemed to have no compunction against drawing an innocent young woman into his bedchamber. Such behavior was not to be tolerated—not if she was to prove her father wrong about her. Mercy was not the wanton her mother had been. She was not so easily seduced. The sight of a bed with an obviously virile man beside it was not going to confound her.

Mercy spent the rest of the evening with Emmy, though thoughts of her charge's intriguing uncle only two rooms down the hall were never far from her mind. She banished them as soon as they surfaced while she engaged Emmaline in helping her to unpack, stopping short when the little girl took a book from the bottom of Mercy's traveling case and opened its pages.

It was her mother's journal, an item Mercy had never seen before Susanna's illness. Nor had Mercy possessed the heart to open it in the weeks since that day.

She would have liked to grab the book away from Emmaline, but the girl's obvious fragility prevented her from acting precipitously. Common sense told her she needed to move carefully with this child, and try not to startle her or frighten her in any way.

Mercy turned away as Emmaline started to page through the book, and picked up the tied bundle of her father's sermons and the few letters he'd kept over the years. Mercy already knew what the sermons contained, for she'd heard him preach similar lessons every Sunday of her life—or rather, every Sunday since her adoption. Twenty years. Susanna told her she'd been about three years old upon her arrival at the vicarage.

Mercy could not help but wonder about that day. Who had brought her to the Franklins? Had she wept at being taken from her mother? Had her mother given her up willingly? Had Mercy possessed a favorite toy or a book as Emmaline did? She would dearly like to know.

Mercy knew the answer to those questions might lie within the pages of Susanna's journal. Deciding she would force herself to open the diary and read a few entries later, she heard Emmaline's voice, reading from the first page. Her voice was clear and stronger than Mercy had yet heard it.

Susanna Franklin's Journal

> *3 August, 1795. I do not understand how my dear husband can expect me to care for another woman's child—a fallen woman, at that, if Mr. Newcomb is to be believed. Robert says it is our Christian duty, but I sincerely have my doubts.*

Emmaline looked up at Mercy. "There are no pictures."

"No. It was my mother's journal," Mercy said thickly, her heart going as cold as her hands with every perfectly enunciated word Emmaline spoke. "But she was not an artist like your mother."

"Is she dead, too?"

"Yes."

Emmaline nodded gravely, and Mercy could see her equating the journal with her own mother's book of stories, gently running her hand over Susanna's precise script. "Her name was Susanna?"

Mercy nodded, not sure whether to feel gratified that Emmaline was talking, or chagrined that the one thing that piqued the child's interest was the journal that Mercy so dreaded reading.

And with good reason, it seemed. Mercy had been merely her mother's "Christian duty." No wonder there had never been a close bond between them, the kind of connection her friends shared with their own mothers. Susanna had taken care of her, feeding and clothing her, giving her guidance as she grew and matured. She'd been strict, but not unkind. Mercy had to give her that.

One day Mercy hoped to have her own children. She vowed that any innocent bairn she bore would feel her mother's love every day of her life.

21 August, 1795. Robert has decided we will call the orphan child Mercy and pray that God will have mercy on her poor bastard soul.

Mercy cringed at the word *bastard*. Susanna had never spoken that awful word aloud in her life— at least, never in Mercy's presence. She reached for the journal, but Emmaline continued reading before Mercy could take the book away.

He says it is our mission to ensure the girl does not follow in her mother's sinful footsteps.

Emmaline closed the leather-bound book and placed it on the small table beside the bed, completely unaware of the turmoil taking place within Mercy's breast.

No child should have to try so hard to attain the approval of her parents—even her adoptive ones.

"What is a bastard soul?" Emmaline asked.

Mercy felt speechless. Emmaline's question struck her on so many different levels, it was difficult to answer. "I-I am not sure, Emmy. I think it means . . . unbaptized."

"But are you baptized now?" Emmaline asked, her voice full of concern.

"Yes," Mercy whispered, so unaccustomed to dissembling, and yet she could not begin to explain to an eight-year-old the true meaning of the word. "My . . . my father was a vicar, so I am sure he saw to it when I was very young." Mercy could not imagine her father neglecting that essential duty.

She slipped the journal into the drawer of the table and closed it tightly. "Shall we go and read from your mother's book?" Her hands were shaking and her stomach felt queasy. She'd been no more than a Christian duty to the couple who'd raised her.

She needed some distance from the hurtful words in Susanna's journal. And she didn't want to try to explain any more bleak passages to Emmaline.

She barely understood them herself.

"Yes, please," Emmaline replied, though Mercy barely heard her.

The few short passages Emmy had read wounded Mercy deeply. Susanna had not been able to say much about Mercy's arrival at the rectory, mentioning only that an old friend of Reverend Franklin had brought Mercy to them. The Franklins had agreed to raise her—and they'd taken what Susanna had called "an acceptable" sum of money for her keep—promising to keep her origins secret . . .

Like a small, nearly colorless wraith, Emmaline left the bedchamber and went across to the nursery. Mercy followed, feeling dazed, but relieved that Emmaline had a purpose in mind. For Mercy could not have given the child instruction on anything at the moment.

She had to pull herself together. She supposed she'd always known the Franklins possessed little affection for her and even less love. Mercy had striven to do her best, but had never understood why her best was not enough.

The journal would give Mercy some insight into her parents' thoughts and feelings. But after her first taste of it, she wasn't sure she actually wanted to know any more.

She sat down with Emmaline in a small, cushioned divan that was hardly larger than a chair, and opened the picture book. The little girl's situation was not too far different from Mercy's own—her true parents were gone, and the only one to care for her was an uncle who seemed to have very little connection with her.

As they paged through the book, Mercy could see that Emmaline was not actually reading her mother's stories. She'd memorized them.

It didn't matter. Judging by the way Emmy read Susanna's journal, it seemed her reading skills were quite advanced for her age and would need more challenging fare than the primers on the bookshelf. Mercy did not allow herself to think about having to broach Lord Ashby's library for appropriate reading materials, but concentrated on building rapport with Emmaline. The late Lady Ashby's tales were a far better way to begin than reading Susanna's disheartening words.

Even so, Mercy could not avoid the journal much longer. If she wanted to learn anything more about her origins, she would have to face up to the task. Perhaps she would read a little bit of it before she retired for the night.

* * *

"Easy, Parker," Nash said through his gritted teeth. "That's my hide you're working on."

"Aye, and the surgeon told me to show you no mercy, my lord."

Mercy. There was that word again, reminding Nash of the woman whose green eyes flashed with such ire when talking to him. Her disapproval could not have been clearer.

And she had plenty to disapprove of. Nash was an abysmal guardian to his niece. Seeing her through Miss Franklin's eyes, he realized that his brother's child was unkempt and far too thin. He knew he ought to have replaced her nurse immediately with someone more acceptable than the disagreeable battle-ax he'd dismissed, but it was too late for regrets. He could only hope Mercy Franklin would suffice for now. After all, how many caretakers did one small child require?

More to the point, how many more could he afford?

"Your shoulder is awfully tight, sir," Parker said. He was several years older than Nash, and a sprinkling of silver had rained through the temples of his brown hair over the past year. Parker had been Nash's batman for years, and the transition to valet suited him well. In addition, he'd become expert in performing the healing massages prescribed by the army surgeons who'd seen to Nash after the explosion. The burn scars had tightened the skin at the top of Nash's shoulder, but its present good condition was a testament to Oscar Parker's nagging and harassment as much as the heavy exercise Nash performed every day.

"It's tension, Parker. Who knew that becoming earl would be such a trial." Or that the images of John Trent's horrible death would stay burned into his brain after nearly a year.

"You've a headache again, I see."

"Too much reading." And too much remembering. He never knew what would set off the memories that haunted him. A loud pop of the fire, the shattering of glass, a sharp shout . . .

But sometimes less than that. Occasionally, Nash would see some old thing in the Hall that reminded him of the early years when his parents were alive, laughing together and finding humor in their sons' antics. And when Nash read his father's script in an old ledger or came across a bit of his mother's intricate needlework, a deep sense of loss would overtake him.

"Get some spectacles, sir. They'll lessen the strain on your eyes."

That might be true, but there didn't seem to be any cure for the troubling memories. No doubt he needed a diversion.

Nash sighed as Parker rubbed a layer of liniment into his shoulder. He closed his eyes and imagined Parker's hands were those of Miss Franklin's, and the scent filling his nostrils was the subtle fragrance of lilies that she wore. How much gentler would she be? How much better would a woman's touch feel?

It had been a very long time since any woman had taken *that* kind of notice of him, looking beyond the scars that marred the side of his face and clouded his eye. And yet Mercy Franklin had barely seemed to perceive them. She'd looked directly into his eyes when speaking to him, never flinching at the sight of his damaged visage.

"Did you meet the governess, Parker?"

"No, sir," said Parker. "But the lads told me she's a comely thing, if a bit stiff."

Aye, she was comely. The stiffness was likely due to her parentage, being a vicar's daughter. No doubt the man had not stood for any foolishness.

As Arthur had not. Nash had not considered it before, but life must have been quite bleak for Emmaline after Hoyt's death. Arthur had never had much patience, and, knowing Georgia, he doubted she had shown any interest in the girl—not when she'd been the one who'd engaged Nurse Butterfield.

But Nash could not be too critical. While their rearing of Emmaline might have been severe, Nash's bordered on neglectful. He supposed he should have been more aware and attentive.

"You've never had a problem loosening them up, my lord, have you, now?"

"Loosening what?"

"The ladies, sir. The ladies."

Ah. He had lost the train of conversation. " 'Tis unseemly to seduce the help, Parker."

"I suppose you're right, sir."

He knew he was right, but it didn't stop him from thinking about Mercy Franklin coming to him in his bedchamber. He fancied her wearing naught but a pretty chemise, something completely at odds with her straight-backed demeanor.

Nash flinched when Parker dug the heels of his

hands into the hollow beneath his shoulder blades and groaned with discomfort when the man started rubbing. "Of course I'm right. Besides, I need money, and the only way I can get a sufficient amount to improve this place is by marrying it. I can't waste my time on a priggish little governess who doesn't have what I need."

What he meant was that Miss Franklin couldn't possibly have the wealth he needed. Nash wasn't so sure about the rest. Beneath her apparent severity, he'd seen a soft regard for her young charge, even though she barely knew Emmaline. She'd been smiling and chattering like a little bird when he happened upon her in the governess quarters, and Nash had been captivated by the small dimples at each side of her mouth. Fortunately, not so captivated that he missed catching her when she fell from the chair.

"Have you any prospects, then?" Parker asked.

"Not yet. But I received a few invitations when we were in Keswick today. And I'll be entertaining here after I get things in order."

Parker made a rude noise.

"What?"

"*Here*, my lord? That will take more than a wish and a prayer, if you don't mind my saying."

"I'm not completely without resources, Parker."

"Of course not, my lord. The house is . . . The house can be . . . Er, have you thought of the London season? Bound to be a horde of marriageable heiresses there."

Nash shuddered and sat up. "I'm hoping like hell to avoid it."

"Don't blame you in the least, my lord, but you

might consider it. Going down there would be a whole sight easier than making this pile of stone presentable."

Nash shook his head and stood. He had no intention of parading himself before a gaggle of simpering debutantes and their marriage-minded mamas. Not unless he had no other options.

"That's enough for now, Parker. You're dismissed." Nash had assigned him a room near the other men, for he did not care to encourage his valet's tendency to hover.

"Yes, sir," Parker said, and took his leave. Nash collected the shirt he'd discarded and went into his dressing room. He looked forward to sinking into the steaming tub of water that awaited him there. All that could possibly make the evening better would be having Mercy Franklin there to attend him.

Mercy hadn't known that the markedly carnal sensations that roiled through her veins at Lord Ashby's touch would bedevil her all night. She could not attribute her sleeplessness to the unease and questions she'd known ever since her mother's revelations about her adoption, or to the words Emmy had read aloud from her mother's journal. She could not credit her new bed and surroundings, either, for they were entirely adequate. She'd been so far beyond merely tired after her day's journey and the work she'd done to make her room ready, she should have been able to sleep.

But once in bed, Mercy had not been able to forget the melting awareness that coursed through her veins when Lord Ashby had caught her, or the shivery heat that skipped across her shoulders beneath his arm when she supported him all the way from her quarters to his bedchamber.

She knew her reaction was entirely inappropriate. Mercy had so very often heard her father preach—both in church and at home—about the dangers of licentiousness. He'd admonished her particularly, refraining from mentioning the ruin of her true mother, of course, but making it clear he believed that Mercy was more susceptible to sin than anyone else.

She'd resented his unfounded insinuations. She was as virtuous as any other young woman in Underdale, even if her father could not believe it.

And yet Mercy found herself yearning to feel those heated sensations again. It was as if she were fulfilling her father's worst opinion of her. She turned over and pulled the blanket over her shoulders, wishing she had mustered the nerve to write to Andrew Vale before coming to Ashby Hall. If she'd sent him a letter right after Susanna's death, she might now be on her way to Whitehaven, where her former suitor had his own small church. She would be en route to the life for which she'd been prepared, and not trying to sleep within the walls of a moldering old ruin of a house. She wouldn't be wasting these precious hours in the dark, ruminating on a rude and rough nobleman who managed to set her blood on fire in spite of herself.

Staring into the darkness, Mercy decided she would not allow herself to dwell on the possibility that Mr. Vale had married someone else since the previous summer when she'd last seen him. He had been newly assigned to his church, and so he might still be getting himself established. There would be plenty of young ladies vying for his attentions, though, for he was a very attractive young man.

Reverend Franklin's refusal of Mr. Vale's proposal had been maddening and frustrating, but there had been nothing Mercy could do about it. And Reverend Vale had had no choice but to honor her father's decision, or defy it and prove himself unworthy of her. There'd been no possible way for Mercy to win the equation.

She decided there was no better time to write the letter than now, but she had no pen or paper. Hoping to find what she needed in the schoolroom adjacent to the nursery, she rose from her bed and lit a lamp, then wrapped a shawl around her shoulders. She went into the nursery and found Emmaline asleep but fitful, her blankets kicked askew. The fire had burned low, so Mercy added some peat, then pulled Emmaline's blankets over the little girl's shoulders. She gently smoothed her hair away from her face.

The child's eyes opened. "Mama?"

"No, dear. It's Miss Franklin. Are you warm enough?"

Mercy's bare feet were freezing. She guessed Emmaline must be cold, too. She pulled up an extra blanket before sitting down on the edge of the bed.

"I dreamed . . . Papa carried me to Mama's room," she whispered, her chin quivering with distress. She reached up and clutched Mercy's shawl tightly in her small hand. "We were laughing, and then everything was . . . was . . . red. And I could not breathe. I jumped down, away from Papa, and ran and ran . . ."

Mercy drew the trembling child into her arms, holding her and rocking her gently until her body stilled and she went back to sleep. The poor child must have bits of memory from the time she'd lost her mother, and Mercy wondered if any of her own dreams reflected her early years before the Franklins.

She would never know.

She eased Emmaline down to the mattress and covered her, but did not leave her right away, in case she awoke or needed comfort again.

No doubt Claire Rogers would say it was not a governess's place to soothe her charge this way, but holding this child felt exactly right to Mercy. She realized with chagrin that caring for Emmaline might be the closest she would come to motherhood, for her chances with Reverend Vale were tenuous at best.

Mercy sighed. Any other father would have welcomed a son-in-law such as Andrew Vale. He had a good living, was kind and respectful, and was exceedingly handsome, with his suede brown eyes and lovely blond hair. Mercy felt herself blush when she recalled her longing for him to kiss her.

Perhaps she *had* inherited an unhealthy wantonness from her mother, though surely her response to Lord Ashby's touch had been an aberration, a reaction to a strange situation that had caught her— had caught both of them—off guard. Now she knew what a mistake it had been to offer her assistance after he saved her from falling.

Somehow, in spite of his injured ankle, he'd managed to get up the stairs and all the way into the nursery corridor. For that matter, he'd hurried to her side to prevent her fall. Mercy thought it likely that he could have gotten himself to his bedchamber.

But even now, strange sensations shuddered through her at the image of the utterly masculine earl standing beside his massive bed, looking at her as though beckoning her.

So absurd.

He was a thoroughly contrary man, his demeanor not attractive in the least. Whatever strange sensations Mercy might feel, she could easily quench them. She had much to do in the next few days, beginning her lessons with Emmy and writing to Mr. Vale, which she vowed to do upon the morrow. It would be an extremely delicate letter to which she would need to give her full attention.

She needed to know if he was yet unmarried, and if so, whether he was still interested in courting her.

When it seemed fairly certain that Emmaline would sleep through the rest of the night, Mercy tucked her shawl around her shoulders and left the nursery. She closed the door quietly and turned to the corridor, only to collide with a large, solid body.

Chapter 9

"**L**ord Ashby!"

Nash caught Miss Franklin's elbow and held her there, suspecting that she wanted naught but to make a quick exit to the privacy of her bedchamber. She stood so tentatively in her chemise and shawl, her feet bare, her hair in disarray, and ready to bolt.

Every nerve in his body tightened in reaction to her.

She smelled like sweet rain, fresh and alluring—so incredibly different from his hideous nightmare of fire. He didn't know if that was what had awakened him, or if there'd been some stealthy noise outside his room.

The candlelight cast her cheekbones in high relief. Her lashes were thick and black, beautifully framing her sleepy eyes, and Nash could easily conjure the way they would lie against her cheek in slumber. It wasn't difficult to imagine her soft body lying against his in the darkness of night, soothing away the harsh memories that plagued him.

He took a deep breath and released her arm, resisting the urge to touch the silken, black filaments that curled over her shoulder. But the force of his desire to touch her was nearly overwhelming. "You are up rather late, Miss Franklin. Is anything amiss?" Though she clutched her shawl tightly to her chest, the visible portion of her simple white chemise seemed to glow in the candlelight.

It was as soft and feminine as he could have hoped.

She took a step back. "No, I— Emmaline was having a nightmare and so I—"

"She must have had a very loud nightmare if you heard her from your bedchamber." He wondered if Miss Franklin's little foray across the corridor had been the cause of the sounds that woke him.

"She— My lord, might we discuss this upon the morrow?"

The governess took another step back, and Nash allowed himself a moment to peruse her lushly feminine form.

He gathered his wits and reined in his lust. "Did you hear anything when you left your room, Miss Franklin?"

"Hear anything?" she asked curtly. "No. All was quiet."

She glanced around as she spoke, and Nash could not help but relive those moments in his bedchamber when he'd felt a compelling desire to lift her into his arms again and take her to his bed. But she was a proper young lady, and quite rightly uneasy in his presence.

"You heard no doors closing?" he asked, tamping down his frustration. "No footsteps on the stair?"

"Nothing. I-I don't even know why I could not—"

"Could not what, Miss Franklin?"

"The house is strange to me. I am unfamiliar with its normal creaks and noises."

"Then you admit there might have been something?"

A faint line appeared between her brows. "Yes—No. I do not know, my lord."

Nor did Nash, but he could not seem to help badgering Mercy Franklin. "All is well, then? There is nothing you need to report about my niece?"

She appeared baffled at his abrupt change of subject. "No, my lord. N-nothing is wrong," she said. "Now, if you'll excuse me, the floor is cold and it is entirely unseemly for me to be—"

"Not at all, Miss Franklin. I'll bid you good night. Unless you'd care to assist me to my bedchamber again . . ."

"Since you arrived here on your own two feet," she said acerbically, "I trust you can go back the same way."

Mercy stood with her back against the inside of her tightly closed bedroom door and forced her breathing to return to normal. She felt heated and chilled all at once, the sensations of her restless dreams coming back in force. She could not believe she'd actually hoped Lord Ashby would touch her again, perhaps draw her close and say something quite . . . quite . . .

Oh, how ridiculous. She'd never been a fanciful girl, but Lord Ashby brought out the worst possible inclinations in her. Not only was her body far too sensitive to his presence, he somehow made it impossible for her to govern her wayward tongue. It did not matter that he'd put her in an untenable position, keeping her in the shadowy corridor in her night-clothes while he asked his questions. She was in his employ and needed to be mindful of her place.

Mercy had never been inclined to display such insolence as she did with this exasperating man, and yet she knew his irritating manner was no excuse for her behavior. No doubt her friend Claire Rogers would chide her for her impertinence. Yet the earl seemed to derive some satisfaction from mocking her. How ought she to respond to that?

By avoiding him altogether.

With some careful planning, Mercy might be able to evade him for the duration of her employment at Ashby Hall, which she hoped would not be long. And if she encountered him again, she would take care to follow the strictest protocol.

In other words, she would hold her tongue.

Once Mercy wrote to Mr. Vale, she did not think it would take much time for him to send his response. Perhaps only a fortnight. Mercy doubted Lord Ashby possessed any such sense of etiquette. Clearly, he had no awareness of proper social decorum, as demonstrated by their inappropriate interchange just now.

In any event, Mercy had not heard any sounds out of place in the house, and wondered if Lord Ashby had concocted his tale of rogue noises for the purpose of detaining her outside her bedchamber, wearing naught but her chemise.

That possibility was really quite infuriating, and Mercy's blood boiled at his inconsideration. She had no doubt he'd enjoyed her discomfiture.

She climbed into her bed and gave the bolster a

violent shake before yanking the blankets up to her shoulders. If the earl had intended to be maddening, he could not have been more successful.

She just wished he did not make her body quiver with an awareness that created an unwelcome heat in the core of her being.

When morning came, Mercy washed and dressed, then listened for sounds of footsteps going past her door before broaching the corridor to walk across to the nursery. She did not care to encounter . . . anyone . . . on her way to Emmaline's room.

The arrangement of rooms at Ashby Hall was quite different from the house Claire Rogers had described in her letters, and completely unacceptable in Mercy's opinion. But it was not a governess's place to demand a change. She could not tell the earl to move the master's bedroom away from the nursery any more than she could order him to stay away from her.

Nor could she quell the nervous anticipation of another midnight meeting outside her bedchamber.

In direct opposition to such a daft notion, she'd dressed in a modest frock, a gown of celery green with a high neck and sleeves that fell just below her wrists. She brushed and pinned her hair carefully, leaving no loose ends to give anyone the wrong impression.

When Mercy entered the nursery, Emmaline was still in her nightclothes, kneeling beside her bookcase, looking at the picture book they'd read the night before.

Mercy wondered if she ought to discourage Emmaline's fascination with her mother's book. Perhaps her attachment only encouraged the kind of dreams that had upset the child's sleep the night before.

And yet the book was one of the few items Emmaline had of her mother. It did not seem right to take it away when the girl had already lost so much.

If Mercy owned something of her true mother's . . .

She wished she knew more about the woman who'd borne her, and knew it was time to delve into Susanna's journal, even though the passages Emmaline had read were disturbing. Mercy could not help but suspect the rest would be just as difficult to take.

But she might learn something of her origins, something more than the trifle Susanna had told her before she'd died. And Mercy longed to know. Later, when their morning lessons were done, she would try to eke out a few minutes to read a bit more. Perhaps after she wrote her letter to Mr. Vale.

"Good morning, Emmy," Mercy said quietly so as not to startle the girl out of her intense concentration.

Emmaline glanced up at her, then closed the book and put it away, ever so carefully.

" 'Tis my guess that Mr. Blue will not be coming up with our breakfast as he did with supper last night." At Mercy's request.

"No."

"Well then, we must go down to the kitchen and see what we can find." And make arrangements for all their meals to be brought up to the nursery.

Claire had mentioned that the nursemaid in her household always gave instructions to the kitchen staff for the nursery's food requirements. Then a footman would bring the meals to them. Clearly, that

would not be the case at Ashby Hall, since she'd had
to go down to the kitchen the night before and request
supper. She should have made it clear then that she
expected all future meals to be brought to the nursery.

"Let's get you dressed, then."

She found some reasonably clean clothing for
Emmaline and functioned as nursemaid once again,
helping her with buttons and laces. When the little
girl was ready, they walked downstairs together, and
Emmaline went directly into the kitchen, where there
were six men seated around the large worktable. The
child immediately took her place between two un-
shaven men in shirtsleeves, and when a bowl of some
sort of gruel was placed before her, she began to eat.
Emmaline was clearly accustomed to this practice.

But Mercy had no intention of allowing it to continue. She had never before met the daughter of an
earl, but she had been a guest in the homes of a few
of the local gentlemen near Underdale. Their daughters were treated in a vastly different manner than
this. Mercy could not imagine Squire Claybrook's
daughters being squeezed into a place at the table
between men such as these.

They were savages who had no sense of decorum
and not the slightest practice of good table manners. She cringed when Henry Blue speared a piece
of bread with the point of his knife and bit off a large
piece of it without even removing it from the knife.

Their crude example was the last thing to which
Emmaline should be exposed.

Mercy debated whether to remove her charge
from the table immediately and instruct someone to
take her breakfast into the dining room or up to the

nursery, or allow this meal to continue and make the change for future meals.

"Sit yourself down, missy," said the oldest of the group. He was the fierce bald man who'd gazed at her with such disdain when she'd encountered him before. The man had a broken tooth beneath his dense brown mustache, and he raised his thick, winglike eyebrows as he chewed openmouthed and pointed in Mercy's direction with a spoon.

"I beg your pardon." Mercy would give no quarter, or she'd be lost.

He gestured to a place at the end of the table just as Lord Ashby came into the kitchen from one of the outer doors. He brought in the cold air from outside, smelling of fresh air, leather, and horses.

The men all came to their feet, pulled off their caps if they wore one, and put their fingers to their forelocks. "Morning, Captain."

"Be seated, men. You know you needn't salute me any longer." His dark hair gleamed in evenly clipped layers and his face was freshly shaven, his square jaw reminding Mercy of polished granite. He removed his dark green coat, which left him in rolled-up shirtsleeves and waistcoat. He wore no collar.

Neither the heated impressions of Mercy's dreams nor the chance nocturnal encounter with Lord Ashby had prepared her for the sight of his bare forearms or the deep notch at the base of his throat, grazed by a few dark hairs rising from his chest. She struggled to gather her thoughts as he handed his coat to one of the men, who carried it out of the room.

So much for maintaining her distance, she thought, chagrined.

"Miss Franklin, you do not break your fast with us this morning?" he asked.

"My lord, this is quite irregular."

"Where's my tea, Bassett?" he asked the bald man.

"On the stove, sir. Steeping nicely."

The earl slightly favored his injured ankle as he walked to the stove and poured himself a cup, and Mercy could not help but glare at his strong back and the bold line of his legs. He wrapped his large, blunt-fingered hand around his cup as though its handle did not exist, then turned to focus his gaze upon Mercy.

"Where is Miss Franklin's tea?" he demanded.

"My lord, Lady Emmaline should not be put into the position of . . . of . . . fraternizing with your men."

"Do you want her to eat all alone, upstairs?" he asked with a frown creasing his brow.

She did not understand how such a damaged face could be so compelling. His unharmed eye was pale gray with flecks of blue, and seemed to miss naught. His injured eye was slightly cloudy, but Mercy did not think it was blind, for it moved in tandem with its mate and seemed to spear her with awareness.

He looked at her with a purely masculine potency that set her nerves on edge.

"Of course not, my lord. But there is proper decorum and unacceptable—"

"Do you wish to quarrel again, Miss Franklin?"

Seeing the governess bristle, her back going as stiff as the crisp blade of a lethal saber, was one of the rare pleasures Nash could enjoy these days. The other was the hot bath he often sank into after Parker's massages. Sometimes they relaxed him enough so that he could sleep without dreaming.

Last night had not been one of those occasions. Something had awakened him. Perhaps it had been the dream of the exploding farmhouse, or maybe he'd heard the same cries from the nursery that had awakened Miss Franklin.

Nash took in her presence like a long drink of cool water after a hard ride. Her eyes were only slightly darker than the pale green of her dress, and if she thought those nondescript sleeves and her high collar could disguise her conspicuously feminine attributes, she was vastly mistaken. Even the severe style of her hair served to accentuate her delicate features rather than mask them.

"I do not quarrel, my lord," she said, her tone as prickly as ever.

He could not help but enjoy the look of pure indignation on her face. She was a surprisingly bright spot in a long tunnel of dark days, and he could not resist provoking her. Not when it was so very easy and she reacted by biting her full lower lip and releasing it ever so slowly through her teeth as she pondered her next words.

"My lord," she said, and if Nash was not entirely mistaken, she was actually tapping her foot. "This . . . *arrangement* . . . at mealtime is not suitable for your niece."

"She is hungry, is she not?" he asked, intentionally misinterpreting her words. "I should think a growing child would—"

"I should like to speak with you, if you don't mind." Her color was high, her eyes flashing daggers in his direction.

He was about to tell her to go ahead and start talking, but noticed that the men were far quieter than usual. And Emmaline was there, sitting among them, no doubt listening carefully to every word. "Come with me, then. To the library."

"But Lady Emmaline—"

"Is perfectly all right here with Henry Blue. Isn't that so, Private Blue?" Nash asked rhetorically, looking forward to a few moments alone with Miss Franklin. He could feel waves of anger rolling off her, and every nerve in his body reacted. She would be a fiery one in bed.

"Yes, sir."

He took the pretty governess's arm and started to draw her out of the kitchen, but Philip Lowell came into the room just then and delivered news that changed Nash's direction.

"There's a carriage coming up the drive to the Hall, my lord."

He was expecting no visitors, nor did he want any. "Tell them to go away, Lowell."

"No, my lord."

Nash shot Lowell a lethal glance. "That was a direct order, Mr. Lowell," he said, even though direct orders were not quite the same anymore, and certainly did not apply to civilian stewards.

Lowell ignored him. " 'Tis likely Mr. Carew, and he's come to call in a bright new landau with a driver and two footmen. He is not a personage you ought to snub, my lord."

Nash resented the intrusion, but he recognized the need to play the engaging host to his neighbors. He would have preferred they wait until he was ready for them.

"My lord," said Lowell quietly, raising his brows expectantly. He said no more, though Nash knew what was on the tip of his tongue. Nash could not play the reclusive lord of the manor, not if he was going to make local alliances and perhaps even find a rich wife to finance Ashby's restoration.

He held back a colorful word and gave the governess a curt nod of his head before abandoning her and starting for the door. "Miss Franklin, I'm afraid we'll have to postpone our chat."

But not for long. After his hour-long gallop, Nash was in the mood to engage with the tidy little governess who most definitely had a burr under her saddle.

"Harper," he said as he unbuttoned his dirt-speckled shirt and started to pull it from his trews, "go and find Sergeant Parker—he's likely in my bedchamber. Tell him to bring a clean shirt and coat to me in the library."

The sight of Miss Franklin's blushing face stopped him cold. Her eyes seemed to be locked upon the triangle of flesh and hair he'd exposed with his unbuttoning, and he felt a wrench of arousal, a bold fullness that had been quite absent for the past year.

Chapter 10

The governess quickly turned away and Nash realized belatedly how indelicate their informal interchange must seem to her . . . Perhaps worse than their encounter outside her bedroom the night before.

Unless she felt it, too. A hot rush of awareness raced through him at the thought of her putting her hands upon his naked chest. Sliding her fingertips down to his most sensitive—

No. A vicar's daughter would be immune from such fevered longings, and shocked to know she'd been the subject of his intensely carnal thoughts.

Not that she would ever find out. Emmaline was in dire need of Miss Franklin's services, and Nash had no intention of seducing his niece's governess. While it would solve one of his problems, such a liaison would raise a host of complications he did not need.

He left the kitchen and the issue Miss Franklin wanted to discuss, and started for the library alongside Philip Lowell. Perhaps he would send Lowell back to deal with whatever Miss Franklin wanted. Staying clear of her would be the most prudent thing.

But Nash couldn't quite make himself form the words that would eliminate his reason to converse with Miss Franklin after the visitors were gone.

Parker was already coming down the steps, carrying a change of clothes. "In the library, Parker," Nash said, putting his inappropriate thoughts of Miss Franklin from his mind.

From the privacy of the library, Nash heard Grainger open the door and greet the visitors, then admit them to the house.

Nash quickly changed clothes and Parker tied his neck cloth, with some difficulty, since Nash could not manage to stand still.

Lowell returned to the library. "Aye, 'tis Horace Carew, and his daughter, Miss Helene Carew."

Nash did not remember meeting any Carew in years past, though the name was familiar. He glanced at Lowell. "*Carew*. He owns a number of acres that abut all that marshy land at the southern end of my estate. Right near the Ridge path. He owns Strathmore Pond."

"Aye, my lord."

Nash considered the details of the plat map he'd studied at length. The southernmost acres of the estate were rough with slate-laden crags and low-lying fields that flooded often, making them useless. Or, useless until he could afford to hire an engineer to come in and drain the land. Then he would have some ditches dug to channel the excess water that accumulated in that area during heavy rains.

"I wonder what he wants," Nash said.

"He's likely come merely to give you a proper greeting."

Perhaps he wanted to begin a joint improvement of those waterlogged acres. "We'll see, won't we?"

Nash left the library and went into the drawing room, where a tall, distinguished man stood before the fire. The gentleman was well dressed and appeared old enough to be Nash's father.

Seated nearby was a young woman in a vibrant pink coat with some frilly off-white trim on its edges and a perfectly matched hat with feathers. She sat straight in her chair with a benign smile on her utterly charming face, giving her an air of elegant sophistication. Nash needed no more than one good eye to see that she was a lovely blond. When he came into the room, the lady turned and gave him a brilliant smile, which faded only the slightest bit when she caught sight of his scars.

Nash had become so used to it, he barely noticed her reaction.

"Lord Ashby, 'tis very good to meet you!" the gentleman said, coming toward Nash with his long, narrow, outstretched hand. "I am Horace Carew."

Nash grasped his hand and shook it. The silver-haired man was thin and angular, his chin long and pointed, his nose slightly hooked. He looked every inch the gentleman, but for the malformed finger on his left hand. It looked as though an accident had crushed the tip, and now there was no nail at its end.

It was naught compared to Nash's scars.

"Allow me to present my daughter, Miss Helene Carew." Since she remained seated, Nash could not be certain, but the lady seemed to have inherited her father's height, but not the same unfortunate nose. She was quite stunning.

"It's a pleasure to meet you." Nash took her hand and gave a short bow over it, catching a whiff of some exotic perfume.

"We've been remiss in welcoming you home, my lord," said Carew. "I understand it's been some time since you were last here."

"Not since my eldest brother's funeral."

"Ah yes—we'd left for Edinburgh by then and were obliged to miss it." A thoughtful frown creased his brow. "My condolences on that, and your more recent loss, as well."

Nash gave a nod. It was an awkward moment, but there was no help for it. Speaking of deaths in one's family was never easy. He'd had to miss Arthur's funeral because he was in hospital at the time, apparently fighting for his life, if the army quacks were to be believed.

"Rumor has it that you were at Waterloo, my lord," Carew said.

"Aye. I was there," Nash replied simply.

"We read reports of the day, of course." Carew took on the expression Nash had seen many times before. It was one of morbid curiosity—a thirst for details Nash had spent months struggling to forget. No one seemed to understand the personal agonies that had occurred that day. The taste of blood and fear, the loss of friends, the anguish of injuries to flesh and bone—all the things Nash wished he had never had to witness.

"'Tis said some of the bloodiest action was at a farmhouse—what did they call it, Helene? Oh yes, Hougoumont," he said before she could reply. "That's it."

Nash chewed the inside of his cheek and tried to think of some answer that would not offend this potentially valuable neighbor. "Aye. I was at Hougoumont." He changed the subject abruptly. "You must be fairly new to the district, Mr. Carew."

"We came up from London about six or seven years ago. I bought the Hartfield property, down south of the Ridge path. We still call it Strathmore Pond, just as Mr. Hartfield did," Carew said, accepting the change of subject while verifying what Nash had already deduced. "We're enjoying the country life, running a few sheep."

Nash guessed it was more than a few, judging by the cut of their clothes and air of wealth that seemed to swirl about them. He had no doubt that Mr. Carew had a few other business interests that kept him and his daughter in expensive clothes and perfumes.

"We thought it was time we came to pay our respects, isn't that right, my dear?"

"Yes, Father," Miss Carew said, keeping her eyes downcast. A demure pose, to be sure, but Nash was fairly certain her real reason was that she wasn't quite sure where to look. His damaged countenance made a lot of people uncomfortable. "It's been some time since we visited Ashby Hall."

"The past few years have been rough on the place," Carew said. He did not glance around the drawing room, so Nash took him to mean the estate itself, and not just the house.

Admittedly, Carew was right on all counts. The fields, the herd, and the house.

"Aye. I have a great deal of work to do. We're still

taking stock of the situation here before we institute a plan."

"I believe there are a few Ashby sheep grazing down in your eastern quarter."

Nash knew where every one of his remaining sheep were. He'd ordered his men to ride all through the fells to look for them and count them. It was too early to bring them in for shearing, but he wanted to know how many of Ashby's Herdwicks remained on his lands. Their numbers would tell him how many he would need to purchase in order to build up the herd.

Besides hiring a head shepherd, Nash decided he would need at least one good sheepdog to help bring in the flock when it was time. As he recalled from his youth, sheepdogs could be more valuable than a human shepherd in the field.

"You may be right," he said, still assessing his guest, wondering if there was some particular reason for his visit.

Carew sat down beside his daughter, and Nash took a seat across from them. Miss Carew glanced around the room, her eyes alighting upon every piece of dusty antique furniture, every vase, picture, and bauble, giving him a chance to appreciate her striking features.

He could not fathom why she was unwed. She appeared older than Miss Franklin, by a few years at least, long past the age most young women married. Based on her father's apparent prosperity, she would have a better than average dowry, which should have made her very appealing as a wife. Nash would have to make some inquiries to see if he could determine exactly what Carew's finances were, and what his daughter's dowry would actually be.

He wondered if Carew would have any interest in marrying his daughter to a destitute nobleman.

It was not unheard of. There were many instances of wealthy gentlemen's daughters marrying impoverished noblemen for their titles. Perhaps this was what the Carews had in mind, although Nash could see that his rough visage was not particularly appealing to the young lady.

Miss Carew was flawless, and would surely have drawn the attentions of every young bachelor in London. Nash wondered why her prosperous father had decided to remove her from London society to rusticate here in Cumbria. A scandal, perhaps?

Her beauty, along with a good reputation, might be preferable in a wife, but both were completely unnecessary to Nash's purpose—unlike the dowry, which was essential.

Nash decided to foster his acquaintance with these people, for both father and daughter were likely to be of great value to him. He relaxed in his chair as he considered the possibilities. "Ashby is in need of some careful husbandry, Mr. Carew. I'd be interested in getting your advice on a few of the issues we're facing here."

Carew laughed good-naturedly. "No doubt you can use some good counsel, my lord. Ashby lands have been slowly declining especially since your brother—since Arthur—inherited it."

"Arthur was smart as a whip, but never much of a manager," Nash said, resenting Carew's assessment of his brother, honest though it might be. It was well enough for Nash to admit his late brother's short-comings, but he didn't appreciate hearing it from an arrogant stranger.

But he tempered his annoyance. Horace Carew was obviously very successful, and Nash decided he wanted the man's goodwill. He might even court the man's daughter.

"I'm pleased to find you willing to ask for advice. Intelligent as the last Lord Ashby might have been, advice was something to which your brother had a severe—and quite detrimental—aversion."

Nash rubbed his forehead as the early twinges of a headache daggered through his skull. "Do you know of anyone in the district who has a good dog or two he'd be willing to part with?"

"Hmm," said Carew, his formidable brows coming together in thoughts. "Metcalf Farm, down east of Keswick. You probably know Sir William."

"Oh, aye. I once knew them well."

"I would not be surprised if he had a few spare dogs."

Nash reminded himself it was past time for a visit to the old squire who'd been a friend of his father all those many years ago. Perhaps the older man even had some opinion on what had occurred the day Hoyt had died.

Carew turned to his daughter. "My dear, you were going to ask Lord Ashby . . ."

"Oh yes." She faced Nash, but he could sense her reluctance to do so. "Are you planning on joining the social circuit here in the Lake District?"

"I'm afraid I don't know much about it, Miss Carew." He took in her graceful posture and perfect manners. She would make an ideal wife—if she could ever become accustomed to his face.

He ought to court her. Ought to see if he could charm her beyond her aversion to his appearance. Nash had an unholy urge to inform her that all his important parts were in good working order. If he hadn't been certain before, his interactions with Mercy Franklin had proven it was true.

He returned his attention to the conversation. "Hasn't everyone already gone to London for the season?"

"Not everyone goes south, my lord," said Carew when his daughter did not immediately reply. "There will be some folderol at the assembly hall in Keswick next week, and after that, I'm sure there will be house parties and whatnot. Plenty to do. There always is. Am I right, Helene?"

The young lady nodded.

"That's good to know. I was thinking of hosting a house party here, to reacquaint myself with my neighbors."

"I'm sure that will be a very welcome event, my lord," said Miss Carew. Her skin was as clear as white porcelain, and her golden hair framed her face in intricate ringlets. Nash could not imagine a more beautiful woman . . .

And then his thoughts turned again to Mercy Franklin, whose quiet beauty would turn heads if she ever loosened her hair and donned something less severe. Showed a bit more skin, as Miss Carew did.

Nash could easily imagine her delicate collarbones and the sweet hollow at her throat, and he could not stop himself from thinking about touching it with his tongue. A fancy ball gown would display her enticing curves far better than any frock he'd seen on her thus far, although the color of today's gown set off her magnificent eyes to perf—

Carew cleared his throat and gave his daughter a pointed look, just as Mercy Franklin walked past the door with her young charge. Nash could still feel the anger radiating from her skin. It seemed not so very different from the heat he'd felt as she stood so close to him in the middle of the night, wearing only her thin night rail.

His mouth went dry and his body reacted just as it had the night before. Miss Franklin was nothing like the cool, practiced socialite who sat before him now, with her eyes trained on a spot somewhere behind him. He had an implacable desire to take Mercy to his bedchamber and remove her clothes, piece by piece while he kissed her.

"Would . . . would you like some assistance, Lord Ashby?" Miss Carew said, and Nash wondered if she had lost her mind.

Then he realized that he was the one whose hold on sanity was compromised.

Chapter 11

"I-I mean . . . I could help you with your guest list." Miss Carew made her suggestion hesitantly, pulling Nash's attention back to his guests in the drawing room. He slid his suddenly damp hands down the tops of his thighs and gathered his thoughts while Miss Carew glanced from her father, then back to him. "I could provide you with a list of those whom you might wish to invite."

"That's most gracious of you, Miss Carew, and would be very helpful. But there are a good many details I need to take care of first." Such as finding some satisfactory servants and a shepherd to manage the sheep. Getting them to shovel out the dust and mildew that had accumulated in the year since Arthur's death. Putting Miss Franklin out of his thoughts and concentrating on wooing a suitable female.

"If we can be of any help, my lord . . ." said her father.

"Thank you. I'll be certain to ask you. In the meantime, may I offer you some refreshment? Tea, perhaps?"

The visit lasted an hour, during which time Carew

spoke of various neighbors and several improvements that were being undertaken all over the district. He mentioned the flooding in the Ashby acres that bordered Strathmore land, and asked if Nash had any plans to improve the area.

"Aye. But there's a great deal more that needs to be done before I turn my attention there."

"True enough," he said. "What do you think of all the tales of boggarts down there on the ridge?"

"Boggarts?"

"Yes. People say they've taken up residence on the ridge there. Bob Danner says they made his mule go lame."

"You believe that nonsense?"

Carew laughed. "Of course not. I . . . just didn't want you to be surprised by the gossip."

Nash didn't recall any talk of boggarts on Ashby land in years past. The malicious fairies were real enough to the country folk, with run-ins and mishaps usually occurring after dark. And the injuries were always vague enough to be attributable to anything other than the victim's clumsiness or foolishness. But Nash was no bumpkin who subscribed to the old superstitions. He didn't believe in boggarts *or* curses, no matter what the townsfolk might say.

"I wonder if the boggart rumor keeps people from using the Ridge path."

Carew nodded. "I believe it does, my lord."

"That's all right, then. I don't fancy the notion of Gypsies or any other vagrants loitering on my land." He had enough problems as it was.

Before Mr. Carew and his daughter took their leave, they extended him an invitation to sup with

them in a few days' time. Nash did not look forward
to an evening observing the ways in which Miss
Carew could evade his glance, but knew he could
do naught but agree to visit their estate. He saw them
out soon afterward.

Walking outside with them, Nash could not help
but take note of their lavish carriage and the handsome servants who'd accompanied them to Ashby
Hall. Several of Nash's men had come out to pass
the time with Carew's driver and footmen. It seemed
only Lowell and Grainger were absent.

Nash walked outside and bid his guests good day
as Lowell emerged from the house to escort them to
their conveyance. Nash returned to the Hall.

If he was not convinced of Carew's affluence
before, his carriage and the servants in livery were
proof that the man had a great deal of wealth at
his disposal. Nash wondered if he knew anything of
the deer stalking party during which Hoyt had been
killed. Perhaps he'd been one of the hunters that day
and knew more than what was contained in Peter
Wardlow's report.

The notion that Hoyt's death had not been accidental would not leave Nash alone. He could not
imagine what the motive for murder would have
been, because there was no one to profit from Hoyt's
demise besides Arthur.

Whatever Arthur's failings were, he wouldn't
have harmed Hoyt for any reason, much less for the
Ashby title and estate. He'd had a very good living
up near Thursby, and with all his connections, had
begun to advance in the church. After Hoyt's death,
Arthur's letters had conveyed his shock and dismay

at the loss of their brother. He couldn't have been responsible.

But who was, and why? Ashby was an entailed estate for the most part, although Nash's grandfather had added hundreds of additional acres of land that were not part of Ashby proper. Hoyt had bequeathed it all to the next earl, so Arthur had inherited it all.

It made no sense, but Nash could not shake the feeling that someone had shot Hoyt intentionally.

He wondered if his brother had possibly offended someone. Maybe he'd broken a promise.

Or perhaps there'd been nothing at all, and the magistrate in Keswick was correct. Maybe Hoyt's death had been a horrible accident after all, and Nash's misgivings were entirely mistaken.

London, England

In a Fleet Street tavern, Gavin Briggs met with an old judge who remembered Daniel Hayes, the father of Windermere's two granddaughters. "Hayes was a brilliant pleader. Very solid future ahead of him. Damned shame what happened."

"Do you remember anything about his children?" Gavin knew it was a long shot, but he asked Judge Morton anyway.

"Children?" The old man shook his head. "I didn't know he had children. But I met Mrs. Hayes. A stunner, she was. But he wasn't exactly ill-favored himself."

"Have you any recollection who Mr. Hayes's associates were? Friends, perhaps? Business partners?"

The judge frowned. "Why do you want to know all this? The man is long dead. Twenty years at least."

"There is some interest in finding out what happened to his daughters."

"They'd have had relatives somewhere, would they not?" the judge asked, with typical legal curiosity. "The court would have appointed a guardian."

Gavin evaded the assumption and hoped the judge would let it slide. "I don't really have much information about them."

The judge shrugged, and Gavin breathed easier for the moment. "Barker might know something. Davis Barker. Still in Milford Lane, practicing law. Brilliant man. He and Hayes were very good friends as I recall."

As Gavin walked to the address given him by Judge Morton, the small hairs at the back of his neck prickled, giving him the oddest sense of being watched. He took a surreptitious glance around and saw no one suspicious. But after all his years of stealthy work for the crown, he knew better than to ignore his instincts.

He wondered if someone from his past life as one of Lord Castlereagh's spies had caught up with him, but quickly dismissed the thought, realizing that someone else had a far more compelling motive for following him . . . for finding Windermere's granddaughters.

His search for the lost Hayes girls suddenly became far more interesting than simply the means to a fat financial reward. He wondered if anyone besides Baron Chetwood might have an interest in finding Windermere's granddaughters. He doubted it.

He'd checked into Chetwood's background and found it was naught to be proud of. The man was a member of the infamous Hellfire Club, and spent his money on loose women, gaming, and racing. There did not seem to be any activity too depraved for the man's tastes. His damned club had resources of the darkest, most corrupt kind.

Windermere's heir was a poor candidate to become a duke of the realm, but it would not be the first time the highest title in the land was held by a scoundrel of the first order.

The Windermere estates were vast, but the duke also held a great deal of unentailed wealth and property. And he'd indicated he intended to give all that was not part of the entailment to his grand-daughters. Gavin did not need to wonder how far Chetwood would go to ensure none of Windermere's wealth—entailed or not—went to anyone but him. The man's grasping character was obvious.

Gavin felt he was being watched, and could not shake the idea that Chetwood had sent someone after him to prevent him from finding the duke's granddaughters.

Or worse, to find them first, and prevent them from being able to inherit. And there was only one way Gavin could think of to accomplish that.

Gavin continued on his way, behaving as though naught was amiss as he went into a paved courtyard that abutted Milford Lane. A number of law offices bordered the courtyard, as well as a few narrow alleyways between buildings. Gavin slipped through one of them and came out into Milford Lane, doubling back a good distance from where he'd ducked out. If anyone had been following him, he was behind them now.

He hastened into Barker's office and found it a beehive of activity, with clerks working at desks and orders being called out from the offices in the rear. Looking back through the heavy pane of glass in the door, he saw no one come out of any nook or cranny in pursuit of him.

He removed his hat, turning to face one of the clerks. "I'd like to speak with Mr. Barker, please."

"Have you an appointment, sir?" the man asked, pinching the bridge of his nose. His expression was harried and he looked as though he'd raked his fingers through his overly long hair one time too many.

"No, but I will take only a moment of his time."

"We are getting ready to plead a very important case, sir. There is no spare time."

"Honestly. Two minutes. Please just tell him I'm investigating the whereabouts of Daniel Hayes's daughters. I'm sure he'll speak with me."

Clearly put out by the request, the clerk went to an office door and knocked. A muffled voice beckoned the man inside, and he closed the door behind him. A moment later he stepped out and summoned Gavin. "Only a few minutes, mind you. We are on a very tight schedule. What's your name?"

"Captain Gavin Briggs."

The clerk returned to the office, announced him, and beckoned Gavin inside.

Barker was not quite as old as Gavin's father, but seemed as prosperous as he was harassed. The weight of the law seemed to rest upon his thin shoulders. His hair was the color of dull steel, and a pair of magnifying spectacles rested upon the end of his nose. Thick law tomes lay open on Barker's desk along-side stacks of notes with scribbles and ink stains. He rose from his chair and shook hands across the desk, removing his eyeglasses as he sat back down. He speared Gavin with a razor-sharp gaze. "I understand you're asking about Daniel Hayes? Or more rightly, Hayes's children."

Gavin nodded and took out a letter with Windermere's seal on it, and showed it to the barrister. "I've been asked to look into the disposition of his grandchildren."

Barker narrowed his eyes. "Disposition? What do you mean?"

"Do you know what happened to them?"

A deep crease formed between Barker's brows. "It was a long time ago."

But Gavin doubted the man ever forgot anything. "About twenty years."

"Right. I remember Mrs. Hayes's father was a duke. But they were estranged. He sent someone . . . Give me a moment . . . Newton, I think it was. A Mr. Newton— No, it was Newcomb. Mr. Newcomb came for them. Took them from their nurse and escorted them up to their grandfather in the lake country."

"Correct. Newcomb was the duke's estate manager." What Barker told him was information Gavin already had. He needed something more. "But the manager did not take the children to the duke."

"The duke was named guardian. Are you saying the man does not know where his grandchildren are?"

Gavin gave a nod. "The estrangement extended to

his daughter's children. Now he wants to find them. Reconcile with them."

Barker sighed. "I assume there is some reason the old man can't ask Newcomb. Dead, probably."

"Right again. And the duke has found no record of where Newcomb took the children." Neither had Briggs. There'd been no pertinent information in Newcomb's papers.

"Not that the old man deserves it," said Barker, rubbing a hand over his jaw, "but you might be able to track down the Hayes nurse. Nelly Thornton was her name. She could very well have had more knowledge of the events after Hayes's accident."

"Nelly Thornton?"

"I happen to know she went to work for another colleague right afterward—Mr. and Mrs. John Payton."

"Are the Paytons still in London?"

Barker dipped his pen into the inkwell and began to write on a sheet of foolscap. "Yes. I know them well, and they—or their children—have likely kept in touch with Miss Thornton. Here is their address. Tell them I sent you."

"Thank you for your time, sir," Gavin said before he stood to take his leave. "By the way . . . I am the only agent with authority to search for Windermere's grandchildren. If anyone else comes around asking, I'd appreciate it if you wouldn't mention any knowledge of the children."

Barker gave a nod.

"By the way, would you mind if I took a rear exit?"

With the latest lead in his waistcoat pocket, Gavin went out to the courtyard and made his way through a maze of alleyways, certain that he could lose anyone who might be following him. Several streets away, he hailed a hackney cab and rode to his hotel, then ordered tea and set himself up near the window in his room to wait. And watch.

Ashby Hall

Somehow, Mercy managed to keep her expression impassive as Lord Ashby left the kitchen. *He'd come disturbingly close to removing his shirt right there in front of her in the kitchen!* Mercy felt her face heat and hoped no one else would notice it. No decent woman would react the way Mercy did—with heated anticipation of seeing the man's bare torso.

She tried to distract herself from such an improper notion by searching the kitchen for a tray. But the fear that she might be what her father believed—a loose woman just like her mother—gave her pause.

So much for trying to avoid the man who plagued her dreams as well as her waking moments. His appeal was far more potent than mere handsomeness, and Mercy was ridiculously susceptible.

That was going to change now. She had to get Emmaline and the schoolroom in order so it would rarely be necessary to venture into the kitchen or any other part of the Hall again. And she would make certain never to come out of her bedchamber at night. Perhaps she ought to move her bed into the nursery and sleep even closer to Emmaline.

Yet she could almost hear Claire Rogers admonishing her that it was a nurse's place to sleep near the children. If Mercy served in both capacities, Lord Ashby might not ever hire a proper nurse for Emmaline.

As needy as the child was, Mercy did not want to serve as nursemaid, giving baths, doing laundry, and seeing to meals for the entire duration of her employment here. There would be enough to do to prepare lessons for the girl.

Ignoring Mr. Bassett's hostile glare, she rifled through the kitchen cupboards and located a tray in a storage area. Taking it to the table, she placed Emmaline's bowl as well as her own on it. "Come with me, Emmaline," she said.

"Where're you off to, miss?" Bassett asked in a gruff tone.

Mercy girded herself with the authority she could only assume she had. "We shall be taking our meals in the nursery, Mr. Bassett."

The thickly built man stood. He was a bit taller than Lord Ashby, and a great deal meatier. When he sent Mercy a fierce frown, she took a step back. "Why would you want to eat up there when you can sit here in the warm kitchen? With us?"

Mercy stood her ground. Thanks to Claire Rogers, she knew what was correct and proper, but that didn't prevent her heart from thudding uncomfortably in her chest. "Surely you do not take offense, Mr. Bassett. Young ladies—*the nieces of earls*—do not take their meals in kitchens."

She'd never before confronted anyone, certainly not a burly, red-faced stranger who seemed more than a bit hostile toward her. "From n-now on, Emmaline and I shall be eating in the nursery." She glanced around and looked at every one of the men's faces. "Every meal, unless otherwise specified."

"Now, you can't be changing all our ways here, miss," Mr. Bassett protested, backing down slightly, which helped to bolster Mercy's courage. She hoped it indicated that the man was more mouth than trousers, as her mother would have said. Or perhaps he held back because he did not yet have clear orders from the earl.

"Our way has been working well for the past month, ever since we got here. So I don't see why you need to change anything. Especially not when carting all your meals upstairs adds more duties to what the lads already must do."

Mercy refused to be intimidated. "I don't expect you to see why, but that is how Lady Emmaline will be taking her meals in future. And there may be other changes as well."

Lifting the tray, she avoided Mr. Bassett's eyes and instructed Emmaline to come away from the table. The little girl stepped over the bench without argument and accompanied Mercy out of the kitchen. Mercy felt a bit dazed after her little confrontation with Mr. Bassett, so she proceeded as quietly as Emmaline, past the cavernous medieval hall near the much smaller drawing room, where the door stood open.

Inside was Lord Ashby, who had made a startling change in his appearance since putting on more formal clothes. Despite his fine attire, Mercy could still feel an underlying roughness to his edges, but now she noted yet another dimension to his bearing. He was every bit the lord and master of Ashby

Hall. He was now an imposing figure in a dark coat and waistcoat, with a crisp-looking collar and his neck cloth tied perfectly below his square chin. In spite of his obvious potency, Mercy knew her father would never have approved of him as a suitor—not that Lord Ashby would ever court her. But Reverend Franklin quickly would have detected the earl's lack of piety and disapproved of his apparent disdain for propriety. Her father would have turned over in his grave if he'd seen her pulling off the man's boot in the middle of the road.

Or speaking to him in the insolent manner that was becoming such a habit. A most improper one.

Lord Ashby took no notice of her and Emmaline as they hesitated momentarily, for he was speaking to a fashionable young lady who wore an expensive rose-colored pelisse with cream lace and a matching hat. Even her shoes that peeked out from beneath her skirts radiated extensive wealth.

Mercy felt a pang of something exceedingly unpleasant, a feeling she couldn't quite place. Surely it was not envy, for she hadn't a jealous bone in her body. She'd been on friendly terms with the wealthy members of the parish, including Squire Claybrook's daughters, and had never coveted their clothes or any of their possessions.

And yet the attention being given the attractive young woman by Emmaline's uncle made Mercy feel distinctly tense. No, not tense, exactly. She could not quite define how it made her feel.

Perhaps it was the woman's blatantly opulent attire that bothered her. Such ostentation served no purpose beyond demonstrating a person's wealth, which was no measure of one's worth. Mercy had never aspired to such a wardrobe, although owning a few gowns that complemented her coloring and her figure would not have been amiss. But her father had frowned upon any sort of vanity—as much as he'd abhorred impropriety—and Mercy's gowns reflected his tastes.

Lord Ashby was fully engaged by the beautiful lady, whose narrow-brimmed hat bobbed as she spoke in a quiet tone. He must have gotten dressed quite quickly in order to receive his guests—and Mercy felt her face heat at the thought of seeing his bare chest. Of course he had not completely disrobed in the kitchen, but she knew he had to have removed his clothes nearby, possibly in plain sight of anyone who might pass by.

Mercy had found him even more imposing as he'd absently unfastened the buttons on his shirt. She still felt a tingling awareness of his purely male intensity—of the power and strength of his body and the intractable force of his will.

She heard her father's stern voice in her head. *Such useless nonsense, Mercy. Get on with your work.*

She started up the stairs. "Who are those people with your uncle?" she asked Emmaline

"I don't know," the child replied.

Which was just as well, for Lord Ashby's guests were none of Mercy's concern. She should not have been anywhere near the drawing room in the first place, and would not have been if proper protocol had been followed. There was a servants' staircase off the kitchen, and they should have used it.

But she'd have remained within Mr. Bassett's

sights for far too long if she'd taken that route. And she had to admit she was a coward at heart.

She and Emmaline went up to the nursery, and Mercy put thoughts of Lord Ashby from her mind. Her reaction to the man was entirely improper, and she knew better. Besides, Emmaline was in need of her attention.

As they finished eating their breakfast, Mercy instructed her young charge. "'Tis not really proper for a young lady of your standing to dine with the servants, Emmaline," she said gently.

Emmaline did not respond.

"I am sure they are all fine men, but you must always be mindful that you are the lady of the house."

Emmaline looked up at Mercy with puzzlement in her eyes.

"You are an earl's daughter—the current earl's niece. There is some decorum which must be followed."

The girl shrugged, and Emmaline decided she needed to write to Claire for a few more specifics on protocol. Claire's charges were the children of a viscount, but Mercy didn't think their code of behavior would be any different from what would be expected of Emmaline.

She did not want Emmaline to be confined by an excessive number of rules, though. Mercy had lived with far too many of them throughout her twenty-three years.

And yet, at the moment, she found she could not even abide by the simplest one—to keep a civil tongue in her head.

Chapter 12

As Nash changed clothes, it occurred to him that the game had changed since he'd last wooed a woman. Granted, his past amorous campaigns had not been about finding a wife, but about luring a willing woman to his bed.

Helene Carew might agree to wed and bed him, but Nash didn't think she'd ever be particularly willing. Not when she couldn't even look at him.

Perhaps the marriage would succeed if he made sure she did not have to look at him too often. He would douse the candles in their chamber when he bedded her, and after he got her with child a time or two, he could find himself some living quarters and absent himself from Ashby Hall. No doubt his countess would be capable of seeing to the raising of his heir. Miss Carew was likely a competent sort, if a bit dull.

He could not dwell on thoughts of the happy life his parents had made for themselves at Ashby Hall, or the affection they'd openly displayed for each other, for their sons to see. Such a marriage was not in Nash's future.

Feeling disgruntled by the duty that had been imposed upon him, he left the hall and started walking. Unconsciously, he headed toward the chapel.

It was an ancient little stone building, a remnant of a flurry of pastoral building projects at Ashby from the sixteenth century. Hoyt and Arthur were buried in the tidy churchyard beyond the chapel, as well as Nash's parents and many previous generations of Farrises.

When Nash arrived, he was appalled to see what a neglected mess it was. His parents had wed in that chapel. So had Hoyt and Joanna. There was a history here that was being slowly decimated by time.

The enormous task and responsibility of restoring the Ashby estate struck Nash full force, and he recognized fully now that he had no choice but to court Helene Carew. He had no business thinking about the voluptuous warmth of Mercy Franklin's body. At least, he could not think about Mercy until after he'd courted, wedded, and bedded Miss Carew. After he had an heir on the way, he doubted his wife would care much where he chose to bestow his affections.

Fortunately, Helene was not a hag or giggling minnow. She was a perfectly acceptable female specimen, one who would make a decent sort of wife, if not a particularly tender one.

It was her money that had the power to seduce him, not her beauty or her impeccable manners.

As Nash walked, he thought of all that could be done with Carew funds. He hoped Horace Carew would not try to dictate how Nash used the dowry. He had a feeling the man might be a meddler, especially when it came to money . . . and his daughter.

Sir William Metcalf would surely be able to advise Nash on the best way to build up his herd. Sir Will always knew who had the best lambs to sell, and he could tell Nash what price he ought to pay for them.

While he slowly replenished the herd, the Hall itself needed far more serious attention than his men had given it to date. It was obvious that the former housekeeper had done little more than keep her own quarters and Emmaline's in order.

None of his men knew anything about running a household. Childers might be surly, but he could cook army fare, and Lowell had experience in keeping books, though he seemed a bit too anxious to get Ashby back on its feet and profitable.

As often as Nash had told him his expectations were unrealistic, Lowell had insisted they would manage to show a profit by year's end.

The men who'd come to Ashby with Nash were grateful to have a home and were willing to perform whatever tasks were assigned to them. But someone had to know what needed doing.

Bassett had taken charge of the younger men, but he'd spent most of his life in the army, and that was what he knew. He had not yet realized that Ashby Hall was not a barracks, with men engaging in wrestling matches, races, and swordplay to stay busy and fit between battles. There was actual work to be done in the house.

If only Grainger were not quite so elderly, the old butler might have a hand in directing the work that needed to be done. But he was absentminded at best, spending countless hours polishing Ashby silver. He barely remembered the day Hoyt was killed. Nash kept him on only because he suspected the old retainer had nowhere else to go. Just like the rest of his men.

What Ashby Hall needed was an experienced housekeeper, if Nash was going to host any sort of a party there. But he didn't know of any competent woman who would accept her board and lodgings as sole payment for her services. And until the estate had sufficient meat and wool to sell, there would be no other payment.

It occurred to Nash that Miss Franklin might be able to give her assistance in this area. As a vicar's daughter, she must have observed—or even participated in—some basic housekeeping tasks. Maybe he ought to have Lowell ask her what she thought needed to be done.

But the thought of providing Philip Lowell with a reason for seeking out the comely governess did not sit well. Nash decided to see to it himself as soon as the occasion presented itself.

He walked into the cemetery. There was an overgrown, cobbled path that led to an ancient vault, in which the earliest earls and their families were entombed. More recently, the Ashby earls had taken to less grandiose graves. He located Hoyt's monument, and then Arthur's, flanking the graves of their parents, with their wives beside them.

Dropping down on one knee beside Hoyt's headstone, Nash brushed away a few dried leaves and
  d to understand why he was the one who had been
      when all of them were gone. He bowed his
          ntly vowed to find out exactly what had

happened to Hoyt and to do whatever was necessary to preserve his family line. He would carry on, no matter what he had to do to make Ashby the earldom it once was.

He left the cemetery and returned to the house, where he saw Emmaline with her governess. They were walking together and talking quietly—or it seemed Miss Franklin was talking and Emmaline listening.

They wore shawls over their dresses, but their heads were bare. Miss Franklin's hair was arranged in her usual neat knot at the back of her neck, and she had done something pleasing with Emmaline's hair—put it in a long plait that was held together at the end with a blue ribbon. The child looked almost relaxed in her governess's presence, reaching up to slip her small hand into that of Miss Franklin's, and Nash fancied that his niece might have enjoyed such walks with her mother had she survived the birth of her second bairn.

Perhaps she'd ridden on her father's shoulders in this garden lane, the way Nash and his brothers had done with their own father.

He felt the powerful pang of grief that had somehow escaped him as he knelt beside the graves in the cemetery, and abruptly turned away from his niece and her governess. He headed for the house, hoping Parker would be ready to massage the knots out of his neck and shoulders.

Once Mercy had sorted out an arrangement for Harper or Roarke to bring their meals to the nursery, she and Emmaline settled into a routine. A very busy regimen of lessons and exercise—usually outdoors.

But even after a few days together, the little girl remained reserved, though Mercy felt she was making some progress.

There had to be a way to break through the invisible walls with which Emmy had surrounded herself. Unfortunately, nothing came to mind, other than allowing her to read more of Susanna's journal. That had piqued Emmaline's interest as nothing else Mercy had yet seen.

But Mercy was still not ready for that. Every night while getting ready for bed, she'd thought about picking up the diary, but had not been able to face it. But she would, soon.

She didn't understand why Emmaline was so interested in the diary, unless it was because Susanna's writing was more personal than the printed books in the schoolroom. Emmaline had had no difficulty reading Susanna's words, but Mercy knew the concepts were far too advanced for a child Emmaline's age. Which was why she'd closed the book that first night at Ashby Hall, and put it away in the drawer of the table at her bedside.

Thinking back on her days at St. Martin's, Mercy recalled her own childhood and the activities she'd enjoyed with friends. That was key—she had not spent a lot of time alone. She'd had chores to do, and prayers. And she'd been allowed to have friends. Playmates.

Perhaps that was the solution.

"Emmaline, do you know of any other children who live nearby?"

"No, miss."

No, of course she wouldn't. Mercy suspected that the child's former nurse had been remiss, or perhaps simply unsociable, for Emmaline should have had contact with some of the neighboring children.

Claire Rogers had mentioned frequent, pleasant outings with her children in London, and meeting playmates in various parks near their home. Mercy wondered if Lord Ashby knew of any families with children nearby.

She knew she should not feel even the slightest twinge of anticipation at the thought of seeking out her employer, especially since she'd made such a point of avoiding him. Instead of speaking to Lord Ashby about neighboring children, Mercy decided that church was the answer. The vicar or his wife would surely know who Emmaline's playmate prospects were.

As Mercy worked to engage the little girl, she noticed a few minor successes. Emmaline spoke more often, offering more than just a one- or two-word response.

They walked around to the front of the house, just as two horsemen rode up. Lord Ashby and Mr. Lowell.

The earl wore the dark green coat he seemed to favor, and it hugged his broad shoulders like a caress. He had not shaved, so there was a shadow of whiskers on his chin. Mercy felt her breath catch when he made a masterful leap from his horse and came toward them, greeting them with a slight bow. "Miss Franklin . . . Emmaline . . ."

"Good morning, my lord," Mercy said, sounding

ridiculously breathless to her own ears. "We were . . .
we're just taking a short walk."

"Have you been to the summerhouse yet?" he
asked.

"Summerhouse?"

"Aye. An ancient marble pavilion"—he touched
her shoulder and turned her to face a tree-lined
path—"down there."

A shudder went through Mercy at his touch, centering deep, inside places she hardly knew existed.

"Shall I show you, Miss Franklin?" Mr. Lowell
asked, coming forward.

Lord Ashby handed the steward his reins. "Perhaps I shall escort you myself. Lowell, take the
horses to the stable."

"Yes, my lord."

Mr. Lowell went in one direction, and the earl led
them in another. Emmaline tightened her grasp on
Mercy's hand, and Mercy collected herself for their
impromptu outing together. Whatever Lord Ashby
said to her, she would not respond with any of the
impertinence she'd shown him before. Not in front
of his niece.

"You are not comfortable around horses, Miss
Franklin." His statement had to have been based on
their first interchange when he'd asked her to bring
his horse to him.

"No. My father did not find it necessary to keep
horses in Underdale. So I am not so very accustomed
to them."

"Underdale is a small town on the coast, is it not?"

"Yes. I could see the sea from my window."

"Ah. Is there a beach?"

She nodded, pleased that the conversation was moving along in quite the conventional manner. "Yes, there is a lovely long, white, sandy beach."

The earl looked down at his niece. "What do you think, Emmaline? Do you suppose your governess would ever pull up her skirts and walk barefoot in the sand by the sea?"

Emmy smiled shyly and nodded while Mercy felt her toes curl inside her shoes. Lord Ashby's tone had turned low and seductive, calling to mind the embarrassing moments when she'd stood barefoot with him, more than half undressed outside her bedroom. Her heart fluttered within her breast.

It seemed her respite was over. He was resolved to making her uncomfortable.

"Perhaps she even dipped her feet into the sea."

Mindful of Emmaline's presence, Mercy bit back a sharp set-down. She was perfectly capable of maintaining her poise in order to give the child a creditable example. Even though she felt she might explode.

"Did you . . . swim, Miss Franklin?"

Mercy felt sure he was making an oblique reference to the practice of disrobing down to one's chemise to swim. "Of course not, my lord. The sea is far too cold at Underdale."

A change of subject was needed. She pointed toward a long, low hedge. "Emmaline, do you see all those shoots that are just coming up just this side of that hedge?"

"Yes."

"Those are daffodils, and they will flower, I think, next week."

"I like daffodils," Emmaline said, and it seemed to Mercy that their little walk and Lord Ashby's casual tone did much to ease Emmaline's stiffness in her uncle's presence. "May we cut some of them when they flower?" Emmaline asked.

Mercy glanced at Lord Ashby. "If your uncle allows."

"Of course you may."

The pavilion came into sight, a circular building with a domed roof. There was a covered colonnade to provide some shelter, but the interior was closed up, and ivy and other vines had grown into its walls.

"It does not appear to have been used in quite some time."

Lord Ashby stood still, gazing at the building before them. "No. Not in a very long time."

There were nights when Nash knew it was better to avoid his bed than go up to it, only to wake in the night, feeling his flesh and the room around him burning. Not that anything was actually burning, but the sensations of that day at Hougoumont would not let him be.

He could wish for dreams of Mercy Franklin, but that was a different kind of torment. He'd tried to avoid her, but it was a halfhearted effort at best. He could not resist stealing a glimpse of her fine eyes, her beguiling mouth and tempting curves. No matter how plain her gown or severe her coiffure, the punch of desire hit him every time he caught sight of her.

Nash feared he could not allow her to remain at Ashby Hall, not if he was going to establish a successful marriage. He might have no experience at being a husband, but he had the notion that his wife would not appreciate seeing him lusting after his niece's governess.

A particularly virulent nightmare woke Nash and he sat up suddenly, in a trembling sweat. He brushed a hand across his face and stood in a desperate attempt to dispel the images of John Trent's death and the horrible sensations of his skin burning off his face.

He'd had other injuries, too, but they'd have been far worse if Bassett had not dragged him from the fallen timber. As abrasive as the sergeant could be, Nash owed him his life.

He pulled on a pair of trousers, then lit a lamp and left his bedroom for a quick trip to the library for something to read—something to take his mind off his dream and put him to sleep.

He went down the corridor toward the staircase, but stopped at Mercy Franklin's bedroom door. What he wouldn't give for another rendezvous like the one they'd shared on the night of her arrival at Ashby Hall. This time, he would slip the narrow little sleeve of her chemise from her shoulder, and see how much of her tender flesh he could bare. He wanted to touch her, wanted to assuage his desire with a taste of her lily-scented skin. He would warm her delicate feet in his hands, then slide them up her legs and . . .

Nash's heart gave a little jolt when he found her bedroom door open. An invitation, perhaps.

He stepped into the door frame and looked into the

room, but found it empty. The fire had burned low in the grate, and her bed had not yet been touched.

Guessing she must have heard Emmaline call out, he went across to the nursery and quietly opened the door.

There, he found his niece sound asleep in her bed, her governess curled up in a chair beside her. She wore a simple dark banyan over her chemise, but her feet were bare again. Her eyes were closed and she was breathing deeply.

A lamp on the table beside her had burned low, and a book lay open in her lap. She'd been reading to Emmaline.

Nash stood quietly, taking in the scene before him, then turned abruptly and went to the fireplace. He needed a distraction to drive away the sudden ache of loss that pinned him with an unexpected stab of grief.

Emmaline was warming to her governess, and had not seemed quite as shy with him during their walk to the pavilion. Even so, Nash did not need his niece's—or anyone else's—affections. It was enough that she was being taken care of adequately, that he was there to see to her needs. He swallowed back the lump of anguish that always came upon him when he thought of Hoyt, and knelt to build up the fire.

Then he returned to Miss Franklin and slipped the book from her hands, placing it on the table. He bent down and lifted her, cradling her against his body as she nestled her head against his chest, without waking her.

He'd wanted to feel her body against his, but not quite like this. In spite of the absurd erection he now sported, he carried the governess to her own bed-chamber and lowered her to her bed. He thought about removing her banyan, but just pulled the blanket over her and left the room.

Hard and aching for something he would never have.

Chapter 13

"Shall we take a walk outside?" Mercy asked Emmaline. Really, they ought to be practicing penmanship or working out sums, but the sun had come out, and Mercy was sure that children ought to spend time outdoors whenever the weather was decent.

Emmaline's pretty eyes sparkled for a moment, and Mercy took heart in that brief flash of interest. She was making progress with her pupil, and she knew that was as important as making sure the child could read and write and do sums. She hoped Emmaline would soon feel as comfortable with her as she'd have felt with her mother.

Mercy corrected herself. That was *not* what she wanted at all. She wanted Emmy to feel comfortable and confident in her own skin, able to stand up for herself and not be afraid, whatever situation arose. She wanted her to establish some kind of bond with her uncle so that when Mercy left Ashby Hall, the child would not feel abandoned as she must have done when her father and then her other uncle had died.

Because Mercy fully intended to compose her

letter to Andrew Vale as soon as she put Emmaline to bed that night. She was not going to get caught up in the book she'd chosen from the library as she'd done the night before, or fall asleep while she read. Somehow, she'd made her way into her own bed, though she could not remember doing so.

In any event, there was much she could do for Emmaline in the fortnight or so before she would receive a response from Mr. Vale in Whitehaven. Emmaline was not the fragile doll her uncle seemed to think she was, and she hoped he'd seen that during their outing to the pavilion the day before.

"Let's find your coat, Emmy. And we'll take a ball, too. It'll be fun to toss it to each other."

It took only a few moments to dress appropriately and locate a door that led to one of the gardens. Soon they were outside in the bright sunshine. The trees were in bud and there was an abundance of tender, green shoots spearing up from the black soil.

"Doesn't the sun feel wonderful?" Mercy smiled and tipped her head back to soak up some of its warmth. She saw that Emmaline followed her example and did the same.

Mercy felt sure the child only needed some kind attention and she would blossom, just like the gardens she had so painstakingly cultivated at home.

"The garden seems to be overgrown," she said, not expecting any response from the young girl who stood by her side, mimicking her movements. "See the rhododendron bushes? I wonder what color their flowers will be."

"Pink," said Emmaline.

"You noticed," Mercy said happily. It meant the

child had not been oblivious. "I see the bushes need pruning. I wonder if your uncle intends to . . . No, likely not." She'd seen no signs of upkeep anywhere on the property, inside or out. There were only Lord Ashby's army cohorts, who were unlikely to have been trained to maintain a garden, especially one of this size and complexity.

"This was once quite a garden," she said.

Emmaline nodded. "My papa . . ."

"Yes? Did your papa keep a nice garden?"

She nodded. "Inside."

"In the house? He kept plants?"

Perhaps he kept a green room and grew his favorite plants there. Mercy would have to take a look for it when she had time.

"Papa used to take me on his shoulders . . ."

Mercy put a comforting arm around the little girl's shoulders. Her own father had never done anything so frivolous, but she had seen other parents playfully engaged as Emmy described, carrying their children that way. She was glad to know Emmaline had such pleasing memories of her father.

"Do you like to play games, Emmy?"

The girl shrugged in response.

"Come now. There must be something you enjoy doing. Perhaps a hiding game?"

Emmaline shook her head and Mercy tried to recall some of the games played by the children back in Underdale. "Have you ever played hoops and sticks?"

"No."

"What about jacks?"

Emmaline shook her head.

Feeling quite at a loss, she took Emmaline's hand and moved her several paces away from where Mercy would stand. "We'll play a bit of catch, then."

She turned to glance at the house and saw the dingy windows of her own bedchamber. Not far from it would be Lord Ashby's room. Her face warmed at a fleeting memory of something entirely improper . . .

Had she pressed her face against Lord Ashby's chest during the night? No, she decided it must have been a dream.

Quickly, she looked away from the house and started walking down one of the garden paths with Emmaline. She had no business gazing up at the windows of the most maddening man she'd ever met.

Nash rode into Keswick alone since Philip Lowell was nowhere to be found. He assumed Lowell must be out with the men, taking stock of the herd.

He wanted to talk to Magistrate Wardlow again, and did not need Lowell to do so. Riding directly to the Moot Hall, Nash dismounted and tied his horse, then went inside.

It surprised him that it no longer felt quite so strange to be recognized and greeted as "my lord" by everyone he encountered. He was treated with far more deference than he'd ever enjoyed as a captain in Wellington's army, and was quickly shown to the same office where he and Lowell had met with Wardlow before.

But not before he heard whispers of the cursed Ashby lords.

He shrugged them off as superstitious pap and

entered the magistrate's office. Wardlow stood when Nash came in, but quickly rolled up some documents that were on his desk and shoved them aside, even as he bowed and greeted him.

Nash took a seat, casting a quick glance toward the documents. Maps, if he was not mistaken, and he wondered why Wardlow was so averse to letting Nash see them. What could possibly be so bloody confidential that the highest-ranking nobleman in the district should not be allowed to see it?

"How can I be of service to you this morning, my lord?" Wardlow asked. He was a short man with wide side whiskers and nondescript features. Nash remembered him vaguely from years before—he was the son of a local squire, and close to Hoyt's age. "I thought we'd gone over all your questions when you were here—"

"Something was missing from your reports of my brothers' deaths," Nash said. "If you recall, you did not have the list of men who attended my eldest brother's stalking party. Have you found it?"

"I-I don't believe I, er . . . actually made one at the time, my lord."

"That seems rather remiss, wouldn't you say? Makes for an incomplete record, doesn't it? Perhaps you could write down the names now . . . You were present at Ashby Hall that day, were you not?"

"Yes. Yes, I was."

"You were one of the shooting party, correct?"

He had not seemed nervous when Nash and Lowell had visited before, but the man seemed quite out of sorts now. He rubbed his face and tugged at his waistcoat more than once as they talked, causing Nash to wonder if his groundless suspicions had some merit.

He tamped down the grief and the sick feeling that rose in his chest. Wardlow could be edgy for any number of reasons that had naught to do with either Hoyt or Arthur. But he glanced toward the maps and saw that one of them was not entirely hidden.

"Yes," Wardlow said, "but I was late getting out to the fields that day. Your brother was . . . was shot before I even—"

"Who else was there, Wardlow?"

"The usual, my lord. Men of good standing in the neighborhood."

"How many?"

"Ten or twelve," he said. "My lord, if I may be so bold—you, er . . . seem to think there was something nefarious about the incident."

Nash didn't know what he thought. Accidents happened every day. But not to the two elder Farris brothers, in quick succession.

He tapped the desk. "Nefarious or not, I'd like that list. And I'd also like to know who attended Baron Landry's house party at Braithwaite. The one to which my brother Arthur never arrived."

Wardlow picked up his quill and dipped it in ink, but hesitated before he began.

Nash prompted him. "Perhaps you could start with Viscount Allerdale? I assume he was there."

Wardlow nodded and wrote the old man's name, then added several more without further encouragement from Nash. He stopped when he'd put down half a dozen names, and looked up at Nash, frowning. "It was some time ago, my lord."

That might be true, but if Nash had been present at a shooting party when the host had been killed, he was bloody sure he'd remember the name of every man present. "What about Horace Carew?"

"Right." Wardlow added the name. "Mr. Carew was there."

"Carew mentioned that he and his daughter did not attend Hoyt's funeral."

"No, that's correct. They left for Edinburgh the following day. If I remember right, there was some family matter he had to attend to."

Interesting that he would remember that small detail, but not the men who'd been present when Hoyt died. But, as Lowell had pointed out, Nash had no good reason to suspect any foul play in the deaths of his brothers. But it seemed far too coincidental for comfort. He did not believe in curses any more than he believed in boggarts.

When Wardlow finished making his lists, Nash folded them and slipped them into his waistcoat, then stood to take his leave.

First, he tipped his head toward the maps Wardlow had shoved aside. "New surveys are being done here, Wardlow?"

Wardlow sucked in his cheeks. "Aye, my lord. All over the county."

"On whose authority?"

"Well, uh . . . the crown's, of course."

Nash narrowed his eyes and wished he knew more about an earl's prerogative. He tried to remember what kind of authority his father had wielded, but failed. "Every acre?"

"Yes, my lord."

"I'd like to see the ordnance maps."

"They are incomplete, my lord. They've only just begun—"

Nash reached out his hand. "Nevertheless . . ."

Wardlow retrieved them and handed them to Nash, who spread them out on the desk.

Several properties had been drawn. Some were north of the lake, a few south. Ashby was there, the lines matching what he'd recently seen while studying his own plat maps.

"What is the purpose of these new surveys?"

Wardlow cleared his throat. "Taxation, I suppose, my lord."

He stepped away from the desk thinking he could barely afford the taxes that had already been assessed.

He left the Moot Hall and stopped short when he saw Philip Lowell standing outside the draper's shop, talking with Horace Carew. It seemed more of a conversation than just a passing greeting. Likely they'd known each other for some time.

"Lord Ashby!" called Mr. Carew.

Nash nodded briefly, wondering what reason Lowell had for coming to Keswick. He tied his horse and joined the two men outside the shop.

"My lord," said Lowell, "I was just about to return to the Hall."

"Excellent," he said bluntly. "I will see you when I return."

"Very good, my lord," the steward replied. "I'll get my horse and . . . Good day, sir," he said to Carew.

When Lowell had left them, Nash turned to Carew.

"You and my steward seemed deep in conversation."

Carew laughed. "Not at all. He merely wondered if I'd commissioned my landau to be made locally."

Nash glanced toward the expensive carriage, which stood at the ready nearby, with its liveried driver and footmen waiting for Carew's return. Why should Lowell care about the man's landau? It would be some time before Nash could afford such an extravagance.

He turned to the question that had bothered him since his interview with Wardlow. "Carew, you did not mention that you were present at Ashby Hall on the day my brother died."

Carew appeared puzzled. "I did not suppose you wished to speak of that terrible day, my lord."

"I don't, particularly. However, I find myself puzzling over exactly what happened. How did my brother happen to find himself in someone's line of fire?"

Carew's expression turned somber. "He was delayed at the Hall and came out after the rest of us had scattered. He was shot before he ever reached his sector."

As Nash pondered Carew's words, his daughter exited the shop and came to them. She bowed to Nash and greeted him with a smile that did naught to lighten the gravity of her father's words.

"Miss Carew, it is lovely to see you again," he said.

"My lord," said Carew, "my daughter and I would be honored to have you join us"—he tipped his head toward the Market Street Inn nearby—"for luncheon."

Carew could not have been more obvious. The man was making use of their serendipitous meeting to put Nash and his daughter together.

Nash considered the dowry that would likely be hers, and thought again of Lowell. He could not believe his steward's conversation had been about a lavish landau.

Perhaps the man wanted a more lucrative position at Strathmore Pond. Obviously, Carew's estate was a great deal more prosperous than Ashby.

Or maybe Lowell was offering himself as Helene's suitor. He was a wellborn gentleman, and with his family's connections, he could introduce his wife into the highest levels of society.

Nash refrained from gritting his teeth, and accepted Carew's invitation.

Chapter 14

Nash spent the rest of the day in a dark mood. He felt ill-tempered and edgy after his encounter with Peter Wardlow in the Moot Hall, then seeing Philip Lowell with Horace Carew.

Sometimes Lowell's impatience with the situation grated. Ashby could not yet afford a headman to oversee the sheep herd, but Lowell did not seem to grasp the pacing of good sheep husbandry. Even Nash knew that naught was to be done in spring. The real work began in summer, when the sheep would be herded to their pens and sheared.

Nash jabbed his fingers through his hair, feeling another headache coming on. Obviously, it was not easy, having to build up the estate from practically naught. But Lowell and all the others could damned well leave if they did not wish to remain at Ashby and work toward its success.

He got up from his chair and paced. Worrying about Lowell's intentions was pointless. He needed the man to help interpret the numbers and notations in his brothers' ledgers. After that, he could leave, for all Nash cared. He would find someone else to keep Ashby's books.

In any event, Nash now had in his possession the list of guests at Hoyt's deer stalking, as well as those who had attended the Landry house party. He would invite them all to Ashby Hall, soon.

His agitation persisted in spite of his resolve. His luncheon with the Carews had not improved his spirits, even though Horace had unmistakably encouraged Nash's courtship of his daughter. He'd blatantly left them alone together to go outside and greet an acquaintance he spied through the window. And he'd suggested that Nash attend the subscription ball that would soon be held in the assembly rooms in the very inn in which they dined.

Nash supposed he ought to attend the ball, but Helene's *incessantly* bland manners had grated on his nerves. After a quarter hour of the most vapid conversation possible, he concluded that she possessed no opinion of her own. She agreed with every word he said, or quoted her father when he asked her a direct question. And she listened to him so bloody *earnestly.*

Nash had to remind himself that her father was in possession of a blasted fortune, and that a large percentage of it would comprise Helene's dowry.

With that in mind, he'd agreed to dine with the man and his daughter the following evening.

He couldn't help but wonder if there were any other heiresses in the district. Perhaps that was reason enough to attend the ball at the Market Inn.

Nash stalked to the library window and shoved the drape aside, catching sight of Miss Franklin and Emmaline down in the garden. They were playing some sort of jumping game, and the governess's hair had come loose from her chignon to curl seductively down her back.

He could almost smell the lilies in it from where he stood, and he uttered a low curse as he turned away from the window. He did not know what lessons were taking place in the schoolroom, but he had not engaged a governess to *play* with his niece.

A knock at the door drew him away from the window, and Lowell came into the library, carrying the mail he'd picked up in town. He placed it on Nash's desk and proceeded to unseal the letters. "My lord, Harper and Roarke found a small grouping of sheep that haven't yet been counted up on Paswick Fell."

Nash swallowed his ire. He would deal with Miss Franklin later. "How many, Lowell?"

"Twenty-four."

"Any lambs?"

"Aye. Several."

It was good news, but an additional twenty-four sheep would not get them in the black this year.

"What errand took you into Keswick today, Lowell?"

"We seem to be in constant need of eggs, my lord," he replied. "So I've made an arrangement with a local farmer to buy some chicks."

Nash gave a nod. It was not unreasonable.

"And Miss Franklin asked me to acquire some seeds for her to plant a kitchen garden."

Nash felt his spine contract with irritation. The steward had paid far too much attention to Emmaline's governess since her arrival, notifying Nash every time the woman sneezed. Or so it seemed. And now he was her errand boy?

"She sent you to Keswick for seeds?"

"Not exactly, my lord. She mentioned that our diets might improve if she could grow some herbs and vegetables for the kitchen."

"And?"

"I said that I had an errand in town and would pick up what she needed."

How very accommodating, Nash thought acerbically, but he said naught. At least she was not some timid miss who needed to come running to him with every question or every time one of his men looked askance at her. As long as she was dealing with Emmaline, that was all that mattered.

And yet . . . he glanced out the window again . . . perhaps it was time to ask the governess about his niece's progress.

Mercy's heart warmed at the sound of Emmy's laugh, and she couldn't help but draw the little girl to her breast for a brief hug. It might not be exactly proper decorum, but Mercy's own childhood had been quite devoid of affection. She did not think it was necessary for Emmaline's to be the same.

She would like to see Lord Ashby take more of an interest in his niece, more than the teasing remarks he'd made for Mercy's benefit during their walk to the pavilion the previous day. A close bond between Emmy and her uncle would be beneficial to both of them, although Mercy did not know how to accomplish it without having to spend time in his presence.

If the earl did not make it his business to visit the schoolroom, neither did Emmaline seem to miss his presence, although it seemed she'd relaxed a bit during their walk.

The earl possessed an imposing presence—he was very tall, and his voice deep and commanding—so it was quite easy to see how Emmaline would be intimidated by him. But he was the only family the little girl had, and Mercy had a new appreciation for blood ties.

She wished she had some of her own.

Mr. Lowell came into the garden and Emmaline slipped her hand into Mercy's. He was not nearly as striking as her uncle, but Mercy gave Emmy's small hand a reassuring squeeze. Mr. Lowell might not be an imposing figure, but he possessed a swagger of importance, or perhaps it was just his misplaced masculine arrogance that grated on Mercy's nerves every time he came into the nursery.

She did appreciate the seeds he'd brought her from town, but did not understand why it was necessary for the man to visit the nursery several times each day.

"You look quite lovely today, Miss Franklin," he said, though Mercy knew it could not possibly be true. She wore her black mourning gown beneath her drab brown coat, and her hair was in disarray. She reached up and twisted it back into its neat knot.

She had certainly not dressed to please a man, and yet his smile and the sparkle in his eye smacked of flirtation. She felt vastly uncomfortable with the way he allowed his gaze to drop below her neck, lingering in places it should not.

"Thank you for the compliment, Mr. Lowell."

"And you, Lady Emmaline. Your governess has done something wonderful with your hair again." Mercy became further annoyed with him when he turned the compliment into one for *her*, and not just for Emmaline.

" 'Tis a fine day to be outdoors, Mr. Lowell. We were just playing awhile before going back in to resume our lessons."

"Oh, aye." He turned his face to the sun for a moment. "Lord Ashby sent me to fetch you. He'd like to see you in the library."

"Now?"

Lowell nodded. "Aye. As soon as you can manage it. Alone."

She caught sight of Emmaline's worried glance.

"Do not worry, Emmy. All is well." She turned to look at Mr. Lowell. "If you'll just ask Henry Blue to take Lady Emmaline back to the schoolroom?"

"Of course," he said. "Allow me to escort you inside."

"That won't be necessary, Mr. Lowell. We will wait here for Henry and go inside once he comes along."

"Very well," said the steward, who took his leave, albeit reluctantly.

Mercy smiled at Emmy, relieved to be spared Mr. Lowell's presence. "I won't be long. All right, Emmaline?"

Emmaline nodded as Lowell left the garden to fetch the young man. Mercy's good sense warred with her anticipation of seeing Lord Ashby again, but she decided that this time, she would not allow him to provoke her. She'd had years of practice curbing her tongue and speaking only when required to do so. She was certainly capable of following that dictate now.

Once Henry Blue came to take Emmy to the nursery, Mercy followed them inside and made her way to the library. She found the door standing ajar, and inside was Lord Ashby, sitting at a desk cluttered with papers and thick ledgers. He seemed deep in concentration, holding a pen in one hand and rubbing the injured side of his face with the other.

He was unbearably attractive, and Mercy had not been able to avoid thinking of him, of their strangely intimate moments together since her arrival at Ashby Hall.

She knew how very inappropriate some of their exchanges had been, though each one had touched something deep within her.

Yet this would be the first formal discussion Mercy had had with the earl since her arrival, and she paused at the library door and smoothed her skirts, wondering what Lord Ashby wanted to speak to her about.

Lord Ashby suddenly dropped his hand from his head, looked up, and saw her.

And he did not appear to be in good spirits. "Miss Franklin." His voice was gravelly, as though he had not used it in some time.

She bolstered her courage and walked into the library. She had done nothing to warrant his displeasure. Unless he'd just now learned that she'd changed the arrangement for Emmaline's meals. Or that she'd asked Mr. Lowell to purchase some planting seeds for her . . . "You wanted to see me, my lord?"

He set aside his quill, leaned back, and crossed his hands over his dark waistcoat. "I would like a report on your pupil."

"Emmy?"

He frowned at the shortened name, and Mercy realized he must not have heard it before.

"She likes to be called by her father's pet name for her."

"I see. I also see that you spend a great deal of time amusing yourselves outdoors. What is her status in the classroom, Miss Franklin? Is she an apt student?"

Mercy bristled. "If you bothered to speak to her, you might already know the answer to that, my lord." She wanted to clap her hand over her mouth, but it was too late. She could not unsay the words.

Lord Ashby tipped his head slightly down as he studied her, as though she were some strange creature he had never encountered before. Which could not be too far off the mark, for Mercy had never encountered this side of herself before. She'd never been defiant or rude . . . Perhaps it was because his accusation was so unfounded. *Amusing themselves, indeed.*

"M-my lord, I-I-I mean . . ."

"I know what you mean, Miss Franklin. You are implying that I have neglected my duties with regard to my niece."

"Well, not your duties, surely." After all, he *had* hired her, forgoing all other servants aside from his former military subordinates.

He rubbed a hand across his mouth and chin. "I will admit I have not been quite sure how to approach her."

"She is just a child, my lord." But she guessed he had not had much experience with children. Not as an army officer.

"I will bear that in mind in future, Miss Franklin. In the meantime, shall I rephrase my question? How would you evaluate my niece's classroom skills?"

Mercy clasped her hands together at her waist, relieved that the conversation was moving in a reasonable direction. "She is a very bright young girl, my lord. She can read everything I put before her, and then some. Her arithmetic skills are strong as well, even going beyond simple sums and subtractions."

He raised a brow. Plain interest, Mercy wondered, or surprise?

"My lord, you may have heard that I've forbidden your niece to take her meals in the kitchen with your men."

He looked at her blankly. "Your point being . . . ?"

"It is entirely inappropriate for an earl's daughter . . . or niece . . . to dine elbow to elbow with your staff. Such as it is," she could not help but add.

Ashby leaned back in his chair and gazed at her, and she felt that uncomfortable curling of her toes again. "No doubt you are right, Miss Franklin. But without proper servants and a decent chef, what would you have had me do?"

"Perhaps you should have kept her nurse until there was someone to replace her."

She had done it again. She was quite capable of carrying on a suitably respectful interchange, and yet something about Lord Ashby made her forget all her training. Maybe she did it to fend off the intense attraction she felt.

The earl came slowly to his feet and circled around the desk, his movements half tamed at best, and Mercy wondered if he would chastise her now.

Moving quite deliberately, he came to stand right in front of her. Mercy could not help but take a step back from his powerful presence. He was so very tall, his shoulders enormously wide in his dark jacket and plain waistcoat. His legs were powerful, his booted feet standing apart and solid on the ground. The earl faced her squarely, as though he could frighten her with his damaged visage. But, much to her chagrin, she found his scars far more fascinating than frightening.

She needed to curb this inappropriate attraction. It interfered with her concentration and caused her to lose sleep with unacceptable, fevered dreams. If she had to count the times she'd pictured his strong hands with their blunt-tipped fingers, or thought of the deep timbre of his voice—

"The woman was a shrew, and caused my niece to cower," he said softly, and Mercy could almost feel the sharp rasp of his voice against her spine as he spoke. "I could not abide her, Miss Franklin."

Mercy forced herself not to shy away from him, away from the seduction of his gaze and his powerful, masculine stance.

The earl moved closer, sending sparks of awareness skittering across Mercy's skin. But if he thought he could intimidate her—or even seduce her—he was sadly mistaken.

She raised her chin and faced him head-on. Emmaline needed a nurse, someone with more experience than Mercy. Someone who would stay here and be a companion to Emmy once Mercy left. "My lord . . . is there someone . . . Has Mr. Lowell employed someone—as he did me—to come and function as Emmaline's nurse?"

In spite of his daunting posture, Mercy intended to make it clear that someone needed to see to Emmaline's wardrobe and do her laundry. She needed an experienced nurse to make sure she was eating properly, and to care for her if she became ill. Because Mercy was barely qualified to perform her own duties.

"Miss Franklin, my brother died last summer on the very day I was getting half my face blown off at Waterloo." His voice rumbled through her this time, like quiet thunder before a storm. "I was unable to travel for some time. And now that I have returned to Ashby Hall, I find the estate in . . . shall we say . . . less than ideal circumstances."

Waterloo? She had thought of that possibility, of course, but her lungs seemed to deflate as she imagined the horrors, not to mention the pain, he must have endured that day. Mercy considered the fact that he must have come close to losing his own life in a battle so far from her home that she'd only heard about it weeks later as her father read aloud the accounts of Napoleon's defeat.

By then, Lord Ashby might very well have been struggling for his life. The thought gave her pause, and she found herself softening toward him.

"For now, Miss Franklin, you will be the only one who looks after my niece. You have free rein." His gaze dropped to her shoulder, and Mercy realized that a wisp of hair had escaped her mended chignon. She attempted to push it back surreptitiously, but Lord Ashby's eyes followed her every move with a purely carnal scrutiny. His gaze dropped to her throat and then lower, brazenly assessing her feminine attributes.

Mercy was mortified to feel the tips of her breasts puckering, certain he could not help but notice.

"I-I can accept that, my lord." She crossed her arms over her chest. "But your men . . . Some of them are not what I would call pleased to take direction from me . . . when it pertains to your niece, of course."

The strand of hair must have fallen down again, because Lord Ashby reached for it. He rubbed it between two fingers, the gesture causing an onslaught of radiant heat that coursed from her shoulders to her hands, and especially across her breasts. It was as though a flash of hot sunlight had pierced through her, leaving her singed and raw.

She trembled with sensation.

His touch was thoroughly improper, but Mercy could not summon the wherewithal to step away. She closed her eyes as the permeating heat suffused her, suddenly centering and pooling in her lungs and deep between her thighs. His hand was hot on her shoulder, and when he slid it down her back, Mercy felt herself leaning into his touch. Her heart jolted, its rhythm racing frantically as the pressure of his touch increased.

He eased her gently toward him, and Mercy sensed a ravenous hunger emanating from him.

Her breath caught in her throat when she realized he shared her hunger. He was going to kiss her.

Chapter 15

Mercy longed for that brush of his lips upon hers. An intimacy unlike any she'd shared before.

Abruptly, he withdrew his hand and returned to his desk. He picked up a document and studied it, studiously dismissing her, dismissing the rush of longing that had so possessed them both.

Mercy would have believed the intense moment was naught to him, but for the way he raked his fingers across his scalp, disturbing his layers of glossy black hair.

"I will see that the men understand you are in charge of all matters regarding my niece and the nursery." It was as though he was speaking to the paper in his hand.

Mercy stared at his back. The conversation had not gone at all the way she thought it might, but her mouth had gone dry and her brain seemed incapable of forming the ideas she needed to resume their discussion. She had not been able to put together a single coherent thought since he'd touched her. Since his head had descended toward hers, with the promise of his kiss.

"That will be all, Miss Franklin." He turned slightly toward her, giving her a view of his injured side. It seemed he was intentionally trying to put her off.

Mercy's face burned with mortification at her lapse of decorum, and at his sudden indifference. She didn't notice the odd thickness to his voice, but gave a nod that she was sure he could not possibly see, and quit the room.

Nash had to get outside. Outside and far away from temptation, for Miss Franklin was seduction personified. He derived a perverse pleasure from her brash comments, and had been so distracted by the promise of those plush lips against his that he'd nearly pulled her against his chest and ravaged them.

Once again she had not even seemed to notice his scars.

"Lowell!" he shouted as he strode purposefully from the library. He headed for the door that led to the stable, expecting the steward to hear him and follow.

Nash had waged a savage little battle to gain the strength of will to turn away from Mercy Franklin, even though his heart was thumping uncontrollably in his chest and his groin hardening with unrelenting force. She'd borne the now-familiar fragrance of lilies again, so enticing in its simplicity, so completely opposite to the lady herself. Nash didn't think he'd ever be able to encounter the scent again without becoming aroused.

Roarke joined him in the stable yard.

"Mr. Lowell went into Keswick, sir."

"What the hell for?"

Roarke shrugged. "He didn't say."

Nash swallowed his annoyance. He'd wanted the company of the one man who'd seen the magistrate's report, the one man who'd been present at Ashby on the day Arthur had died. "Get our horses saddled, Roarke. You're coming with me."

"Where do we go, my lord?"

"To the high road where my brother's carriage went over."

Roarke said naught, but Nash noticed a slight lifting of the man's brow.

Nash gave no explanation. There was enough time before dark to ride to the place where Arthur's accident had occurred. And a trip to the high road would surely help him to conquer his preoccupation with Emmaline's governess.

They saddled their horses and started for the road to Braithwaite where Arthur's carriage had dropped off the road.

"Mr. Lowell said it was raining for days when your brother started out," said Roarke.

Nash made a low sound of agreement. There'd been heavy rains and terrible road conditions. It was just like Arthur to go ahead, in spite of the dangers, for there was to be a very prestigious crowd gathered for the weekend party at Baron Landry's house.

Georgia had accompanied Arthur, of course, but Nash was exceedingly thankful his brother had not taken Emmaline along.

It took nearly an hour to reach the fatal spot at the highest point of the fell. Nash knew he'd found the correct location, for he could still see fragments of wood and metal and glass littering the rocks over the edge of the cliff.

Nash dismounted at the site, and Roarke followed suit.

"This must be it," the corporal said. He pulled off his cap and scratched his head, frowning.

"The road is unnaturally narrow here. A carriage could barely get past." Nash turned to look back the way they'd come and shook his head. "They would have been walking up to this point."

"In the rain, sir?"

He nodded. "It's too steep for a team to pull a carriage with occupants. Our custom up here is for passengers to step out of the carriage on steep inclines, whether up or down."

"What could have happened, then?" Roarke began to retrace the steps Arthur and Georgia would have walked, and Nash turned away as his grief threatened to spill out. "Did they walk in front of the carriage, or behind?"

He managed to choke out a reply. "Likely in front."

"Are you sure they would have been walking here? Begging your pardon, sir, if the weather was so bad, wouldn't your brother's wife have refused to get out and walk in the rain and mud?"

"I didn't know her well enough to say," Nash said. But on the few occasions they had met, Georgia had been far more pompous than Arthur, and prickly, too. Nash supposed it was possible Georgia had refused to walk, especially since she would want to be at her best when they arrived at Landry House.

He tried to re-create Georgia's thought process. "I don't suppose she'd have wanted soaked and muddy clothes when they arrived at their destination."

But as socially conscious as Georgia was, she was no fool. He could not imagine that she'd stay inside the carriage when the driver had gotten down to lead the horses, as he must have done. Surely Arthur would have gotten out, though he might have told Georgia to remain inside.

Nash turned and watched as Roarke paced the crumbled stretch near the edge and tried to visualize what might have happened that fateful day.

"I don't know, sir . . ."

"What are you thinking, Corporal?"

He shook his head as if to clear it. "If they were inside the carriage and a wheel went off the edge . . ."

"The whole carriage would have gone over," Nash remarked, wincing as he pictured the screaming horses and the crash of the carriage. Worse, he could almost see his brother's broken body tumbling down the side of the fell, where it had not been found for two days.

A roiling wave of nausea caught him off guard.

"But even if they were all walking, the mud would have been slippery, wouldn't it?" Roarke said, moving away from the precarious edge. "And this road is far too narrow."

Nash shook his head. "You think someone tampered with it? Narrowed it intentionally?"

Roarke put his hands on his hips and looked down the cliff. "Well, sir, I did a lot of trench digging in the army. And I . . . well, I wouldn't overlook the possibility."

Nash came to stand beside Roarke near the edge of the road and looked down. It would take a very determined man to do what Roarke seemed to be suggesting. Who would have done such a thing? And why? It all came back to the question of who would gain from the Farris brothers' deaths.

And there was no one—other than the British government itself.

"They had an experienced driver," Nash said evenly, "a man who was born and raised here in the lakes. He knew the dangers, he knew what precautions to take. He'd have seen the narrowing. And yet he allowed his carriage to go down, and him with it. It doesn't make sense."

Or perhaps Nash was wrong about the Ashby curse.

In the bright morning light streaming through the nursery windows, Mercy felt a tight ripple of awareness slide through her as Lord Ashby stopped inside the doorway. He stood watching for a moment as she brushed Emmaline's hair and braided it into a neat plait.

Mercy had not seen him since the night before, but in the hours since their encounter in the library, she had not been able to stop thinking of his touch, or the cravings he'd roused in her. She could still feel the tingling in her breasts and the heated stirrings between her thighs. He'd intended to kiss her.

And she had been more than ready to respond to his touch.

In a quick glance, Mercy noted that his clothes were the ones he usually favored, fawn breeches and a dark green coat with a black waistcoat and white shirt underneath. His neck was bare, and Mercy found herself wondering how that bit of skin would taste. Like his shaving soap? Like the man himself?

Appalled at the direction of her thoughts, she concentrated on tying a ribbon at the end of Emmaline's plait.

And making her face a mask of indifference.

"Miss Franklin . . ." His voice echoed through her.

She cleared her throat. "There. All finished," she said to Emmaline, avoiding looking up at the earl.

"I have need of some . . . housekeeping advice."

Mercy's eyes darted up to his, in spite of herself. It was the last thing she expected him to say. "Housekeeping? That, my lord, is what housekeepers are for."

"Yes, well, need I remind you that we have no housekeeper here at Ashby Hall?"

"No need to remind me, my lord. The evidence is clear, everywhere I look."

"Which is why I am asking for your opinion. Counsel, as it were."

Silently, Emmaline went into the schoolroom, leaving Mercy alone with Lord Ashby, who came all the way into the nursery. He stood close to her, but at a proper distance. A far cry from his position the previous day when she'd approached him in his library.

"I would appreciate your assistance, Miss Franklin. I intend to hold a house party soon, but the house . . . The house needs work. Thanks to old Grainger, the Ashby silver is presentable, but nothing else is."

"My lord, I—"

"I realize this is beyond the scope of your employment at Ashby Hall. And I assure you, it will only be a matter of consultation." He clasped his hands behind his back and turned to the window, and Mercy wondered if he even remembered their exchange in the library the previous afternoon. "I have the labor to accomplish whatever tasks you assign. My men know about sweeping and mopping and what-have-you. But clearly, there is more that needs to be done. The hall must be made ready."

"I haven't any experience. A house party?" A little flutter of panic rose in her breast. "With overnight guests?"

It was one thing to take little Emmaline under her wing and teach her to read, write, and cipher. But Ashby's reputation would surely rise or fall upon the quality of the party the earl intended to hold.

"Yes, I . . . I suppose so." A crease appeared between his brows, and Mercy suspected he wasn't quite sure what a house party entailed.

Well, neither was she.

"Several, I imagine," he replied.

"Good Lord, it will be a monumental task."

The earl turned back to face her, and Mercy felt an agonizing, all-consuming, wholly inappropriate craving for the rasp of his calloused hands on her skin. She closed her eyes and spun away from him.

"My lord, I would have no idea where to start. My father's house was one tenth the size of Ashby Hall, and we rarely entertained. Only an occasional clergyman visited, sometimes with a wife in tow. Surely that is not the kind of guests you intend to entertain here."

"Indeed not. But I have every confidence that you are up to the task." He tipped his head toward the schoolroom. "Look at my niece. In a few short days, you've improved her appearance immeasurably."

Mercy threw up her hands in exasperation. "A child is nothing like a house, Lord Ashby!"

"Of course not," he said, and Mercy chose to ignore his small smile of amusement. "I merely refer to your competence with regard to her care. Besides her appearance, there is a subtle but distinct change in her bearing since you came."

"You will badger me until I agree, won't you, my lord?"

He nodded. "Until I get my way, yes."

The sight of Mercy Franklin was a respite for Nash after the hellish night he'd spent. He did not think he'd slept more than a couple of hours.

His usual nightmares of the Hougoumont explosion got mixed up with Arthur's carriage accident, and all through the night, Nash had felt as though he were falling off a cliff. Or under a burning beam. Or watching Arthur and John Trent meet their deaths. It was sheer hell.

Miss Franklin had finally agreed to his request, and she'd come down to the great hall with a plan that she'd imparted to his men. It was a systematic approach to making the Hall ready for guests—starting with a thorough cleaning of the place. The men had begun to follow her orders, and as she spoke, Nash could not help but remember their all too brief moments in the library the day before, when he'd come so close to taking her in his arms and kissing her. He was certain she'd have allowed the kiss, for she'd been just as aroused as he.

Nash imagined how she'd taste—not too sweet like an overripe peach, but spicy and unique like some untried delicacy. Her body would fit nicely against his, and Nash considered how the weight of her breasts would feel in his hands, the taste of her nipples on his tongue. He could almost hear her moan of pleasure as he—

"My lord, you are standing in the way," Mercy said sharply, drawing him out of his reverie.

He moved aside as a hint of her lily scent wafted toward him, and Harper and Blue rolled up the carpet upon which he'd been standing.

"The library is next, my lord," she said. "If there is anything you want to remove from that room so that you can work elsewhere without disruption, please do so this afternoon."

"Perhaps I'll have you work around me, Miss Franklin. How would that suit you?"

"It does not suit me at all, my lord." She turned to speak to Roarke. "Take this bucket and start on the windows, Mr. Roarke. There are some clean rags on the mantel."

"Miss Franklin, I had not guessed you would be as fierce as Field Marshal von Blücher."

"Yes, you did, my lord, else you would not have assigned me this impossible task."

Nash started a retort, but when she bent to pick up a cushion that had fallen from a chair, presenting far more bewitching curves than he had ever seen, he was rendered mute. Over her dress, she wore a plain white neckerchief that crossed over the shapely swell of her breasts and tucked into the apron that was cinched tightly at her waist. The neat knot at the nape of her neck had come loose, and his fingers tingled when he thought of its silky softness.

He wanted to sidle closer and touch his mouth to the point in her neck where the scent of lilies was strongest. He wanted to take down that pure white bib and slowly untie the strings at her waist.

But he knew better.

He was expected to dine with Mr. Carew and his daughter at Strathmore Pond that night, and would begin his courtship in earnest. He could not attend Helene Carew properly while thoughts of Mercy Franklin pervaded his entire being.

Nash supposed he should mention that he intended to entertain his future bride at Ashby Hall when it was ready for guests, but he had a feeling such information would hinder the lively exchanges he shared with Miss Franklin. Once she became aware that he had already begun to court Miss Carew, he was fairly certain she would find a way to curb her tongue. She would become distant and respectful, an attitude he was not going to enjoy when it happened.

And it would happen soon.

At least he had all day to enjoy her comings and goings, and the way she delegated housekeeping chores to his men. And while Mercy strode between the great hall and the various receiving rooms, Emmaline sat with paper and pencils on her lap, quietly drawing.

Soundly dismissed by the general whom he'd put in charge, Nash retreated to the library, where he gathered up the ledgers and notes he intended to finish that afternoon.

Mercy's heart swelled at the sight of Lord Ashby hovering near Emmaline as she drew. She wondered if there was something else she could do to ease his awkwardness with his niece, or Emmaline's shyness with him.

Her urge to leave Ashby Hall had diminished over the past few days, and she had lost some of her impetus to write to Mr. Vale. Keeping busy with Emmy had sidetracked her . . . as had Lord Ashby himself. It was difficult to focus her attention on Andrew Vale when she knew the earl was in his bedchamber, just down the hall.

Emmaline's uncle was annoying. No, he was not merely annoying, but maddening, and yet Mercy could not control the purely visceral response he provoked in her. When he was near, there did not seem to be enough air to breathe. Her heart pounded and sparks skittered wildly across her ragged nerves.

She did not need to wonder how his kiss would have felt, for she knew. It would have been amazing.

It *would be* amazing, if she allowed it. Which she could not. Writing to Reverend Vale was a far more practical, as well as safer, bet. The young vicar was a man within Mercy's reach, and even though he did not create in her the kind of maelstrom that Lord Ashby did, he'd been a perfectly satisfactory suitor eight months ago. Of course he was still acceptable now.

If he remained unmarried.

Mercy focused her attention on the housekeeping tasks being performed under her direction. The neglect she saw in every corner of the Hall was palpable, and she could only wonder how the rest of the estate fared. She had not seen many sheep on the hillsides, though there was at least one milk cow housed in the barn near the stable. One of the younger men—usually Henry Blue or Roddy Roarke—did the milking and made sure there was plenty available for Emmaline.

But they needed butter, cheese, and eggs. The fruits and vegetables that were brought up from town were far from fresh, and hardly palatable. Their diet at Ashby was dull and monotonous.

That would change in the coming months. Mercy had been surprised by how quickly Mr. Lowell had obtained the seeds she requested. When she had a few moments' leisure time, she would look for an appropriate plot in which to plant them. Not that she intended to be there long enough to see her crop harvested. If all went as she hoped . . .

Well, she would not count her chickens before they were hatched.

When she saw Mr. Vale again, her fondness for him would turn into something rather more compelling, more exciting, than it had been when he'd asked for her hand. When he gave her a kiss to seal their marriage vows, it would be pure bliss—not the dark promise of sweet savage pleasures she could not even imagine.

Mercy felt a blush creep up from her neck to her forehead and put aside her lascivious thoughts.

Something must be fundamentally wrong with her to entertain such wild imaginings. She had chores to do, and there was no time for such nonsense.

Luckily, Mercy was not expected to do the work of putting the house to rights. Lord Ashby had told the men to follow her instructions, and Mr. Lowell was usually nearby in case of any disagreement.

There had been some grumbling. Childers and Bassett were not pleased with having to do housework, but they did as they were told, albeit begrudgingly. They did, at least, until Mr. Lowell stepped out and Lord Ashby disappeared, and Mercy asked Mr. Bassett to help Henry Blue carry out the carpet.

"I'm not a flippin' footman, missy," he growled. "Get Roarke to do your carrying for you."

"Mr. Roarke has gone to fetch a bucket of water." She wondered where Mr. Lowell had gone. "I would appreciate it if you would just help Mr. Blue now so we can get this chore over and done."

"Well, nobody bloody well cares what you appreciate." He faced Mercy squarely, his face close enough that she could see flecks of brown in his black eyes.

In her peripheral vision, Mercy saw Henry Blue on his knees where he'd rolled up the carpet, and Emmaline on a chair beyond him. Henry gaped up at them, seemingly paralyzed.

Mercy swallowed as Bassett stepped even closer. The dome of his bald head was slightly damp, and his cheeks red. He towered over her, his anger out of proportion to the request. "Mr. Bassett . . ."

Mercy found herself trembling. Mr. Bassett had

been threatening on that first morning here, but this was far worse. She felt he might actually do her some harm.

"Stay where you are, Blue!" Bassett barked when Henry got up and started for the door. "No need to summon Lowell for this."

"Mr. Bassett, sir, I think you should—"

"Shut it, Blue." He did not take his eyes from Mercy as he spoke, and his harsh command achieved the result he'd intended. Henry stood still and silent. Emmaline did not move, but seemed to shrink into her chair, her eyes closed tightly.

And Mercy's fear turned to anger. How dare he frighten the little girl in this way?

"You are out of line, Mr. Bassett." She spoke firmly, putting her hands on her hips and leaning toward him, rising on her toes to gain a bit of height. "I gave you a perfectly civil, perfectly legitimate request."

"I'll be damned if I—"

Mercy jabbed one finger into Bassett's chest. "Your language is offensive, and your attitude is even worse. Either you give Mr. Blue your assistance, or you can leave the house. Now."

"Right," he drawled derisively. "You don't have the authority—"

"Yes, she does, Bassett," came a growling voice at the other side of the room.

Chapter 16

Mercy did not know how long Lord Ashby had been standing in the doorway observing the interchange, but when he walked into the room, Bassett retreated a pace or two. Clearly, the former sergeant had not been aware of his presence, either.

"I'm a soldier, sir," he said. "Not a housemaid."

"And what you *will* be—is without a place to rest your head if you ever again speak to Miss Franklin in that tone."

Bassett's face twisted harshly. "But sir—"

"You all know the importance of making the house ready," the earl said, his tone unyielding. "Miss Franklin is our best resource for accomplishing that task. I expect you and the others to do as she instructs. Without question."

Mercy pressed a hand against her chest and walked over to Emmaline. She took the little girl's hand and led her from the room. "I believe it's time for our lessons, Emmy."

Nash had never felt such a virulent anger. If not for the fact that Bassett had dragged him out from under the burning beams at Hougoumont Farm after the explosion, he'd have tossed him out of Ashby Hall on his arse without a second thought.

But Nash owed him.

"I've already spoken to you once about Miss Franklin, Bassett. You know what I expect of you. I don't want to find you giving her any trouble again."

Clearly agitated by Nash's dressing-down, Bassett looked away, smoothing down his thick mustache. He turned back and pinned Nash with his fierce, dark gaze. "I don't take orders from a woman, sir."

"Miss Franklin did not order you, Bassett, she made a request. A very reasonable request that I was able to hear quite distinctly from the entrance hall."

Bassett grumbled something under his breath.

Nash ignored it. "I need this house put to rights, and I need you and the rest of the men to do whatever it takes to accomplish that. If it means taking direction from a woman, then so be it. Have I made myself clear?"

"Yes, sir." Bassett grumbled his agreement, and Nash knew the man still wasn't happy about the situation. But he refrained from reminding him that *he* owed Nash, too. Because the conclusion of the war meant there was very little employment available for a former sergeant with no skills but those he'd learned in the army.

Before returning to Arthur's ledgers, Nash took the stairs and walked down the hallway toward the schoolroom, where he assumed he would find his niece and her governess. He needed to reassure himself that Mercy was unscathed by her clash with Bassett.

He stopped at his niece's open door and saw

Miss Franklin and Emmaline sitting together on the divan, discussing the confrontation. Mercy had her arm about Emmaline's shoulders, and was twirling a lock of the girl's hair in her fingers. On the table nearby, he noticed a bookmarked volume of *Robinson Crusoe* that had been read and reread by Nash and his brothers years ago.

No wilting violet was this governess—she'd borrowed from his library one of the most daring, adventurous stories ever written, to share with his niece.

He could not help but admire her bold choice in reading. It echoed her boldness in handling Bassett, a daunting opponent if ever there was one.

Neither Mercy nor Emmaline noticed him in the doorway.

"Mr. Bassett was mean," said his niece.

"Probably not mean . . . but just harsh, Emmy. My father was a harsh man, too," she said to the child, "not too terribly different from Mr. Bassett."

Nash wondered how harsh. And whether her father had ever raised his hand to her. If he'd been like Bassett . . . The thought of anyone doing violence to Emmaline's governess had him balling his fists at his sides.

Even Emmaline expressed some dismay. From Nash's oblique angle at the door, he could see a dark frown cross her brow. "He should not speak to you as he did. He said—"

"I know what he said, sweet. And it was not very nice," Mercy remarked. "But your uncle managed him rather well, did he not?"

No, Nash thought. Mercy had had matters well

in hand ever since her arrival at Ashby Hall, and he'd been impressed with her resolute stance. She had not cowered in the least, and had attempted to minimize the confrontation—for Emmaline's sake, he supposed. She had stood valiantly before Goliath, small and feminine, but powerful in her determination. Even so, Nash knew it was a wonder Bassett had not knocked her over merely with his breath.

He walked into the schoolroom. Mercy and Emmaline appeared startled at his entrance, and Nash found himself at a sudden loss for words. Though he'd just seen the governess in the drawing room wearing this very same apron, with her sleeves rolled to her elbows, the sight of her now jolted his heart into a rapid rhythm.

"My lord," Mercy said. Silky filaments of her black hair had escaped her once-tidy coiffeur to curl about her ears and temples. "I— Thank you for interceding just now. I'm not sure how it would have ended had you not arrived."

"You'll have no further trouble from Mr. Bassett."

She had a softer, far more vulnerable appearance now than what she'd displayed to Bassett. And Nash found that his protective instincts had only increased since his exit from the burly sergeant in the drawing room.

Which was absurd.

"All is well then, Miss Franklin?" He put a wry tone into his voice so he would not sound like a total idiot. "You are unscathed?"

"Yes, my lord. But we will remain here in the schoolroom for the rest of the day. Mr. Roarke and Mr. Blue know what is to be done. I daresay they can be the ones to deal with Mr. Bassett if he proves difficult again."

Emmaline slipped her hand into Mercy Franklin's and looked at him, and he thought perhaps it was the first time she'd looked directly at him without glancing away awkwardly. He knew his scars were difficult to look at, and his cloudy eye made it that much worse. But it seemed that Miss Franklin's reassuring touch gave his niece the fortitude to face him.

Nash thought even *he* might be able to face his own fate with the pretty governess's hand in his, then dismissed such a foolish notion. He'd been an army officer for the past thirteen years, in battles that had made grown men consider desertion. He had no "fate" to face—he did not believe in curses or that he would be the next Farris to meet an untimely end.

The only fate he had to face was marriage—to Helene Carew, if his courtship went as planned. Or someone just like her. He could deal with that.

As absurd as it was, he was loath to leave the schoolroom. He could not take his eyes from the neckerchief that crossed the front of Mercy's body, hugging her breasts before tucking tidily into the waist of her apron.

Never before had he found a maid's attire even remotely alluring. Bland colors and high collars had not been especially tempting, either, and yet Nash's eyes were drawn again to Mercy's flushed cheeks, her delicate throat, and the satiny tumble of curls that had escaped her chignon.

He clasped his hands behind his back and cleared his throat. "I am going to a neighboring farm tomorrow morning to look at some dogs. I'd like Emmaline—and you—to accompany me, Miss Franklin."

"But we have our lessons, my lord. And the house—"

"Are you refusing, Miss Franklin?"

Her throat moved as she swallowed thickly, clearly undecided.

"I am not asking you to"—he glanced at Emmaline and tempered his next words—"to climb up there and take down the draperies, as you have already demonstrated some incompetence in that area."

She tipped her head slightly in a gesture that could only be construed as annoyance. But Nash could not keep himself from provoking her. He supposed it kept him from taking her into his arms and doing what his body had been demanding since their first meeting on the road when she'd taken his foot in her hands and presented him with her lovely derriere.

She gave him a nod. "Whatever you wish, my lord."

Her acquiescence was just that. A surrender, and nothing more. The governess had indicated no particular desire to accompany him, but agreed to it because he'd essentially ordered her to come with him.

Nash was accustomed to giving orders, but this was one he wished had been taken as an invitation.

Mercy knew she should not feel quite so eager for the proposed outing with Lord Ashby. Her ridiculous attraction to the earl bordered on becoming an infatuation that could only bring her heartache. He was her employer and nothing more.

But he could seduce her so easily; Mercy had to guard against the potent longing he roused in her. Naught could ever come of it.

"What are you working on, Emmy?"

The child handed over her neat folder of drawings, and Mercy saw that they were quite skilled, even though they had been done with a childish hand. There were pictures of the fireplace in the great hall, and a few of Henry Blue, and one of Mr. Bassett and his angry face. There were pictures of birds and other fauna . . . With encouragement and perhaps some lessons, Emmaline would become an accomplished artist. "These are very good," Mercy said.

A deep blush appeared on Emmaline's hollow cheeks.

"I wonder . . ." Mercy said, paging through the pictures.

"What, miss?" Emmaline asked quietly, and Mercy was pleased that she'd managed to pique Emmaline's interest.

"You're obviously quite an artist," she said. "Destined to become as good as your mother, at least."

"Me?" Emmaline squeaked.

"I think so, Emmy. Look here." She pointed to the detail and shading of the wings of a dragonfly. "And here." She shifted to a picture of a sheep and the horns she'd drawn on it. "So accurate."

Emmaline gave a timid smile.

"Perhaps you would like to help me with my plant catalog," Mercy said.

"What is a catalog?"

"It's a registry of sorts. I have always wanted to make a list of plants and their characteristics—but

I have no artistic ability at all. Perhaps you would draw the plants for me, and I can write about them?"

Emmaline looked toward the windows. "There are no plants now."

"Of course there are." Mercy went to the window and beckoned Emmaline to join her. "Look at those buds on the plane trees here."

"Plane trees?" Emmaline asked, and Mercy was pleased to have a way to engage the child in conversation. The young girl had started warming to her, and did not seem quite as leery of her uncle.

"Aye. In Underdale, we call them plane trees. You've probably heard them called sycamores. See the rough bark on their trunks?"

Emmaline nodded.

"Perhaps you can draw some of these trees for me. For my catalog."

"Will it be like a journal? Your mother's journal?"

Emmaline's question took Mercy aback. "Yes, perhaps a little," she replied, recovering herself. She'd managed to avoid reading the journal so far, though she knew she ought to rouse the courage to do so.

As they stood looking out the window, Lord Ashby came into view far below, banishing all thoughts of Susanna's journal from Mercy's mind.

She could not recall ever seeing anyone move with such strength of purpose. He had changed clothes again, and was wearing far more formal attire than he'd worn before in her presence, and Mercy could not help but wonder at his destination. He walked to the edge of the drive and mounted the horse that Mr. Harper held for him.

And then he rode out of sight.

* * *

Nash knew he should not waste his money this way, but he took a detour into Keswick on his way to supper with the Carews at Strathmore Pond. In town, he purchased tickets for everyone at Ashby Hall to attend the ball that was to be held in the large assembly rooms at the Market Street Inn. The men needed a break from their daily routines. After Bassett's confrontation with Miss Franklin that afternoon, Nash realized he had kept the men isolated far too long. They needed to realize they were no longer in the army.

He included a ticket for Miss Franklin, although he was not sure she would agree to attend. Did vicars' daughters dance? Drink punch? Socialize the way the rest of society did?

Nash intended to find out.

Not that it could possibly matter to him. Except that Mercy Franklin could stand in a corner and attract the attention of every young gentleman at the ball. How could she not? With her alluring eyes and her captivatingly feminine form that tempted him beyond reason every moment of every day, all the bachelors in the district would fall over one another to dance with her, court her.

Nash ground his teeth together at the thought of it, but . . .

Dash it all, if he had to attend the ball at the Market Inn, he wanted her there. He *wanted* her to be courted by every marriageable man in the Lake District. He wanted her to notice his flawed face and compare it to the faces of all the other men who danced with her.

Maybe when she looked at him and really *saw* him, he could get her out of his thoughts.

With a long, low sigh of resignation, he pocketed the tickets and started for the bridle path to Strathmore Pond, only to notice Philip Lowell coming from the Ridge path and into the main street, riding toward the Moot Hall.

Lowell appeared surprised to see him, and spoke as though he'd been caught doing something untoward. Nash glanced toward the bridle path behind his steward, but saw nothing. "My lord, I thought you had an evening planned at Strathmore Pond."

Nash tipped his head toward the Moot Hall. "You are on your way to see Mr. Wardlow?"

There was a moment's hesitation. "No, my lord."

Nash waited.

"There is, er . . . a young lady in Lake Road . . ." Lowell indicated a narrow lane entering the main street just past the Moot Hall.

"I see," Nash replied. He guessed the woman in Lake Road could account for the steward's occasional absences from the Hall. But a vague suspicion of something altogether different crept into his mind.

"So, if you'll excuse me, my lord . . ."

Nash moved aside. "By all means, Lowell."

Lowell tipped his hat and rode past, while Nash started for the Ridge path to Strathmore Pond, to his own courtship dance with Miss Helene Carew.

And as he rode, he pondered the possibility that it was Philip Lowell who had somehow arranged his brothers' fatal accidents. Nash knew it was a weak suspicion, for what reason would Philip Lowell possibly have for wanting to eliminate the Ashby earls?

* * *

While Emmy drifted off to sleep, Mercy stayed in the nursery, sorting through the little girl's clothes, looking for something suitable for her to wear on their outing the next day. She chose an acceptable dress and a pair of stockings, which she took down to wash in the laundry room.

She felt a swell of anticipation for the morrow's outing, and spending several hours in Lord Ashby's company. She told herself not to make much of it. He could more readily choose a shepherd dog alone, but seemed to have decided it was a good opportunity to spend time with his niece. And not have to do it alone, for he was not yet comfortable with her.

Emmaline was not exactly comfortable with him, either, and Mercy hoped their excursion would help to assuage some of her unease. The earl's scars were barely noticeable, and Mercy had not given them much more than a passing thought when she'd first met him. Now, she hardly noticed them at all.

Mercy thought that once Emmy accustomed herself to her uncle's appearance, the scars would no longer bother her. And the sooner Lord Ashby and his niece developed some rapport, the sooner Mercy would be able to leave Ashby Hall.

The laundry was obviously a rarely used room, and she met no one there as she washed some of her own laundry as well as Emmaline's, which was a relief, especially after her confrontation with Mr. Bassett earlier. He and the cook, Mr. Childers, were clearly put out by having to take orders from her. Not that any of the housekeeping chores were terribly onerous. None of the other men seemed to mind them.

On the contrary, Harper, Blue, and Roarke had
seemed happy enough to do what she asked of them.
They even seemed to enjoy the occasional short visit
in the nursery when they brought up the meals, passing on their excitement about an assembly ball they'd
heard would soon be held in Keswick. Though they
had yet to receive Lord Ashby's permission to attend,
they were certain he would give it. Eventually.

Mercy's friends had taught her to dance, although
she had never been allowed to attend a dance of any
kind, much less a ball. Her father had not approved
of such frivolity. For Henry's and Roddy's sakes, she
hoped Lord Ashby allowed them to go to the event
they so anticipated.

Once Emmaline was settled in for the night,
Mercy returned to gather the clean laundry from the
clotheslines. She took the front staircase in order to
avoid any of Lord Ashby's men who might be lurking
about, and slipped into the back corridor that led to
the servants' hall and laundry room.

Just as she was gathering the dry laundry into her
basket, Mr. Lowell came in.

"Ah, Miss Franklin, here you are." He gave her a
polite bow. "I understand there was some difficulty
in the drawing room this afternoon. I do hope all is
well now."

In spite of his smile and his overtly friendly attitude toward her, Mercy felt no spark of attraction
to him. The ground did not shift under her feet the
way it did when she stood near Lord Ashby.

Which was absolutely absurd. Ground did not
shift, but even if it did, she was not in the league
of women like the one wearing pink who'd visited

Ashby Hall soon after Mercy's arrival. Mercy had no wealth, no dowry, and only one highly nebulous prospect in her future.

"All is well as can be, Mr. Lowell, for a house without proper servants." She folded Emmaline's dress and placed it in the basket.

"Right you are," he said, giving her a sheepish smile, then allowing his gaze to wander down to her collar, then to her bodice. Mercy turned away and gathered the last of the laundry, unnerved by his scrutiny.

She did not understand him. At times, he was the epitome of gentlemanly courtesy. But sometimes, he played the gentleman rake. Servants were vulnerable and counted on their employers to behave honorably. And yet Ashby Hall was nothing like other houses Mercy had ever heard of. So many men about, and none of them had any true notion of propriety.

"I apologize for not being closer to hand at that moment," he continued. "I might have been able to keep Mr. Bassett in line."

"No harm done." *Thanks to Lord Ashby.* At least he seemed to have decent control over his men, even the obstinate Bassett and Childers. Mercy could not help but wish the earl were present now, for Mr. Lowell was making her uncomfortable in an entirely different way than Mr. Bassett had done.

"Lord Ashby has hopes of ushering in a number of improvements here in the weeks to come," he said, and Mercy heard an edge of something vaguely unpleasant in his words. It might have been sarcasm, but Mercy was not sure.

"I hope that means a housekeeper and some

housemaids. And a nurse for Emmaline," Mercy remarked as she started scouring the shelves and various storage boxes for an iron.

"He is not exactly . . ."

She stopped and looked over at him. "*Who* is not exactly *what*, Mr. Lowell?"

The man found several irons in a cupboard and pointed them out to her. "'Tis naught. Only . . . it will be some time before Ashby can afford any servants."

Mercy gathered the clean laundry into the basket, discomfited by Lowell's disparaging tone and inappropriate conversation. She did not believe a steward ought to be speaking of Lord Ashby's finances to her—a governess—and wondered if he spoke so frankly to the other men in the earl's employ.

She stood looking at him for a moment, wondering why Lord Ashby seemed to trust him so implicitly, for Mercy did not care for him in the least.

"Mr. Lowell, I found the linen cabinets today," she said, ignoring the implications of his pessimistic assertion. "If Lord Ashby intends to entertain overnight guests, then perhaps you ought to assign some of the men to wash and iron the linens you find inside the cabinets. The beds will need to be made up fresh."

She looked forward to a day away from the Hall, away from Mr. Lowell, as well as Mr. Bassett and the others. And far from the housekeeping duties that had been assigned her.

"I will do so, Miss Franklin."

"Mr. Lowell, I am puzzled." As long as Mr.

Lowell seemed willing to divulge secrets . . . "There was some gap between the last Lord Ashby's death and the arrival of the current earl. Was there no one here to supervise the estate during all that time?"

He shook his head. "Just me, and I was entirely without resources, but for old Grainger and an elderly cook who came in daily. And Miss Butterfield, the nurse. You did not meet her, because Lord Ashby dismissed her on his arrival."

Mercy felt her heart clench in her chest and wondered why Mr. Lowell had not dealt with the nurse himself. "That's terrible."

"Lord Ashby decided Henry Blue would be good for the child. But he's a rather large fellow, and rather exuberant. I think she was a little bit afraid of him."

Mercy considered it and thought Mr. Lowell might be correct. For Henry was not only a giant of a boy, he was definitely enthusiastic. He was well-meaning, but seemed to have little sense of restraint. Even so, Emmy seemed fond of him.

Mercy lifted the basket into her arms and left the room.

"Please allow me, Miss Franklin."

He followed Mercy closely, down a dimly lit corridor to a servants' back staircase. No one else was nearby, and the isolation of the setting gave her pause, and she decided it might be prudent to give Mr. Lowell something to do with his hands.

"That will be lovely," Mercy replied.

She climbed the steps at a natural pace, although she felt inclined to hurry. It was ridiculous, she knew, for there was no solid reason that Mr. Lowell should make her feel unsettled. She reminded herself that, although he might not feel quite optimistic about Ashby at the moment, he was an ally, and she had need of one for as long as she was responsible for assigning chores to Mr. Bassett and Mr. Childers.

She took the laundry basket from the steward when they reached the nursery, and she went inside, closing the door behind her. Emmaline was still asleep.

The house was quiet and the hallways in shadows. Mercy did not relish the thought of going back to the laundry room to iron Emmy's dress, so she decided to do it early the following morning. She crouched down and selected a volume of Mr. Wordsworth's ballads from the bookcase before returning to her own bedchamber.

Mercy had resolved to read through the rest of Susanna's journal, as well as write to Mr. Vale. But not tonight. It had been a thoroughly trying day, and she was too tired.

Lowell was gone when she opened the door, and she met no one else as she returned to her own bedchamber. But she noticed a chilly draft coming from the far end of the hall that concerned her. Thinking there must be a window left open, she used the light of her lamp to guide her to the source of the breeze, and found a door standing open.

Behind it appeared to be an attic staircase.

Mercy considered closing the door and going back to her room, but knew it would be most prudent to go up and close whatever window had been left open. Her candle was protected from the draft, so she lifted her skirts with one hand and climbed the narrow flight.

At the top was a long, broad room, with wide wood planks on the walls and floors. The rafters were exposed and there were several dusty trunks lying haphazardly about. Two windows—one of which was wide open—faced into the darkness, but Mercy assumed they opened up onto a roof. She went to the open one and, after setting her lamp and book on a nearby table, she reached for the window and started pulling it down.

"You'll lock me out if you do that," came a masculine voice from the other side of the glass.

Mercy startled. It was fortunate she'd set down her lamp, else she might have dropped it. That surely would have been a disaster.

"Lord Ashby."

"Aye, lass. Come out."

"I-I do not think I—"

"You are not afraid, are you?"

"Of course not. I merely—"

"Then step out. The night is fine and there is a view of the lake from up here."

Mercy wondered how well he could see it in the dark. And whether he was safe out there. Someone should talk him into returning to the *interior* of the house.

She took a deep breath and stepped out, somehow managing to sit down and skim her legs across the windowsill. It was awkward, getting outside with her skirts in one hand, but Lord Ashby took her other hand and helped her to step out. The height was dizzying, but he was right—the sight was incomparable.

Mercy did not think she'd ever seen such a view, even in the darkness. The stars were out and the moon was more than half full, which made it possible to see the skeletons of trees dotting the fells, and a silver crescent of light reflected on the surface of a distant lake. The panorama took her breath away.

"Amazing, isn't it?" he asked.

"Quite." She avoided looking at him, but felt his gaze upon her. He must have had his fill of the excellent view already to bother with the sight of her.

"I used to climb up here as a boy. Among various other high places."

"You must have frightened the wits out of your parents."

"My mother, yes. My father only laughed."

"I cannot imagine," she replied, keeping a stern tone that she hoped was reflective of a staid, responsible governess.

She felt his low chuckle as much as heard it, and it echoed all through her limbs, making her shiver.

"Are you cold? Here." He removed his coat and draped it over her shoulders, the silk of its lining warming her with his heat. Then he turned her to face him, drawing his lapels close together across her breast.

Mercy held her breath. The warmth of the coat felt like an embrace, and she suddenly felt as though she was being swallowed whole, into a lush, velvety heat that flashed through her veins. The earl stood very close, his knuckles still against her chest. Mercy could feel his breath on her face. She fancied that she could hear his heart beating in his chest, perhaps as rapidly as her own.

He gazed at her intently, and Mercy resisted the temptation to reach up and touch the lock of hair that had fallen haphazardly across his forehead in the chilly breeze. He leaned toward her, and Mercy felt as though they were swathed together in some invisible cocoon. He dipped his head slightly, and Mercy knew he intended to steal that kiss he'd wanted the other day in the library.

She knew better than to allow it.

She took one step back and he let his hands drop to his sides, leaving her feeling not only abandoned, but far too wobbly. "Thank you for the coat, but don't you think you ought to return inside? Like your mother, I have no doubt it is dangerous to stand up here. The roof is probably not in very good condition, is it?"

"Do you fear for my safety, Miss Franklin?" His voice was low and seductive, and she realized she had not moved anywhere near far enough away from him.

Nor, to her chagrin, did she want to. She wanted to feel the rush of sensations she'd experienced during their encounter in the library. She wanted him to fill the gaping well of desire that surged so powerfully through her.

"Of course I do, my lord," she said, her voice just a whisper on the breeze. She could not look away from his intense gaze. "I wouldn't . . . wouldn't want . . ."

He lifted one hand and touched the side of her face. He tangled his fingers in a loose strand of her hair, brushing her ear with his knuckles.

"You haven't any idea how exquisite you are, Miss Franklin, do you?"

Mercy swallowed. "You have a talent for hyperbole, my lord."

He ran his thumb across her cheek. "Not in this instance." He lowered his head and brushed her mouth with his own, causing sparks to skitter across her nerve endings.

Chapter 17

The sensation made her more light-headed than the height could ever do. She took a fistful of his shirt in her hand to steady herself, and he seemed to take it as her approval of the kiss.

Perhaps it was.

"I've wanted to do this since the moment I first saw you on the road."

Her unsteadiness only increased as he slid his free hand around her waist and pulled her closer, fully capturing her lips. Heat seemed to roil off his chest into her hand as he angled his head down, maximizing the fit of their lips.

He smelled of shaving soap—but not the harsh kind her father had always used. Lord Ashby's was something spicy and warm, and made Mercy want to fall into a vat of it. She loosened her clench upon his shirt and pressed her hand against the hard plane of his chest, and as he slid both his hands down her back, she felt the earth shift beneath her.

He coaxed her lips open and seduced her mouth with his tongue. Mercy's knees wobbled and her pelvis grew heavy with desire. The only force holding her up was the strength of his arms and the mag-

netic affinity that raged between them. The height of
the roof was far less dizzying than the sensation of
his mouth upon hers. She felt absurdly boneless, her
will separated from her intellect.

He shifted one powerful leg into a highly intimate
position between hers, and Mercy was lost. The
merging pressure melted any resistance she might
have shown as the shock of his body tightly pressed
against hers promised unimaginable pleasures.

Mercy heard a strange little whimper and realized
it had come from her own throat. But as he continued devouring her mouth, torturing her body, sliding
his hands down to her hips to coax her against him
so intimately, she engaged fully in his seduction. She
held him tightly, as though letting go would cause
her to fall into an unimaginable chasm of emptiness.

Mercy hugged him to her, arrowing her fingers
into the hair at his nape, pulling his head down to
hers. She hadn't known a kiss could make her feel so
alive. All her senses were heightened, her body exquisitely aware of his slightest touch. The vague rasp
of his whiskers on her cheek, the press of his hands
against her bottom, the weight of his thigh against
the core of her body—they all created a maelstrom of
sensation that made her crave more. So much more.

He pressed her back against the stone turret wall,
taking possession of her heart with his mind-stealing
kisses. The feeling of being so completely enveloped
in sensation intoxicated her. And when she felt his
hands slide up to the buttons of her bodice, she did
naught to prevent what he intended. With only a few
deft moves, her gown fell open.

His mouth left hers, and Mercy struggled for

breath as he trailed kisses down her throat to the swells of her breasts. She felt his hands cup them, then his fingers brushed her nipples, creating a frisson of sensation that shot directly from her breasts to her womb.

His breath seemed to whoosh out of him. "Mercy . . ."

He tugged on her chemise and bared her breasts, then bent to take one pebbling nipple into his mouth.

Mercy's knees buckled.

It was sheer heaven, the only thing missing was his own chest bared. She craved the feel of their bodies touching each other, skin to skin.

But she whimpered when his tongue swirled around the tip of her other breast, and held his head in place as desire spiraled completely out of control.

He stopped suddenly and spoke, his voice a mere rasp. "Mercy . . ."

She didn't know if he was murmuring her name or pleading for lenience.

The cold air touched her bared breast and caused her to shiver. It shocked her back to earth, to where she was and what she was doing. She caught her breath when she met Lord Ashby's gaze, his eyes full of potent male appreciation as well as a sudden reserve.

Lord above. What could she have been thinking?

He pulled the edges of her bodice together over her bare breasts, and bent so that his forehead touched hers as their hearts slowed and their breathing became normal again.

Mercy knew better than to allow such drugging caresses. She could not put together a single cohesive thought, but somehow knew she had to retreat.

Had to get away before she dug her fingers into his shoulders to hold him there. Before she demanded he continue his all-absorbing kisses.

"No."

He could barely have heard her, because her voice was weak, her throat thick with need.

It was not her body that denied him, but her years of training in Reverend Franklin's house. For Mercy still wanted far more of his kisses and his intimate touches than was at all suitable. She swallowed the thick taste of regret and blinked away her tears of frustration and remorse.

She was not a loose woman in any way. She wanted Andrew Vale to marry her, and not succumb to the heat of desire in the arms of a nobleman who was only toying with her.

"My lord . . ." She had no idea what to say. Or how she would ever face him again.

He eased away, though it seemed not easily. He brought his hands up to her shoulders and spoke, his voice gravelly and deeper than she'd ever heard it. "My apologies, Miss Franklin. I am not in the habit of accosting young ladies in such a way."

Mercy licked her lip, still savoring the taste of him, her desire warring with good sense. She could not dally with this obviously unattainable peer of the realm, for it would be far too easy to care for him. She already felt much too strong an attraction for this lord who struggled with his injuries and his terrible losses every day. She could easily come to love the man who'd dismissed Emmaline's nurse for being unkind to his little niece.

Mercy needed to try to regain her senses. She had

to keep her position at Ashby Hall, at least until she could get a letter to the far more appropriate suitor Mr. Vale—and receive his response. The urgency to write her note to Whitehaven took a massive leap.

She took a step toward the window. "I-I-I will just . . . er, leave you now." She felt like a fool for stammering like a child as she moved away from him. Her legs felt shaky and her heart still pounded as though she'd just run up one of the fells that surrounded the lakes.

"Allow me to assist you, Miss Franklin."

"No! No, please." *Do not touch me, else I might do something completely unconscionable.* "I can manage just fine on my own."

Although she could not. She stumbled slightly and he grabbed her arm, steadying her as she made her way back to the window. She could not look up at him as she sat on the sill and attempted to swing her legs inside without seeming too clumsy. Not that she should even care.

She slipped into the attic and removed his jacket, then turned and handed it to him through the window. "I nearly forgot."

Nearly forgot her wits, and they seemed far too sluggish in returning to her. She would like nothing better than to remain there and explore the heady sensations he wrought in her.

He put both hands on the sill and leaned toward her. "Miss Franklin . . ."

Mercy held her bodice together with one hand, aware that it was far too inadequate a covering. "I accept your apology, my lord."

"That isn't— I . . . want you to know . . ."

"I must go, my lord."

"Aye."

"Emmaline w-will be ready to go with you to the neighbors' farm whenever you wish to go." But Mercy did not know how she would endure a long outing in his presence. Not after . . .

How could she ever face a man who had actually taken the tips of her breasts into his mouth and swirled his tongue around them?

Lord Ashby gave a quick nod, his expression unreadable in the shadows. Mercy hesitated for another moment, even though she knew it was vital that she leave him now, before she abandoned the last of her principles entirely.

But she was loath to go. Loath to give him back his coat. Loath to abandon the pleasures promised in his touch.

Nash must be losing his mind. He'd definitely lost control of his body. He wanted Mercy Franklin with an intensity that was unparalleled in his experience. He knew he should never have touched the alluring governess, not after he'd officially begun his courtship of Carew's daughter during his visit to Strathmore Pond earlier that evening.

Helene had worn an ice-blue gown, designed to seduce a man. It had ridden low on her bosom, exposing her delicate collarbones and the modest swells of her breasts. Her skin was as perfect as porcelain, and she'd worn her shimmering, silvery blond hair in an intricate, artful arrangement of gravity-defying curls that lay in perfect symmetry beside her ears.

And yet she'd had far less allure than the plainly

dressed governess who'd captured far more of his attention than was prudent. Nash needed Helene's dowry, needed the exorbitant sum of money that Horace Carew had hinted at—no doubt to whet Nash's appetite for his daughter.

And yet Nash knew his interest in Helene would not increase any time soon, even though he had an immense attraction to her marriage portion.

He didn't understand how the girl could have so little fire in her. She was as bland as the frocks Mercy Franklin wore, and as cold as the icy color of her gown. He'd gotten Helene to smile a few times, and she'd even managed to look him in the eye once or twice. Unfortunately, he had not been able to keep from thinking of Emmaline's governess all through the meal, of her fine green eyes and delicate floral scent. He'd had to force away images of beautiful Mercy lying under him, responding fiercely as he made love to her in a field of fragrant lilies.

It was probably the reason he'd lost his head with her on the roof. He'd used up all his powers of resistance while dining at Strathmore Pond, and when faced with Mercy in the flesh . . .

He swallowed hard and forced some control into his wayward body. Thinking about Helene helped.

Nash wondered if there was something intrinsically wrong with her for her father to be so very intent upon the match. He could easily take his daughter to London for a season and snag an influential earl or marquess for her.

Then Nash recalled Horace mentioning they'd already tried that route. And there had been no acceptable offers forthcoming. For whatever reason, the

Carews had moved away from London to Cumbria to rusticate in the hilly country of the Lake District.

Not that the fells weren't beautiful and appealing in their own way, but Nash could not help but wonder what had gone wrong in London. He decided to have Lowell write to his solicitor in Town and find out.

Or perhaps not. Nash decided a bit of prudent reserve was in order. He did not fully trust Lowell, especially after seeing him chatting with Carew in Keswick. Nash doubted Lowell had been interested in Carew's landau, but he could not imagine why the older man would lie about their conversation.

Nash decided to write his solicitor himself, and see what he could discover about Carew's reasons for leaving London.

He exited the roof, closing the window behind him. Mercy's scent lingered in the attic room, and Nash inhaled deeply. He shuddered, aware that he'd never wanted a woman more than he wanted Mercy Franklin.

She had slid her hand up the side of his face, not even slowing when it met the rough skin of his scars. From the beginning, she had not flinched from the sight of him.

Nash did not know how it could be possible, but his heart gave a strange tug at the thought of Mercy Franklin being unaffected by the damage to his face.

Descending the stairs, he decided to have Parker increase the intensity of his massage tonight. Nash knew only the pain his valet could inflict would give him any respite from the intensity of his arousal. He only wished the man could magically eradicate the taste of Mercy Franklin from his tongue.

And the notion that his damaged visage made no difference to her.

London, England

Once Gavin Briggs located the man tailing him, he took a back way out of the hotel and hailed a hackney cab to take him to the Payton house. From the Payton housekeeper, he acquired the address of the nurse who'd taken care of Windermere's grand-children all those years ago. Quickly returning to his cab, he gave the driver the woman's address in Cheapside.

He was fairly certain there was no one following him this time, but he ordered the cab to stop well before he reached Miss Thornton's neighborhood, and walked, taking a roundabout route to the river's edge. He strolled down Old Church Street, turned into the embankment, losing himself in the crowd of pedestrians that walked along the riverside. He continued with them for several blocks, then took a quick turn into Flood Street and back toward Miss Thornton's house.

It was nearly dark, and not the best time to call on an elderly lady. But fate had taken him there at this moment, so he proceeded to the address given him. He arrived at the neat little house, knocked on her door, and hoped for the best.

A modestly dressed dowager came to the door, carrying a lamp. She pushed aside the curtain and looked at him through the glass. "Who's calling?"

"I am Captain Gavin Briggs, ma'am. I'm here on behalf of the Duke of Windermere to speak to Miss Thornton." He held out the duke's letter, even though the old woman would not be able to read it through the glass.

"Just a moment." She let the curtain fall, and Gavin heard her footsteps as she retreated into the house. A moment later, she returned and unlocked the door.

"Miss Thornton is not well, Captain Briggs. If you will make your visit brief and to the point?"

"Of course."

He followed the woman into an unassuming sitting room and saw a very frail-looking lady sitting in a cushioned chair. Her hair was a dull gray, pulled back into a tidy little bun, but her hands shook and her eyes were glassy. She was clearly not well. "Miss Thornton, thank you for seeing me."

He took a seat across from her, while his escort, the woman with the lamp, waited impatiently.

"You wished to speak with me, Captain Briggs?" Miss Thornton asked, her tone one of puzzlement.

"Yes, ma'am. I'm trying to discover what happened to the Hayes children." He got up and set the duke's letter on the low table between them. "I understand their grandfather, the Duke of Windermere, sent a man to collect them and remove them to the Lake District. Is that correct?"

The elderly nurse frowned, giving a little nod of her head. "The saddest time I can ever recall."

"Do you remember where the children were taken?"

Her frown deepened as a dark suspicion crept in. "No, Captain Briggs. I wasn't told. The duke's man came . . . What was his name? Wait, I'll think of it."

Gavin eased back in his chair and watched while the elderly nurse collected her thoughts and memories. After all, he'd given her no warning, no time to think back on those days after the drowning. It would take her a moment.

"Newcomb. That was it. He carried a writ of some sort from the duke. Brought a nursemaid with him, too, named Thornberry. I remember because her name was so similar to my own. But not her temperament," Miss Thornton added with a grimace. "She was a severe character at best."

"Where did they take the children?" Gavin repeated.

She gave him a puzzled expression. "To the duke, is what we were told. To their grandfather."

"At Lake Windermere?"

"Yes. I was to pack up all their things and have them ready in just half an hour. They cried, poor little things. Cried for their mama every day after her death. I've taken comfort over the years in the knowledge that they had a home with their grandfather." She frowned deeply. "Are you saying . . ."

Gavin considered his words carefully. "No, ma'am. I've just been asked to do a bit of an investigating into Mr. Newcomb's actions twenty years ago. Do you know if Miss Thornberry returned to London?"

"No," she replied. "I remember she was hired specifically to travel with the Hayes children all the way north. *I* would have gone with them, if only I'd been asked."

But that would have been the last thing Windermere would have wanted. His intent had been to sever all connections to their old life. No doubt the duke had ordered Newcomb to be circumspect so as to avoid any talk of his decision to disown his orphaned grandchildren.

"Miss Thornberry was quite anxious to complete her journey with the children and return to her home in Oxfordshire. There was a position waiting for her there with a young couple expecting their first child."

"Did you ever hear the name of the family with whom she would be employed?"

She pressed a parchment-pale hand to her chest. "No, sir. Now you have me worried. Those were the sweetest children I've ever nursed, and their parents some of the finest people. He was very rich, you know. But never put on any airs. Treated all of us in service very well. So did the missus. Gracious, she was. And very beautiful."

"Yes, so I've heard."

"Is this about their father's estate? It had to have been substantial."

Gavin puzzled over that statement for a moment. He had not thought about the possibility of a Hayes estate. "Ma'am, I'm not at liberty to discuss the details."

"I understand," said Miss Thornton, although Gavin knew she could not possibly understand. Even he wasn't privy to every detail—certainly nothing about a Hayes estate. It cast the Hayes daughters in quite a different light.

"Was there a solicitor involved when the children were taken from their home?" Gavin asked.

"Solicitor?" Miss Thornton repeated. "No. Fleming—the butler—read the directive from the duke and told us what we were to do. It was very official, the letter with its seal. Just like the one you carry, Captain Briggs." She gestured toward the document on the table.

Gavin stood and bowed, considering this new twist. The duke had not mentioned anything about Daniel Hayes's wealth. Surely a man as astute as Windermere would not have missed something so consequential. Gavin wondered whatever happened to their money.

Wherever it went, the key to finding out was their grandfather, the duke.

Gavin stood. "Miss Thornton, thank you very much for your time." He glanced at the companion. "If anyone else comes round asking questions about the Hayes children, you'll be sure to turn them away, won't you?"

Miss Thornton gave a worried nod, and Gavin started for the door.

"Thank you again, ladies. I'll see myself out."

Perhaps when he found Sarah Hayes's children, he would suggest that they write a few lines to their old nurse, just to reassure her.

Chapter 18

Ashby Hall

Nash slept badly, and not because of the painful muscle stretches Parker had had him do. The massage and hot bath afterward should have relaxed him, but neither had done the trick. He dreaded his impending outing with Mercy, and yet craved it like nothing else in the world.

He was a ravening fool.

The morning was overcast, but Nash did not think it would rain, which was fortunate. Since Ashby's carriage had been destroyed in Arthur's accident, there was only a small barouche for him to take all of them to Metcalf Farm. He had Harper get it ready, then sent Henry Blue to fetch Miss Franklin and her pupil.

To be sure, this would be a far easier trip on horseback, alone. But Nash had not been able to refrain from inviting Emmaline's governess any more than he'd been able to resist taking that incredible taste of her while they stood together on the roof the previous evening.

As far as it had gone, it had been much too little.

Thinking of that kiss made him hard all over again. He could almost feel her fingers in his hair, and taste the sweet flavor of lilies on her skin. He'd wanted naught but to take her to his bed, and undress her slowly as he kissed every inch of her body.

She'd shown that she was no passive miss, neither submissive nor unresponsive. She would be as fiery as a thunderstorm, and just the mere thought of pulling her beneath him and sliding into her body sent a jolt of fire vaulting through his veins.

Nash did not think he was mistaken in believing their kiss had been her first. Her reaction had been ingenuous, as he should have anticipated. She was a vicar's daughter, after all, and likely quite sheltered all her life. He ought to be horsewhipped for seducing such an innocent.

And yet he could not regret it, not when she looked at him without seeing the damage done to him at Hougoumont.

He glanced around the stable yard, reflecting that he hadn't thought there could be anything new for him to experience. With a full and rich childhood growing up with his brothers and boyhood friends, and then his years at school and in the army, he'd led a life fuller than most. He'd flirted with death too many times to count, and taken a considerable number of beautiful women to his bed.

But none had been like Mercy. The breathless sounds she'd made, the weight of her breasts in his hands, the press of her feminine mound against his straining cock . . .

Bloody hell. He felt the early twinge of a headache and tried to rub it away as Harper brought the small barouche from the stable. Nash knew that sitting next to Mercy Franklin was going to be torture. If she decided to brave his presence this morning, he was sure she'd make certain Emmaline sat between them all the way to Metcalf's and back.

And it was just as well.

Soon his two traveling companions appeared, both wearing hats and warm clothes. Miss Franklin's brown coat covered her fine form, as she'd no doubt intended, and Emmaline's presence provided any number of reasons for her governess to avoid meeting his eyes.

He wondered if she would stammer again as she'd done during her retreat the previous evening. Her shy withdrawal had captivated him far more than it should.

"Good morning, Emmaline." He did not wait for his niece's response, but turned his gaze directly toward the governess, so completely prim now in her demeanor. So different from the siren he'd held in his arms the night before. "Good morning to you, Miss Franklin."

She gave a little bow. "My lord," she said quietly, then bent down to speak to Emmaline, who appeared surprisingly neat and clean, her shoes polished, and no holes in her stockings. Due to Mercy's effort, no doubt.

" 'Tis polite to say, 'Good morning, Uncle,' " she said to the child.

Emmaline spoke softly, but at least her greeting was audible.

"Shall we get started?" he asked.

He opened the door to the barouche and lifted

Emmaline in, then took Miss Franklin's hand. She thanked him without really looking at him as she stepped up into the conveyance, settling herself on the far side of the seat, with Emmaline in the center, just as he'd predicted.

Nash, who was rarely disposed to small talk, started the conversation. "Do you know anything about dogs, Emmaline?"

"No," she said.

"We're looking for a particular type."

Emmaline looked up at him then, but Mercy still didn't meet his eyes. She fiddled with the buttons on her coat, then shifted in her seat in order to smooth the thick fabric of the coat securely beneath her.

Nash could not contain a small smile. He had gotten to her as deeply as she had affected him.

"Aye. We need a working dog. But not one we'll keep in the house. This dog will help the shepherds herd the sheep when it's time to bring them in for shearing. Sir William has always kept eye dogs. They're very effective herders."

"*Eye* dogs?" Mercy asked, her curiosity finally piqued.

She could have no idea the effect of her clear gaze, looking at him as though there were no facial defects to be seen. Her striking eyes were beautifully bordered by long black lashes, and Nash had a rushing desire to see those dark crescents resting upon her cheeks as she slept.

He would nestle her close, tucking her head beneath his chin as he wrapped his arms around her slumbering body.

"Eye dogs, yes." He cleared his throat. "They can

control the flock with a look in their eyes. They're fast and agile, and so smart it seems as though they understand what you say to them."

Mercy tossed a skeptical expression in his direction.

"Miss Franklin, have you ever had a dog?"

"No," she said simply. She had turned away again, but was blushing quite charmingly at what she thought was his jest. How he longed to make her blush with his touch. Perhaps later, he would manage another little inadvertent rendezvous with her. Not that he'd planned last night's encounter, but he relished it nonetheless.

"I believe we might need a demonstration once we get to Metcalf's," Nash said with a grin, feeling far different from the man who'd been thrown from his horse a few days before. Surprisingly enough, his headache had receded. And it was amazing to discover he could still smile. "What do you think, Emmaline?"

"Yes."

As they rode, Mercy turned to a very effective avoidance technique of pointing out the various shrubs and trees they passed that were coming into bloom, telling Emmaline which ones she would like the child to draw for her "catalog."

"What catalog would that be, Miss Franklin?" Nash asked. She could avoid him all she liked at the moment, but they would return to Ashby Hall together, and she could not elude him forever.

"As I once mentioned to you, I have an interest in plant life, my lord," she replied, keeping her tone neutral and distant. "And I have started a directory of sorts—a catalog of the flora to be found here in the Lake District."

"And my niece is to illustrate it for you?"

"Emmaline is a very good little artist," Miss Franklin said, smiling down at the child. "I would very much appreciate her help in creating my catalog."

Nash noticed the wording of Mercy's request, giving Emmaline credit for her talent and asking for her expertise without being condescending, or mentioning any lessons. He'd never been quite sure how to converse with Emmaline, but now he took Mercy Franklin's lead.

"It should be your decision, Emmaline," Nash said. "Would you like to do the drawings?"

She glanced up at him in surprise.

"It's your choice."

Emmaline's brows came together as though she'd never had a choice in anything. Nash feared that was probably true, and his admiration for his niece's inexperienced governess increased yet again. Somehow, Mercy had known just how to draw Emmaline from her quiet little retreat from the world.

Riding in Lord Ashby's barouche was the last thing Mercy wanted to do. Last night on the roof had been a breach beyond belief. Even now she blushed at the thought of what they had done, for she had been raised far better than that.

And yet her behavior proved she was no better than what the Franklins believed of her mother.

She'd been so rattled by her encounter with Lord Ashby on the roof that she'd been unable to write

her letter to Andrew Vale. Thoughts of the earl's
touch had made logical, rational thought impossible,
and she'd had to lay down her pen and postpone her
writing until later. She would do it today. After they
returned to Ashby Hall, she would suggest that Emmaline take a short nap, which would give Mercy
the opportunity to compose her letter in private.
Without Lord Ashby's exceedingly potent influence.

Yet here she sat in the small barouche, not two
feet away from him as he drove them over hills and
dales, so much larger than life itself that Mercy
could scarcely breathe. He wore casual attire, dun-
colored trousers and dark blue coat—the same coat
he'd wrapped around her shoulders before kissing
her senseless on the roof.

The only way Mercy could distract herself from
thinking of Lord Ashby's kiss was by pointing out
the fresh young shoots of the plants that were about
to emerge, and talking to Emmaline about the catalog they would make together.

But still, her eyes wandered far too frequently to
Lord Ashby's muscular thighs, resting so casually
beside Emmaline's, and his large, heavily veined
hands as they held the horse's reins. Mercy could
almost feel his blunt-tipped fingers on her breasts,
stroking them until she'd moaned with desire. Even
now, she could taste the spicy flavor of his mouth
and smell the earthy scent of his soap.

She'd never been kissed before, not even by Mr.
Vale, the man who'd asked her to marry him. Mr.
Vale put his lips to the back of her hand, of course,
but never anything more. And none of his touches

had caused a melting sensation, the way Lord Ashby's slightest glance could do.

Mercy hadn't known a kiss could make her feel so alive. The earl had a way of making her feel as though her blood was on fire, without even touching her. And now that he *had* touched her, she knew a deep tension, a coiling of yearning for something she could not name. It was an intense sensation of physical craving that had kept her from being able to sleep for much of the night.

She had been right to stop the interlude on the roof, and yet she would dearly love to feel more of Lord Ashby's caresses. She was a fool to allow herself such longings, and fully aware that she could never compete with fine ladies like the one who had come to visit Lord Ashby in all her pink finery. No doubt the woman had some favored social standing in the community, not to mention a substantial dowry.

If Lord Ashby gave any thought to marriage, Mercy knew it was not with her. And any other sort of liaison would be entirely unacceptable.

The earl clucked his tongue and their horse took them across a pretty stone bridge over a noisy little beck. On the other side of the bridge stood Metcalf Farm. Mercy found it a pleasant, pastoral setting with a large, stone manor house with its gray slate roof, nestled at the foot of the tall fell they'd just descended. There were a barn and a stable, and one other outbuilding, all enclosed within a low stone wall. Geese pecked for food at the ground near the beck, and two swans floated nearby. The house itself was surrounded by tall deciduous trees—some oak and maple, and a stand of lovely old birches.

"When your father was a boy," Lord Ashby said to Emmaline, and Mercy discerned a slight wistfulness in his voice, "we frequently came to Metcalf's to play knights and villains with Sir William's son, Jacob."

"My papa?" Emmaline asked, the first thing Mercy had heard the little girl say to him without being prompted. She looked up at him with more curiosity than fear.

"Aye. And a serious young boy was he."

"Am I . . . am I like him, Uncle?"

The earl gave a contemplative smile, and Mercy's heart contracted tightly at his melancholic tone. He did not often appear vulnerable, but Mercy knew it must be very painful for him to think of the brothers he'd lost. "Aye, I believe you are."

Lord Ashby appeared weary, as though he had not slept in a fortnight. And yet, for some reason Mercy did not understand, his demeanor was far less stilted when he talked to his niece now. And Emmaline was not quite as stiff with him as she'd been before. Perhaps it was the mention of Emmaline's father, which brought back fond memories for both of them. Clearly, this outing had been a very good idea for the two of them, in spite of Mercy's misgivings.

A well-dressed, silver-haired lady came out of the house when they pulled into the drive, and hurried toward the barouche with two footmen behind her. The woman smiled broadly when she saw Lord

Ashby, and bighearted warmth seemed to spill from her deep brown eyes and plump bosom.

"Nash Farris, you rascal!" she called out as she approached the barouche. "'Tis been a full month at least since your return to Ashby Hall, and only now do you come to visit!"

"Scold me all you want, Lady Metcalf," Nash replied with a pleased smile, "for I truly deserve it. Though I might ask why you and Sir William have not come and graced my hall with your presence."

The lady sobered. "If you must know, my Will is not in the best of health of late."

"I regret to hear it," Lord Ashby said gravely. "Perhaps our visit is not—"

"Here now! Of course it is! He'll be so happy to see you, lad."

Mercy smiled at the lady's obvious affection, but could not think of Nash Farris as a lad at all, not with those shoulders, that hard chest, or the rasp of whiskers she'd felt during his kiss.

Before a groom was able to come over and assist, Lord Ashby opened the door of the barouche and jumped down, then lifted Emmaline to the ground. "This is Emmaline, Hoyt's daughter. Emmy, say hello to Lady Metcalf."

Emmy cast a surprised glance toward her uncle at the use of her pet name, then quickly greeted Lady Metcalf in her usual shy manner. The dame took Emmaline's hand and chattered about Nash having such a lovely little niece.

But Lord Ashby had already turned to Mercy.

She felt her heart thud in her breast in anticipation of his touch. He placed his hands upon her waist and hesitated for an instant, probably not long enough for Lady Metcalf to take note, but Mercy could not have been more aware of every moment his hands were upon her.

He swung her down to the ground and released her, turning to face Lady Metcalf. "With us is Miss Mercy Franklin, Emmaline's new governess."

Mercy bowed properly, although she did not feel even slightly respectable at the moment, not when a rash of utterly carnal thoughts and objectionable yearnings were coursing through her, entirely against her wishes.

But Lady Metcalf welcomed Mercy warmly in spite of it, then turned to Lord Ashby, taking hold of his arm and looking directly into his scarred face. Her expression was one of deep concern. "What happened to you, lad?"

Mercy was surprised by the direct question. She'd heard no one else speak so candidly to the earl. Except perhaps herself, and she was determined to curb her unruly speech.

"I was in the wrong place at the wrong time. A wall exploded and caught me by surprise."

A wave of horror flowed through Mercy at the thought of such a violent attack and the earl being in the thick of it. Her throat tightened at the thought that he might have been killed.

"It was that last horrible battle, wasn't it? Waterloo." Lady Metcalf reached up and patted his face as a mother might do to an ailing child.

The earl shrugged and took her hand gently away from his face. Mercy did not think Lady Metcalf had caused him any pain, but it seemed he was uncomfortable with the attention given his scars. "Aye."

"We were so fearful for you when we heard that nasty little Frenchman had the brass neck to leave his island prison and start up again," she said, shaking her head. "Well, come in and say hello to William before he drags himself up off the sofa to see for himself who's here."

Lord Ashby seemed to forget their purpose of acquiring a dog when Lady Metcalf took Emmaline's hand again and started for the house, warmly enveloping the little girl into her motherly warmth. "William took ill last June," Lady Metcalf said, "only a week before Arthur's accident, or we'd have been up at Ashby Hall, doing what we could . . ."

"What happened? What ails him?" the earl asked with obvious, deep concern.

"He suffered a stroke. Lost the power of speech for a time, and he's still got some weakness on one side." Lady Metcalf sighed. "He's not been the same since that day."

"Are you sure our visit won't affect him adversely?"

"Heavens, no. He'll be like my old Will again when he sees you."

Mercy could not imagine Nash's frown growing any darker. It was clear he hadn't known of Sir William's illness, and it troubled him.

Lady Metcalf spoke to Emmaline. "Did your uncle regale you with tales of the times he and your father caused havoc with my son here at Metcalf Farm? No? Well, we'll just have ourselves some tea and I'll see what I can remember about those scoundrels. I'll tell you all their secrets," she added with a wink.

Emmaline was clearly overpowered by the warm and wonderful lady, and found herself unable to withdraw, as was her wont. Mercy gave her an encouraging smile when she looked back for reassurance.

"Lady Metcalf will help loosen her up," Lord Ashby murmured close to Mercy's ear, and shivers of awareness coursed through her nerves. "No one can keep their reserve in the old girl's presence."

"Not even you?"

"Ah, I stand corrected. I believe there might be two ladies who can cause me to lose my reserve, Miss Franklin."

Mercy's eyes shot forward, and she was hardly able to trust her ears. He was flirting with her!

"Thank you for making my niece presentable," Lord Ashby said quietly, setting Mercy off balance once again.

"It was nothing, my lord."

"Aye, it was. Laundry is no simple affair, and we both know it."

Mercy could always count upon Lord Ashby to say or do the most outrageous things, and she dearly hoped he would not make reference to her lapse with him on the roof. She would die of embarrassment if he mentioned it.

She knew she should have found some excuse to avoid this outing. Riding so close to him in the barouche had been difficult enough, and now they were to behave as though naught had passed between them the night before. She had to pretend she was unaffected by his proximity and his simple thanks for seeing to Emmaline's clothes.

And yet Mercy hadn't had any choice but to accompany Emmaline on this trek with her uncle to visit the Metcalfs. Emmy would likely have resisted going if her governess had not come along. And since Mercy had not known what the situation would be at Metcalf Farm, she'd thought she ought to be there in case Emmy needed her.

Having met Lady Metcalf, Mercy now knew that her presence was unnecessary. Lady Metcalf radiated the kind of warmth and kindliness Mercy had always wished her mother had possessed, and she saw that Emmy could not resist the older woman's genuine affection.

"William, my dear!" Lady Metcalf called as they entered the house. "We've company. You will never guess who has come to call!"

The servants took their coats, and they all retired to a small sitting room at the back of the house. There were three wide windows across the far wall, with a view of the sheep-dappled fells beyond. Facing the windows was a frail-looking man—little more than a skeleton, Mercy thought—half reclining on a divan. His white hair was thin and mussed, but his muddy brown eyes brightened when he caught sight of Emmaline. He looked up at Lady Metcalf, and Mercy noticed that one side of his face sagged slightly.

"What have we here, Edwina?" His voice was not strong, but Mercy could see that he had once been a force to be reckoned with.

" 'Tis Hoyt Farris's girl. Is she not the image of her lovely mother?"

"Aye, that she is. Joanna was a beautiful lady—just like her daughter, it seems."

"And bringing her to visit is Nash. The pretty young lady with them is Miss Franklin."

"A pleasure to make your acquaintance, Miss Franklin." He turned to Lord Ashby. "Nash Farris, you young bounder—so you've finally decided to take a wife!"

Chapter 19

Mercy felt her face burn with mortification. She started to deny it, but Nash—Lord Ashby— laughed aloud and prevented her from speaking. He went to Sir William and went down on one knee beside him, taking his hand in a firm grip. "It is going to take far more than a beautiful face to get me to the altar, Will."

A ball of emotion welled in Mercy's chest and she felt it might explode then and there. She'd been perfectly aware that she was not a woman he would ever consider taking to wife. And yet his advances had unlocked the most improbable of yearnings within her.

Oblivious to the emotions rushing through Mercy, Sir William smiled at Nash, nodding weakly. "You were always the worst of the lot, lad."

"No, I wasn't. That was Arthur." Lord Ashby's expression turned boyish as he spoke, and Mercy realized he was speaking fondly of his late brother. He'd suffered so many losses in his family, and then the horrors of battle. Even though she'd recently lost her parents, Mercy could not imagine the kinds of sorrows Lord Ashby had endured.

Sir William chuckled at the earl's quip. "Aye, but only if the criteria were for being a fussbudget. I was speaking of foolhardy, brash, impudent, overconfident—"

The earl laughed out loud. "Never say I was foolhardy!"

"Ha!"

They enjoyed the joke for a minute or two, then Lord Ashby spoke of the reason for their visit. "We've come for a dog, Sir Will."

"What dog?" Lady Metcalf asked.

"A herding dog. You've got a few of those, haven't you?" he asked facetiously.

"Of course we have. More than enough, truth be told. You can have your pick."

"I thought Emmaline might like to choose," Lord Ashby said as he stood.

"Well, let's have our tea first," said Lady Metcalf with a happy smile. "You stay here with Will, my dear Nash, while we ladies get things ready."

Nash should have anticipated that the house would seem horribly empty without Jacob Metcalf. He'd been killed at Salamanca in '12, and Nash had seen Sir William and Lady Edwina only once since then. They might have gone on living, but the sorrow hadn't gone out of their eyes.

He wondered how Horace Carew could have neglected to mention William's ill health. They'd spoken of Metcalf Farm—it would have been appropriate for him to speak of it then.

He almost wished he hadn't come here, hadn't seen their lingering pain. He sat down on a cushioned stool beside Will and looked closely at him. It was unlikely the man had much time left. He was hardly more than skin and bones, his hands and neck mottled with a purple discoloration. Nash was no physician, but he knew such a symptom could not be good, and it saddened him. He and his brothers had spent many a day and night at Metcalf Farm, running wild with Jacob, who'd become like a fourth brother to them. Jake had been Arthur's age, but closer in temperament to Nash.

Nash knew Jacob's parents had been sorely disappointed when he'd bought his commission and gone to war. They'd had only one child and heir, and he'd died without issue.

"You could do worse, you know," said Will.

Nash raised a questioning brow.

"Miss Franklin. She's a lovely thing. Don't think I cannot see those pretty dimples on either side of her mouth. Or that deep blush that crosses her cheeks. Only the most passionate of women can pink up that way."

Nash's discomfort grew. Passion was the last thing he ought to be pursuing now, though looking at Mercy made him forget his intentions of marrying a fortune and restoring the Ashby estate. Almost.

She was a serious threat to his plans. He supposed he could dismiss her from her post and send her back to Underdale. But that would be grossly unfair. Mercy had done nothing wrong but to succumb to his formidable desire for her.

When she met the district's eligible young men at the subscription ball and started collecting suitors, Nash would be able to put her from his mind and focus on wooing Helene and her handsome dowry. As quickly as possible, he would sire an heir or two and focus his full attention on the estate. "Sir William—"

"And you wouldn't be the first lord to make off with the governess."

Unfortunately, the very same thought had occurred to him last night while he lay awake in an agony of lust. "Aye. But I have need of a wife with a substantial dowry. Not to put too fine a point on it, Sir Will, but Ashby is in ruins. Arthur's investments were calamitous, so there are no funds for improvements. A large number of our herd has died off, and I can't say that we'll have more than a handful of lambs this spring. If I'm to make anything of the place, I'm going to need money."

"You're right, I suppose, lad. The wealthiest man in the district is Horace Carew. And he has a daughter."

"I know. I had supper at Strathmore Pond last night. With Carew and his daughter."

A twinkle lit the old man's eyes. "She'll do, eh, my boy? She's a comely lass."

Yes, she was. But Nash knew she would never be able to set his blood on fire as Mercy Franklin did. He steeled himself against falling prey to thoughts of what could never be. "Her father is in favor of a match between us. He gave me his blessing to court her."

Sir William chuckled.

"What is it?"

"Hoyt once mentioned that Carew suggested *he* marry the daughter. But your brother couldn't even consider remarrying after he lost Joanna. He politely declined the offer."

Nash rubbed his forehead. "He did?"

"Aye. Seems the man is determined to make his daughter a countess."

"Well, she could do worse, eh?" But it bothered Nash that the Carews didn't seem to care which brother Helene wed. It was the title they wanted, and the face of the man who owned it did not seem to matter.

Sir William allowed his gaze to drift to the scene outside the window. The sky was beginning to clear, and the hills rose up in all their early spring glory. Metcalf Farm had always been a jewel in the district.

And Nash was fairly certain Sir William would soon be leaving it. He rubbed the dull ache that rose up in his chest and wished he had not come here today. He needed a dog. And some advice.

But not another loss.

"If I wed Miss Carew . . . it won't be . . ." He nearly choked on the words. "It won't be anything like my parents' marriage."

It had been years since Nash had thought of the glow that enveloped his mother and father when they were together. Hoyt and Joanna had shared it, too. They'd had something that went far beyond mere satisfaction or contentment with their spouses.

Even if Nash wanted a similar bond with the wife he settled on, he could not afford it. Neither his finances nor his heart could take it.

"No. Few marriages are like theirs," Sir William agreed. "Only the lucky ones."

The inevitable weighed heavily on Nash's heart.

He stood and walked to the window. "Miss Carew cannot abide my scars. Or my clouded eye."

"She'll accustom herself, will she not? Becoming a countess will likely trump such a minor drawback."

Nash doubted it. But finding himself loath to expend any more energy on thoughts of Miss Carew when the memory of Mercy Franklin's kiss was fresh in his mind, he changed the subject. "I need someone to manage the estate, Sir Will." Lowell might be good with numbers in ledgers, but he didn't know anything about sheep farming.

William pursed his lips. "Are you asking for my advice?"

"Aye."

"Is old Grainger still up at Ashby?"

Nash cast Will a questioning glance. "Hoyt's old butler? Aye, he is. Why?"

"He has a brother, George. A widower. One of the best sheep men at Windermere, though I've heard he's moved into his son's house. He'd likely come up to Ashby if only to get away from his daughter-in-law and be closer to his brother."

"I can't pay—"

"That's what I'm saying, lad. George and Giles were always close. Giles has no other family. George knows everything about running a farm like Ashby. He will likely steer you back onto your two feet for the mere pleasure of escaping his son's house to live on the same farm as his brother. He did very well for himself down Windermere way."

"Where is he now?"

"His son's house is down near Ambleside. Ask Giles Grainger. He'll have George's direction."

"I'll do that."

"George knows every sheep man in and about Keswick. He might know of a few who will come work for you for naught but their keep until Ashby's put back to rights."

Nash nodded, thinking of the valuable resource he'd had under his roof and not even known it. And then he wondered how Lowell would take to having his position usurped by a country sheep herder.

Maybe the reason for his brothers' demise had had something to do with the management of the herd. But Nash could not think what it could possibly have been. A healthy, plentiful herd meant a substantial income, and a steward would only profit from such a situation.

He was grasping at straws.

Nash decided to deal with Lowell later, after he learned whether George Grainger would actually come to Ashby. "I'll need shearers come summer, Sir William. Will you lend me yours when it's time?"

"Aye. Of course. Or . . ." He looked away. "Edwina will see to it. I'll speak to her."

Nash did not want to acknowledge what Will was saying—that he might not be there to make sure the Metcalf shearers were sent to Ashby Hall.

The kitchen was a warm and bustling place that reminded Mercy of Lady Metcalf herself—cozy and comfortable, though she was clearly in charge. The cook gave them a sociable smile, then reached into a hot oven to pull out a pan of hot, savory cake, which she turned out onto a wooden block.

" 'Tis my husband's favorite treat—Cook's gingerbread." The lady's features sobered slightly. " 'Tis about all we can get him to eat these days, is it not, Cook?"

"Aye, m'lady, he likes my gingerbread, all right," said the woman. "Soothes the stomach, it does." She pinched off a small piece from the corner of the loaf and gave it to Emmaline, whose eyes brightened at the treat. It was quite clear the child had not received any such coddling—at least, not in a very long time.

"Has your uncle told you of his antics here at Metcalf Farm, Emmaline?" Lady Metcalf petted Emmaline's head.

Emmaline shook her head, and some of the bashfulness left her demeanor as she chewed the ginger cake.

It was a novelty for Mercy, too, who was unused to so such casual conversation and pleasant female company. The Franklin household was usually quiet, bordering on austere. Her father had required silence in the house in order to concentrate on his studies and his sermons. But even when the family came together at mealtimes, there was little discourse, other than the lessons Reverend Franklin chose to impart.

"Ah, your uncle was a wild one. The youngest of the bunch. I believe the worst was the time he set a wager to see which of the lads could climb the highest in that tree there." She pointed out the window at a tall, thick oak that was only just budding. Emmaline's shoulders seemed to loosen as she listened to the older woman talk.

Lady Metcalf's eyes crinkled with amusement at the memory. "Nash was the first one up, of course. He was always the first to climb to the top of something—the barn roof, the highest fell." *Or a roof-top*, Mercy reflected. "On that particular morning, Arthur managed to climb higher than anyone—even Nash."

"What happened?" Emmy asked, forgetting to be bashful.

"Even a well-practiced climber like Nash knew when to stop, but Arthur was out to prove something that day. Which he did." Lady Metcalf chuckled while the cook shook her head and clucked her tongue.

"He proved what a pigeon egg he could be."

Emmaline let out a tiny giggle that brought a smile to Mercy's lips.

"Arthur went into a panic when he realized how high he'd gone. Nash and my Jacob knew when to stop, and they were far below him."

Emmaline's eyes grew wide as she waited for Lady Metcalf's next words, and even Mercy found herself hungry to hear more of Nash's boyhood antics. She could easily imagine him as a carefree lad, his face clear and unscarred, his sculpted lips smiling widely.

"Your father—the sensible one—came into the house to get help. But your uncle . . ." She shook her head. "Always too impatient for his own good. Leaving good sense behind, he scrambled up and perched himself right next to Arthur to reassure him and talk him into climbing down."

"Did Uncle Arthur climb down?" Emmaline asked, so engrossed in the tale she lost her shyness for the moment.

Lady Metcalf gave a nod. "Oh, aye. With Nash talking to him quite calmly, giving instructions and

even encouragement, Arthur managed to get his two
feet back on the ground." She put one hand against
her heart and looked up at Mercy. "We'd all come
out of the house in a panic by then, certain that one
of them would fall. But that Nash—he was as sure-
footed as one of those African monkeys."

"How old were they?" Mercy asked.

"Hmm. Nash was about ten, and Arthur twelve."
Lady Metcalf looked at Emmaline. "Your papa was
only thirteen, but he had more good sense than the
other three altogether."

Emmaline's smile broadened, and Mercy's heart
clenched tightly in her chest. She knew what it was to
be alone, but at least she was an adult, not a vulnerable little child like Emmaline, who seemed to have
been an afterthought in the years since her father's
death. That had been two years ago. A very long
time in Emmaline's life. It was far too long since
she'd had anyone who cared anything about her.

"Did Papa scold Uncle Arthur?"

Lady Metcalf laughed. "He did a great deal of
scolding that day. Even *his* papa—your grandfather—hardly needed to say a word more. Arthur
never climbed again. At least not that I ever heard."

And yet Nash still liked heights, Mercy thought, if
his presence on the roof last night was any indication.

"Your poor uncle, lass," Lady Metcalf said, turning to speak directly to Emmy. "You must be very
kind to him now that he's home. I cannot imagine the
suffering he must have endured with those injuries."

Nor could Mercy. But Lady Metcalf seemed to be
addressing something other than the earl's scars. A

tiny crease appeared in Emmy's brow, and she gave the lady a questioning glance.

"Oh, aye. To be burned so. 'Tis a hard thing for a robust man so used to good health to be brought so low. Like my William. You must always try to understand how difficult it is for your uncle, lass. He's had some very difficult times, too."

Emmy sat quietly as she took in Lady Metcalf's words, but she gave a slight nod.

"I'm sorry Sir William is ailing," Mercy said to Lady Metcalf. Her father had had the same look about him in the days before his death. A quick but devastating stroke had taken him, weakening one side of his body and rendering him incapable of speech. Sir William seemed to have suffered much the same ailment, though not as rapidly devastating.

"I'm sorry Nash had to see him ailing so. He's been through quite enough—losing both his brothers . . ."

Mercy felt the same. Much as he tried to hide his reaction, she'd seen how shaken the earl had been by Sir William's obvious infirmity. He was far more tenderhearted than he wanted anyone to know.

Lady Metcalf gave Mercy a sorrowful smile. "It's been nigh on a year since the stroke. William has done fairly well, but 'tis not right for a robust man like Will to be so incapacitated." She sighed sadly, then brightened. "We'll just take his ginger cake and tea into the parlor, and see how he does, won't we, Emmaline?"

"Yes, ma'am," Emmaline replied quietly, though her manner was not quite as tightly closed as it had been only a few days ago. Her intelligent eyes observed everything going on in the tidy kitchen, from the cook with her steaming pots, to the two maids who came to arrange the tea things on two trays.

A proper form of decorum was being followed here that was not present at Ashby Hall. Every servant showed deference to Lady Metcalf, who was quite obviously in charge, but not overbearing. She was a smiling force to be reckoned with, and Mercy could not have provided a better lesson in home management or the expectations of a noble lady for Emmaline. She hoped they would have the opportunity to visit again soon.

"It looks as though all is ready," Lady Metcalf said. "Emmaline, go along with Mrs. Jones and Ruthie and tell Sir William that we'll be there presently."

A look of utter panic crossed Emmaline's face, but Lady Metcalf patted her shoulder and said, "You can do it, lass, and I need your help with this."

Surprisingly, Emmaline took a deep breath and went after the maids.

"Now, Miss Franklin," Lady Metcalf said, turning to Mercy once Emmaline and the maids had gone, "you must tell me what's been going on at Ashby Hall."

"I'm going to look into Hoyt's death," said Nash.

"In what way?" Sir William asked.

Nash rested his elbows on his knees and leaned forward, keeping his voice down. "I've gotten at least a partial list of the men who attended the deer stalking. And I'm going to ask every one of those men some questions."

"You think the shooting was suspicious?"

Nash hesitated. "I don't know what to think. Except that if someone wanted Hoyt dead, a shooting accident would be the perfect ruse."

"Have you talked to the magistrate?"

Nash nodded. "Mr. Wardlow had little to say, and his report was not what I'd call thorough. I had to force him to create a list of witnesses."

"He's never had to deal with an incident like the one that killed Hoyt. I doubt there've been any other accidental shootings within a hundred miles."

"Which is what makes me all the more suspicious. Can you think of anyone who might have had a reason to want my brother dead?"

"Hoyt? Of course not. He was a popular, sensible fellow. And we know Arthur was the only one who would have profited by his death."

"But Arthur would never have harmed Hoyt. Besides, he was fifty miles away on the day of the shooting."

"And now Arthur is dead, too," Will remarked. "I didn't really think of Hoyt's death as anything but a terrible accident until Arthur's carriage went over the side of the high road."

Grief, heavy and volatile, ignited in the pit of Nash's stomach, causing a slow burn. "And now?"

"Does it not strike you as being a bit too coincidental? Two perfectly healthy young brothers—who hadn't even reached their prime—dying accidentally within a year of one another?"

Nash shook his head, thinking of Philip Lowell. "How would anyone profit by my brothers' deaths?"

Sir Will narrowed his eyes. "I don't know. But it might be wise to watch your back, Nash. It seems somebody wants the Ashby line to end."

As it would do with Nash's death. There was no one to become earl after him—no male relatives, no distant cousin who could inherit. The earldom would become extinct, with Ashby lands reverting to the crown.

It occurred to Nash that the king was the only one who would actually profit by the demise of the Farris family, but that was absurd. The Ashby estate was nothing special. In fact, it was a wreck. Why would Prince George want it? To raise sheep on it?

"What do you know about the land surveys being done?"

Sir Will gave a lopsided shrug. "I hadn't heard. But every now and then, someone commissions one."

A dull ache rose up between Nash's brows. "What about the crown?"

"What about it? You mean the surveys were ordered by the crown?"

"That's what Wardlow said."

"I suppose so, then."

The ache in Nash's forehead intensified with Will's next question. "Have you written your will yet, lad?"

Nash looked away. "Aye. While I was in the army. Not that I had much to bequeath to anyone. I suppose I ought to change it now, though there's not much for Emmaline to inherit."

"You have unentailed lands that could go to your niece."

Nash raised a brow as Emmaline followed two maids into Sir Will's sitting room, and came to stand beside him. It was a change from her usual, timid attitude, and it took him by surprise.

She twisted her neat plait of blond hair between her fingers and spoke so softly, Nash had to strain to hear her. "Lady Metcalf and . . . and Miss Franklin will come in a moment."

He felt an overwhelming urge to reassure her somehow, but hesitated, unsure of her reaction if he touched her. Doubtful of his own.

Sir William patted the chair beside him, relieving Nash of the need to act. "Come and sit close to me, child."

Emmaline kept her head down and did as she was instructed.

"Tell me what you like to do. Are you a climber like your uncle?"

Nash could see Emmaline's eyes grow wide, even as she kept them averted. "I like to draw."

"Are you any good at it, lass?" Will asked.

"Yes," Emmaline replied simply, and Nash felt a swell of pride, as well as gratitude, rise up in his chest. "Miss Franklin said . . ." She licked her lips and spoke somewhat louder. "Miss Franklin said I am very good." Hoyt's daughter had begun to flourish under Mercy's care.

"Did Lady Metcalf tell you about the time your uncle climbed that big oak tree there?" He pointed to the tree that was an infamous part of Nash's childhood. Or rather, Arthur's. Nash could not recall ever feeling so frightened, not until a year ago at Hougoumont Farm, when John Trent had shoved him aside and was killed for his trouble.

Far too many emotions warred inside Nash's chest. And he did not want to feel any of them. What he wanted was to get outside, choose a dog, and take his leave.

But Lady Metcalf came into the room, with Mercy walking beside her. Nash stood, clasping his hands behind his back as he walked to the window and looked up at the high branches of the big oak tree. He could see the very notch where Arthur had perched that day so long ago, when Nash had felt a truly desperate fear for the first time in his life.

"Are you waiting for us, gentlemen?" asked Lady Metcalf, bringing a much-needed breath of fresh air into the room. "How lovely."

She was clearly not about to allow her husband's illness to dampen the tone of their visit, and Nash welcomed the change of mood. His was bad enough without having to think of Will Metcalf's impending demise.

"Miss Franklin, will you pour?"

Mercy did as she was asked, her graceful hands taking over the gentle ritual he had not had the opportunity to observe in many a long month. Watching her was a balm to his nerves. His headache receded.

As usual, her hair was neatly bound at the back of her neck, but one recalcitrant, silky curl had escaped its mooring and lay softly against the delicate skin of her cheek. He ached to take her into his arms again, and wished he had taken their interlude on the moonlit roof a great deal further.

He should have carried her down to his bedroom

and made love to her properly, kissing every inch of her body as he undressed her, pleasuring her until she cried out his name in ecstasy.

She handed him his tea, but Nash looked at it blankly for a moment while he scrambled to gather his thoughts.

Such wayward fancies would not do. Not at all.

"I've decided to send Mrs. Jones to you at Ashby Hall, my lord," Lady Metcalf announced.

Nash took the cup from Mercy, but could not keep his hands to himself. He allowed his thumb to graze her fingers, and as a jolt of energy arced between them, he was only partly aware of the rest of Lady Metcalf's words.

"Mrs. Jones can serve as your housekeeper until you find someone who suits you better."

A *housekeeper*, she'd said. She was sending Mrs. Jones to help put Ashby Hall to rights. Mercy could go back to the schoolroom, and Nash could entertain as much as he needed. It wasn't that he wanted guests wandering about the house, for he preferred the quiet at Ashby Hall. But how else was he to gather together those men from Hoyt's fatal deer stalking?

"Are you certain, Lady Metcalf?"

Perhaps he was rushing things. There was so much that still needed to be done at Ashby Hall, it would be some time before he could host any sort of party there.

Then it occurred to him that he would likely encounter a good number of the very men he wanted to speak to at the Market Inn ball. He could ask his questions there, and listen to the gossip.

"Our needs are simple here at Metcalf Farm," said Lady Metcalf. "Ruthie Baxter will go and help out in the nursery, but mind you don't let any of your men get fresh with her."

"Of course not." Nash was the only offender in that realm, the only one who'd taken improper liberties with anyone in Emmaline's nursery.

Nash wondered if Mercy would meet a handsome young swain at the Keswick ball. He recognized that it was part of his reason for buying her a ticket to the event—to give her the possibility of a situation somewhere other than at Ashby Hall.

And yet he dreaded the prospect of seeing her wooed by the local bachelors, and perhaps married to one of them, knowing her husband owned the right to kiss her, to touch her, to bed her . . .

He trained his gaze upon Lady Metcalf, because the barest glance toward Mercy made him lose his resolve.

"I think we can spare a couple of our young grooms, too, don't you, Will?" Edwina asked.

Sir William nodded. "We'll help the lad get the place into a decent condition so that Miss Carew will have no complaint when she comes to it as a new bride."

The sudden silence in the room was deafening.

Chapter 20

Oxford, England

Gavin Briggs stopped at the inn in the main road in Oxford, some distance from the university. He went into the taproom and ordered a glass of ale, then sat down to take his ease before going on to find the bookseller who'd employed Miss Thornberry as his child's nurse twenty years ago.

He didn't have much to go on to find her, but he'd succeeded in the past with far less.

He was more concerned with the possibility that whoever had been following him in London was still tailing him on this journey. A skilled man might have taken a coach, or even ridden past Gavin on horseback, and Gavin would never have known his true purpose.

He'd seen no one who'd roused his suspicions, and yet there was still that eerie prickle at the back of his neck, warning him that something was not right.

Gavin was tired. He was tempted to just finish the drink, take a room, and deal with it all later, but it was early enough that he could still go round to a few bookshops and ask some questions. He could sleep when the shops closed for the day.

He left the inn and took what he hoped appeared to be a leisurely ride north, keeping to the streets west of the university. Since he would be staying the night no matter what he discovered in Oxford, he secured lodgings in a small lane near the canal. Stabling his horse for the night, Gavin started walking the streets nearby, stopping in various shops to browse. He didn't limit himself to bookshops, because he didn't want to leave a clear trail for whoever might be behind him.

He questioned every bookstore owner, but it seemed none of them had heard of Miss Thornberry.

Finally, at the end of the day, he came upon a well-heeled book-selling establishment with fresh paint on the outside and glossy oak shelves creating narrow aisles inside. It was full of books as well as students, browsing at their leisure.

It was nearly closing time, for it would soon be dark. Gavin selected a book and approached the proprietor—a very prosperous-looking man—and asked him if he'd ever known a Miss Thornberry.

The man quirked a brow. "Aye. She was in my employ for several years."

"And now?"

"Still lives in Oxford, though she is married now. What's your interest in her?"

"For a very short time, she served as nurse for my . . . client, who needs to have a few questions answered."

"Who is your client, might I ask?"

"No. But I can tell you this much: He is a very high-ranking nobleman who would take it seriously amiss if you did not share what information you might have about your family's former nurse."

"Is that a threat, young man?"

"Not at all." He noticed a man walk past the shop window, wearing a greatcoat and a hat pulled low on his head. He did not appear like any of the young students who were on the street. Gavin turned back to the shopkeeper. "I just need to know where I might find Miss Thornberry in order to ask her the questions my employer would like answered."

He placed his coins on the desk in payment for the book while the man picked up a pencil and jotted down an address on a scrap of paper. He turned it to face Gavin. "Last I heard, she lived here."

Gavin glanced about, looking for anyone who might be paying too close attention to the trans-action. He looked down at the address in Norfolk Street and memorized it, then tore the scrap into pieces and pushed them back across the desk. Years of clandestine work for the crown had taught him never to carry such information on his person.

And if the man who'd just passed was the one who'd been on his trail, he would not want him to find Miss Thornberry first.

"Thank you very much," he said. Tucking the book under his arm, he left the store and started back to his room by way of a few more shops that had not yet closed.

He kept his eye out for the man in the greatcoat, but did not see him anywhere. Yet the sensation of being watched grew even stronger as Gavin walked toward the canal.

Candles were extinguished and shops closed. It

became dark in the streets, and Gavin joined the stream of students and other pedestrians, hoping to lose himself in the crowded streets. He suddenly took a detour, ducking into a narrow alley to watch for his pursuer. Standing in the shadows, he pressed his back against the wall and watched, hoping to catch sight of the man looking for him.

A sudden attack from the other direction startled him, and then the man in the greatcoat came at him in a full frontal attack.

The blow to his belly doubled him over, but he struck out with one elbow and caught his secondary attacker off-guard. The man grunted and released him, and Gavin charged at the man in front.

He butted him in his midsection, knocking him down just as the second man recovered and came at him, delivering a vicious blow to his jaw. What a fool he'd been to assume his pursuer was working alone. He should have known better.

He circled the bearded attacker, hoping for an opening to attack, but the other man recovered and kicked Gavin's feet out from under him, knocking him down.

"Hold him down, Hank!" rasped the one in the long coat. The man tried to pin Gavin to the ground, but Gavin rolled away and came to his feet.

But there was no place to go. Both of them were quickly on him, like cats on a fresh kill.

Darkness fell far too quickly in that alley. Gavin could barely see as a pitched battle ensued. He fought hard, using every trick he'd learned during his tenure as one of Lord Castlereagh's agents.

He used his fists, his knees, and feet to defend

himself, but he was outnumbered, and he felt his opponents gaining the upper hand. They were brutal with their fists, giving him a pummeling that made him taste blood. He felt dizzy and off-balance, and just when he thought it was over, he took a sudden hard blow to his back—a strike that had to have been caused by a heavy rod, either metal or wood.

It knocked the breath out of him and he pitched forward, losing his grip momentarily on one attacker's wrist. The man beneath him took advantage and rolled to the top. But when Gavin caught the gleam of a knife coming at him, he got a burst of strength from somewhere and grabbed the man's jacket, shoving him aside. He heard the knife drop to the ground.

"Get the knife, Hank!"

Gavin scrambled to reach the blade before Hank, but could not see it. The other one came at him again and again, jabbing and punching, using whatever he could find in that dark alley to hit him with. Finally, the bearded one—Hank—pinned Gavin against the rough brick wall.

"Where are they, Briggs?"

"Don't know who you mean," Gavin rasped.

"Windermere's granddaughters."

Gavin brought up his knee and struck hard, but his opponent merely grunted and tried to thrust the knife into Gavin's gut.

Gavin caught his arm just in time, and the two men battled silently with the knife between them, only inches away from each other's vital organs.

Hank suddenly struck out blindly, and Gavin turned the knife, making the fatal thrust into the other man's abdomen. "Briggs . . . you bloody . . ." the man said through a revolting gurgle.

He slid down to the ground in a heap.

"Hank?" the other one asked, unsure of what had happened. Gavin wasn't about to tell him.

But his partner groaned just then. "Bertie, I'm . . ." With Hank's final sigh, Bertie dropped whatever weapon he had in hand and took off running. Gavin went after him, but he'd been badly beaten. His jaw was bruised and his ribs screamed in pain with every breath. He could not catch up.

It was not ideal, leaving Bertie to discover his trail once more. Even though Gavin could lose him again, he knew there were ways of picking up a cold trail. He'd used some of those ways himself, many a time.

Gavin cursed under his breath. Now that he knew how deadly serious Bertie's mission was, he had to make doubly sure the man did not find the granddaughters.

There was no longer any question that it was Chetwood who must have hired Bertie and Hank. It seemed clear the baron intended to see that Windermere's grandchildren were never found.

What a vicious, greedy bastard. The Windermere estate could certainly afford some very generous grants to the young ladies who had been discarded in their infancy. But Chetwood wanted it all.

Gavin dragged himself to the stable where his horse was housed and managed to mount it. He didn't bother to go back to his room, but started looking for Norfolk Street before Bertie had a chance to regroup.

*   *   *

Nash could not believe Sir William had just announced to everyone in the room that he intended to make Helene Carew his wife. He shot Sir William a look of pure astonishment, but the older man was oblivious to Nash's exasperation. Had he always been so obtuse?

First the remark about Mercy being his intended . . . Now this. Likely it was his illness that made him less than circumspect.

Edwina finally broke the silence. "Miss Carew? Of Strathmore Pond?"

Nash gave a slow nod, purposely keeping Mercy out of his line of vision. If her clattering cup was any indication, Sir William's revelation had upset her, and rightly so, for he'd had no right to take such wildly improper liberties with her on the roof. Even if he had not set his sights on Helene Carew, he should not have touched the innocent governess in his household.

"I've never cared much for that Horace Carew," Edwina said. "But his daughter will have a pretty dowry. You could make much of Ashby with it."

"He wouldn't be marrying the old man, Edwina," said Sir Will.

"And I don't know if I'll marry Helene, either. I haven't proposed. I haven't agreed to anything yet." Nash surprised himself a little with those words, and though he felt some measure of relief, the weight of his responsibility still weighed heavily on him.

"But you mentioned her father is in favor of the match," Will said.

Nash nodded. "He encourages it."

"Of course he does," Edwina argued. "What untitled father would not dearly love to snare an earl for his daughter's husband?"

"Might we speak of something else, Lady Metcalf?" Nash blurted. "There *is* no imminent betrothal."

But there would be, soon. Nash couldn't avoid it, but he had no intention of discussing it with everyone who might have an opinion on the subject.

Miss Carew was going to make a far different kind of wife than his penniless Mercy would ever do. Nash knew that life with Helene was going to lack color. There would be no energy, no fire in the marriage.

He could not help but reflect that where Mercy had stood toe to toe with him, Helene was reserved to a fault. She could not possibly understand the meaning of *interaction*.

Mercy had strong opinions and was not afraid to share them. Helene's coy conversation bored him.

There was no question that Helene was pleasing to the eye. A man would have to be dead not to notice her. But Nash could not imagine enjoying her exquisitely good looks in the bedchamber. He feared she would be more concerned with maintaining her poise than sharing the kind of pleasure he'd tasted with Mercy.

For a man who'd never thought of becoming a husband, it was irksome to realize he would have to endure his marriage rather than enjoy it.

As long as her money was good, Nash didn't care. Much.

"You mentioned grooms, Lady Metcalf?" he asked. "Do you have one or two to spare?"

"Davy Colton and Charlie French will do," she

said, glancing at Will. He nodded in agreement. "They're good lads and they're used to my spring cleanings."

"I will not deny we need the help, Lady Metcalf. And appreciate it greatly. Up till now, Miss Franklin has been doing double duty—instructing my men on what needs to be done, as well as teaching Emmaline." He caught sight of Mercy inadvertently as he spoke.

Her face was devoid of all color, but she had gotten up from her chair and was collecting the cups and all the rest of the trappings of their tea. Nash wanted to tell her to leave them, that the maids would see to them.

But he remained silent, his eyes fixed on her hands, so awkward as they let the cups jangle against the saucers.

There was nothing Nash could say to her now, so it was fortunate that Lady Metcalf was there to break the tension in the room.

"Very good, then it's settled," she said, apparently unaware of Mercy's sudden awkwardness. "Now, shall we see about choosing a dog for you?"

She patted her husband's shoulder and called for a footman to fetch their cloaks.

Mercy took a sharp breath when she felt Lord Ashby's hand at the small of her back, ushering her out to the yard behind Lady Metcalf and Emmaline. Her pulse took up a rhythm as mad as when he'd lifted her down from the barouche. Before she'd known about his intentions regarding Miss Carew.

She scuttled away from him and caught up to Emmaline, where the little girl took her hand as if it was the only thing that kept her grounded.

Though perhaps it was Emmy's hand that was keeping Mercy steady, because she felt incredibly off-balance. It was bad enough that she'd surrendered to his fevered touch and honeyed kisses. Learning that he was in the midst of courting Miss Carew had shocked her to the roots of her being.

She blinked back tears, mortified by those moments she'd spent with him on the roof. Lord Ashby had made her feel wanted, given her a sense of being desperately needed. He'd held her as though he cherished her.

How foolish a notion.

She did not know what she ought to do. Now that a nurse was coming to Ashby Hall for Emmy, Mercy could leave. She could go away from the man who had the power to wound her soul.

How much worse would it be when he brought his bride to Ashby Hall?

Mercy hadn't any idea where she would go. There was nothing for her back in Underdale, and, like a half-wit, she had not yet made time to write Reverend Vale. He was her means of escape.

It was not that Mercy didn't care for him . . . She liked him very much and knew they would deal quite well with each other. *He* was her future, and Mercy intended to write him immediately upon their return to the Hall. There would be no further procrastination.

Mercy kept her distance from Lord Ashby as they walked around to the back of the house. She half listened to Lady Metcalf's little anecdotes about Hoyt and his brothers until they reached the area where the infamous oak tree stood.

Of course Nash had rescued his older brother. He was brave and daring, and must have had a warrior's soul, even then. But Mercy resented the wave of sympathy she felt over his terrible losses. The three Farris boys had had a life together, had shared a closeness Mercy could only imagine, having no sisters or brothers of her own.

Though perhaps she *did* have some siblings, somewhere. She felt a deep regret that she would never know them, wondering at the same time if perhaps there was a way. There could be a clue to her origins in her mother's journal, but Mercy had stayed clear of it ever since Emmy had read the first disturbing entries.

The grassy area where they stopped was within sight of Sir William on his sofa, which was obviously Lady Metcalf's intent. He was not well enough to come out, but his wife made certain to include him, despite his infirmity. The closeness of the older couple gave Mercy a wistful feeling that did not abate even when one of the grooms trotted out of a barn with three dogs running by his side. She and Mr. Vale would surely develop the same kind of closeness that Lady Metcalf and her husband obviously shared.

But Mercy did not think she would ever again experience the kind of passion she'd felt the night before, for anyone but Lord Ashby.

She swallowed her dismay and turned to observe the dogs. They had glossy black coats with white markings, and they followed the young boy's whistled commands exactly.

"Oh look, the clouds have gone," Lady Metcalf

said, taking a seat on a chair near a heavy wooden table that had been set up by the oak tree. "Watch, Emmaline. See how they mind Davy. All he needs to do is whistle, or move his hand, and they understand what he wants them to do."

"You thought I was having you on, didn't you, Miss Franklin?" Lord Ashby asked quietly.

A burst of heat flooded her veins. "H-having me on?"

"About the eye dogs." At least he had the grace to appear sheepish. *Having her on, indeed.* Right on the roof of his run-down old wreck of a hall. And she had let him.

"I have yet to see them control anything with their eyes, my lord." Her voice was taut, uncompromising. She had to get through this visit, and afterward, she would see to it that there was no reason to find herself alone with him again. "So far, they've done naught but obey the lad who brought them."

Lady Metcalf let out a good laugh. "Ashby did not jest, Miss Franklin. Our dogs are quite intimidating to our poor little lambs!"

"We'll need a demonstration, Lady Metcalf, of course," said the earl.

"Certainly, you rascal. And then you can choose."

The dogs were enthusiastic but perfectly behaved as they approached with the boy. Emmaline edged close to Mercy when they came near, their tongues hanging out and their tails madly wagging. Obviously, they were also intimidating to shy little girls.

Lady Metcalf told them something of each dog— their names, ages, and personality quirks—while Lord Ashby knelt to study their hips and eyes, then look into their mouths. He had a natural facility with the animals, stroking and examining with a proficiency that was no surprise to Mercy. His hands were large and strong. Of course the dogs respected his touch. She had felt it and hadn't been able to stop herself from yearning for more—

Realizing she was ogling the earl, she took in a gulp of air, and when she turned away from him, caught sight of Sir William watching them through the window. He was frowning fiercely, and an uncanny awareness brightened his eyes. Mercy hoped the man had not been able to sense the turmoil that roiled through her.

Embarrassed to have been caught with her raw emotions so tightly drawn on her face, she turned toward Lady Metcalf and Emmaline. Whatever she'd shown was fleeting, surely. Sir Will could have no idea what she felt.

Especially since Mercy herself did not really know.

"You must watch closely, Emmaline," said Lord Ashby. He caught Mercy with his gaze, his hard gray eyes studying her as though she were some kind of complex puzzle he needed to solve.

"Miss Franklin, give me your hand."

Mercy froze inside, unsure if she'd heard him right. He must know she could not have further contact with him.

She clasped her hands together. "I would rather not, my lord."

"You are not afraid of him, are you, Miss Franklin?"

"Of course she isn't," Lady Metcalf said indignantly. "Miss Franklin, show the child there is naught to fear."

Feeling cornered, Mercy reached out to the tail-wagging animal.

"Approach him where he can see you. You'll want to pet him nicely. Give me your hand."

The earl's words seemed to mock Mercy, but they quaked through her nonetheless, making her knees feel slightly wobbly. *Pet him nicely?* Mercy told herself he was only engaging in a bit of callous teasing, but for what reason, she could not fathom.

Her eyes started to burn and she knelt to scratch the dog behind both ears.

"See Emmaline? Your governess has the right of it," said Lady Metcalf. "Now 'tis your turn to try."

Emmaline joined her, and after a moment, seemed quite comfortable. She cast Mercy and Lady Metcalf a pleased smile, then a bashful one toward her uncle. After a month of avoiding looking at him, it seemed the child was finally warming to her uncle.

Mercy looked up at him and noticed that his expression was as somber as she'd ever seen it. And as his gaze bored into hers, the persistent, unwelcome fever she'd felt with him on the roof returned to warm her blood.

There were decisions to be made. Once she wrote to Mr. Vale, she needed to be patient and wait for a reply before doing anything else—such as advertising for another post. Not that she'd had a great deal of luck with the first one. Mr. Lowell's query was the only one she'd received.

Mercy took a deep breath and concentrated on Emmaline. That was her task at the moment, not worrying about her exit from Ashby Hall.

"Come around and look at Dexter's eyes," the

earl said to his niece, and Emmaline actually did as she was told. "His are both clear and sound—not like mine."

Emmaline looked up into her uncle's eyes without recoiling at all. "Does it hurt you?"

"Not anymore," he replied quietly, and Mercy's heart clenched tightly in her chest.

"Will you part with Dex?" the earl asked Lady Metcalf, and Mercy knew he realized that Emmaline's question was the most important thing that had occurred on their outing.

So did Lady Metcalf. "I'll give you all three. On loan, of course," she said.

But Lord Ashby refused her offer. "We need no more than one. Our herd is badly depleted, so I won't need quite so many sheepdogs until I can build it back up."

"I see. Davy, take Dex out to the field and show Lord Ashby what he can do."

They watched the dog crouch low to the ground as he rounded up the sheep on the nearby hillside and started to drive them toward the stone wall. "See how he controls the sheep, Emmy?" Lord Ashby remarked.

"Perhaps what he is doing is protecting them, my lord," Mercy said impulsively.

He gave her a curious look. "Are you suggesting the dog has some affection for the sheep, Miss Franklin?"

Mercy shrugged. "Maybe it is all just a game to him, and he doesn't really care one way or the other."

Chapter 21

Nash would have enjoyed his morning spent with Emmaline's governess a great deal more had Sir William not mentioned Helene Carew. It had spoiled Mercy's mood, and rightly so.

Nash was a cad.

There was no denying it. And the only way he could make amends was by making sure she was introduced to a few likely bachelors at the ball in Keswick. She needed a suitor—someone appropriate and available.

"When will Dexter come to Ashby Hall?" Emmaline asked, and Nash realized the change in her attitude toward him was real. She was far less timid than before, her voice stronger, her speech more direct. Nash did not know what kind of magic Mercy and Edwina Metcalf had worked, but his niece was far more relaxed with him now.

Which was not the case with her governess.

"Later today, I think," Nash replied to Emmy's questions, casting a sidelong glance at Mercy. She kept her eyes on the road ahead. "He'll come with the grooms Lady Metcalf is sending to help with the housework. I imagine they'll bring him along with the nursery maid." The housekeeper was unable to come to Ashby Hall until the morrow.

They had gone to Metcalf Farm just for a dog, and now he found that his haven was about to be invaded by servants—competent servants who would turn Ashby Hall into the kind of place he believed he wanted: a suitable setting for a house party.

Nash's headache had flared back to life with Sir Will's untimely announcement about Miss Carew, and he still felt Mercy's fury.

He'd told them he hadn't yet proposed to Helene Carew, but that did not make his offense any less galling. Mercy had every right to be incensed, for no honorable man would ever trifle with a woman—an innocent woman—as he'd done with Mercy.

But he had not been able to resist her. She'd been a force to be reckoned with from the moment he'd first encountered her in the road, and he knew he would always compare Helene—or any other prospective bride—to her. She was a fiery swallow of fine Scotch whisky to Helene's bland draught of cow's milk. One intense and passionate, the other chalky and dull.

"You and Lady Metcalf seemed to get on well, Miss Franklin," he said. "I suppose you told her all about the dismal state of affairs at Ashby Hall."

"Not at all, my lord."

"No need to prevaricate." He should not even try to engage her in conversation. What could he do but pursue a wealthy woman for his bride? It did not matter how wildly he might desire Mercy Franklin.

"Very well." She turned and looked directly in his eyes without flinching. "Lady Metcalf asked some pointed questions, and I answered them truthfully. Far more truthfully than . . ."

Far more truthfully than he'd been with her. But she stopped before voicing the words, in respect to Emmaline's presence, no doubt, because Nash had not known her to mince words before.

"Lady Metcalf and my mother were very good friends," he said.

Mercy nodded. "Yes, she spoke fondly of Lady Ashby. *Your mother*, I mean."

"I know who you meant."

There was color in her cheeks and her hat was not particularly effective at keeping her hair contained as neatly as she seemed to prefer. Nash could almost feel the silken strands whipping against his fingers.

He looked back to the road and tried to put his wayward thoughts into some semblance of order. Fate had decreed many abhorrent events in Nash's life, and would soon force him to spend his life shackled to a beautiful but insipid source of capital.

Facing the reality of his future caused him no end of frustration, and he turned to Miss Franklin and spoke bluntly. "There is to be a subscription ball in Keswick on Sunday. The whole district will attend. I've bought you a ticket."

Nash kept his eyes on the road, but felt Mercy turn to look at him.

"I have no interest in going to any ball, my lord."

"Everyone from Ashby is going." His tone left no room for refusal.

"But not I."

"You are not going to defy me, are you, Miss Franklin?"

He turned and cast a glance at her. If sparks could have burst from her eyes, they would have done so then. But she held back, apparently unwilling to engage in a contest of wills with Emmaline as a witness.

They rode the rest of the way in silence. Nash didn't know if he could force Mercy to attend the ball, and he wasn't sure he really wanted her to go. He envisioned every bachelor in attendance swarming around her, bringing her refreshments and asking to be her dancing partner.

And Nash had no interest in witnessing it.

But then, it was not necessary for him to go—not unless Helene and her father would be in attendance.

He swore silently but viciously. Nothing about his return to Ashby had been simple. Perhaps he should just forget about the estate and go back to Lord Wellington. Surely the victor of Waterloo could use an adjutant who had battle experience.

A storm was threatening when they returned to the Hall. But it was no worse than the fury Mercy felt within.

How dare Lord Ashby order her to attend the Keswick ball. She had absolutely no interest in socializing with anyone in Keswick. In fact, the sooner she was able to leave Ashby Hall and this district, the better.

Tears welled in her eyes when she thought of Nash going to the ball, dancing with Miss Carew. What did he think she would do? Welcome the chance to watch him court someone else after he'd seduced her so thoroughly the night before?

She curbed her anger. Emmaline was not at fault here, and Mercy had a duty to deal fairly with the child. Just because her uncle was a scoundrel—and because Mercy had allowed herself to succumb to her attraction for him—was no reason to take out her temper on his niece.

Mercy and Emmaline went up to the nursery, and while Mercy sharpened a pen tip and took out a clean sheet of foolscap, Emmaline sat down with a book on her lap, but did not open it.

"May we read more of your mother's journal now?" she asked, yawning.

The question knocked the wind from Mercy's lungs. "Not now, Emmy," she managed to reply. "I have a letter to write, and you need to read a few pages of *Pilgrim's Progress*. Then perhaps Ruthie will have arrived and you can show her around the nursery."

Emmy nodded. "I like Lady Metcalf."

"Yes, I could see that. She is very kind, isn't she?" Mercy remarked. "And she has a very winning manner."

Emmaline toyed with the edge of the book, then looked up at Mercy. "Why won't you go to the ball, miss? My uncle . . . He wants you to go."

Mercy clenched her teeth. She did not know what Emmaline's uncle wanted, other than to court another woman while he made improper advances toward her.

And she had succumbed, mightily. She could not go to a ball where she would be subjected to the sight of Lord Ashby dancing with Miss Carew and every other eligible lady in the Keswick district. His duty to the earldom had become quite clear with Sir William's words. He needed a wealthy wife.

"I haven't a ball gown," she finally said. Even Emmaline would understand that she could not attend a ball wearing any of her plain day dresses.

Emmaline's expression turned thoughtful. "May I show you something?"

"What is it?"

The child stood and reached for Mercy's hand. "Will you come with me?"

They left the nursery and went to the attic door. Emmaline opened it and started up the same staircase Mercy had climbed—much to her detriment—the previous night.

"Emmy . . . I don't think we ought—"

"No, please. There's something . . ." she said quietly.

Mercy followed Emmaline up the stairs and into the large attic room. The little girl went right to one of the trunks and opened it, pushing the heavy top over the side.

She looked up at Mercy. "See? You can go to the ball with my uncle."

"What do you mean?"

"My aunt's dresses. They're here."

It took a moment for Mercy to understand. "Emmy . . ."

In the shadowy light of the attic, Mercy could see a froth of silks and satins neatly folded in the trunk.

"There will be dancing," Emmy said. "My papa used to dance with me."

Mercy slid an arm around Emmaline's shoulders

and tried to think of a way to explain her true reason
for declining to go to the Keswick ball. She could
not. At least, not to a child.

"I like this one," Emmy said. She peeled back a
few gowns on top and revealed a gown made of deep
scarlet satin and trimmed in gold thread. "Will you
take it out?"

"Emmy." There was no point in it, because she
was not going to any ball.

"Please?" Emmaline asked, sounding more timid
than Mercy liked. The little girl had come a long
way today, and Mercy did not want her to lose any
ground.

"All right, but just to look. I'm not going to the
ball, Emmy."

She carefully slipped the gown out from under
the ones on top and held it up for Emmaline to see.
Mercy knew little of current fashion, but this was a
beautiful dress. Its sleeves were short, and gathered
at the shoulder. The waist was high like Mercy's
gowns, but the neckline was lower than any she had
ever seen. Even so, it was a tasteful dress, and had
a matching pelisse lying just below it in the trunk.

Holding the gown up in front of her, she tried to
imagine how she would feel wearing such a beautiful thing.

"No," she said abruptly, taking it down from her
shoulders. "I—"

"It will fit you, miss," Emmy said. "I know it will."

Before Mercy could say anything more, they heard
Henry Blue calling to them from the doorway. She
used the distraction to lay the dress carefully on top
of the others in the trunk, and hoped Emmy would

forget her silly notion. "Come. We must see what Henry wants."

They found him standing at the bottom of the stairs with Ruthie Baxter beside him, the nursemaid who had been sent from Metcalf Farm. Her hair was as red as Henry's, and she appeared to be only about fifteen or sixteen years old. Emmy had been charmed by her friendly manner and vividly colored hair, and Mercy felt Ruthie would be yet another positive influence on the child.

They returned to the nursery, and Mercy encouraged Emmaline to show Ruthie around herself, and she noted that it was a far different tour from the one she'd given Mercy. Emmaline was still a reserved little girl, but far more talkative and . . . *engaged* with Ruthie.

Mercy remembered having to pry every word from Emmaline's lips on her own arrival at Ashby Hall. Now, she was speaking more freely, and, most important, her fear of her uncle had faded significantly.

Emmy and her new nursemaid were getting along well, so Mercy left them alone, saying they would visit the laundry and kitchen on the morrow and discuss Ruthie's duties.

Mercy retreated to her bedchamber. She closed the door and stood with her back against it. She had not anticipated becoming quite so attached to her young charge.

Or to her uncle.

He might have denied his betrothal to Miss Carew, but Mercy had seen with her own eyes the terrible condition of his house and estate. And Mr. Lowell had confided that the earl did not even have funds for proper servants. Mercy did not doubt that Miss Carew would bring a generous dowry to her marriage. How could Lord Ashby turn it down?

How could he have taken such liberties with her when he knew he would have to wed soon?

Torn between anger and hurt, Mercy went to the small writing desk and began her letter to Mr. Vale. This time, she was determined to finish it and find someone to post it for her.

"Dear Mr. Vale," she penned, and followed with the usual pleasantries. Then to the meat of the letter. "With the deaths of my parents, I find myself in the employ of the Earl of Ashby near Keswick, as governess to his niece. It is not ideal, but alas . . ."

Mercy stopped and crossed out the last line, realizing it might take a few attempts before she achieved just the correct tone. Once she had the wording exactly right, she would write the missive on a clean sheet of paper, and send it off.

When she finished final draft, she opened the drawer of the table beside her bed and took out Susanna's journal. She supposed now would be a good time to delve into the diary, but the day had already been long and distressing. She could not yet face it.

Besides, she felt angry enough already.

She slipped her letter to Mr. Vale into the pages of the journal, then put it away. Straightening her collar and cuffs, she went to check her appearance in the mirror, and grimaced at the state of her hair. Her coif was as disordered as her emotions.

She removed the pins that held it in place and brushed it, reminding herself that it was best for her to leave Ashby Hall. Emmaline would soon forget about the governess who'd helped her to overcome the worst of her shyness, and Lord Ashby would soon have the funds he needed to pay Ruthie and the houseful of other servants that were needed here.

Mercy smoothed her skirts, then took her lamp and went down to the servants' hall, where she located the housekeeper's bedroom. There was not much to be done to prepare for Mrs. Jones's arrival, just a quick dusting and the application of fresh linens to her bed. A low rumble of thunder gave Mercy pause, and she knew a storm was coming. She quickly made up the bed, then left the room.

All was so quiet, there didn't seem to be anyone in the house, not even the old butler. She ventured into the kitchen and saw pots simmering on the stove, but none of the earl's men were in evidence. They must have had some errand away from the Hall, or perhaps they were out on the property doing chores. Even the earl.

Which was perfectly fine with Mercy. Her anger had not abated in the least, and she did not wish to see Lord Ashby now, anyway.

Once again, Lowell was nowhere to be found. The rest of the men were playing at swords, but Lowell had likely gone to visit his female acquaintance in Lake Road.

Nash did not think the steward would appreciate the arrival of Grainger's brother. It would be one thing to hire a shepherd to manage the flock, but Sir William indicated that George Grainger was much more than that.

He would take Lowell's place.

And Nash needed someone like him to do just that. Lowell had helped him plow through Ashby's account books, but it had become clear he knew nothing about raising sheep. It was a complicated business, one that Lowell did not really understand. And he was far too impatient with the pace at which Ashby would become profitable.

Perhaps Nash ought to dismiss him, but on second thought he realized it might be more practical to keep him close. That way, he would know what the man was up to . . . and why. Nash could not fathom what Lowell could have gained by the deaths of the Ashby earls, though something he'd seen that afternoon in Arthur's last ledger had made him curious.

He took Roarke from the fencing match, and together they rode the Ridge path to Ashby's southern acres that bordered Carew's land. It was rough and craggy, and the lower ground was marshy.

"In town, they say there's some kind of nasty fairy that goes about causing trouble near here."

"Boggarts."

"What's that, my lord?"

"It's what they call them here. The nasty fairies. They're just a superstition."

Roarke gave a nod, but did not seem to be entirely convinced. He swallowed and glanced around. "Are we looking for something here, my lord?"

Nash did not remember any talk of boggarts on Ashby land when he was a lad. Surely that was something he would have loved to explore with his brothers and Jacob Metcalf. Which meant that the boggart story was a fairly recent one. He supposed that if a superstitious man's mule had gone lame near there, he would blame it on some spritely force.

"I found a notation in one of my brother's ledgers . . ." Nash said. "Someone offered to buy this land. I want to know why."

It had been Horace Carew, and he'd indicated that he wanted more grazing land for his sheep. This section of Nash's land was unentailed—he knew it from studying the maps—so Arthur could have sold it off. He *should* have sold it, if only for the income.

And it had been surveyed recently. Nash wondered if Wardlow had been entirely honest in his explanation of the survey. Had the crown really commissioned it, or had someone local ordered it? It occurred to him that someone who hoped to buy the land might want a new survey.

"It looks useless to me, Lord Ashby. Rocky. Good for nothing. You can see the slate in the water, there."

"Aye." Nash wondered if Carew was still interested in the land, and whether he'd be interested in negotiating a good price for it. Nash had no problem with the notion of parting with it—for the right price. "Let's head back."

With the house empty, Mercy returned to the servants' hall and closed up the linen cupboards. She started back to the nursery, but stopped at the doors of the large conservatory adjacent to the servants' hall. She'd only had time to take a quick peek into the room while the main areas of the house were being scoured. It had intrigued her then, but she'd had no chance to explore it. She had time now, with Ruthie in charge in the nursery. Mercy did not think she would be missed until morning.

She unlatched the conservatory door and stepped inside, onto a light green tile floor that was interrupted at regular spaces by iron grates. Her heart beat a little faster when she took in the walls and ceiling that seemed to be all glass, the panes filmy with age and dirt.

It should have worried her with the storm coming, but she had never seen such a room and was filled with awe at the possibilities.

Mercy's astonishment increased at the sight of row upon row of narrow tables that held discarded clay pots with the dried-up skeletons of plants in them. Several huge pots stood on the floor near the windows, bearing the corpses of long-dead trees.

She glanced at the floor once again and realized the metal grates allowed heat to rise from below. During more prosperous times, the earl would have had stoves burning during the cold months of the year.

Mercy sighed. The room was heaven on earth, and would be a wonderland of green with new plants in all the pots. The estate could have fresh fruit and vegetables all year round. If Mercy were staying—

A loud clang outside startled her, and she went to a window. Using her fingers to rub away the foggy coating, she saw Lord Ashby's men fencing, only they did not seem to be using harmless fencing foils. They were sparring with their war sabers.

They'd all abandoned their coats and were in shirtsleeves, their hair and skin moist with their exertions.

Lord Ashby was among them.

Mercy's throat constricted at the sight of him, his shirt buttons open and his sleeves rolled up to his elbows as he battled Mr. Bassett. She held her breath as the sergeant lunged and Lord Ashby dodged the blow.

She felt as though a vicious fist had taken hold of her stomach and twisted. "Lord above, what can he be thinking?" she murmured. If Mr. Bassett killed him . . .

Her earlier anger toward Lord Ashby paled at this newest madness. What would happen to Emmaline if yet another Farris man were killed? Hadn't Emmaline suffered enough losses in her young life?

"I cannot believe they're jabbing away at one another this way."

She stormed out of the conservatory in search of a door that would lead to the courtyard where they performed their dangerous antics, fully intent upon ordering the thoughtless, irresponsible man to cease.

When she found the door, she flung it open in a blaze of white-hot fury.

All movement in the yard stopped. Ashby's men turned and stood gaping at her as though she were a lunatic, escaped from the attic. Her gaze came to rest upon Lord Ashby, who lowered his sword as he looked at her.

Mercy could not form the words that had balled into a lead weight at the back of her throat. She clenched her teeth, still furious, but vastly discomfited by the sudden attention she'd garnered.

Ashby started toward her. His white shirt hugged his shoulders and torso like a second skin. A sheen of perspiration lit his face, but his expression was dark and forbidding.

Her anger became a liquid ripple in her blood, only slightly tempered from the way it had been when she'd pulled open the door.

"Was there something you wanted, Miss Franklin?" the earl said ominously. He towered over her, a warrior in battle. Untamed. Savage.

Mercy stepped back, and the door slammed shut behind him. The little light from outside disappeared as Lord Ashby continued to stalk her until he'd backed her into a far corner of the room.

"You . . . Can you not use wooden swords, my lord?" she asked, or rather, she demanded, balling her fists at her sides. She felt the wall at her back and knew there was nowhere to go. A fleeting memory of being backed up against the garret and kissed with a ruthless tenderness crossed her mind.

"Hardly," he said, his voice low and dangerous. "What would be the point?"

He lowered his head, his face only inches from hers. Mercy could smell the scent of sunshine and horses and sweat on him. She swallowed.

"Your niece," she said, her voice a mere croak, coming from deep in her throat. "She relies upon you, my lord. To stay alive!"

He moved in closer, and Mercy felt his breath upon her face. He tipped his head slightly, angling as though determining the right placement to fit his lips to hers.

Mercy swallowed dryly. Wanting it, wanting to feel his lips upon hers. And yet so furious . . .

Her limbs seemed to soften like warm honey, but

her body drifted toward him like iron to lodestone. Her breasts felt heavy. Her heart thudded in her chest.

"I have no intention of dying, Miss Franklin." His voice was satin-rough in her ears. "At least, not any time soon."

"B-but your swordplay . . ."

He lifted his hand to frame the edge of her jaw, brushing back a few wisps of her hair. "You have such little trust in my swordsmanship, then?"

Her thoughts blurred. She could not think when he touched her, when his mouth inched so close to hers. She could barely recall why she was so angry.

"I am going to kiss you, Miss Franklin."

Her eyes drifted closed. His chest touched her breasts, the contact drawing them into tight, exquisitely sensitive peaks. His scent filled her. He dropped his hand to her waist and drew her even closer. She felt his mouth only a hairsbreadth from hers.

"Lord Ashby," called a harsh voice from outside, "as soon as you're finished playing nursemaid to the nursemaid, might we get back to it?"

Mercy recognized Mr. Bassett's voice, and was surprised Lord Ashby did not react to the man's insolence. He ignored Bassett and covered her with his body, taking her lips beneath his own.

He speared her mouth with his tongue, teasing her with exquisite intimacy, inflaming her blood with his hard body pressed against hers. His desire was unmistakable and Mercy felt her own, puddling deep inside her.

Some vague whisper at the back of her mind insisted she should not want him, should not crave more of his breath, his touch; more of his soul. But his kisses were merciless, making her respond as ferociously to his seductive onslaught as he demanded.

He suddenly broke away and grabbed her hand. He pulled her alongside him to the first open room—the housekeeper's bedchamber—kicking the door closed behind him, drawing her into his arms once again.

"I've waited forever for this," he whispered, and in her haze of desire, Mercy believed she must have, too.

Chapter 22

Nash cupped Mercy's face and kissed her lips while caressing her shoulders and back. With purpose he pulled her tight against him, letting her feel the heat of his arousal, the depth of his desire.

He kissed her as though that intimate contact was the only thing keeping him alive, and he groaned when she dragged her fingers through his hair in an insistent demand for more. He complied, sucking her tongue into his mouth, then stabbing his own into hers. Her kisses consumed him.

She pressed her breasts into his chest, and Nash could hold off no longer. He ripped at her buttons. And as the rain suddenly began drumming violently at the window, Nash managed to pull open her bodice. He shoved her sleeves down her arms and broke the kiss, pressing his lips to her bare shoulder, then the sweet mounds of her breasts that rose above her chemise.

"I want you."

His words were punctuated by a crash of thunder. The storm was upon them.

Nash managed to dispense with her dress, then ripped his own shirt off. His naked torso pleased her, and she slid her hands up his chest and over his shoulders, drawing him in, seducing him with her own desire.

Her stays presented little challenge to him, and once Nash had the garment loosened, it fell to her feet. Still kissing her, he lowered her chemise off her shoulders and it slid down, though it caught on the peaks of her breasts.

"Mercy . . ."

Lowering his head, he bared her breasts and caught one pink-tipped nipple in his mouth. Her head fell back as he circled it with his tongue, and her deep sigh rippled through him like molten honey. He laved the other breast, the familiar scent of lilies filling him as his hands slid in eager paths down her body.

He smoothed his battle-roughened hands to the soft mounds of her bottom and pulled her against his erection, her nakedness against his trews. "Mercy . . ."

He felt her hands on his bare chest, tentatively sliding through the hair, testing the taut plane of muscle she found, and he nearly jumped out of his skin when she touched his nipples. "God, yes." His voice was an unholy rasp, his need a fierce torment.

He caught her gaze, but she pulled his head back to hers, then kissed him with a passion that whirled them into a world of their own.

He unfastened his trews, but before he could divest himself of them, could not resist touching her. He slid his fingers into the triangle between her legs, finding her already so hot, so moist. He heard a whimper, but she offered no resistance as he parted her swollen folds and stroked her.

"You're so beautiful, Mercy."

He shoved his trews off and lifted her into his arms. He walked to the bed and laid her on it gently, anxious to be inside her. But it was too soon. He wanted so much more.

A look of panic crossed her delicate features, and Nash knew that what he intended was irrevocable. "No, sweet, don't cover yourself."

"But you . . . your fiancée . . ."

He slid one hand down her thigh, and when he reached her knee, eased it away from its mate. "I have no fiancée."

"My lord . . ."

"Nash." He moved down her body, skimming his lips over her satiny skin while he probed the hot slick confines of the feminine flesh between her legs. "I am Nash."

"Ooh . . ." she said on a sigh.

The rain pelted the window, but they were co-cooned together in the snug little bedroom. The only light was faint, but Nash could see her beautiful eyes and lovely feminine curves. He could not remember wanting anything more than he wanted Mercy Franklin. Now.

She inhaled sharply when he swirled his tongue around her navel and then moved lower. "Oh! I . . . I . . ."

He descended further, and Mercy arched into his mouth. She was made for this—made to share her body with him. With only him.

Nash heard her moan and felt her hands tangle in his hair when he licked between the folds of her sex. He blew his hot breath on her and she shivered, making a small, intensely erotic cry. He found the sensitive bud at her apex and swirled his tongue gently around it.

He ravished her gently, patiently pleasuring her as her limbs went taut with desire. She was too close and he wanted more from her. He withdrew suddenly. Changing his angle, he reached down and took hold of her ankle, then pressed hot kisses to the sensitive skin behind her knee.

She gave a pleading sob. "Please!"

Nash knew he was tormenting her. And he knew that next time, she would be the one doing the tormenting. For there would be a next time, and the plain-speaking governess was nothing less than a tigress.

She arched against him in a plea for release, and Nash could not resist her demand.

He returned to her damp nest of black curls and hovered over her for a moment before flicking his tongue across the acutely sensitive bud. He felt her gasp of breath immediately as she tightened and cried out. But Nash continued his erotic torture, feathering his tongue over her as he used one finger to enter her vulnerable feminine vault. Her damp flesh pulsed over him, and he wanted nothing more than to possess her fully in the most intimate way a man could have a woman.

He prowled over her, his hands moving up beside her until they reached her head. Resting on his elbows, he cradled her face in his hand and positioned himself between her legs, his shaft poised at her entrance. "I cannot remember a time before wanting you. You are mine, Mercy Franklin."

He moved slowly, teasing and nudging until he was barely inside her.

"Nash . . ."

He wasn't sure if it was supplication or worry, but he kissed her mouth again and pushed inside all at once, then held perfectly still for one long moment. She was so tight, so hot. Virgin until this moment.

The sensation of being inside her was almost too exquisite to bear. He feared he might lose control and come before she had time to adjust to his invasion, and he moved again. "Sweet heaven . . ." he rasped.

He felt her swallow.

And when she wrapped her legs around his hips, he knew that everything he could ever want was here.

He moved inside her, setting a rhythm that created a sweet tension between them. He felt her fingers dig into his shoulders, and when he looked into her eyes, he saw an expression of wonder, of astonishment. Of raw greed.

She wanted more.

Nash could do naught but comply.

He slid one hand beneath her bottom and tilted her to enhance the friction between them. They moved together, their bodies as one, their pleasure escalating with every stroke. Her breathing became rapid puffs of air, and she suddenly dug her nails into his skin, shuddering and crying out as she tightened around him.

A fount of some deeply buried emotion sprang up in Nash's chest, and his own orgasm poured forth, a ripping, primal cataclysm that convulsed him with pleasure while it tore every vestige of restraint from him.

He squeezed his eyes tight and shuddered violently, gathering Mercy close as he collapsed beside her.

The room was silent but for the savage beating of their hearts and the rasp of their rapid breaths.

"You are so incredibly perfect," he finally said.

Mercy lay against him, her eyes drifting closed as Nash skimmed the fingers of one calloused hand across her back. His touch aroused her even now, when she should be gathering up her clothes and leaving. She ought to regret what had just happened, for there would be repercussions.

Her body was sated, but her mind whirled with questions. He had denied having a fiancée, but Miss Carew's name had not been idly spoken by William Metcalf. Nash might have denied a betrothal, but he must be seriously considering marrying her—or he would not have mentioned the woman to his old friend.

"I don't want her, Mercy," he whispered, his words intruding on the thoughts she had not yet voiced. "It's been you, from the moment I fell off my horse and you told me to go hang."

"I never said that."

He pressed a kiss to her forehead. "You wanted to."

"Perhaps I should have. And then gotten back on the mail coach and returned to Underdale." A nervous, shivery breath escaped her as her world quietly split apart.

She thought of the letter that lay pressed between the pages of her mother's journal, and the little ripple of panic became a tidal wave. She could not send it now, not after this. She could no longer even imagine a life as Mr. Vale's wife.

Nash lifted her chin and looked into her eyes, his expression one of pure desire, and Mercy forgot all about Andrew Vale. He lowered his head and kissed her, his fervor unabated. He pulled her hips against him, his shaft hard and ready, her own body soft and wet and willing.

He ended the kiss but held her so close she could feel the beating of his heart.

"I had to consider marrying Miss Carew because of her dowry. Because Ashby is destitute."

And the estate would remain destitute if he did not wed her. Tears welled in Mercy's eyes. She did not want to speak of Miss Carew now, but she understood the reality of the situation.

And it hurt desperately.

She would have been satisfied with Reverend Vale. If her father had given his permission, Mercy would have wed the young vicar and gone to live with him in Whitehaven, offering him but a bland imitation of passion. With Andrew, she would never have known the depth of emotion that Nash Farris could rouse in her with just a glance. She would never have understood what it was to love someone with every beat of her heart and every fiber of her being.

She swallowed back her tears, but the back of her throat burned, nonetheless. Lightning flashed, illuminating the room momentarily. "I ought to get back to the nursery. Ruthie has only just arrived, and Emmy—"

"You're crying, Mercy." Nash cupped her face with his big hand.

It was unbearable. "No. I just—"

He kissed her again. "Stay with me."

She shook her head. "Your men will wonder where you've gone. Or what you've done with me."

"No one will wonder. They have their duties. They won't have any idea where I am."

"Nash . . ."

He slid his thigh between her knees, and Mercy's nerves skittered wildly.

"I would make love to you again, but it's too soon for you, sweet." He continued to caress her, pressing gentle kisses to her forehead and cheeks. Her tears subsided. Her fears, along with the tense reality she faced, finally eased from her body, and she drifted to sleep under his gentle touch, leaving her worries for a later time.

Banbury, Oxfordshire

Gavin Briggs wasted no time in getting out of Oxford. He knew Hank's body would be found sooner rather than later, and a stranger with bruised ribs and a purpling jaw would be the first man the magistrate would want to question. Gavin had no interest in staying in Oxford for an inquest.

Nor did he want to encounter Bertie again, the blackguard who'd gotten away from him in that treacherous little street. Gavin hoped Bertie had fled for good and hadn't found Miss Thornberry or somehow discovered the information she'd given him. But he could not be sure.

He hastened out of town as quickly as possible and went to ground in Banbury so that no one would find him.

The ride was painful, but he managed to cover the fifteen miles to his destination, then take a room in a dingy little inn as far out of the way as possible. There was no time to waste recovering from the beating at Hank's and Bertie's hands before heading up to Lancaster, to the rectory where Miss Thornberry said she had escorted a three-year-old Lily Hayes twenty years before.

He would have to leave before dawn to keep ahead of Bertie, in case the bastard found the Thornberry woman and got the same information out of her.

Gavin learned that Windermere's grandchildren had not been kept together. A second nanny had been hired to take one of the sisters to Edinburgh, escorted by an associate of Newcomb. Miss Thornberry did not ever hear his name, but she'd somehow gleaned the name of the Edinburgh family who was to take Christina.

More surprising was the information that the two girls were twins. Miss Thornberry remembered them as being identical and inseparable.

He cursed the duke once again for the heavy-handed cruelty he'd demonstrated, not only for abandoning the two sisters after their parents' deaths, but in separating the children when their world had been essentially destroyed. Gavin could not imagine

a more contemptuous worm of a man than Windermere—but then he thought of his own father. Hargrove was no better.

As Gavin crawled into a relatively clean bed, he
had a firm plan in mind. He would go first to Lancaster and see if Lily still lived there with her adoptive
family. But he was not hopeful. By age twenty-three,
she was likely married, though someone was bound
to know her.

Gavin figured an inheritance from her long-lost
grandfather would be a welcome thing, in spite of
what she might feel for the old man. Once he found
her and delivered her to her grandfather, he would
begin his search for Christina in Scotland.

But for now, sleep was all Gavin wanted.

Nash lay in the dark listening to Mercy's breathing, absorbing the sweet sound into his soul. He inhaled her scent and felt the brush of her eyelashes
against his chest. He was dangerously close to
making an even greater mistake than taking her to
bed. He felt far more vulnerable now than he had in
the past year, ever since his injury. Since his brothers' deaths.

He didn't like it.

His plan had been so perfect. Miss Carew would
never have inveigled her way into his heart, which
suited him well. With Helene, there would have been
no danger of Nash losing everything he cared about.
Whatever happened with Carew's daughter, as long
as her money was made available to him and she
gave him a son, he would not have cared. He could

have gone about his own business, and she hers, only to meet when necessary.

But now there was his fiery Mercy, who noticed none of his flaws but all of his foolishness.

It had grown late, and the storm was subsiding, the rain only a gentle patter now on the ground outside. Mercy's sleep was restless, but Nash gathered her close and stroked her back to help calm her agitation. He'd known better than to seduce his niece's governess.

But now that he had, he wanted to stay there with her all night, lying together on that narrow bed in the servants' quarters until dawn when he woke her and sent her back to her own bedchamber and he went to his.

Chapter 23

Ruthie had not even seemed to notice Mercy's absence for most of the night. And Emmy was content, sitting on her bed and watching while her new nursemaid unfolded all her old clothes to make assessments of which dresses were salvageable and which ought to be given away.

Mercy felt like an extra thumb, in every way. She was barely an adequate teacher, and she was surely not the kind of wife Nash needed.

"I can use these old dresses to make you a brand-new frock, Lady Emmaline." Ruthie held up two gowns that were made of complementary cloths. "Until your uncle . . ." She turned to Mercy. "Have we any funds for new cloth?"

Mercy gave a quick shake of her head. "We'll have to ask Lord Ashby." But she knew the answer. There would be no funds unless Nash married Miss Carew.

Tears welled in her eyes and she walked to the window to wipe them away without calling attention to her distress.

She had given herself to a man who could not marry her. In spite of his denials, Mercy knew that

Nash had commitments and responsibilities, none of which could include her.

She was dismayed by her lapse in the morals she'd been taught, in the principles governing decent behavior, and in her own good sense. She hardly recognized herself.

And yet it wouldn't have happened with any other man. Only with Nash Farris, Earl of Ashby. She loved him.

Mercy's thoughts were as bleak as the sullen sky. Her throat felt thick and raw, and she could not think what to do. Resign as she'd planned?

She thought of Andrew Vale. In all good conscience, could she send him the letter she'd written? Marry him if he still wanted her, despite loving another? Despite having had intimate relations with the man she loved?

A sudden chill came over her, and she rubbed her arms against it. If she did not go to Whitehaven, what then? Find another governess post somewhere?

She turned suddenly, feeling as close to despair as she'd ever done. "It's going to rain again, Emmy. Why don't we go outside for some air before it does?"

Nash shoved his fingers through his hair and tried to set aside his thoughts of Mercy and his hunger for her. But memories of her sensual sighs and the scent of her silken skin consumed him, even as he turned his attention to his brothers' ledgers.

He let out a rasping sigh. There was work to do. He could not allow himself to be so thoroughly sidetracked by a woman, as utterly bewitching as she was. He'd been a disciplined officer with far better control than that. Becoming earl had not changed him so very much.

But he realized meeting Mercy Franklin had.

He'd stopped at the nursery door to catch a glimpse of her, but she and Emmaline's new nursemaid were completely immersed in a discussion of his niece's wardrobe. They hadn't noticed him and he had not wished to intrude, though he had a nearly crippling urge to take Mercy away and find a private little space where he could peel away every layer of her clothing. He wanted to kiss the few patches of skin he might have missed the night before, and feel the smoothness of her naked skin against his.

He squeezed his eyes shut at his memory of the exquisite pleasure of sliding into her, of feeling her wet heat surrounding him, flexing around his shaft.

Mercy had been quiet, allowing the red-haired nurse to take the lead in their discussion of fabrics and colors. He hoped she was reliving their stolen moments in the servants' quarters, remembering the intimacies they'd shared.

How could she not? It was all he'd been able to think of since they'd parted in the darkest hours before dawn. He'd suffered no nightmares, and felt no twinges of a headache when he lay with her. She was his balm, far more healing than any massage Parker could devise.

Nash took his leave of the group of females, promising himself he would come back later and collect Mercy for a few moments alone. He went downstairs with every intention of accomplishing some work, and found the butler in the dining room.

"Grainger, Sir William Metcalf told me that your brother is a sheep man down near Windermere."

"Aye. George is the best in the Lake District. Lives with his son now. Though he doesn't like it much."

"Do you think he'd like it any better here? At Ashby Hall?"

Grainger looked at him quizzically. "You want him, my lord? For the herd?"

"Aye. I have need of an experienced sheep man. Someone who can help me rebuild what we once had. I'd like to hire him to advise me and . . . eventually share in the wealth when we're back in the black."

Grainger smiled and gave a quick nod of his head, obviously pleased. "George is not far—his son's farm is at the north end of Lake Windermere. Hardly a day's ride, my lord. If you were to send one of your men for him now, he could be here tomorrow, or perhaps the day after, if he has any business to close."

"Very good, Grainger. Will you have Mr. Bassett send Harper and Roarke to me in the library?" Harper knew the Lake District well and could find his way to Ambleside today, collect George Grainger, and have him back at Ashby Hall on the morrow. Once he gave his appraisal of the situation at Ashby, Nash would know how to proceed.

"Yes, very good, my lord."

Nash went into the library and saw that the steward had placed the morning's post on his desk. There were two letters, both unsealed, as usual.

Nash unfolded them and read quickly, massaging his forehead as he did so. The letters were from army officers he'd contacted—neither of whom had ready funds to lend. Of course they regretted not being able to help, etc., etc.

He dropped both missives onto the desk and sat back, wondering if he would ever hear from his other friends. He was not yet defeated, though it seemed strange that he had not received replies from Randall and Fitch—two of his closest comrades—for they had both insisted Nash contact them if he had any need. Nash had written them immediately upon his arrival at Ashby Hall, and there had been more than enough time for them to reply.

He wondered if any of the mail could have been lost. Or *misplaced*.

The fire gave a loud crack, startling Nash, but at least it did not immediately take him back to Hougoumont Farm this time. He took a deep breath and thought of Mercy's kiss and the soft press of her body against his, and was soon able to function again.

He'd meant it when he told Mercy that Helene was not for him. Nash's own funds would have to suffice for now, and when he needed rams for the mating later in the year, Nash had decided to ask Sir William to borrow a few. Surely his old friend would understand Nash's need to conserve his money and put off any significant purchases until he was better able to afford them.

He also decided to delay his house party, since it would cost money he needed to put into the sheep. Besides, he would likely meet several of the men from Hoyt's deer stalking at the ball. He doubted it would be as productive as having them all together and talking freely at Ashby Hall, but he might be able to glean some of the information he sought.

Feeling slightly more settled on the issue of his humble finances, he took Arthur's ledgers from a drawer of the desk. Poring over the pages, he searched for the notation about the land Carew had wanted to buy.

He finally came upon the page, very near the end of Arthur's neat entries. "*South acres a boggy mess, but they are mine*," he had written, underscoring the word *mine* twice. Then, he had added: "*Once again, NO to Carew.*"

Which implied that Horace Carew had offered at least once before to buy the land. Nash could not imagine what was so bloody appealing about those acres. They would never be good grazing land, but perhaps Carew intended to complete the improvements Nash had in mind. Maybe the man hadn't wanted to say as much to Arthur.

He wished Arthur had noted what price Carew had offered, for that would put Nash in a better position to negotiate. But in the absence of that information, Nash decided to ask Sir William what he thought the land was worth, boggarts and all.

Then Nash would ask for ten percent more.

He got up from the desk and went to the window, catching sight of Mercy with Emmaline, playing catch with a ball, and felt a surge of emotion unlike any he'd experienced before. He allowed his gaze to wander over the governess's fetching form, wanting nothing more than to go down to the garden and take possession of her now.

Philip Lowell's arrival interrupted Nash's musings, but did naught to abate his intense craving for her.

"Yes, my lord? You wished to see me?" He caught sight of Arthur's ledger on the desk. "Did you find something of interest?"

"Not really. I just wanted to have another look at this note my brother made about the land he refused to sell to Horace Carew."

Lowell's expression was devoid of expression, but a flush of color rose up on his neck. Nash found it curious. "I don't understand."

"'Tis naught," Nash replied. He returned to the desk and closed the ledger. "Just thinking about why Mr. Carew would want a handful of useless acres."

"If he offers to buy them from you, I hope you'll take the offer."

Nash regarded him curiously. "Why?"

"Why not? If they're so useless, you won't miss them, and Ashby has need of the funds."

But why, then, would Carew want them?

Lowell shrugged, but Nash sensed more interest than he wanted to show him. "Well, at least, I hope you'll consider it."

"I will," Nash said as Lowell started for the door. "One question before you go, Lowell . . ."

"Yes, my lord?"

"Have you made any progress on finding a sheep man for us?"

"No, sir," Lowell replied. "I've asked everyone in town, but no one knows of any—"

"Very good. Because I've found a man for us. He should arrive tomorrow, or perhaps the day after."

Lowell showed a moment of bafflement, but quickly recovered, and Nash found himself doubting whether his steward had really put forth much effort to find them a head shepherd. He did not know why the man wanted Ashby to fail, but to Nash's growing understanding of the estate's finances, it had started its decline with Lowell's arrival. That had been nearly a year before Hoyt's death.

Was he a villain, or merely an incompetent?

"Who did you find, my lord?"

Nash returned to his desk and sat down. "Turns out Grainger's brother has quite the reputation in the Lake District for managing sheep farms. I'm surprised you didn't hear of him."

Lowell did not blink, but turned directly to practical matters. "How will you pay him, my lord?"

Nash tapped his fingers on the cover of Arthur's ledger. "For now, the man will work for naught, just to be close to his brother and away from his son's wife. A fortunate turn of events for us, yes?"

"Yes, of course, Lord Ashby. You will not find many who sell their labors so cheaply."

"As you've done yours?"

"Of course not," Lowell said, though Nash detected a slight hesitation before the man's reply. Clearly, he *was* sorry.

"I'm glad to hear it." Nash managed to keep any sarcasm from his voice.

Lowell turned to go, but Nash stopped him. "One more thing . . ." He looked at the steward carefully, wondering if he had the wherewithal—and the motive—to orchestrate his brothers' accidents. "I'd like you to make yourself available to take George Grainger around the estate and show him our borders when he arrives," he said. "Probably tomorrow. And Lowell . . ."

"Yes, my lord?"

"From now on, Roarke or Bassett will be picking up the post in Keswick. You have other duties, so there is no need for you to trouble yourself with it any longer."

A muscle twitched near the steward's eye, confirming at least one of Nash's suspicions.

"Very good, my lord." He gave a slight bow and took his leave as Roarke and Harper came into the library for their orders.

Somehow, Mercy managed to get through Emmaline's morning exercise and lessons, but after lunch, Ruthie took over. The girl was not so very much older than Emmy, and was clearly bored with her nursery work. She wanted to play.

"You mustn't have had an afternoon to yourself in ages, have you, miss?" the nursemaid asked. "If you'd like to take some time, Emmaline and I will be fine. Won't we?" she asked, turning to Emmaline.

Since Emmy had taken to Ruthie so well, Mercy agreed. Besides, it was a struggle to keep her mind on the task at hand when all she could do was dwell on what she had to do.

She left Emmaline in Ruthie's capable hands and went across to her bedchamber. She removed her mother's journal from the drawer and took it to the chair near the window, the one from which she'd nearly fallen that first night, only to have Nash catch her just in time.

He could not catch her now, for she'd already

fallen as deeply as she could. She pressed one hand to her breast and tried to quell the futile longings within. Lord Ashby might want her, but the Ashby earldom did not need her. No matter how incredible the experience they'd shared the night before, Nash would have to come to the same conclusion.

Mercy knew how badly it would hurt when he realized what he must do.

Leaving her letter to Reverend Vale in the drawer, she opened Susanna's journal and skimmed past the entries Emmy had already read.

22 August, 1795. Robert promised to keep Mercy's origins secret, and he holds me to that same promise. Not that we really know anything about the child—only that she is unwanted by her own kin. What kind of mother would give away her child? My husband says she cannot have been a moral Christian woman.

Robert intends to take us far away from our Lancaster parish where we've lived all during our married life, to St. Martin's Church in Underdale. No one will know us there, no one will know the girl is not our own. It pains me to leave here.

Mercy wondered if her true family was in Lancaster—the kin who did not want her. Who were they? And what were the circumstances of Mercy's birth? Why had her mother abandoned her to the Franklins? She read on, afraid she might find a rible answer to her questions.

12 September, 1795. The child is already three years old, but barely speaks. And yet she wails all the time, calling for her mama and for "Teeny." And when she is not wailing, she sucks her thumb raw while she looks at us as though she cannot understand a word we say. Robert believes she might be addled. We pray for her nightly.

Mercy felt a striking mixture of sorrow and anger. She was *not* addled, but clearly just a helpless child who desperately missed her mother and someone with the unlikely name of Teeny.

Holding her temper in check, she read on until she came to the following entry.

30 September, 1795. We've moved so very far from St. Edward's and all our friends, just to keep the secret. It is altogether too dishonest and so unlike my dear, forthright husband. But the £5,000 given us by Robert's friend, Mr. Newcomb, went far to convince him of the value of the move. I, however, can hardly reconcile myself to it.

Five thousand pounds! Mercy clutched her chest. The Franklins had been utter mercenaries. The money was a veritable fortune, obviously given to the Franklins for Mercy's keep. They could not possibly have spent it all.

And yet Susanna had possessed next to nothing after her husband's death. Mercy could not imagine what had happened to all that money. More importantly, she realized that she had come from a family of some means. For who else would have handed over such an exorbitant sum of money for the care of an orphan?

> *9 October, 1795. Every time she calls me mama I want to tell her the truth, but Robert has forbidden it. He promised never to tell another soul—including the child—that she is not truly ours.*

So much deceit from the two most righteous people Mercy had ever known. They'd lived a lie every day throughout the twenty years Mercy had lived with them. She found herself softly weeping as she turned the pages, the book a strange and perverse window on her life in Underdale and the parents who were not parents at all, but mere caretakers of a child they did not believe in.

She wiped tears from her eyes and read yet another page.

> *7 April, 1803. We must guard against any sign of wantonness in the girl. Fortunately, she has a knack for gardening, which Robert said we should encourage. He says it will keep her busy and likely prevent her embarrassing us someday.*

Mercy's world trembled on its mooring. Her mother had been a cold woman, but this was so much worse than anything she could have imagined. She opened to the last few pages, hoping her mother would have developed at least some fondness for her toward the end. But alas.

> *3 May, 1815. Reverend Vale should not have spoken to Mercy before asking Robert for her hand. Her enthusiasm for the match indicates an unhealthy passion for the young man. A marriage between them would only encourage an ungodly wantonness in Mercy. We have always worried she would make the same mistakes her mother must have done.*

Mercy closed the book and leaned back in her chair, trembling. There was nothing more to learn, and a great deal more pain that could be avoided. She rose from her chair and tossed the book onto the bed. She had read enough.

Feeling hollow and empty, she took her heavy woolen cloak from its hook and pulled it on, then walked out of her room and down the steps.

Nash was unsure what more to do about Lowell. He didn't trust the man, but he had no real evidence against him, other than a few inconvenient absences and the decline of the estate. Nash was beginning to suspect that was not all Arthur's fault.

He wanted a few moments alone with Mercy to help clarify his thoughts. It seemed like an eternity since he'd last seen her, and even longer since he'd held her in his arms.

He went up to the nursery, assuming he would find her there. Dipping his head into the room, he quickly saw that Mercy was not present. His niece and her new nurse seemed to be completely engrossed in collecting Emmaline's measurements.

The change in his niece was remarkable. She was still a quiet child, but she'd begun to look directly at him when speaking to him, and was nowhere near as nervous around him these past couple of days. Her governess's influence, of course.

Nash went across to Mercy's bedroom and saw that it was empty. A book lay discarded on the bed, with a few folded notes or letters protruding from the pages. A damp handkerchief lay beside it.

He picked up the book and opened it, and saw the name of Susanna Franklin inscribed on the inside cover page. Mercy's mother?

He read the first few puzzling entries and tried to imagine Mercy reading them, seeing that her deceased parents were not her parents at all, but just two people who'd been paid to take her in.

Had she only just seen this? Bile rose in his throat when he thought of Mercy reading this rubbish, of learning she'd been foisted off on a couple who'd not only lied to her for her entire life, but somehow lost the money they'd been paid to take her in. Mercy would not have sought employment as a governess if she'd inherited any of that money. And yet he could not imagine how the Franklins could have spent five thousand pounds on one young woman in twenty years. They'd squandered it.

Even worse was the cold manner in which Mercy must have been treated for all those years. His heart clenched when he read of her crying for her own mother. He knew little about children, but could only imagine how he would have felt being taken from his own parents.

He knew how Emmaline had reacted to losing hers.

Mercy had not told him much about her past. He knew her father had refused her suitors. Nash recalled that she'd hesitated speaking of the second swain, a clergyman like her father.

Hearing of Reverend Franklin's refusal of the man had confused Nash. Wouldn't her father have thought another vicar would suit her?

Her mother gave a feeble explanation for it in her little diary, but the reason noted had been mean and nonsensical. Mercy was intelligent and kind, and conscientious to a fault. She worked hard, shepherding Emmaline out of her desperate isolation, to the point that his niece had not only begun interacting with him, but was allowing the nursemaid to measure her for new clothes. Mercy had stood up to his men—Childers and Bassett, anyway—and gotten them to follow her instructions for getting the Hall into shape according to Nash's request.

He gritted his teeth at the thought that the Franklins would consider their lovemaking depraved when it had been more honest and pure than anything Nash had ever done.

He left the book on the bed and went downstairs. Mrs. Jones had not yet arrived from Metcalf Farm, but Henry Blue was washing windows in the entry hall. "Blue, have you seen Miss Franklin?"

"Yes, sir, my lord. I saw her leave the house not a half hour ago."

"Where did she go?"

"I'm not sure, sir, but she was headed in the direction of the pavilion."

Nash went after her.

The pavilion was a good, long walk from the house, and if Mercy had just been reading Susanna Franklin's words, she was probably upset. He supposed she might welcome a strenuous walk after reading those entries.

Nash had a fair idea how they had made her feel.

He started on the path to the pavilion as a few sprinkles of rain started to fall. He hardly noticed them in his hurry to get to Mercy. He wanted to give her the reassurance she deserved. The Franklins had not deserved her. Far from it. Had they been alive, Nash might well have gotten on his horse and ridden to Underdale to give them a dressing-down more severe than any he'd delivered in the army.

When the rain began, Mercy realized it had been foolish to walk so far, ignoring the looming storm. But her mood had been bleak and she had barely noticed her surroundings. She pulled up her hood against the first fat drops of rain and hurried toward a structure in the distance—the pavilion she'd visited once before with Emmaline . . . and Nash.

She quickly made it to its covered colonnade and moved in close to the wall, just narrowly avoiding getting drenched. Mercy stood still, catching her breath as the rain came down in waves, soaking the hilly lands all around.

Her head bowed, she shivered with the cold, and let her tears fall. She should be grateful, she knew, that she had not been abandoned to the parish poorhouse, or some terrible orphanage. Her life with the Franklins had been reasonably comfortable, in spite of the fact that they had thought so little of her.

She had tried so very hard to please them.

The wind changed and suddenly, the rain started coming down in sheets. Mercy hardly noticed. Her emotions were profoundly raw. She dropped down to her knees and wept, never having felt so alone. She'd spent her life trying to please her parents, always hoping she would soon win their approval. But she'd been hard-pressed to measure up to their high standards, and she knew she'd failed more often than not.

She doubted she would ever measure up.

Her tears of despair flowed as savagely as the rain all around her, and Mercy wished she could just crawl inside the pavilion and stay there forever.

But she would go to Andrew Vale if he would have her, and live her life as his wife. He was a decent man, but Mercy knew she would live out her years feeling empty and aching for the one man who'd touched her soul. The one man who could not offer for her.

She tried to convince herself that it was not so bad a fate. The Franklins had raised her to become a vicar's wife, even though they'd refused a perfectly proper, acceptable offer from Mr. Vale. And her already shaken spirit reeled at the thought that they would have refused every man of character. They'd believed her unworthy.

"Mercy!"

She recognized Nash's voice, but did not want to look up, did not want him to see her in her present state.

Mercy rose to her feet and stumbled away, hoping

to go to the other side of the circular colonnade, even though she knew it was a fruitless endeavor. But she was not feeling quite logical at the moment.

"Mercy." She felt his hands at her back, taking hold of her shoulders and turning her around. He took one look at her face and pulled her to him, holding her tightly as she wept. "Hush, sweetheart. I saw the diary. I know what she wrote, but it's not true. None of it."

She'd left the journal on her bed—anyone could have read it, and obviously, Nash had, at least some of it. She could have disputed his words—that it wasn't the contents of Susanna's journal that mattered— just the sentiments. But she had not the wherewithal to speak, not when her throat burned and her tears flowed so freely. She kept her face buried in his chest and drew on the strength of his arms around her.

"Come inside," he said. "It'll be warmer there. And dry."

She heard the click of a latch, and a section of the exterior wall suddenly swung open, and then they were inside. He closed the door behind him, and with the few small windows in the dome overhead, Mercy got a sense of the interior of the pavilion, a circular room with covered furniture inside. In other circumstances, it would be a lovely summerhouse. But Mercy had little appreciation for such things now.

Nash pulled a dusty Holland cover from a cushioned chaise, and when he came back to her, he kissed her tearstained face, and then gave her mouth a gentle brush with his lips. He led her to the chair and sat down in it, pulling her onto his lap.

He loosened her cloak and drew it over them both,

leaning back in the reclining chair as he cocooned them in its warmth.

"You should have left me to my misery," she said, though she did not mean it. His embrace touched her heart deeply, giving her comfort where there'd been emptiness only a few moments ago.

"Not after I found that diary on your bed. I couldn't leave you alone." He rubbed her back, creating a soothing warmth. She blinked away her tears and wiped her cheeks with the handkerchief he handed her. "Feel better now?"

She swallowed. How could she possibly feel better? Her world had shifted beneath her feet in every possible way. She barely knew who she was. The only thing certain was how much she cared for this man who held her close.

All Nash wanted was to hold Mercy in his arms and give her some solace. That diary was brutal. No one should have to read such revolting drivel. She was trembling, but at least her tears had abated.

"You'd never read the diary before?"

"No," she whispered. "I found it after my mother died, but I . . . I didn't want to look inside."

"You didn't know?"

She didn't speak for a moment, and Nash just held her trembling body. "Just before she died, my mother . . . told me I was not really her daughter. She didn't explain."

"Callous of her."

"She was very ill . . . barely capable of speech."

"You are far too generous, sweetheart. She had years to tell you."

"She had a vow to keep."

"And a great deal of money, it would seem."

"Yes. I . . . It must be gone now. We had little enough to live on after my father died, and there was nothing left of that after Susanna . . ."

He gathered her close. "Don't think of it now."

She pressed her cheek to his chest and he felt an unfamiliar tenderness invade his heart. The thought of five thousand pounds should have stirred him, but it held far less importance than Mercy's sorrow. He kissed the top of her head and held her close.

"I know I should not," she said, looking up at him. "It doesn't matter who my true parents are. Or who I am."

He shifted them so that they lay on their sides, facing each other. Her eyes were in shadows, their pale green much darker now, but full of her bright intelligence and utterly appealing. "You know who you are, Mercy, sweet."

He cupped her face in his hand and leaned in to touch her soft lips with his. He'd meant it to be a comforting gesture, but his pulse began a mad clatter as soon as their lips met, seeking an end to this unending craving he felt for her. He loved the feeling of her full mouth pressed against his, and the scent of her skin. But he withdrew, feeling like an unscrupulous rogue for wanting her so desperately now, when she was so vulnerable.

He struggled to cool his excessive passion, but Mercy softened against him, moving her head to seek contact. Like the novice she was, she gave a tentative touch of her lips against his.

Nash groaned.

All his senses came alive. She beguiled him, fascinated him, made him laugh and made him burn. He wanted her desperately.

He opened his mouth over hers, and her response was incendiary. She made a low sound as she wrapped her arms around his neck, slipping her fingers through his hair, angling her head to give him greater contact, shifting her legs so that his hard erection was pressed against her.

Nash ravished her mouth while his hands wandered to her back and then lower, relishing her warm, curving flesh, pulling her lovely softness against him.

"Mercy . . ."

He moved down, pressing kisses to her jaw, then the base of her throat, moving against her as her low whimpers of arousal ignited him. He pulled at her gown, raising it up her legs and past her hips, until he touched her bare skin.

"I want you."

He explored her feminine cleft with his fingers and teased her until she moaned and moved against him in a demanding rhythm.

But Nash was not about to accommodate her. He wanted to be inside her when she reached her peak, wanted to feel her hot sheath tighten around him, squeezing every possible ounce of pleasure from his body.

Chapter 24

He circled his hand around to the front of her body and found her feminine center. He slipped his fingers into the soft triangle there, and nearly came apart when he touched the silken flesh, already moist for him.

She pulled at his shirt, fumbling with his buttons, and he lifted up long enough to pull off his jacket and whip off his shirt. "You, too, sweet."

Soon they were nearly naked, his chest against her breasts. She slid her hand between them to touch his nipples, bringing them to tight, sensitive peaks. She bent slightly and licked one.

Nash groaned, the sensation impossibly erotic, but his heart stopped when she moved her hands down his body and slid one inside the placket of his trews. Still licking his nipple, she circled his cock with her fingers and found him hard and ready. Far too ready.

"Mercy." It was a plea.

He moved her onto him, and he cupped her breasts as she straddled one of his legs. She brought his nipple to a hard peak with her tongue, then moved her mouth to the center of his chest and pressed a softly sensuous kiss there.

His cock surged when she moved lower.

She met his eyes and gave him a quizzical glance before moving farther down. "Aye, love. Just as I did to you." He groaned as she stroked him, bringing her mouth closer to his straining shaft.

"Sweetheart. Yes. There."

She touched her mouth to its tip, and Nash nearly lost control. He fisted his hands in the cushion beneath him and hoped he could last long enough to enjoy her inexperienced ministrations. She flicked her tongue over him, and he gave her encouraging words until she took him fully into her mouth.

Nash let out a growl of pleasure as she swirled over him and around him, performing the incredibly intimate act so innocently and yet so deliciously. He could not imagine a more erotic sight than his sweet Mercy pleasuring him with her mouth.

He relished the wild sensations she created, but when he could take no more, he took her by the shoulders and moved them both, slipping her beneath him.

Nash covered her with his body as he shoved down his trews. He spread open her legs with his own and entered her slowly, unsure how much she could take, or how fast, for she had been virginal only last night. He worried that it might be too soon for her, but then she reached down and took his erection in her hand, and placed its tip at her entrance.

"Please, Nash," came her breathless appeal.

She sounded as desperate as he felt.

He entered her in one deep slide and then stilled.

Tried to steel himself from going too fast, from reaching his own climax too quickly. He wanted her to find the same pleasure they'd shared before. But doubled.

When he started to move, he went slowly, then built a faster rhythm as he rocked against her, all to heighten her pleasure. He kept his eyes on hers, their connection deep and all-consuming. It touched a part of Nash that he'd kept buried for so long he no longer thought he possessed it.

Her nails raked his back and she bracketed his hips with her legs, cradling him and urging him on, building the pressure, increasing the tension, like water boiling in a closed pot. He was ready to explode. He took her mouth in a fervent kiss, angling his body to increase the pressure against her sensitive cleft. He plunged deeper and deeper with every stroke until he felt like a madman, on fire, and crazed with longing.

She came first, crying out as she clenched around him. Her orgasm came in a liquid rush; her spasms drove him on to completion. He buried himself deeply one last time, and then burst within her, his body pulsing with pure pleasure.

Mercy shuddered with a profound feeling of loss when he withdrew from her. She feared she would never feel whole without him, but understood what he had to do to salvage his estate.

And yet it was so very peaceful lying against him on the chaise, listening to his breathing and watching the rain pelt the windows so high above them.

He kept his arms around her, and pressed tender

kisses to her forehead and temple, and then her lips.

They lay quietly, neither one willing—or perhaps able—to speak. All Mercy wanted was to stay in his arms forever, but she knew that what had just transpired should never have occurred. Nor should it have happened the previous night.

"Come to my bed tonight," he said, lightly brushing his hand over her hip.

"I cannot." Not when he was on the verge of pledging himself to another woman. If not Miss Carew, then some other dowry-rich lady in the district.

Mercy knew very well that earls did not marry their children's penniless governesses. She was a fool to allow herself to become so attached.

"Then I'll come to yours," he said, his whisper shuddering through her in a sensuous promise.

"Nash, no. Wh-what about . . ." Mercy skirted the real issue. "What if Emmy needs me?"

"That's why she has a nurse."

"But Ruthie is hardly older than Emmaline. What can she—"

"I am sure she is competent beyond her years if Lady Metcalf sent her."

Mercy gave a shake of her head. Her throat burned. She would like nothing better than to spend the night—every night—in his bed. But it was impossible, and they both knew it.

They lay quietly for a moment, neither one capable of broaching that subject.

"Have you thought of going to Lancaster to look for your family?" he asked.

Mercy swallowed. "No. You saw why I was given to the Franklins."

"Perhaps they were wrong. Or the situation has changed."

Mercy supposed that was possible. Her funds were limited, but she believed she had enough for her passage to Lancaster. Susanna had mentioned a Mr. Newcomb . . . But the idea of traveling to the city was daunting. "I wouldn't know where to begin."

She could almost feel him sorting through the facts he knew, trying to come up with a viable solution for her. But there was nothing he could do. He could not take her to Lancaster himself. He had no funds, either, and he had responsibilities here.

She pressed her cheek to his chest. "I resent them for calling me Mercy. It was as though they believed I had done something wrong, requiring an extra plea for leniency every time my name was spoken."

"You were an innocent child, sweet."

"They believed my mother was not. And that her sin . . . I do not understand the logic."

Nash held her close for a moment, then tipped up her chin and spoke quietly. "I'm sure your real mother named you something altogether different. Something pretty and feminine. A name as beautiful as you are."

He kissed her softly and eased her body closer to his.

Mercy appreciated his attempt to comfort her, but they were both aware that she would never find out her true name.

Nash paced the floor of the library while Mercy made her retreat to the schoolroom and resumed Emmaline's lessons, he presumed, though how she

could concentrate on anything at all was a mystery
to him. It wasn't just the explosive interlude they'd
shared in the pavilion. He did not see how the mean-
spirited words and phrases her mother had written
in her diary could fail to weigh on her.

He hated seeing her so distraught.

Nash knew a few good men whose homes and
families were in Lancaster. Perhaps he could prevail
on them to make inquiries—he knew the name of
the man who'd taken her to the Franklins; perhaps
they could find him.

But if Mercy's true mother had not wanted anyone
to know about her child, she would not welcome
questions.

Nash thought it through. Susanna Franklin wrote
that Mercy had not been an infant when Newcomb
had brought her to them. She'd been about three
years old. That meant someone had kept her until
then. Her mother? Grandparents?

For some reason, her family had not been able to
keep her, and they'd wanted her origins kept secret.

Nash muttered a curse of frustration. He didn't
care who her mother was. The woman could have
been the lowest of harlots, but she'd borne an incredibly intelligent, lively, compassionate—

"My lord?"

It took Nash a moment to realize the old butler
had come into the room. "What is it, Grainger?"

"Mr. Carew to see you, my lord."

"Carew? What does he want?"

"A few moments of your time, he said."

"Send him in."

He greeted the man with a handshake, then gestured to a chair before the fireplace. The same chair in which Mercy had sat and answered his questions when she'd first arrived at Ashby Hall.

Nash was going to get her to agree to come to his bed later, after Emmaline and her nurse had retired for the night. After spending the previous night and the better part of that afternoon curled around her adorable body, Nash wanted more.

"Lord Ashby, 'tis good to see you again."

"Mr. Carew, to what do I owe the pleasure . . . ?"

"I felt like a ride, and decided to pay you a call . . . have a little chat."

"A chat?" On a day like this, Carew felt like riding?

"You and my daughter seemed to get on well during your visit the other night."

Right, Nash thought, *about as well as a spring lamb being led away by the butcher.*

Carew did not seem to notice Nash's reserve, and he continued, "You are planning to attend the Keswick ball tomorrow night?"

Nash raised a brow.

"Word travels fast in these parts, my lord. Surely you remember that from your youth."

"Yes, I purchased tickets for all of us—my entire staff—to go."

"My daughter and I will be present, of course."

"I look forward to seeing you there." But he had no interest in sharing a dance with his daughter, not when the memory of Mercy's touch was so fresh in his mind and on his skin.

Carew leaned forward in his chair. "My lord, I thought it would be advantageous for us to come to an understanding."

Nash's brows came together. "Regarding . . . ?"

"Regarding the commitment I am prepared to make, regarding my daughter's marriage."

Nash was not naïve enough to think a marriage commitment existed solely between a husband and his wife. Unless the wife was a woman like Mercy, with no family, no attachments in the world. "Go on."

"Helene's dowry is substantial, my lord. And, without mincing words, you have need of money."

"So I do," Nash said, with no intention of making it any easier on the man. And he could speak plainly, too. "Exactly how substantial is Miss Carew's dowry?"

The direct question seemed to ruffle Carew's feathers, but he recovered himself quickly. He cleared his throat. "I would rather not discuss specifics, my lord. Not until there is an offer on the table."

"I know it is crass of me," Nash said, though not as crass as discussing his daughter's marriage as though she were a ewe on the auction block. He leaned back in his chair and crossed one leg over his opposite knee. "But there will be no offer without specifics."

Carew stood and turned, rubbing the back of his neck. Nash was accustomed to dealing in a straightforward manner with his men and fellow officers, neither hedging nor dissembling, but giving direct orders. He knew this was not the time for it, but he wondered how far Carew was willing to go in order to wrest a title for his daughter.

"Very well, then. Helene will have upward of twenty thousand pounds when she weds."

The sum made Nash's skin prickle. It was a veritable fortune, at least three times what he'd assumed it would be. But he masked his shock and said naught.

"My lord?"

"The bargain seems rather too one-sided, Carew. What's in it for you?"

"The happiness and security of my daughter."

"And the title, of course."

"Which goes without saying. Becoming a countess would suit my daughter well."

Nash nodded thoughtfully. "Is your daughter not happy and secure now? You are well able to provide for her, is that not correct?"

Something seemed off, but Nash had not been approached very often by wealthy fathers wanting to give him their daughters. Perhaps he was too inexperienced in the ways of fashionable Englishmen to understand the transaction, but he had always recognized that bargains should be two-sided. Each party had to reap some reward. He wondered what Carew's was. The countess title she would gain if Nash married her?

Perhaps Helene was a virago in her father's presence and he could no longer abide her. Nash suspected there was something more to it than that, and more than a worthless title. He wanted to mull over the question that nagged at his mind. *What was Carew getting out of this?*

He wished he'd received word on Carew's activities in London, but no response to his query had arrived yet.

"I shall have to think about it, Carew," he said, though he already knew his answer. "We can discuss it on the morrow."

Carew did not speak for a moment. He stood in front of the fire, his hands on his hips, his expression one of displeasure. "Ashby. You are in no position to bargain."

"No?"

"You will be quite free to bed your little piece once you've gotten an heir off my daughter."

"I beg your pardon?"

"No need to deny it. As I said, word travels."

Nash did not see how the man could possibly know about Mercy. Bristling inside, he stood and went to the door. He opened it, giving Carew a clear message.

"We will speak on the morrow, my lord."

Once Carew had exited the room, Nash went to his desk and sat down. Only his men could have any idea that there was something between him and Mercy, though none of them had witnessed anything but an argument during their swordplay, and nothing more.

He supposed one or two of them might have suspected something more had occurred between them after he left the practice field. But which of them would have spoken to Carew?

Bassett, perhaps, because he was still angry with Nash about having to do housework. But Bassett was faithful to a fault. Rough around his edges, but he would not betray Nash's private affairs to an outsider.

It was more likely Lowell, the wily bastard.

Nash did not appreciate any of his staff spilling his private information, especially tales about Mercy. He was going to have to do something about Lowell.

And be more circumspect with Mercy.

He pulled open the lower desk drawer and re-moved Arthur's ledger. Paging through to the last few entries of June the previous year, he found the notation that had sent him down to the southern fields and read it once again.

"South acres a boggy mess, but they are mine. Once again, NO to Carew."

Nash thought again of the maps he'd seen in Mag-istrate Wardlow's office. Thrumming his fingers on his desk, he wondered if the new surveys were con-nected with Carew's offer to purchase those southern acres. Wardlow had said they were commissioned by the crown, but Nash could not help but wonder.

Carew had not made the same offer to Nash for purchase of the land. But he *had* offered a substan-tial bribe to persuade Nash to marry his daughter. Did he think he would be better able to deal with a son-in-law?

Perhaps it would be best to play Carew's game for a while and see where it led.

Mercy unfolded her letter to Mr. Vale and read it over. She blinked back tears over what could never be. Reverend Vale had seemed a perfectly accept-able—even a desirable—suitor only a few short months ago. Mercy had been fond of him and cer-tain that love would grow. She knew she would make him a good wife, for she was well versed in the work-ings of the church, and knew what was expected of a vicar's wife.

Even if her heart was not in it.

She tossed the letter into the fire. She could not

become Reverend Vale's wife now, not when she knew how love ought to feel. Not when Nash Farris possessed her heart, her body, and her soul.

Mercy had never realized how much it would hurt. She wished he were still just a captain in the army, for then they would have a chance. But as Earl of Ashby . . . Mercy shivered and drew her shawl tight around her shoulders. She understood that he had a solemn duty to his heritage, and it could not include her.

She had to leave, for she was not made to be a paramour. And that was all she could be to him.

Perhaps she would go to Lancaster and try to find Mr. Newcomb and get some answers. If not, there would surely be some kind of employment there, for it was a large city. Perhaps she would find a family who had need of a governess.

She took out her money and counted it, quickly calculating whether she had enough to pay for her passage to Lancaster on the mail coach, and how long she could last without any income. If she was very frugal, she could do it.

Even though her heart would break when she left Ashby Hall. When she left Nash.

Underdale, Cumbria

The irony of coming all the way back to the north country was not lost on Gavin Briggs as he hastened from St. Martin's Church in Underdale. He'd been given his commission in the Lake District, and found himself almost back to it.

It was alarming to learn that someone had arrived before him, asking the same questions he'd asked.

Gavin didn't know how that was possible, but the urgency of his mission just doubled. Or tripled. Lily Hayes—or Mercy Franklin, as she was known in Underdale—had taken a post as governess somewhere near Keswick, and Gavin's adversary knew it. No doubt he—Bertie, most likely—was galloping to the Lake District even now.

It seemed everyone in the parish was willing to talk about the poor Franklins, the vicar dying so suddenly without providing any financial security for his wife and daughter. And then to have Mrs. Franklin succumb so soon after her husband—it was unthinkable.

So was the possibility that Bertie, or some other agent of Baron Chetwood, would find Miss Franklin first.

Gavin was not as interested in the reward money at this point, not after all he'd learned about the life the duke had arranged for his granddaughter. He just wanted to be sure she received her due from the callous old man.

He was so certain he'd stayed ahead of Bertie. On his arrival in Lancaster, he'd visited St. Edward's Church and discovered that the current housekeeper had been a laundry maid at the same rectory years ago. At that time, the vicar and Mrs. Franklin had taken in a young girl child, but they'd left abruptly for a new assignment in Underdale soon afterward.

The woman mentioned that she had also done laundry for a number of other families in those days, including a Mrs. Mayer, who'd hired her soon thereafter as a maid of all work in her household. The very same Mrs. Mayer had a brother by the name of Rolf Newcomb.

Gavin could hardly believe his luck.

The housekeeper remembered a great deal of detail about those early days when Mr. Newcomb brought Lily Hayes to the Franklins' rectory. She also remembered Lily as a beautiful child, but very fussy, perhaps even ill.

Mrs. Franklin had not been pleased with taking in the child, and the housekeeper did not really understand why they'd done it. In any event, she was the one who'd directed Gavin to St. Martin's Church in Underdale, where he learned about Mercy Franklin's life there, and the necessity of taking the governess post near Keswick.

The housekeeper at Reverend Franklin's last post had not mentioned speaking to anyone else about the family, and Nash did not know how Bertie would have learned about Underdale, unless he'd discovered something about Mrs. Mayer and followed that lead.

Regardless of how he'd gotten his information, it was imperative that Gavin get on the road immediately. He had the information he needed without talking to Mrs. Mayer, which was fortunate. There was no time to waste.

Chapter 25

Seeking surcease from his headache, Nash went up to the nursery. He found Emmaline sitting on the divan with a book while her young nurse sat in a chair opposite her, sewing. The nursemaid stood immediately upon Nash's entry into the room. He bade her to resume what she was doing.

"Where is Miss Franklin?" he asked.

Emmaline shrugged, and Ruthie gave him a blank look. "I'm not sure, my lord," she said.

The room was snug and warm against the light drizzle outside, and Nash wondered where Mercy could be. Surely not outside. He felt a rush of contentment when he thought of the pleasurable hour they'd spent together in the pavilion, and knew that the bad taste of Horace Carew's visit and Lowell's mischief would recede when he saw her.

He picked up a book from the top of Emmaline's bookcase and opened it to the place where it was marked. "You and Miss Franklin are reading this?"

"Yes," Emmaline said.

"And how do you like the adventures of Mr. Crusoe?"

She gave him a meek smile, but her eyes glittered. "It is a very exciting tale, Uncle."

Nash sat down beside his niece. "Is this where you left off?"

She nodded.

"Shall we read a page or two while we wait for Miss Franklin?"

Robinson Crusoe was an old favorite of Nash and his brothers. As young lads, they'd played at being marooned on a faraway isle.

"If you don't mind, my lord, I'll just go down to the laundry, then," Ruthie said. "I've some ironing to do."

Nash nodded and the nursemaid took her leave. Nash began to read, remembering how much he'd enjoyed the reading time he and his brothers had shared with their father. He would not mind providing interludes of the same kind for his niece.

Nash started reading, but he could not put Helene Carew's twenty thousand pounds from his mind. It was surely enough to convince any sane man to wed. Especially one who had a great deal to lose by refusing it.

Carew's offer was more than he had ever expected. As Helene's husband, Nash would have everything he needed. Her incredible fortune would provide the means to turn Ashby into a creditable estate, and a way to give Emmaline the London seasons she would need when she came of age. Nash would gain a beautiful wife who did not seem to yearn for Town life, nor would she make unreasonable demands upon his time, for she did not appear likely to become overly attached to him. The situation was perfect.

Nash had never wanted a wife for whom he cared

too much—that was a sure way to make himself vulnerable to the kind of paralyzing losses he'd endured over the past few years—his brothers, Jacob Metcalf, and John Trent. He would not do it again . . . he would not become close to anyone again.

And yet as he sat beside Emmaline, he knew he did not wish to return to the cold distance that had existed between them when he'd first come back to Ashby Hall. He had begun to care for her and would not give up their tenuous bond for any reason.

He thought again of Helene Carew and her twenty thousand. She possessed everything he needed.

But he didn't want her.

Mercy's pulse skittered madly when she came to the nursery door and saw Nash reading to his niece. His voice was deep and rich, a pleasing sound that infused her body with futile hopes and desires. A thick pooling of emotion filled her chest and she feared she would never again breathe normally. Not when Nash was so far out of her reach.

Emmaline leaned close to him, his big body dwarfing hers, but they looked comfortable together. His reading cadence seemed to enthrall his niece, and she listened avidly to every word.

A hint of a smile touched Nash's lips and Mercy averted her gaze from it, hardening her heart. She could see that Emmaline and her uncle would do well together after she was gone.

Nash looked up and saw her. "Miss Franklin. Would you join us?"

Mercy hesitated for an instant, but found that she could not refuse.

She pulled up a chair near the divan and sat down as Nash resumed reading. But she barely heard the words.

Emmy and her uncle enjoyed the reading until they reached the end of the chapter, and Nash closed the book. It had grown dark outside, and Ruthie appeared with warm water for washing.

"I suppose it is time for bed," he said, suddenly seeming completely out of his element.

"Thank you for reading to me, Uncle," Emmaline said quietly.

"It was entirely my pleasure, Emmy," Nash said, then walked to the door, where he stood for a moment, still looking a bit lost. Mercy swallowed, wanting him quite desperately.

She averted her eyes, going to the little girl's bed to turn down the blankets.

"I'll just leave you ladies to it, then," Nash said. He quit the room, leaving Mercy feeling hollow and cold inside. She'd insisted they could not share a bed again . . . And she knew it was right, even though she feared she would always feel a horrid emptiness in his absence.

Mercy bade Emmy a good night and retreated to her own bedchamber, somehow managing to keep her tears at bay as she undressed and prepared for bed. She added peat to the fire, and though it flared with heat, it did not warm the void inside her.

She blew out the lamp just as her door opened and Nash slipped in.

"Nash!" Good sense warred with the acute need she felt for him.

"I could not stay away." He pulled her against

him, crushing his mouth over hers in a primal kiss over which he clearly had no control. Mercy's heart swelled almost painfully at the harsh, labored sound of his breaths.

She hadn't wanted him to stay away, either. Not really.

He molded her to the hard planes of his body, and she wrapped one leg around his, opening her body to him. She scarcely had time to think when he lifted her into his arms and took her to the bed, easing her to the mattress and lying down beside her. He ravaged her mouth, seeking the most sensual connection with her tongue as he pulled her chemise from her shoulders.

Mercy worked on the buttons of his shirt and he retreated long enough to yank it over his head and toss it to the floor. He came back to her half naked, and she ran her hands down the hard muscles of his shoulders and back.

"Mercy, love."

He trembled as he nuzzled her throat, and Mercy set aside her worries to give herself fully to the one man who would ever own her heart.

Nash tugged Mercy's chemise down to her waist and she arched, giving him full access to the breasts he so loved to suckle and taste. She held his head in place while he spread his fingers down her belly, eliciting a pleasurable gasp from her lips.

She opened for him and he ventured lower, sliding his fingers into her feminine cleft. He touched her where she was most sensitive, and her breath came out in a thick gasp when he pleasured her with his thumb while slipping one finger inside her.

He'd never known how deeply gratifying it could be to build such pleasure in his lover, to make her writhe and cry out for more.

He wanted her desperately; needed her more than he'd ever thought possible. Rising up, he took her mouth again in a deeply passionate kiss, an intimate melding of mouths that bore witness to the intensity of what he felt for her.

She was ready for him, which was a relief, for he could not wait. "I want to be inside you, Mercy. Now."

He did not have the patience to remove his trews. He tore them open and, without hesitation, she opened for him again. He drove inside her, sheathed himself deeply as he watched her eyes darken in the flickering firelight. "Mercy, love."

She tightened around him, and Nash was overcome with the exquisite sensation of being enveloped by her, of becoming an integral part of her. He filled her, moving gently inside her as he deepened his thrusts. Sparkles of pure, hot sensation skittered across his every nerve.

"More," she whispered against his mouth.

"Aye, love. All I've got."

She wrapped her legs around him and pulled him in deeper, as if inhaling all of him into her body. He buried himself inside her as he wrapped his arms around her and gave her his full length, claiming her with his body and his soul, demanding she give him hers.

Her climax came suddenly and he captured her cry with his mouth. She bucked against him wildly, and her inner contractions brought him to his own release, a turbulent furor of sensation that raged like fire inside him. He shuddered, holding himself deep inside her, in awe of the relentless bond between them.

When he could move again, he lowered himself to his side, staying sheathed within her.

He smoothed a rich, inky black curl back from her forehead. And as they lay tangled together in the bedclothes, Nash was content to stay intimately connected, holding her while she drifted off to sleep.

Mercy knew she was asleep. The comforting smell of lilies surrounded her and she saw a little girl playing in a field of the tiny white flowers—she felt she was seeing herself at a very young age—dark-haired, smiling, and plump-cheeked. Happy. She was holding someone's hand . . . a gentleman in a dark coat and tawny breeches. "Papa."

The word came to her and she knew it was her father. She was dreaming of her true father. She felt it deeply.

"Teeny," she whispered. "Where is Teeny?"

She saw the little girl again, but now she was weeping, and Mercy felt the child's despondence to the depths of her soul. There was nothing Mercy could do to comfort her, not even tell her where Teeny was. She did not know who or what Teeny was . . . and the word, or name, made Mercy feel vaguely unsettled.

She saw her father again, and then a dark-haired woman who must be her mother. Her father lifted her into his arms, and just as she was about to look into his face . . .

He was gone. There was no field of lilies, no gentleman in tawny breeches. Her mother had disappeared and Mercy was alone and afraid.

A desperate sadness choked her. She could not breathe. Not when they'd abandoned her. She was lost. Panic threatened to swallow her. Suddenly, she was falling, and there was no one to catch her.

No one but Susanna and Robert Franklin.

Nash woke to the sound of quiet distress. A whimper and then a sob. A few disturbing words followed. The fire had burned low, but there was sufficient light for him to see tears on Mercy's face, and he knew she was dreaming something distressing. He rubbed her back to soothe her, and pressed gentle kisses to her forehead and cheeks.

He felt an unfamiliar tug in his chest at the sound of her distress, and wished he could ease her anguish as she'd done for him. She treated him as she would any whole, undamaged man. She was honest and audacious, and sweetly nurturing with Emmaline. She could be diplomatic, but candid when necessary. God knew she'd been blunt with him when she'd first arrived at Ashby.

He wanted to wake her and crush her to him, never to let her go. But he contented himself with a few comforting caresses as her disturbing dream subsided and she relaxed once again.

Nash had had his own nightmare, but it was not like the ones that had plagued him ever since Waterloo. This one had more to do with the Ashby curse than any real, tangible battle.

Something Sir William had said during their visit

to Metcalf Farm came back to him. Sir Will had mentioned that Horace Carew had wanted Hoyt to marry Helene. Nash had dismissed it as Carew's obsessive desire to see his daughter with a title before her name.

But Hoyt had refused the man's offer and now he was dead.

Carew had made an offer to Arthur to buy the southern Ashby land, and Arthur had refused. Now Arthur was dead.

Nash had discounted Roarke's comment about trench digging on the high road to Braithwaite. He could not imagine someone going to the trouble of shoveling away the side of a cliff in order to commit murder. Carew had to have an incredible motive in order to stage the murders of two earls.

But what could it be?

He did not seem deranged, but only a madman would murder two men so that a third might wed his daughter. And as for the land he'd offered to buy, Nash had looked at it and had seen nothing special about it. Sheep would not even graze there.

Nash pressed a kiss to Mercy's head and slid away reluctantly from the warmth of her body. He would prefer to stay, but the questions preying on his mind would deny him any more sleep.

Something woke Mercy. It had likely been her dream, since it had been comforting and disturbing at the same time. Which was an obvious contradiction in terms.

She'd seen fleeting images of her mother and father. She knew they must be her parents, for they were unfamiliar to her in any other way but this. She curled her hand closed, nearly able to recall how it felt to have her tiny hand enclosed within her papa's large one.

Perhaps her mind had created those dream images because she'd been thinking so much about Susanna's journal and her true mother. The name Teeny haunted her, as did the floral scent that had permeated the dream.

But maybe the people she'd seen in her dream were pure fiction, just like the Robinson Crusoe adventures she and Emmaline had been reading.

It was still dark in her bedchamber, but Nash had already left. She would have liked to slide up against him and taken her ease in his warmth. But it was not possible, not now or any other time. She should never have taken him into her bed last night.

It was Sunday, so there would be no mail coach today. Mercy swallowed away the burning in her throat, thinking about how difficult it would be to wait until the morrow to leave. Everyone would go to the ball, but Mercy knew she could not face it—she could not bear to watch Nash being courted by all the marriageable ladies of consequence.

She found her clothes and dressed quickly, then went to the nursery, where Ruthie was getting Emmaline ready for church in a gown she'd laundered and altered.

"Emmy, you look beautiful," she said as a wave of emotion threatened to choke her. She had not intended to become so attached to the little girl. But it had happened nonetheless.

Mercy turned away as Grainger came along with

Mrs. Jones in tow, which gave Mercy an excuse to leave the nursery before she succumbed to her tears.

She welcomed the opportunity to show the housekeeper around the Hall before church, for it kept her from dwelling upon her impending departure from Ashby and those she had come to love so dearly.

Nash stood looking out the library window, lost in thought. He'd gone up to the nursery in hopes of stealing a moment alone with Mercy, but the new housekeeper informed him that she and Emmaline had already left for Sunday services in Keswick.

He had kissed her lightly as he left her bed before dawn, of course, but he craved her now. Just a touch, or even better—another taste of her before she left for town.

Feeling bereft of her presence, Nash pondered his suspicions about Carew, but could come to no reasonable conclusion. Sitting down at his desk, he puzzled over the letters that still lay there. Notes from Fitch and Randall were conspicuously absent, and Nash suspected he had removed the mail run from Lowell's responsibilities a few weeks too late.

Nash could not imagine any reason why the steward should want Ashby to be unsuccessful. Failure meant there would be no wealth to share. Or at the very least, the estate's profits would be delayed yet another few years. And Lowell was already impatient to see profits that would not materialize until after the shearing and the wool was sold.

He went in search of Lowell to query him directly, but learned that he'd also gone into Keswick to church. It was frustrating, but Nash was determined to talk to him before they all left for the Market Inn ball. He wanted answers to his questions.

By late afternoon, Mercy had not returned to the Hall. Nash knew that Henry Blue had escorted her and Emmaline into Keswick, so he was not concerned. He assumed she wished to stay away in order to avoid any further discussion about going to the ball. She'd been adamant against going.

Perhaps that was better, for Nash intended to confront Horace Carew with his suspicions at the ball. And since Nash did not know who he could trust—even the magistrate—he did not want Mercy to be there.

But before he acted on any of his suspicions, he decided to ride up to Metcalf Farm and discuss them with Sir William and his wife.

Mercy learned that the mail coach would arrive in Keswick the following morning at half past seven. She could slip out of Ashby Hall at dawn and easily walk the distance to be on time for it. Well, perhaps not so easily. She would be carrying her traveling cases . . .

And she would be leaving all that she had come to love.

Emmaline would be all right. She had Ruthie now, and was not quite so terrified of her uncle. They'd developed a tenuous bond that would only grow stronger with time.

But Mercy would miss the little girl.

Once again, she reminded herself that leaving Ashby was for the best. Nash could acquire a handsome dowry—whether it belonged to Miss Carew or someone else did not signify—and Mercy might even find her true family. She knew her present course was for the best.

Henry had taken them to church in Keswick in Nash's little barouche, and they stayed after the service so that Mrs. Swan could introduce Emmaline to some of the well-heeled children of the parish. Ruthie joined in the play, encouraging Emmy to do so, too. Afterward, Mrs. Swan invited them to the rectory for a light breakfast.

Mercy was torn between accepting—thus avoiding returning to Ashby Hall and facing Nash—or declining so that she *could* see Nash. She yearned for a few moments alone with him before her departure, even though she knew it would hurt deeply to know it would be the last time she would see him.

Chapter 26

On Sir William's suggestion, Nash looked for the last ledger kept by Hoyt and his manager. It was one of the earliest accounts he'd examined on his return to Ashby, and at the time, it had made little sense to him.

He lifted it from one of the library shelves, then sat down at his desk and paged through the entries, realizing that his vision was a good deal better now than it was when he'd first read it. Perhaps the physicians were correct, and his vision actually would improve.

Nash skimmed through the notations Hoyt and his manager had left for each other on a weekly basis, sometimes more often. Every entry had something to do with the sheep and the land, or tenants and their rents. There was nothing out of the ordinary in any of the entries he read until he reached the last quarter of the year 1814.

There were listings of the number of lambs weaned, and ewes returned to the fells. The manager had noted how many wethered males had been turned loose. He documented how many twinters they had, how many thrinters, and so on. Hoyt had written instructions to his manager on negotiations with wool dealers and meat merchants in Carlisle.

And then Nash saw it. *"Decline Carew's offer. Plan to improve those acres next summer."* It was dated 10 October, 1814, four days before Hoyt's hunting party. Four days before his death.

In a rush of stunned outrage, Nash pulled out Arthur's last journal and flipped through the pages until he reached the entry he sought. The notation had been made on the sixteenth of June, just two days before Arthur's accident. Suddenly, it did not seem so implausible that someone had intentionally tampered with the high road to Braithwaite—the only road Arthur would have taken to reach the Landry house party.

Nash sat back in his chair as nausea and disgust roiled through him. *Ashby curse be damned.* His brothers had been murdered for a piece of worthless land, whether through marriage or purchase . . .

And yet it could not be worthless, not if murder had been committed over it. Nash needed to revisit the property and see what he and Roarke had missed the last time they were there.

He dressed quickly and set out early for the ball, starting toward the Ridge path once again, but pulled up short when a man on horseback approached him from the main road.

"Begging your pardon, sir," he said, "I'm looking for Ashby Hall."

"You've found it," Nash replied. "What's your business here?"

"I'm John Stone, sent by Mr. Gerald Hardy in London to deliver a letter."

It had to hold some importance for Hardy to have sent a special courier all the way up to Cumbria with it.

"Mr. Hardy is my solicitor," Nash said. "The letter will be for me."

"You are Lord Ashby?" the man asked, though his notice of Nash's scars was obvious. Of course Hardy had described him.

Nash nodded.

Stone took the folded missive from his waistcoat and handed it to Nash, who gave him several coins in return. "You've had a long ride."

"Aye, my lord."

"Go into the house and tell Mrs. Jones I sent you in for a meal. You will find sleeping quarters near the kitchen where you can spend the night before you return to Town."

"Many thanks, my lord."

Nash looked at the seal and the handwriting on the outside page, recognizing both as belonging to his solicitor. He rode some distance on the Ridge path, out of sight of the house before he unsealed the letter and unfolded its pages. Reading quickly through the salutations, Nash got right to the point of the note.

A potent wave of anger and grief hit him as he read, and when he was through, he slid the letter into his waistcoat, grateful that Hardy had seen fit to send such a detailed reply so quickly. Now there was no question in Nash's mind about what had happened to his brothers.

Mr. Hardy believed the man Nash knew as Horace Carew was really H. Carew Emerson, a charlatan who had swindled thousands of pounds from investors all over England. His most recent deception had occurred in London, with a spurious canal scheme. Some believed Emerson was really an American, and had gone back across the Atlantic to live in luxury on his ill-gotten goods. Whatever the case, he had disappeared without a trace several years ago.

Emerson also had a daughter named Lottie, said to be an exquisite beauty with white-blond hair.

Shaken by all that he read, Nash continued down the Ridge path. When he arrived at the spot where he and Roarke had visited before, he dismounted at the top of the rocky crest. Looking down into the boggy land below, just as he and Roarke had done on their last visit, he saw that the standing water had receded slightly. The reeds and grasses looked taller than they had during the earlier visit.

Nash glanced around and saw nothing of note—it looked exactly as it had before.

Leading his horse, he walked down to lower ground, soaking the boots Parker had just polished in the muck below. He looked in every direction, and saw naught of interest until a streak of black caught his eye.

It was a thick, dark line in the rock face hovering right at the water level where he and Roarke could not have seen it before, since the level had been higher. Nash went in closer, and the shallower water allowed him to see what it was that formed the distinctive black strip.

It was a band of coal. It was a thick, rich hint of the deposit below that would make its owner incredibly wealthy. This was what Horace Carew—or H.

Carew Emerson—had been trying to gain possession of for the past two years. He'd spread tales of boggarts to keep everyone away from the site, so no one else would discover the deposit, and created the Ashby "curse" to account for his brothers' untimely deaths.

Two years of lies, deceit, and manipulations were about to end. If not tonight, then as soon as Nash could summon a judge or the lord lieutenant of the district.

After a long afternoon of visiting in town and avoiding Nash, Mercy returned to Ashby Hall with Emmaline and Ruthie. When she learned that Nash had already left for Keswick, she should have felt relieved. There would be no argument about her attending the ball, and she would not have to face telling him that she was leaving Ashby.

And yet she wished he had stayed long enough to ask her just once more to accompany him to the ball.

But he had not.

The house was nearly empty. Nash's men had already gone into town, and once Henry left for Keswick, Grainger and Mrs. Jones would be the only ones remaining in the Hall. Mrs. Jones was a fair cook, and she put together a supper for them. Mercy relaxed her rules long enough for Emmy to eat in the kitchen.

But Mercy had no appetite.

She went to her bedroom, and as she started to pack her things, she recalled her first encounter with Nash Farris.

The memory of his outrageous demands brought

a painful little laugh to her throat and tears to her eyes, but she wiped them away and continued folding her clothes and placing them inside her traveling boxes. She could not think about all that she was leaving, for it was far too painful.

She thought of Nash at the Keswick ball, so tall and appealing, his broad shoulders and strong legs so tempting . . . Every woman there would want to dance with him. He'd said he didn't want Miss Carew, but Mercy felt certain that others would be present—well-born ladies with fortunes to bring to a marriage.

She did not have a chance with him. Earls did not marry governesses, and Mercy could not live as his mistress.

But she did not know how she would live without him, either.

She finished packing and left her bedchamber. Intending to spend the rest of the evening reading with Emmaline, she entered the hallway and noticed that someone had left the attic door open. She paused as a fanciful, entirely hopeless thought struck her.

She could not give up Nash.

Her breath caught at the notion of fighting for the man she loved—and not giving up the way Andrew Vale had done when faced with her father's refusal of his proposal.

Mercy bit her lip as she eyed the open door of the attic. She would never know who her parents were, and never have the money Nash needed.

But they had other resources that would surely grow over time. She had only to convince him that her love was enough.

Mercy crept slowly toward the attic door, feeling very unsure of what she was about to do, and yet utterly convinced that she had to try to win him.

She climbed the attic stairs and located the trunk containing the late Lady Ashby's clothes. Lifting the lid, she removed the scarlet gown and pelisse, and held them up to her shoulders.

Could she do this? Did she have the nerve and the power of will to trust that Nash cared for her as she did him? That he would not wish to gain a wealthy wife at the cost of losing her?

Mercy took a deep breath and carried the gown down to her bedroom before she could change her mind. She dressed quickly, and when she came out again wearing Lady Ashby's gown, with her hair artfully arranged, Emmaline and Ruthie were coming up the stairs.

"Oh my, Miss Franklin, you look beautiful!" Ruthie cried.

Emmy said naught, but her eyes grew wide, as did her smile.

"Thank you, Ruthie," Mercy said. "Has Henry left for the ball yet?"

"No, miss. Shall I fetch him?"

Mercy gave a nod.

It seemed as though everyone in the Lake District was present in the assembly rooms at the Market Street Inn. And Nash was still reeling from what he'd seen on the Ridge path and in his brothers' journals. Hardy's letter was the spoon that made the pottage come together.

A few of his men had arrived, although there was

still no sign of Philip Lowell or the Carews. Nash
had been tempted to go directly to Strathmore Pond
and confront Carew with his discovery, but stopped
halfway there.

Confronting the villain alone, in his own territory,
was far too dangerous. Nash no longer had the slightest doubt that Carew was responsible for Hoyt's and
Arthur's deaths, and he knew the man wouldn't be
pleased to have his crimes—any of them—exposed.

But Nash intended to survive the confrontation
when it occurred. He intended to go home fully
intact to Mercy later that night. He just wished he
understood Lowell's part in all this. Hardy specifically stated that he could find nothing on anyone
called Philip Lowell, suggesting that Nash search
through Hoyt's old correspondence for the man's
references. Nash wondered if Lowell was aware of
the crimes for which Horace Carew was responsible.

The ball was held on the uppermost floor of the
inn, and the doors had been pulled open, leading
onto wide balconies outside. The air inside was
pleasant and cool, but Nash knew it would become
heated once the dancing began.

He did not intend to stay that long.

The orchestra started the first set, and Nash allowed himself to be taken under Reverend Swan's
wing to be introduced to the various landowners
who were present. They all seemed to have daughters, many of whom were exceedingly comely, and
most certainly in possession of adequate dowries.
But none of them was of any interest to Nash. There
was only one woman for him, and the stubborn chit
had remained at home with his niece at Ashby Hall.

For which Nash was grateful. He did not know quite how he was going to react when he saw Carew, but he didn't want Mercy anywhere near.

"My lord," said Reverend Swan as a small, white-haired gentleman in a maroon coat and bright yellow waistcoat approached them, "may I present Lord Lieutenant Sir David Milner."

Milner made his bow. "My lord, may I offer you a belated welcome to the district, as well as my apologies for neglecting to pay a call to Ashby Hall?"

Nash could not believe his good luck. "Not at all, Sir David." He could not have planned it better—having Cumbria's ultimate civil authority present when he accused Carew of murder. And if Magistrate Wardlow had any part in Carew's scheme, he would also answer to Milner. "I wonder if I might have a word?"

"Of course." They took their leave of Swan, and Nash found a private alcove away from the crowd, where he showed him Hardy's letter and told the man what he'd discovered.

Milner frowned fiercely. "This is most disturbing, Lord Ashby."

Nash looked at him solemnly. "Aye. It could not be more so."

"And you expect Mr. Carew to attend tonight?"

Nash gave a nod. "He told me he and Miss Carew planned to be here. I expect the magistrate as well."

The two men conferred for a few moments more, and when Nash returned to the ballroom, he avoided being drawn into the dancing. Prowling the periphery of the main assembly hall, he felt very much like a bear with a thorn in its paw. Quite unsettled and decidedly unfriendly.

Magistrate Wardlow appeared with his wife on his arm. Nash waited for the man to greet his acquaintances, and when his wife left him to join some ladies near the refreshment table, he started in the man's direction.

He stopped suddenly when a vision of perfection stepped into the room. Nash's breath caught in his throat and his chest swelled with a fierce kind of tenderness when he saw her.

It was Mercy.

The music faded from his ears, as did the flickering light of the sconces and chandeliers above him. All he could see was her.

She wore a gown Nash had never seen before. Its vivid color accented the glossy darkness of her hair and her lily-pure complexion perfectly. The low-cut neck and simple lines of the dress complemented her fine figure. She'd done something incredibly beguiling with her hair, and her eyes sparkled like exotic jewels.

His fingers itched to touch her.

Young men swarmed around her, barely allowing her to move into the room. And while Nash's heart quaked at the sight of her, he forgot his reasons for thinking it was best that she stay away. He did not know why she'd changed her mind about coming, but he drank in the sight of her, very glad that she had.

She hardly seemed to notice the horde around her, but glanced about the ballroom, as though searching for someone. Her eyes lit on him . . . And she smiled.

He did not think he'd ever seen anything as arresting or beautiful as Mercy's smile. And by God, he loved her. He intended to marry her, and not some cold, indifferent dowry with a woman attached. Only Mercy could assuage the deep, desolate pit that had been his soul until now. She filled the void in ways he would never understand.

Pushing through the crowd, he made his way toward her, then stopped before her, his heart surging with love as he made his formal bow. He took her hand and looked into her eyes, and for a moment he could not move. He wished they were alone, because then he'd be able to take her in his arms and kiss her sweet mouth.

Instead, he took her hand and led her away from the group. "If you'll excuse us, gentlemen . . ."

"My lord," someone protested, "the lady has only just arrived."

A few others called out, asking her for a dance.

Nash took her to the dance floor, and just before the orchestra started its next set, asked her to dance with him. Mercy smiled again and took his hand, then lined up with the other couples for the quadrille.

Nash barely noticed the other dancers. He executed the steps of the dance, but kept his full attention on Mercy—the tilt of her head, her graceful arms, her agile steps enthralled him. He did not understand how he could ever have entertained the idea of marriage to any other woman.

The dance ended, and Nash bowed to Mercy, then placed her arm in the crook of his elbow and retreated from the dance floor. He found a relatively quiet space and bent to whisper in her ear. "You are the most beautiful lady here, love."

She blushed madly, the color rising from the swells of her breasts, then blooming on her cheeks like the petals of a rose.

He lifted one hand and nearly caressed her bare neck before remembering himself and what proper etiquette demanded. "One day I will adorn you with jewels."

She touched his lapel. "I don't want jewels, Nash. I only want—"

The sight of Horace Carew startled Nash and brought him back to a harsh reality. "Wait, Mercy." He took her arm and drew her away to where Sergeant Bassett stood with Oscar Parker. "I want you to stay with my men while I take care of some business," he said.

He was loath to leave her, but at least she would be safe with Bassett and Parker.

"But Nash—"

He would have kissed her to reassure her, but such an act would draw unwanted attention, as well as damage Mercy's reputation. Already, Nash noted far too many pairs of eyes trained in their direction, speculating on the new earl's female interest.

No one but the Metcalfs had met Mercy, although Carew knew of her. Someone at Ashby Hall had been talking out of turn, and Nash believed he knew who it was. Lowell. And he was standing before Helene Carew, his eyes locked on hers as though she were the only woman in the room.

Nash watched him for a moment, frowning as a distinct possibility came to mind. The steward was in love with Helene. His frequent, unexplained absences might not have involved a lover in Lake Road, but trysts with Miss Carew herself.

And if her father was so determined to see her married to an Ashby earl, it might be enough motivation for a lovesick madman to rid himself of the competition. And yet Arthur could not have been construed as any kind of competition.

It was the land, the coal-veined land.

Nash left Mercy in Bassett's capable care, although she did not appear too happy with the arrangement. He started making his way toward Carew, collecting Lord Lieutenant Milner on his way. "Here is the gentleman I wanted you to meet, Sir David," he said when they reached Carew. Nash drew the men out of the music-filled ballroom and made the introductions.

"Carew, I just discovered that there is a piece of Ashby land that interests you."

Carew appeared nonplussed by Nash's remark. His eyes narrowed and he tightened his lips for an instant before speaking. "I do not know to what you refer, my lord."

"My late brothers both made notations about your offers to purchase some worthless Ashby land. I found them quite interesting."

"Lord Ashby—"

"What do you say, Carew . . . are you still willing to buy?"

Carew pulled on his waistcoat, a vague sign of some discomfiture, which gave Nash a fleeting sense of satisfaction. "I only thought to relieve them of that worthless property, and it made sense since it adjoins my land. Your brothers were in need of funds, and I had the wherewithal to make the improvements necessary."

"Improvements?"

"Why, yes. The land is flooded."

"How very generous of you."

A number of gentlemen had come out of the ball-room and were standing close enough to hear, but Nash was indifferent to his audience.

"You also proposed that my widowed brother marry your daughter, did you not?"

Carew glanced around at the men who had gathered nearby. "My lord, I don't see how that is—"

"It was an attempt to get control of those worthless southern crags, wasn't it?"

Carew glanced away from Nash, then looked at Milner. He set his jaw, clearly of the belief that he was above any sort of questioning. "My lord, perhaps we can discuss this at a more appropriate time."

Nash ignored the suggestion. "I would like to ask you this: If I also decline your offer to wed Miss Carew, will I soon meet with a freak, accidental death?"

"That is preposterous, my lord. For you to suggest—"

"Ah, Mr. Wardlow!" Nash called to the magistrate. "Come and join us."

Wardlow tried to stutter an apology and move away, but Milner beckoned Wardlow to him and the man joined the group, albeit reluctantly.

"Just to be sure I'm clear on what would happen," Nash said to Wardlow. "If I die without an heir, Ashby land will revert to the crown, is that right, Magistrate?"

"I b-believe in Ashby's case, that is so, my lord." He rubbed his face with his hand, his eyes darting nervously between Milner, Carew, and Nash.

"But the crown will not want my poor, neglected acres, will it?"

The color drained from Wardlow's face, and he was clearly at a loss for words.

"What say you, Wardlow?" Nash asked.

"My lord, I am not an authority on the laws of—"

"No doubt the crown will want to rid itself of such worthless land quite quickly, will it not?" Nash interjected.

Carew spoke angrily then. "I see what you're getting at, Ashby, but it just doesn't hold—"

"Ah, but it does, Mr. Carew," said Sir David as the men around them grew eerily quiet. "I find it very curious that both of Lord Ashby's brothers died under suspicious circumstances after declining to sell you their land." He turned to Wardlow. "Mr. Wardlow, did you not—"

"I had naught to do with it, Lord Lieutenant!" Wardlow cried out. "I-I-I . . . Mr. Carew said they were accidents!"

Carew jabbed his fingers through his hair. "I never said—"

"Aye, you did!" Wardlow said in alarm. "You told me there was no need to go into any great depth with the inquests because no one would—"

Carew turned on him. "Get hold of yourself, Wardlow!"

"I want no part of it anymore, Carew." He turned to Milner, his face flushed now. "I did not want the surveyor to alter the property lines, sir. The coal rightly belongs to Lord Ashby."

The music in the next room stopped just as Wardlow made his damning statement, resulting in an astonished hush. Now everyone knew that the two had been involved in a deadly plot to seize valuable land from Nash's brothers.

"Coal?" someone said.

"There's coal on Ashby land?"

A loud hum of excited banter followed those words, everyone wondering what was going on and how the discovery of coal would affect Keswick and the rest of the district.

"Gentlemen! Gentlemen!" Milner shouted over the din. "I believe it is time for us to take this discussion to the Moot Hall."

"Now, see here," Carew protested just as Nash's men made their appearance. One stood behind Carew, the other next to Wardlow. Nash looked for Mercy and saw that she was flanked by Henry Blue and Corporal Childers.

"Miss Carew, too. *Lottie*, I think you call her."

Carew blanched at Nash's words, as the magnitude of his misfortune became clear.

"Lowell."

The steward had protested Helene's removal by Sir David and Nash's men. Blue and Childers had needed to restrain him. He sat down heavily on a bench in the gallery outside the ballroom, where Nash decided to show him the letter from Gerald Hardy.

Lowell perused it carefully, then swallowed thickly and looked up at Nash, his face ashen. "I was no part of this, my lord."

Nash believed him. "But you have worked against Ashby ever since you arrived."

He gave a weak nod. "I'd hoped that if Ashby remained insolvent, Helene's father would not be so keen on marrying her to its master."

Nash shook his head in disbelief. "She could not have married Arthur."

He put his head in his hands. "No. I thought it a terrible tragedy when your eldest brother died, but . . . I believed I had a chance with Miss Carew when Lord Arthur inherited." He looked up at Nash. "Your brother alone was responsible for his own failures. He would not listen to anyone's advice."

"Clear your possessions out of Ashby, Lowell. I don't want to have to see you again." In utter disgust, Nash walked away.

His anger dissipated the moment he set eyes on Mercy, sitting in a chair on the far side of the ballroom with Childers beside her and several young men surrounding her. She was unreservedly stunning, and Nash felt exceedingly fortunate that she was his. He could not wait to take her home, away from all these handsome swains who were clearly smitten with her.

He started in Mercy's direction, only to be sidetracked by a man he had not seen in over a year, a man whose presence commanded attention no matter what the setting.

"Briggs!" Nash exclaimed. The captain wore a

greatcoat and gloves, and he looked bruised and worn. Nash could not imagine what mission would bring him to Keswick.

"Captain Farris," Briggs replied, taking Nash's outstretched hand, flinching slightly at the sight of Nash's scarred face. "I did not expect to see you here."

He was as tall as Nash, and dark-haired, with a fresh cut on his lip and bruises on his jaw and the crest of his cheek. They had not known each other well, but Nash was aware that Briggs had been an elite agent of the crown who'd carried out secret operations during the war. Clearly, he was on some assignment now.

Nash drew him to an outside terrace, away from the crowd in the ballroom. "What happened to you, Briggs? What brings you to Keswick?"

"I was involved in an altercation with two dangerous men," he replied. "I killed one, the other is likely here somewhere."

"In Keswick?"

"Aye. Or he may be out looking for a place called Ashby Hall, as I am."

A feeling of dread roiled in Nash's gut. He'd thought it was over—the threat against his person, his estate. "I am Earl of Ashby. You're talking about my home."

Briggs frowned with surprise. Everyone knew that Nash was a younger son. "I thought—" He stopped and gave a sympathetic bow of his head. "My condolences, my lord."

"Who's the man, Briggs? And why is he looking for Ashby Hall?"

"Do you know a young woman called Mercy Franklin?" Briggs seemed preoccupied, and tautly vigilant.

"Why do you ask?" Nash said, loath to disclose anything about Mercy until he understood why Briggs sought her.

"I've been charged with the task of finding her."

"For what purpose?" Nash asked, keeping his eye on the throng that had gathered around the woman he loved.

"I believe she is in danger."

"From whom?" Nash asked.

Briggs turned and looked about the ballroom, searching the crowd. "An assassin."

Nash felt as though he'd slipped into one of the strange, laudanum-induced dreams he'd had right after being injured at Waterloo. "*An assassin?* To kill *Mercy?*"

It made no sense at all. *Nash* was the one Carew had wanted to murder.

"I'm here to see that she comes to no harm," said Briggs, "and take her to her grandfather. Where is she? At Ashby Hall?"

Nash gave a puzzled shake of his head. "She has no grandf—"

"My God, who is that?" Briggs asked, catching sight of her as she rose from her chair and started toward him.

"*That* is Miss Franklin," Nash replied as he went to meet her. "And be warned, Briggs, she is mine."

Whatever Briggs had to say about assassins and a grandfather would have to wait. If Mercy was in danger, then Nash wanted to get her away from the swarming crowd and into a safe location.

Nash met her halfway, and when he turned, he saw that Briggs was no longer in the open terrace where Nash had left him. When he saw the captain prowling on the opposite side of the room near the outer gallery, the hair on the back of his neck prickled.

Nash could hardly credit that an assassin was after Mercy, but Briggs had not come all the way to Cumbria on a bad hunch. "I need to get you out of here," he told her.

She looked confused as well as disappointed. "Nash, I—"

"Quickly, sweet." He took her by the shoulders and shepherded her out of the ballroom, quickly finding an empty servants' staircase that led to an isolated hall below. They started down, but Mercy stopped abruptly halfway down. "Nash, wait! Where are we—"

"Keep moving, love."

"No!"

When he turned around to face her on the step above him, the stubborn woman placed her palm on his chest. "I have something to say."

"Mercy, love. Not—"

"Nash, I know I told you I wouldn't come tonight, but—"

He cupped her face in his hands and touched his lips to hers. His heart pounded with urgency, though he did not know if it was because of his desire to make love to her, or his need to keep her safe.

"Please," she said, taking hold of his arm, "let me say this . . ."

"Quickly, love. There is some danger . . ."

"The only danger is my giving up."

He looked at her, puzzled but impatient.

"I love you, Nash. I . . ." She swallowed and her eyes brightened with tears. "There might be other women with better pedigrees, and rich d-dowries. But no one will ever love you as I do. I—"

He dragged her into his arms and kissed her fully, his love and desire eclipsing everything else. But the necessity of getting her to safety prevailed, and he broke away. "Mercy, sweet, I love you with all my heart." He took her hand and kissed the back of it. "There is no one in the world like you . . . And—though I would rather have proposed in a more suitable setting—will you be my wife?"

"Nash! Oh yes!"

"Mercy, love—if we don't find you a safe place—"

Mercy had no chance to savor Nash's brief proposal before the door above them opened and a bruised and battered man in a dark greatcoat came through it. "Lord Ashby, he is not here. But we must get—"

"Who? Who is not here, Nash?" Mercy asked, feeling quite alarmed.

"Captain Briggs, allow me to present my fiancée, Miss Franklin."

"Ma'am." Briggs gave a quick nod. "We need to get you to a safe location, where there are not so many people about."

"Why? What's going on?"

"I'll explain everything later," Captain Briggs said. "But we need to go. Now."

* * *

Ashby procured a private sitting room in the inn, and the two men checked the doors and windows before Gavin felt that he could at least partially let down his guard. He had seen no sign of Bertie anywhere near the inn, but he knew the man could be lying in wait somewhere.

Or he could have given up on Mercy and already be on his way to Edinburgh, looking for Christina.

Fortunately, Lord Ashby had brought a number of his men with him when he'd left the army, so Miss Franklin ought to be safe enough when they returned to Ashby Hall.

Gavin studied Windermere's granddaughter and tried to fathom how the old curmudgeon could possibly be grandfather to such a delicate beauty.

"What's this all about, Briggs?" Ashby asked.

He'd put his arm around Miss Franklin's waist, though the woman did not look as though she needed much support. She was clearly a hardy soul, and ready for the news Gavin brought.

He removed Windermere's warrants from his coat and handed them to Ashby. "My lord, my mission was to find a young lady bearing the name Mercy Franklin."

Ashby and Miss Franklin read the document together. The earl looked up at Gavin, frowning, and then spoke in measured words. "What is the meaning of this document, Briggs? What has the Duke of Windermere to do with Mercy?"

Miss Franklin frowned with puzzlement as she read the document. Of course, it contained nothing beyond Briggs's authority to search for Windermere's granddaughters.

"As it happens," Gavin explained, "in the past few weeks, I have followed a trail from the duke's estate in the lake country down to London . . . from the connections of Sarah and Daniel Hayes, and then to the rectory of Reverend Robert Franklin. All in search of Windermere's granddaughter—Reverend Franklin's ward."

Miss Franklin dropped the duke's letter to the ground. Ashby tightened his arm around her waist.

"Explain, Briggs." Ashby's tone was harsh and demanding, as Gavin supposed his own would be if their situations were reversed.

"Of course. Miss Franklin," Gavin said, "perhaps you ought to take a seat while I tell you what I've learned."

She did so, though Ashby remained close by, keeping her hand in his.

"You were orphaned at the age of three."

Her brow creased and Ashby gave a gentle squeeze of her hand.

"Your mother was Sarah Barton, the daughter of Hadley Barton, Duke of Windermere. When she married Daniel Hayes—your father—the duke disowned her."

"Why?" The word was a mere wisp of air, and Gavin was unsure how to answer it. Rejecting one's own young? It boggled his mind, although his own father was just such a cold-hearted bastard.

"I cannot explain it with any certainty. Mr. Hayes was a well respected, successful barrister in London, but he had no noble blood."

"And that is why . . . ?" She turned to meet Lord Ashby's eyes, then looked back at Gavin. "What was my name? What was the name my parents gave me?"

"Lily. You were Lily Isabella Hayes."

A gasping sob escaped her, and Ashby knelt and drew her into his arms while she wept. He caressed her back and murmured quiet, private words in her ear. When she had calmed, she wiped her eyes. "What else?" she asked him. "What more can you tell me of my family?"

"Your grandfather is very ill," Gavin replied. "Dying. He regrets his actions now, and wishes to make amends. To you . . . and to your sister."

"My—my sister?"

"Yes. Christina."

"Chris*tina*. Oh, Nash," Mercy cried, and Ashby held her close. "I remember now. She was Teeny. My Teeny."

"She was your twin, Miss Frankl— Miss Hayes."

It took several minutes for Mercy to compose herself. "I'm not sure I care to meet my grandfather," she finally said, and Nash could not blame her.

"I can certainly understand that, Miss Hayes," Briggs said, though he frowned in consternation. Nash realized the man would not likely receive payment if he didn't produce the Hayes sisters for their grandfather.

"I would like to meet my sister though." Her voice sounded stronger now.

"That can be arranged . . . as soon as I find her."

Nash spoke up. "Is there anything we can do to assist in the search, Briggs? I take it Christina might also be in danger?"

"'Tis likely, and I believe the danger to Miss

Franklin, er . . . Miss Hayes—has diminished significantly. There are far too many witnesses here. Everyone will soon know that Mercy Franklin is Windermere's granddaughter, so Bertie will be less inclined to strike."

"Bertie?"

"The heir's man."

Ashby scowled. "Windermere's heir does not want the duke's kin found?"

"That's the only conclusion I could come to. Baron Chetwood is not what I would call an upstanding subject of the crown. And the two sisters are to receive a substantial inheritance out of the duke's estate. My belief is that Chetwood intended to prevent that. He is a greedy sot."

Mercy stood abruptly and wrapped her arms tightly around her. "Where is my sister? You said Edinburgh."

Nash would have gone to her, but he realized she needed a moment to collect her thoughts and gather her emotions.

"Twenty years ago, Christina was taken to a family in Edinburgh. I don't have much to go on at the moment, but there will be clues . . . There are always clues," Briggs said.

Mercy, or Lily, as Nash needed to start thinking of her, walked quietly to the door. He went to her then, and stood behind her, gently placing his hands on her shoulders.

"I'll go to him," she said, "but only for the inheritance he wants to give me. I'll have a dowry then—"

"Lily," he said softly, loving the sound of her pretty name. Her back seemed to melt against his chest. "Don't do it for me. We'll be all right without taking anything from Windermere."

"No. I think I *do* want to see him," she said. "I want to see the viper who separated my sister and me, the man who would not take us in when our parents died. And then I'll take his money . . . for Ashby."

Nash pressed a kiss to the top of her head. "Aye, then. We'll go. But not until after we're married."

Chapter 27

Mercy did not know if she would ever become accustomed to being called Lily, but she was going to try.

They had returned to Ashby Hall under heavy escort, and then secured the house against any intruders, although none of Nash's men had found signs of any. Captain Briggs had said he would leave at first light to get ahead of Bertie in his search for Christina. And he was a man who evoked one's trust.

"Lily, my sweet Lily." Mercy loved hearing her true name on Nash's lips, and she wanted to leave behind every trace of her old life with the Franklins. She leaned back into Nash's arms as she stood in his bedchamber, looking out at the tall, dark fells that surrounded Ashby Hall.

He stood behind her in the candlelight, nuzzling the side of her neck. "Have you any idea how very deeply I am in love with you, Lily Hayes?"

She smiled and he turned her around, then started working on the fastenings of her beautiful ball gown, pressing light, tantalizing kisses across her shoulders as he did so. When the gown was fully opened, she shrugged her shoulders free of it and slid her arms up to Nash's strong, broad shoulders.

He drew her into his arms as carefully as he would handle a delicate bit of china. "You are so very precious to me. You complete me in a way no one else ever could."

She cupped his face and brought him down for her kiss, molding her body against his.

"I am so sorry about your brothers, Nash. Mr. Carew's actions were unforgivable."

He swallowed, but said naught. She felt his sorrow to the roots of her soul, and vowed to be his comfort for the rest of their lives.

"You know we needn't go to Windermere, love," he murmured.

She pressed kisses to his jaw and neck. She spread his shirt wide and allowed her lips to wander lower, to his throat, his chest. She knew how he loved it when she touched his nipples with her tongue.

Nearly as much as she did.

"I'll only go to make us safe," Lily replied. Captain Briggs said he believed there would continue to be a threat from her grandfather's heir, but only until Lily claimed her bequest. After that, Baron Chetwood would have no reason to eliminate her, for the gift could not be un-given.

"I'll keep you safe, my love." He took her mouth in a searing kiss, then broke away, touching his forehead lightly to hers. "I do not know how you reached so very far into my heart. But you are everything to me, my audacious little governess. Let us ride to Gretna tomorrow and make our vows. I do not want to wait for the banns to be read."

Lily smiled and touched his face, answering with a heartfelt whisper. "Yes."

At Avon Books, we know your passion for romance—once you finish one of our novels, you find yourself wanting more.

May we tempt you with . . .

- **Excerpts** from our upcoming releases.

- Entertaining **extras**, including authors' personal photo albums and book lists.

- Behind-the-scenes **scoop** on your favorite characters and series.

- **Sweepstakes** for the chance to win free books, romantic getaways, and other fun prizes.

- Writing **tips** from our authors and editors.

- **Blog** with our authors and find out why they love to write romance.

- **Exclusive content** that's not contained within the pages of our novels.

Join us at
www.avonbooks.com